IN
SHEEP'S
CLOTHING

IN
SHEEP'S
CLOTHING

MARY MONROE

KENSINGTON PUBLISHING CORP.
http://www.kensingtonbooks.com

DAFINA BOOKS are published by

Kensington Publishing Corp.
850 Third Avenue
New York, NY 10022

All Kensington titles, imprints and distributed lines are available at special quantity discounts for bulk purchases for sales promotion, premiums, fund-raising, educational or institutional use.

Special book excerpts or customized printings can also be created to fit specific needs. For details, write or phone the office of the Kensington Special Sales Manager: Kensington Publishing Corp., 850 Third Avenue, New York, NY 10022, Attn. Special Sales Department. Phone: 1-800-221-2647.

Dafina Books and the Dafina logo Reg. U.S. Pat. & TM Off.

ISBN 0-7582-0345-4

First Hardcover Printing: September 2005
First Paperback Trade Printing: August 2006
10   9   8   7   6   5

Printed in the United States of America

ACKNOWLEDGMENTS

Thanks to the following:

Karen Thomas for being my editor and my friend.

Andrew Stuart for being the best literary agent in the world as well as my friend.

Peggy Hicks and Roxann Taylor, my publicists at Tri-Com, for organizing my tours and interviews. Oops! You two are my friends, too.

Maxine Thompson for making me feel so special on your radio shows.

Lauretta Pierce for creating my website.

Kar Kar, Xavier, and Rasha for letting me have some peace.

Special thanks to the many bookstores and reading groups. Without your support I'd still be doing day jobs from hell.

A very special thanks to the devil who stole my identity! You gave me the idea for this book!

To my readers, I hope you will enjoy this one, too. Please visit and sign my guestbook at *www.Marymonroe.org*. This is my sixth novel, but brace yourselves because I'm just getting warmed up.

Thanks to Janet Salessi at the Plaza Travel Agency in San Francisco for answering my questions.

CHAPTER 1

I didn't know if the gun aiming at my head was real or not. But the sudden wetness between my legs told me that my bladder malfunction was real. So was the sweat that had saturated my hair and covered my face like a facial. I expected to look like a wet duck by the time my ordeal was over that dreary Friday afternoon. And the way things were going, it looked like I'd be a dead one, too.

"You might die today, bitch." My assailant didn't raise his voice or even speak in a particularly menacing tone. He was just as cool and casual as he'd been when he entered the store a few minutes earlier. A moment before he had given me a possible death sentence, he'd asked, "Do y'all take checks?" Before I could respond, he had whipped out a gun. Just the sight of it would have been enough to bring me to my knees. It was a long, dark, evil-looking weapon, complete with a silencer. His threat streaked past my head like a comet and bounced off the cluttered wall behind me. It even drowned out the piercing, ongoing screams of the spoiled Porter baby in the apartment across the parking lot.

"Please . . . please don't hurt me," I managed. "I'll do anything you want me to. Please . . ." I had never begged for anything before. I never dreamed that the first thing I would beg for would be my life.

It seemed like every part of my body was in pain. My throat felt like I had swallowed a sword and my stomach felt like it had been kicked by a mule. Cramps in my legs made it hard for me to remain standing. Even my eyes were in pain, throbbing like I had run into a door. But that didn't stop me from staring at what I thought at the time was the last thing I'd see on earth: the face of my killer. And on the last day of one of the most miserable jobs I'd ever had before in my life at that.

"You goddamn right you gonna do anything I want you to do! You stupid-ass heifer! I'm the one with the gun!"

"Well . . . please do what you have to do and leave," I pleaded, ever so gently. It was bad enough that I had already emptied my bladder. Now my stomach felt like it was about to add to the puddle of pee that had formed on the floor around my feet. I heaved so hard I had to grab onto the counter and cover my mouth.

"Look—I just et lunch. If you puke in front of me, I'm gonna whup your black ass before I kill you!"

I had almost used a "sick" day that morning. I had almost asked to work the evening shift, but had decided not to because it was the shift that most robbers usually chose to do their dirty work in our neighborhood.

"Bitch, don't fuck with me today!" My tormentor waved his gun at me as his spoke. His beady black eyes shifted from one side to the other as thick yellow snot trickled from both sides of his wide flat nose. This seemed to embarrass him. He turned his head so abruptly his knitted cap slid to the side, revealing neat, freshly braided cornrows. With a loud snort he swiped his nose using the sleeve of his baggy plaid flannel shirt. "Do you wanna die today?" This time his voice sounded like the thunder I'd heard just before he had entered the store.

"No, I don't want to die today," I told him, my voice barely above a whisper. A purple birthmark about a square inch in size and shaped like a half-moon occupied a spot directly below his right eye.

"Then you better stop *lookin'* at me and do what I told you to do! Open that fuckin' register and gimme every goddamn dollar in it! I ain't playin' with you, bitch! Shit!" He glared at me as he rubbed the mark under his eye. But it would take more than that to remove it. He had been branded for life. You would have thought that somebody with such an identifying mark would have concealed his face. But most criminals were as stupid as they were crooked.

The individual who held my life in his hands reminded me of my eighteen-year-old cousin, Dwan. He was the same age and height. He was even the same shade of cinnamon brown. And, like Dwan, he wore clothes big enough for two people. But my cousin had come to his senses before it was too late and was now in Iraq risking his life to keep America safe for me and fools like the one facing me.

Even as scared as I was, I was so angry that I was not able to keep my thoughts completely to myself. I pressed my sticky wet thighs together, angry that my urine had drenched my favorite pair of socks and my only pair of Nikes. "It's a damn shame that Black folks are the ones keeping other Black folks down. If you just got to rob somebody—why *us?* You know how hard we work for our money!" I yelled. "How can you sleep at night, brother?" I asked, folding my arms. Bold was one thing I was not. At least not under normal circumstances. But even meek women like me had a breaking point. Especially when I thought I was about to die anyway.

"Aaah . . . I sleeps like a baby," the young robber sneered, his eyes rolling back in his head in mock ecstasy. Then his face tightened and he gave me a sudden sharp look. "No wonder you Black women so evil—y'all too hardheaded! Don't know when to listen! Didn't I tell you to keep your hands up in that goddamn air?"

"I can't open the register and do that, too," I smirked, placing my hands on my hips.

"Uh," the bold thief began. He paused and whistled to get the attention of his even younger accomplice guarding the door, not taking his eyes off of my face. "Snookie—everything still cool?"

"It's all good, dude! Hurry up so we can get up out of here!" Snookie yelled back, sounding almost as frightened and nervous as I was.

Armed robberies in broad daylight had become a way of life in certain parts of the south Bay Area. Liquor stores seemed to be the most popular targets. Especially "Otto's Spirits," the liquor store conveniently located between Josey's Nail Shop and Paco's Bail Bonds.

My daddy, Otto Bell, owned the liquor store where I'd been working for the past six years, six days a week, eight hours a day. While I was being robbed and terrorized, Daddy was at home, in his frayed gray bathrobe, wallowing in depression on our tattered couch. This was how he now celebrated Mama's birthday every year. Even though she'd been dead for sixteen years. The sudden thought that I might die on my mother's birthday increased my anger. Not just at the young robber, but at life in general. No matter how hard I tried to enjoy life, things always seemed to blow up in my face. Even the little things. Earlier that day, a drunken prostitute had sprayed my face with spit when I'd asked her not to solicit in front of the store.

"Gimme the money, bitch! I ain't tellin' you no more."

I popped open the cash register and scooped out every dollar. I dropped the small wad of bills on the counter next to the *Ebony* magazine that I'd been reading, and the two bags of Fritos, six-pack of Miller Light, and six candy bars the perpetrator had pretended he'd come in for.

He snatched up the money with two fingers and counted under his breath. "A hundred and seventy-five dollars?" he gasped and looked at me with his mouth hanging open. "Now that's a damn shame." His eyes were as flat as his voice.

"That's all we have," I whimpered, wringing my hands. It was hard not to look at his face. His eyes and the birthmark kept grabbing my attention.

He rolled his eyes then looked at me with extreme contempt. "Stop lookin' at me so hard!" he screamed as he lunged across the counter, punching the side of my arm. His hand, the one with the gun, was shaking. I could not decide if it was because he was nervous or just that angry. "You stingy bitch, you," he roared, grinding his teeth. "I went to all this trouble for a hundred and seventy-five fuckin' dollars." He gave me an incredulous look. "What is the matter with you people? Broke-ass niggers! Don't y'all know how to run a business? Them damn Asians puttin' y'all to shame! At least with them, I get paid right!"

"It's been a slow day and people around here barely have enough money to live on," I explained, my hands back on my hips. "Look— uh, the other cashier will be back any minute so you better leave now while you still can," I said.

He blinked and released a loud breath. He slid his thick tongue across his lips then formed a cruel smile. "Not unless he Superman he won't. I seen that lame old motherfucker leave ten minutes ago. Matter of fact, I know for a fact that old dude was on his way to that massage parlor around the corner to get him some pussy. I been checkin' him—and you—out for two weeks now." Looking around he added, "I done did my homework. I ain't no ignorant punk. I know what's up around here . . ."

"You know Mr. Clarke?" I asked, praying that another customer would wander in and possibly save me. Even if Mr. Clarke had come back in time, he would not have been much help. The last robber had beaten him and Daddy to the floor with the butt of his gun. Then the greedy thug had helped himself to what little money we'd had in the cash register at the time, a sack full of alcohol, and other light items.

"I know everybody and everything that go on in this neighborhood, girl. I ain't stupid." As cold and empty as his eyes were, he managed to wink at me. Then he leaned forward far enough for me to feel and smell his hot sour breath. My face was already sizzling with rage, so it didn't make that much more of a difference. "I know about you and James and I know you give him some mean head," he told me, his voice low and hollow. "If I was a little older, I'd let you be my main woman . . ." He paused and whistled again and yelled over his shoulder. "Snookie, if anybody come up in here—pop 'em in the head. I'm fin to take this stingy ho in the back room and get my dick sucked."

CHAPTER 2

It was March. For most of the people I knew, it had been a pretty good year so far. A few were still grumbling over the fact that California now had a movie star, who had played the *Terminator* of all things, sitting in the governor's seat. Daddy wouldn't even call our new governor by his name. "I can't even fix my lips to pronounce his whole name no how. Arnold Swattzen . . . Swattz*uh* . . . oh, shit! If he don't do nothin' to help Black folks and cut taxes, he ain't nothin' but a terminator after all," Daddy complained.

I had done my taxes myself earlier that morning before the robbery, and I was still upset because I had to pay Uncle Sam three hundred dollars. After that, and what the robber took and did to me, I felt that I'd been "fucked" twice in the same day by two different hounds from hell.

It had been raining off and on for most of the week. The cool air and dark clouds seemed to fit the mood that had already settled over me before the robbery.

The robbers had entered the store just after the noon hour, and the whole episode, the robbery and the violation, had taken only a few minutes. But it had taken the police more than an hour to show up, which was quicker than when they usually arrived to investigate crimes in the inner city. A month ago the jealous ex-husband of a waitress on Mercer Street had stormed her apartment waving a tire iron. By the time the cops showed up, the woman, her new lover, and the pit bull she'd bought for protection had all been beaten to death. I was one of the fortunate ones.

Before the cops arrived, I snatched a bottle of Scope off a shelf, rinsed out my mouth, rearranged my clothes, and composed myself. My urine had almost dried on my jeans but I smelled like a nanny goat. Several other customers had entered the store during that hour, but I'd turned them all away and placed the "closed" sign in the front window.

I told the cops as much as I could. How much money had been taken, the robbers' clothes, and how they sounded. The only thing I left out was the sexual assault. How do you tell a cop, one who didn't seem to care anyway, that a robber had made you suck his dick, too?

"Did the perpetrators harm you in any way, miss?" The young white policeman couldn't look more bored if he tried. With a grunt and a sigh, he paused and chewed on a toothpick as he scribbled on a notepad. He was the same officer who had come to take a report the last time we got robbed six weeks ago. "Did they touch you?"

"No, they did not," I lied, rubbing the sore spot on my arm where I'd been grabbed and dragged into the dim broom closet–size rest room to be further humiliated. "They just took the money and some beer." I slid my tongue across my lips and clenched my teeth. I knew then that I would never look at oral sex the same again after this day.

"And do you think you could identify the suspects in a lineup? Maybe look at a few mug shots?" Lineups and mug shots would not have done any good even if every face I looked at was the face of the boy who had robbed and assaulted me. I knew enough not to identify my assailants. From past experiences I knew that it would only make the situation worse. I knew of too many shady lawyers who got their clients released on bail long enough for them to come back to retaliate.

I started to shake my head but stopped because it was now throbbing on both sides. My assailant had gripped my head like a vise, and held me in place between his hairy legs until he had had his way with me.

"I'd never seen them before and they had on masks," I lied. I looked away from the policeman because I didn't like the indifferent look on his face.

My mind went off on its own. It didn't matter what I said. I knew it would do no good. I'd given a lot of thought to what I'd experienced. I'd been lucky that all I'd given up was the money, the beer, and a clumsy blow job. It was times like this that I really missed my mother. She had always soothed me when I was in pain by buying me something nice. She had rewarded me with a new bike when I was seven after I'd been hit by a car. She would take me on shopping sprees at the mall every time one of the neighborhood bullies harassed me. There was not a time I could remember that I didn't get some type of reward from somebody to help me get over some trauma. Until now.

The policeman cleared his throat to get my attention back. "You said you'd never seen them before, is that right?" he mumbled.

"That's right." I nodded.

"Well, if the perpetrators had on masks, how would you know that?"

"Wh . . . what?" I stammered. It wasn't bad enough that I was already flustered. But now I was being grilled like I was the one who had committed a crime.

The policeman massaged his forehead with his thumb and gave me an exasperated look. "Do you want to tell me what really happened, ma'am?"

"I just told you," I wailed, getting angry all over again. I knew what he was thinking. A few of the cashiers in the 'hood plucked money from the cash registers, robbing their employers blind. Then they staged phony robberies to cover the thefts. One of the problems with that was these same thieves blabbed to the wrong people and now even the cops knew about that scam. "Look, sir, this is my daddy's liquor store. If you think I'd steal from my own daddy, you got another think coming. Now if you don't want to take this report, give me your badge and precinct number so I can call up your supervisor and tell him to send somebody out here who can do the job!" I was proud of the fact that I had enough courage to stand up to an authority figure when I had to. But I knew enough about rogue cops to know that that could get me into trouble, or killed, too. And since the cop and I were alone, I decided that it would be in my best interest for me to be a little more docile. "Uh . . . if you don't mind, I'd like to finish this up so I can call my daddy," I said in a meek voice, looking at the cop's shiny black boots.

"I'm just doing my job, ma'am. I didn't mean to upset you."

"Well, I didn't make this up and I hope you believe me."

"I do believe you, Miss Bell. I apologize if I implied otherwise. Like

I said, I'm just doing my job." The cop paused and gave me a quick, weak smile. "Well, if you can think of anything else, please give us another call. I suggest you close up and call it a day. You've been through enough." With a sniff the officer snapped his notebook shut, tipped his hat, and strolled out of the store, whistling like he was on his way to a ball game.

Before I could lock up and leave, Hai Suk, the old Chinese woman who owned the nail shop next door, entered the store clutching a fist-ful of bills. She padded across the floor on her tiptoes like she always did. "Five quick pick, cash value. I feel lucky today," she said, slapping the money onto the counter. Her grin disappeared and she gave me a concerned look. Her eyes were already so narrow I wondered how she could see. But she narrowed them some more and looked at me long and hard. "Trudy, you don't look too good."

"We just got robbed," I mumbled, placing five lottery tickets into her dried hand.

"Again?" Hai Suk asked, shaking her head. "So sorry, so sorry. Last week was my turn. Not much money so crook take nail drill and cell phone, too." Hai Suk turned her head to the side and tapped a faint bruise below her fish-like eye. "Doctor say if robber hit me one inch higher I maybe lose eye."

"You want anything else, Miss Suk? I'm going to close up and go home now." I sighed. It felt like I was breathing through a tube.

The old lady shook her head, her coarse gray and black hair dan-gling about her parched yellow face like a vine. "I see you next time, Trudy."

"No, you won't," I announced proudly, feeling like I'd just re-turned from the dead. I was even able to smile now. "I'm starting a new job on Monday."

"Good for you." Hai Suk waved her hand in the air, then fanned her face with the lottery tickets. She bobbed her head so hard her eyes watered. "I don't like to work so hard. Did I tell you about . . ."

I held up my hand and flashed a smile. "I don't mean to be rude, but I really do have to close up and leave," I said as gently as I could. Hai Suk was like so many of the people I knew. She liked to share her business with the world and she liked to take her time doing it.

Well, this was one day that I didn't have the time to listen to any-body else's problems. I had enough of my own to keep me occupied. As far as I was concerned my ordeal was not over yet. The police had

come and gone and had been of little or no use. The boy who had
robbed me admitted that he had been watching the place. He could
have been peeping from behind a tree right now for all I knew, waiting to pounce again.

Hai Suk gave me a grin and a nod. "I understand, Trudy. I just want
to say I hope next job is better."

"It will be," I said, clicking off the lights and snatching open the
door to let the old woman out. "I'll still come by your shop to get my
nails done," I promised.

I stared out the door for a few minutes, wondering if it was safe for
me to leave. I had some serious concerns because the boy who had
robbed me knew about James and me. If he knew that much, then it
was possible that he knew where I lived. I had never seen him before.
At least I didn't think so. I let out a deep breath and with it went some
of my anger and fear. I had to move forward with my life and put this
behind me. And standing there in that darkened liquor store, that's
just what I decided to do.

I didn't know if my next job was going to be better, but I knew it
would be safer. And I'd make more money so I'd be able to give myself the material rewards I so desperately wanted. Not that any of that
mattered to Daddy, though. He'd been upset ever since I'd started
going on interviews three weeks ago.

Having to go home and deal with a grumpy old man after being
robbed and sexually assaulted was the last thing I wanted to do. But I
didn't have a choice in the matter and that was part of the frustration
I'd been feeling lately.

Changing jobs was one choice I was glad I'd finally made. I had already decided that even if my new position turned out to be the job
from hell, I would make the best of it.

As soon as I got a job offer Daddy fussed about it so much he had
chest pains. He thought that that, and a slew of his other ailments,
would make me change my mind.

"What if I need to get to the hospital?" he had asked when I told
him I'd accepted the job I'd been offered.

"Miss Plummer from across the street said she'd keep an eye on
you," I told him. "She used to be a nurse."

"And how do you plan to get to San Jose?" he asked, wheezing
louder and harder than usual. "That's twenty miles from South Bay
City. You know I need the car to get around in," he whined.

"I'll take the bus until I can afford a car of my own," I told him.

"San Jose is a big city. It ain't no safe place for no woman to be roamin' around."

"I've been to San Jose dozens of times, Daddy, and nobody has ever bothered me. The only place I've ever been bothered is right here. . . ."

CHAPTER 3

Icould barely keep my attention on the road as I drove home. South Bay City was a mostly blue-collar city with a little more than fifty thousand residents. To see so many of the city's young Black men hanging out on the street corners on this particular day infuriated me more than it normally did. I ran a red light when one hissed in my direction to get my attention so he could wink at me.

I knew most of the individuals holding court on the streets, so I knew that the majority of them didn't have the time or the desire to go to school or work. And it was no wonder. Why would anybody want to work when they could rob and assault people like me and get away with it? The fact that so many criminals didn't have to deal with any consequences for their crimes had a lot to do with the mess I eventually got myself into.

The noisy old Chevy that I shared with my daddy made enough noise to wake up the whole street we lived on. But Daddy was already hanging out the front window of our living room with an exasperated look on his tired face when I pulled into our driveway.

Even though it had stopped raining, dark clouds hovered over our house making everything seem just that much more menacing. Every door in our house had *two* dead bolts. And Daddy and one of his friends had put bars on every window except the one in the front where Daddy liked to roost. I couldn't figure out why I was so worried about the same boy coming to the house to take even more from me. And, as old and feeble as Daddy was, he would do everything he could to protect me.

"Trudy, what you doin' home so early? Who's mindin' the store?" he yelled before I could even get into the house.

"We got robbed again, Daddy," I told him, watching the expression on his face turn to one of anger. "There were two of them this time. Teenagers."

A horrified look appeared in a flash on Daddy's tired face. He leaned farther out the window. "They didn't hurt you or nothin', did they, baby?" Daddy's eyes watered and his lips quivered. "I can't have nobody messin' with my girl. You all I got left."

My feet felt so heavy I could barely lift them up the three steps to the front porch. "They didn't hurt me, Daddy. They just took the money and ran," I muttered, my eyes looking everywhere but at Daddy's face. It was hard for me to look in his eyes and lie.

"Oh. Well, wipe your feet, come on in this house and get dinner started. James just called here 'cause wasn't nobody answerin' at the store. He was wonderin' where you was at."

I didn't speak again until I got inside. Dragging my feet across the living room floor, I dropped my thin, discount-store windbreaker onto the back of the wing chair facing Daddy as he stood in front of the couch, with his tacky housecoat looking more like a body bag. One thing I was proud of was the fact that even though we didn't have much money, our house was nicely furnished and never cluttered. Our outdated plaid furniture and dull brown carpets were clean, and everything else was always in its place. And even though we recycled mayonnaise jars and used them for wineglasses and some of our pots and pans didn't have handles, I was proud of everything we had. But that didn't stop me from wanting something better.

"Daddy, if you don't get a security camera, the store'll get robbed on a regular basis from now on. And the next time we won't be so lucky. The guy had a gun," I said, running my tongue across my lips.

Despite the heavy dose of Scope I'd used to rinse out my mouth after the assault, and the three sticks of Dentyne I was smacking on now, the vile taste of the stranger's most intimate body part was still in my mouth. At least it seemed that way to me. I took a sip from an open bottle of warm beer on the coffee table but it didn't help. The inside of my mouth still had that unholy taste in it.

Knowing that I was not that wild about beer, especially when it was room temperature, Daddy gave me a blank look as he fell back onto the couch he was so fond of. "Where was brother Clarke at?" With a groan, Daddy wobbled back up from the couch and snatched my windbreaker off the chair and hung it on the hook behind the door. When it came to his house, he was the neatest man I knew.

"Getting his weekly 'massage,' " I sneered. I tossed my well-worn denim shoulder bag onto our coffee table, the top of which contained an empty candy dish so pristine I could see my face in it.

"Them suckers didn't take my new radio off the counter, did they?" Daddy asked, plopping back down on the couch again with a painful moan.

"No, they didn't take your new radio, Daddy." I was too restless to sit, so I stood in front of him with my arms folded, shifting my weight from one foot to the other like I had to pee again.

Daddy looked me up and down with his hooded eyes narrowed and his gray mustache wiggling like a caterpillar above his lip. I was glad that the urine on my jeans had dried completely now, but it had left a stain. "And you say they didn't touch you or nothin'?"

I shook my head, turning before Daddy noticed my soiled clothing. "No, they didn't."

"Well, I'm sure enough glad for that." Daddy sighed and fanned his face with a rolled newspaper. "I thawed out them neck bones."

I finally eased down onto the arm of the couch, crossing my legs. "Daddy, I wish you would close that place up or sell it or something. It's getting too dangerous."

"And what we gwine to do for money?" Daddy's eyes were too busy watching one of Ricki Lake's daily sideshows on the television, one of his favorite pastimes. "Hmmm?"

"I'll be making a lot more at my new job. As long as I work, I can help you out. And with James's salary, we'll do fine," I insisted.

Daddy whipped his head around and gave me a hard look. "You the one marryin' James, not me. I can't expect that man to support me. Besides, that mama of his ain't about to let nothin' like that happen. What's wrong with you, girl?"

I sighed so hard my throat hurt. "I'm tired. I want to take a hot bath and go to bed. I got a lot of things I need to do before Monday. I need to go out tomorrow and get some office clothes, I need to learn the bus schedule to San Jose, and I need to practice my typing."

Like me, Daddy bought almost everything he wore off a clearance rack at a discount store or from a secondhand store. Size, style, and color didn't matter. His housecoat was two sizes too large. The tail swept the floor as he followed me to my tiny bedroom near the front of our one-story stucco house. He stood leaning against the doorway. "And what you know about workin' a travel agency, Trudy? You ain't had no experience."

"I'm just going to be a secretary. I have done some clerical work so I know all I need to know. Besides, I'll finally get to do a little traveling," I said, sitting down hard onto my squeaky bed.

My room was slightly larger than a walk-in closet. It barely accommodated my twin bed and a few other pieces of furniture. But it was the only room in the house where I felt comfortable anymore. And it was the only place in the house where there were still traces of my mother. I had insisted on keeping some of her clothes. One of her favorite sweaters, pink cashmere, was in my closet. A small framed photograph of her occupied my nightstand. Right next to it was a picture of James Young, the man I had agreed to marry. I had been counting on James to "rescue" me for the past ten years.

"Travel so you can end up just like your mama did?" Daddy barked, rubbing his chest. Daddy's numerous ailments, his "bad" heart being the crutch he used most, had all started right after my mother's death and had become more profound over the years. When he wanted to make me feel guilty about something, or sorry for him, he threw in complaints about his arthritis and high blood pressure. "I just hope I live long enough to see you get married . . ."

"Don't you start that again because it won't work. James doesn't want me to work after we get married so this might be the last time I get to see what having a real job is like. Besides, working for a travel agency sounds like it'll be a lot of fun. I might even be able to get you some traveling discounts."

"You can get me all the discounts you want. I ain't gwine no place." Daddy paused as a sad look appeared on his face. "Not now, not never. If your mama hadn't been so hot to see the world, she'd be here with us right now."

Flying or anything else that had to do with traveling was a sore subject with my daddy. Mama had been a flight attendant for Pan Am. She had divided her time between our house and an apartment that she had shared with several other flight attendants in New York because Daddy had refused to quit his job and move to the East Coast.

Mama had been called in at the last minute to replace a sick coworker. That was also her last day at her job. Her last day period. A terrorist group had placed bombs on the plane and it exploded over Lockerbie, Scotland, four days before Christmas in '88, when I was twelve. Daddy was still in mourning. And, in a more disturbing way, so was I.

My grief was so extreme it often interfered with the decisions I made. I had chosen not to go away to college, even though I'd been offered a scholarship. At the time, it seemed more important for me to be close by in case something happened to Daddy. I had even settled into a relationship with James mainly because Daddy liked him. The feelings I had for James were not the feelings I wanted to experience in a relationship with a man. The passion I felt for him was mild, but he offered me protection, companionship, and security. And, not that it was that important, he also provided safe and regular sex. My life had become such a routine and so predictable that you could set a clock by it.

I had no idea how drastically it was about to change.

CHAPTER 4

I looked a lot like Daddy. I had inherited his medium-brown skin, kinky black hair, and small black eyes. I had thin lips and a narrow nose for a Black woman. By looking at me, most people couldn't tell that I was biracial. And I didn't go around broadcasting it, or bragging about it the way some mixed race folks did. My mother had been the only child of a so-called liberal White couple who had marched and protested all over Berkeley during the sixties.

Daddy had found out just how liberal his wife's family was when he married her. He'd been cussed out by Mama's family and she'd been disowned. I had never met any relatives on my late mother's side and didn't even know if they were still in Berkeley.

Some of Daddy's family still lived in Tennessee. And almost every Black person in Lubbock, Texas, was related to us. Daddy's deceased parents had moved to California while he was still in Vietnam. When he got out of the army he decided to settle in California. Four of Daddy's five siblings and their families were scattered all over the country. Uncle Pete, the family nitwit, was the only one who had also moved to California.

My only sibling, Gary, had died at nineteen in an automobile accident two years after Mama's death. Along with Daddy, my brother had been the center of my universe. Gary's death devastated me. I couldn't even go to his funeral. I stayed at the home of a girlfriend until some old sisters in the neighborhood helped Daddy dispose of Gary's belongings. When Goodwill came to get Gary's bedroom furniture, I discovered one of his Prince cassette tapes stuck behind the dresser drawer. The sight of it caused me to have a panic attack.

I crawled into Daddy's bed that night, wrapping my arms around his lumpy body so tight he could barely breathe. "You can sleep with me tonight, but don't you do this no more. It ain't natural," Daddy said, his face pressed against my hair. His bedroom was so dark and quiet that night I felt like I was in a tomb. I wanted to speak but couldn't find my voice. Somehow I managed to nod my head enough for Daddy to feel it.

I was all Daddy had left and he took full advantage of that. I'd had a lot of friends growing up, but I had not had a normal life as a teenager. Instead of parties and football games, I'd spent the best part of my youth sitting in the house listening to Daddy complain about his declining health. He had been a sergeant in the army so he knew how to manipulate people. Most of the time I felt like a puppet and Daddy was the one pulling the strings.

I'd had a few boyfriends along the way but the only one Daddy had accepted was James Young.

James was an only child, and when his meddlesome, bossy old mother, Mavis, wasn't running his life, he was running mine. He told me how to dress, how to act, how to behave, and even how to fuck sometimes. It would be more accurate to say that he *tried* to tell me what to do, because no matter what he suggested, I usually did what I wanted to do anyway. But James was a good man. He worked hard as a department store manager at the South Bay City Mall. He didn't smoke or do drugs, but he had a passion for beer. He was Daddy's first and most frequent customer after Daddy quit his job as a mechanic for United Airlines and opened the liquor store.

"James asked to take you to the movies this comin' Saturday night," Daddy informed me, six months after I'd graduated from high school. In addition to business college three days a week and an occasional clerical temp job, I worked behind the counter at the liquor store. My social life consisted of an occasional night out at the local clubs with a few of my girlfriends left over from high school.

"James who?" I asked.

"Mavis Young's boy," Daddy snapped.

"That James?" I yelled. "James is not my type," I said casually.

"Well, he more your type than some of them other scoundrels you done dragged to this house. He clean. He got a good job and he ain't never been in jail."

"And he's homely," I added with a smirk, which was not really that true. James was no Denzel, but he was fairly attractive. Even with a nose too big for his narrow face and thick black hair so knotty that he had to tame it with strong pomade.

"You ain't no glamour girl yourself," Daddy decided. "You'd do good to reel in a catch like James."

True. I was not in line to be the next Miss Black America, but I could be considered more than a little attractive with the right makeup and hairdo. But Daddy didn't like me wearing makeup and elaborate hairdos. He insisted that it attracted the wrong kind of attention. My plain face, limp ponytail, and tame clothes kept him off my back. However, that didn't stop men from asking me out. Even Mr. Clarke, the retired cook who worked part-time at Daddy's liquor store, made passes at me between his frequent trips to the local massage parlors.

I went to the movies with James that Saturday night and before I knew it, he was the only man I went out with. And since nobody else seemed interested enough in me to consider me wife material, I accepted James's unexpected marriage proposal five years into our relationship.

When it dawned on me that I was about to give up my freedom before really experiencing it, I took control of my own life so to speak: I signed up with an employment agency and I was willing to take any job I could get.

I had no idea what I was getting myself into.

CHAPTER 5

With James and Daddy being such good friends, James didn't have a problem with me working for Daddy. He encouraged it. He didn't have to say it, but I knew James well enough to know that he saw it as a way to keep me out of trouble and under his control. As a matter of fact, he considered it more of a "pastime" than a family obligation or a real job. He laughed and made jokes every time I complained about the long hours I put in at the liquor store, telling me I was lucky because I'd never had to do a real job. He sang a different tune whenever I mentioned working elsewhere.

"Most women would give anything in the world not to have to work," James told me when I shared my intentions with him. "My mama has never had to work a day in her life."

"Things have changed, baby. And your mama never wanted to work," I reminded him. James's mother and I got along all right. Especially since she was the only one who supported my desire to work for a few months before James and I got married. However, she had her own agenda: money. No matter how much James gave her it was never enough, so she was always asking him for "mo' money." With my own money, I wouldn't have to depend on James and that meant more for Mavis. With James's help and her widow's pension she lived well. But she was a small-minded, small-town woman who wore her greed like one of the many expensive hats she wore. I knew that with Mavis on my side, I'd be able to do what I wanted to do as long as I was bringing in some money.

Other than the movies, a few clubs, and the malls, the only other place that I went to on a regular basis was James's apartment, which was only six blocks from Daddy's liquor store. James had to drive past the store to get home, so it made sense for him to purchase his beer there, even though Daddy's prices were a little higher than some of the chain liquor stores. James was one who believed in Black folks supporting Black businesses, even the numerous liquor stores that dominated the Black neighborhoods. With alcoholism being such a big problem in the Black community, it made me nervous to know that someday I would inherit a liquor store. But I'd already made plans to sell the business and open a coffee shop as soon as Daddy passed on. The same people who liked to drink alcohol also liked coffee, and it didn't make sense for them to have to go all the way across town to the nearest Starbucks. James didn't know about my long-range plans, and I didn't plan to tell him until after we were married.

Visiting James's neat, inexpensive one-bedroom apartment next door to a car wash was something I still looked forward to. When we weren't wallowing on his three-legged couch, an old telephone book in the place of the missing leg, we spent our time in his bed. We sat on metal folding chairs in front of his fifty-three-inch, high-definition TV. Because he watched so much television, the TV was the only "luxury" item he owned. James could have afforded a larger apartment, but in addition to helping support his mother, he was also saving to buy a house. His car, a dull blue Nissan Sentra, was six years old.

What James didn't know was that Daddy had stashed away ten thousand dollars to give to us toward a down payment on a house once we were married. It was part of the money that Daddy had collected on one of several life insurance policies my mother had had. I saw no reason to share this information with James until the time was right. Money did strange things to people.

"Besides," I told James, "I could use the money I make to help pay for the wedding. And working for a travel agency, I could probably get us a good deal for a cruise or something for our honeymoon," I chirped. I was puzzled as to why James had such a bewildered look on his face that night as we sat on his couch watching television a week ago.

James gritted his teeth and shook his head. "We don't have to go on no honeymoon, and you know I make enough to pay for every-thing we'll need." He abruptly stopped talking and gave me a thoughtful look. "You do not have to work. Once we get married, the house, and the kids when they come, will be more than enough to keep you busy," he said, bobbing his head.

"Well, let me do this just for my own peace of mind. I don't ask for much, James, and I don't think that me working at a travel agency is asking for too much. It's just for a few months, anyway."

"You can do whatever you want to do, Trudy. I'm just letting you know what I think about it." James let out a heavy sigh and gave me a sharp look. "You are going to do whatever it is you want to anyway, right?"

"That's right," I said defiantly, folding my arms.

"Then why are we discussing this in the first place? Did you think you needed my permission?"

"Look, I don't need permission from you to do anything," I snapped, holding my hand up to James's surprised face. "My daddy's name is Otto Bell. I just thought it made sense for me to tell you before I did it."

We argued a few minutes more, but I calmed James down the best way I knew how. While he was busy watching a *Sanford and Son* rerun and sipping from his sixth can of Miller Light, I was busy licking his naked crotch.

CHAPTER 6

My training at Heald's Business College had prepared me well for my job interviews. In addition to the secretary's position at the Bon Voyage Travel Agency in downtown San Jose, three other places had offered me jobs. I'd eagerly accepted the job at the travel agency and showed up for work the following Monday after I'd been robbed at the liquor store.

Compared to Daddy's liquor store and the few other places where I'd done clerical work, Bon Voyage was the height of glamour. A few years ago I'd temped as a receptionist for a sausage-making factory in nearby Santa Clara. I'd left after three days when I found out that a man's finger got caught in one of the grinding devices and ended up in a package of link sausages. After that I worked for a halfway house and then an old folks' home, one just as bad as the other. I had seen enough despair to last me a lifetime. Working for a glamorous travel agency in downtown San Jose was just what I needed after enduring all of that.

Bon Voyage shared a huge beige building with several other businesses. There was a bank on one side and a deli on the other. The clerical employees worked on the ground floor where huge posters of exotic places covered every wall in the reception area. A rack with travel brochures stood a few feet to the side of my desk. Facing my desk was a desk occupied by a receptionist whose main job was to greet and announce customers. The other employees of Bon Voyage occupied offices on the second floor, which they shared with the employees from a small insurance agency.

"We keep the front door locked at all times. We've had a few problems with the homeless people from the park down the street. Someone has to be in the reception area at all times to let customers and delivery people in. Even during the lunch hour. Now that you're here you'll share that responsibility with the receptionist." Speaking to me was Wendy Barker, the woman who had been assigned to train me. Wendy was also the woman whom I was replacing. She had recently been promoted to bookkeeper. Her cluttered workstation was a cubicle a few feet behind my desk.

Standing by the side of my desk, Wendy rambled off a short list of tame do's and don'ts. Why she felt she had to frown at each one was a mystery to me. Helping keep the break room neat and calling in if I had to take the day off were nothing compared to what I'd already had to put up with at my other jobs. "This is not an easy place to work for. If the going gets too rough for you, I advise you to leave right away. Don't hang around here wasting anybody's time, even your own," she said in a firm voice, shaking a finger in my face like I was five years old. That gesture alone let me know that I would have to feed Wendy with a long-handled spoon. There was nothing I hated more than people who patronized me, especially now that I was approaching thirty. "Do you think you can handle this job?"

"I know I can," I said, nodding my head. I smiled when it was appropriate, but I went out of my way to avoid giving Wendy the impression that I was someone she could dominate. "Is there anything else?" I asked, looking at my watch, then the telephone on my desk.

Wendy let out a weak gasp. "Uh, no, I guess not. A lot of this stuff you will learn as you go along."

"Good. Now if you don't mind, I'd like to get to work," I said in a firm voice but with a huge smile. Wendy stared at me with her mouth slightly open. "Thank you so much for taking the time to show me the ropes. And by the way, where did you get that blouse?" I asked with a raised eyebrow.

"Uh, this old thing? It was a gift from me to me after I had my son," Wendy said with a blink and an eager smile. I could tell that she enjoyed any attention she could get. And something told me that Wendy didn't get many compliments.

"It looks very nice on you," I said.

"Th . . . thanks. Maybe that's why my son's godmother tried to take it away from me." Wendy let out a hesitant chuckle. Then she sucked in her breath, stood up straighter, smoothed the sides of her skirt, and patted her hair. This made me think she was fishing for another compliment.

"I'm not surprised. You have nice taste. I bet you've had your colors done, too," I chided.

Wendy's eyes widened and she stood up even straighter. "I sure have! You're the first person to bring that up." Wendy looked at me with admiration. "Here, let me hang up your jacket. There's a coatrack in my cube." I had Wendy figured out from day one, but I still planned to feed her with a long-handled spoon.

So far everything was going the way I wanted it to. It was going to be a real challenge to act and speak properly on a regular basis after dealing with some of the ignorant people I'd dealt with at the liquor store for so many years. It was a good thing I could shift gears as well as the next woman from the 'hood.

The Bon Voyage receptionist, Pamela Bennett, was a petite woman in her early thirties with a potbelly. She had chalky white skin, thick curly red hair, and a face full of freckles. Pam stared in silence from her desk as Wendy hovered over my desk with a clipboard in one hand and a tall Styrofoam cup of coffee in the other. Both Wendy and Pam wore stylish dresses, dangling earrings, too much makeup, and heels that made me cringe in pain from just looking at them.

Wendy cleared her throat and lifted her chin as if to establish a level of authority. She was more attractive than Pam. Her blond hair was long and silky, but the dark roots and her slightly pockmarked skin worked against her. She looked to be about thirty, but one of the first things she had told me was that she had just celebrated her twenty-third birthday.

After hanging up my jacket, Wendy darted back out of her cubicle to my workstation. "Do you have any kids?"

I shook my head. "Not yet, but I plan to," I said proudly.

"Well, too bad you can't use a child-care problem as an excuse when the real reason you need a day off is to get over a hangover, like me and Pam." Wendy gave Pam a conspiratorial glance and they both laughed. I didn't think her comment was funny but I chuckled anyway. Then she cleared her throat and leaned toward me, brushing the top of my head with her narrow chin. "And between you and me, don't ever forget your place," she whispered. She followed that with a smile. That's when I noticed her slightly crooked yellow teeth.

"Excuse me?" I leaned back to avoid Wendy's breath, which smelled like stale weed and coffee.

Wendy glanced at Pam again before she continued. "Well, you are just a secretary and to some people that's just a glorified servant. Do not, I repeat, do not refer to the travel reps here as agents. Bon Voyage is a one-of-a-kind travel agency and the reps want to be called reps." Wendy gave me an annoyed look. "These travel reps all think their shit don't stink so they expect us clerical folks to keep our nose up against their butts. Dennis Klein and Joy Banning are pretty harmless. Lupe Gonzalez is the only one you can trust, and the one you'll really have to keep your eye on is that Ann Oliver."

"Is she the owner?" I asked, glancing at Pam who had just snickered and clapped her hands together. I played with the top button on the jacket of one of the new suits I'd purchased. Even Daddy had commented on how good I looked in red before I'd left for work that morning. But he'd also criticized the length of my skirt and the nail tips I'd spent money on.

"She acts like she is," Pam volunteered. The tiny steps she took over to my desk and the grimace on her spotty face made it seem like she was in pain. She straightened the brochure rack as she watched and listened.

Wendy gave Pam another conspiratorial look. "Ann wishes," Wendy snapped. "The way she prances around this place you'd think she was the queen of the Nile. The way Mr. Rydell lets Ann behave around here she must be sucking his dick." Wendy paused and looked at me for my reaction. I just blinked. "We're pretty loose around here so I hope you don't have virgin ears." She dipped her head and looked at me with her eyes bugged out.

"Hell, no," I scoffed.

"I didn't think so. Now, Mr. Rydell, he's the dude who interviewed you and hired you. He's the owner. Despite the fact that he's totally clueless, he's as cool as they come. He's into that affirmative action shit so he lets minorities get away with murder. But even as big a bitch as Lupe is, for a Mexican she's pretty smart, so she knows her place. I'd rather deal with her than Ann. That heifer's ass gets kissed more than the Pope's ring. No wonder she walks around here like she owns the place." Wendy gritted her teeth and gave me a critical look. "She's Black, too, but you'd never know it with the snooty way she treats our Black clients." Wendy lowered her voice and leaned across my desk. "No offense, but I am sure you know how some Black folks behave when you give them a little power . . ."

I had led a sheltered life so far and had never been one to speak my mind, but Wendy's attitude forced me into a defensive mode. "Power can be a dangerous thing in the wrong hands," I said, grinding my teeth. My sarcasm went right over Wendy's head. She didn't bat an eye or change her direction. It took all of the strength I had to keep from saying something really harsh. But since Wendy had already shown me that she had such a narrow, opinionated view of minorities, the last thing I wanted to do was reinforce her beliefs. I was already wondering if I'd made a mistake accepting this job.

"I have my own ways of dealing with people like Ann," Wendy said smugly, giving Pam a smug glance and a nod.

Racism was not new to me. I had dealt with it almost every day of my life. However, I decided that Wendy was more of an ignoramus than she was a racist.

"Just do your job, and watch your step and your back. If things get too tough for you, don't worry: there's a liquor store down the street." Wendy leaned closer and whispered. "And I keep a big bottle in my desk drawer that I don't mind sharing."

"And I have enough breath mints for an army," Pam added with a grin.

"I don't think I'll need any alcohol to do my job," I said firmly. If anybody had a reason to drink, it was me. But if working in Daddy's liquor store for so many years, where I had access to all of the alcohol I wanted, hadn't sent me running to a bottle every time I had a problem, nothing would.

I was wrong.

CHAPTER 7

Before I met Ann Oliver, just knowing that she was Black made me feel more at ease. One of the things that I had hated about some of my temp jobs was the fact that I had often been the only Black person on the premises. Even in a state as liberal and racially diverse as California, being alone around too many White folks was something I was not used to. The funny thing about that was my White mother had felt the same way! She had always worn her hair in elaborate braided hairstyles that had been made popular by Black women. She'd danced, cooked, talked, and imitated mannerisms associated with Black women. "Trudy, think of me as a Black woman in a White woman's body," she had told me once when I was nine, laughing as she said it. It was funny to me then, but once I got older I realized how hard life must have been for a woman like my mother. But she'd made me feel proud to be Black. I cherished the sisterhood I shared with my Black female friends.

I looked forward to my first encounter with Ann with nervous anticipation. But after hearing all of the catty things that Wendy and Pam had said about her, I had some valid concerns. Some unpleasant experiences lingered in the back of my mind.

I had worked more than one temp job that had included some of the most unpleasant Black people on the planet. One conceited woman at an engineering firm—a low level file clerk at that—had gotten her kicks by correcting me whenever I used bad grammar, which was why it was so important for me not to make that mistake again. It had been years since I'd even said ain't.

Another so-called sister had advised me in a very harsh way to stop wearing a particular blouse with an African design, insisting that it made me look militant. Even after having dealt with Black folks like those two women, and witnessing the regular fights among the folks in my neighborhood, I still regarded Black folks very highly. I still thought of other Black women as sisters. I had no idea that my first encounter with Ann Oliver would turn out to be such a disaster.

Two days after my first day on the job she returned from a trip in Martinique where she had toured with a church group. I arrived at the office that morning fifteen minutes late. Ann was already in the reception area wrestling with that brochure rack, which had already become a major thorn in my side. It seemed like every time somebody got near that damn thing they had to straighten the brochures.

Ann whirled around to face me before I could even shut the door. "You've missed three calls," she barked at me with a wild-eyed look. It was hard to believe that she was showing so much emotion over some missed telephone calls.

Pam, peeping from behind a folder at her desk, cleared her throat as Ann strutted across the floor like a prize-winning poodle. She had on an expensive-looking cream colored pantsuit. Her thick shiny black hair was in a French twist. Gold hoop earrings dangled from her ears, a matching locket adorned her swan-like neck. All of the new work clothes that I'd purchased did update and improve my appearance. But the generic suits, blouses, and pumps I'd purchased from a couple of discount stores and a factory outlet looked it. I didn't own much jewelry or any other adornments, so I'd purchased some new silver metal clips to hold my shoulder length ponytail in place. Even with all my improvements, compared to Ann I looked and felt as dowdy as a fishwife.

"I'm Gertrude Bell, but I go by Trudy," I said nervously, taking my seat as Ann approached my desk. She was a stunning woman, even with the pronounced scowl on her face and her flaring nostrils. She was about my height and weight and medium-brown skin tone, but the most obvious similarities ended there.

Her face, which was probably quite average, was made up like a super-model's. Hunter green eye shadow enhanced her shiny black eyes and

long silky black lashes. There was just a hint of blush on her high
cheekbones. She had a set of teeth so white and perfect they looked
like a toothpaste ad. This woman was definitely in control, and had
enough confidence for both of us. I never felt so drab and frumpy in
my life.

She stopped in front of my desk and slapped one hand on her hip,
a sparkling charm bracelet dangling from her wrist. "I know who you
are," she said in a flat tone. "If you don't want your first week to be
your last, I suggest you get to work on time. Do I make myself clear?"
One perfectly arched eyebrow arched up even more. Getting impatient because I was taking too long to respond, she lifted her chin and
gazed down at me with her eyes sparkling like black diamonds.
Which, by the way, were not covered by a pair of schoolteacher-looking
glasses like the ones I wore. The way that heifer sniffed, looked around,
and rubbed her nose, I regretted the fact that I had splashed myself
with the knock-off version of Eternity perfume after I'd showered that
morning. "You're being paid to do a job and do it right. Being on
time is not asking for too much. Next time you roll in here late, I'll
have Wendy dock your pay."

My purse was still dangling from my shoulder and I still had my
new imitation leather jacket on. I removed my glasses, patted the side
of my head and smiled so hard my cheeks ached. "Yes. It won't happen again," I mumbled, so stunned I couldn't stop blinking.

"See to it," Ann snapped. Clutching a tall coffee cup with her name
on it in big bold, black letters, she turned on her stiletto heels and
marched toward the elevator that led to her office on the second
floor where she reportedly ruled.

Pam leaped up from her seat and skittered over to my desk shaking
her head. "Looks like you got off on the wrong foot with her," she
said, giving me a look of pity. "She's not that bad, though. She could
be your best friend, or your worst enemy. That's the way it was between her and Jeannette, the Black girl who used to do Wendy's job.
One day Ann took her to lunch. The very next day when Jeannette
came to work twenty minutes late, Ann called her into her office and
beat her down for an *hour* about how important it is to be punctual.
She's especially brutal when Marty's not around to keep her under
control."

"Who is Marty?" I asked.

With a hint of impatience in her voice she said, "Who is Marty?

That's Mr. Rydell's first name. He interviewed three other girls for your job but if he picked you that means he likes you. Now don't let that go to your head. A jackass in a suit is still a jackass. Martin is what he prefers, but Ann is the only one who can get away with calling him Marty to his face. Remember that," Pam said with a serious look and a controlled nod.

"Do whatever she wants you to do, if you want to keep this job," Wendy warned, tiptoeing from the small room behind her cubicle where the office supplies were kept. "And just to let you know, Ann's got a long reach. She gave Jeannette such a bad reference when she tried to get a new job, the poor girl is still unemployed."

I nodded. "Which drawer do you keep that bottle in?" I sighed.

CHAPTER 8

No matter how much I complained about my life I did have a lot to be thankful for. I was thankful that I was still young enough to make the changes in my life I felt I needed.

Unlike a lot of the women I knew, my daddy had been in my life from day one. He had never abused me in any way. Well, there were times when his whining and complaining got on my nerves enough to give me a headache, and he was overly protective, but my daddy was the most important person in my life. Despite the fact that the Bible told us to put our mates before our parents, or something like that, I knew I'd never put James, or any other man, before my daddy. The one thing I believed with all my heart and soul was that I could count on Daddy to do anything in the world for me. Even die. I couldn't say that about James or any other man in my life.

I knew that I couldn't really be happy if Daddy wasn't. His alleged bad health kept me under his thumb up to a point, but we both knew that things would change once I got married. The thought of Daddy being in the house alone was not a thought I allowed to enter my mind too often. Other than me, he didn't want to share his beloved house with anybody else. I found that out when I suggested moving a couple of his wayward cousins from Lubbock, Texas, in with us because nobody else in the family would. "Heeeel no!" was the way Daddy had reacted, screaming the words in such a violent way he lost his breath. "After what I went through when I was growing up with them lowlife, no-workin', countrified niggers, they ain't fin to come to California and finish drivin' me crazy." My only other hope was for Daddy to settle down with a lady friend. But that was highly unlikely, too. He had not been in a serious relationship since my mother's death. However, there was an old sister here and there who he visited from time to time. Most of them I never got to meet and didn't even know about until I found a package of condoms in Daddy's shirt pocket one day when I was preparing clothes for the laundry. His current lady friend was a retired waitress who lived on the south side of town in a trailer with her three grandsons. The boys' parents had died in a nightclub fire when the youngest boy was a baby.

I'd only seen Miss Sadie once, but she'd been a vague part of Daddy's life off and on for the last two years. They got together at her place and they didn't have to worry about her grandsons getting in the way because they were all in and out of jail or shacking up with their lady friends most of the time anyway. I'd never met the boys and after all the things I heard about them from Daddy, I didn't want to. I had a fairly blessed life and I wanted to keep it that way.

One of the biggest blessings in my life was my best friend, Freddie Ann Malone. She was the only other living person who was as important to me as Daddy and James.

Freddie had been my best friend since seventh grade when her family moved to South Bay City from Oakland. When I returned to school the Monday after attending my mother's funeral, Freddie was sitting in the seat behind me in Mrs. Reichard's homeroom.

I was still preoccupied and numb from the shock of losing my mother in such a horrible way. But even with that on my mind, I knew from the first moment that Freddie was one of a kind.

Before even introducing herself, she tapped me on the back and leaned toward me and whispered in my ear. "I heard about what happened to your mama so I took my babysitting money and got you a sympathy card. I didn't bring it today because Mrs. Reichard said she didn't know exactly when you'd be coming back to school."

I rotated my neck so that I could see her face. "Thanks," was all I could manage.

My new classmate was a very sweet and likeable girl. It was a good thing she had that going for her because she was more than a little homely. She had long wavy brown hair and the high-yellow skin tone that a lot of Black people would have sold their souls to the devil to have. But she had a long face, bulging eyes, and big ears that she didn't even try to hide underneath her long hair.

Even though I was still grieving the loss of my mother, I felt sorry for this girl.

"I'm Freddie Ann Malone." She smiled, revealing yet another flaw. There were gaps between her teeth like a rake.

"Is that short for Fredericka?" I asked, hoping that this sad sack wasn't looking to latch on to me, which would certainly lower my social status even more. My drab clothes, thick glasses, and shyness caused me enough grief.

I'd like to say at this point that, at the time, I'd held the position as the plainest girl in my class with a personality to match. At least that's what my classmates had decided. Even though I was not considered "classically" ugly, I had been compared with every unattractive famous Black individual you could name, which I won't because some of the ones on the list *think* they look good.

And on the subject, some of the kids who criticized me should have been wearing dog collars themselves. However, a lot of my misfortune had to do with the fact that I wasn't allowed to do anything to enhance my appearance. Makeup, an up-to-date hairdo, contact lenses, and trendy clothes would have made my younger years a lot easier to get through. "Looks aren't everything," Mama had told me, which explained why she'd dressed me the way she had. She used to brag about all the tacky granny dresses she had once owned. In every picture I'd ever seen of her as a young, barefoot, hard-core hippie, she'd worn long bone-straight hair full of flowers and beads. She'd looked so proud posing with Daddy with his huge, globe-shaped afro and equally tacky clothes. I often thought that life would have been more exciting for me if I'd been a teenager during the sixties. But since I'd been born too late, I had made up my mind to make the best I could out of my life.

"No. Freddie Ann is the name on my birth certificate. It's special and so am I."

Special was a mild way to describe Freddie Ann. She made no secret that she was as proud as a person could be without being a braggart. She boldly displayed a framed photograph of herself, her parents, and her four younger siblings on top of her desk. Her father looked like a gnome himself, but somehow he had convinced her that she was the most beautiful girl in the world. It seemed odd that the other members of Freddie's family in her photo were reasonably attractive. By the time we got to high school, she had become one of the most popular girls in our school.

Freddie's confidence was contagious. The popular boys wanted to get in her pants, the popular cute girls—who still had low self-esteem—wanted to hang with Freddie, hoping to absorb some of her confidence.

I was proud to call Freddie my best friend. I was lucky to have a friend like her to call up when I had a problem. Daddy was always there for me, but I knew better than to take up his time with petty issues only another woman could understand. I didn't like to share too much personal information about myself with a lot of people. Some of the individuals I knew had such long tongues they couldn't keep their mouths shut. Even with a vague piece of information they would spread rumors like manure. Of all the people I knew Freddie was the only one I knew with whom I could discuss my disastrous first encounter with Ann.

CHAPTER 9

Less than an hour after she'd first approached me, Ann Oliver sashayed back into the reception area holding a large, flat white box, carrying it like it contained a pizza. As soon as I spotted her my entire body got so rigid I felt like I had turned to stone. My throat felt dry and obstructed, like a big fuzzy lump had suddenly formed in it. The huge sip of vodka from Wendy's bottle hadn't really helped that much because it seemed like my brain was just sitting inside the middle of my head with no activity going on. I didn't even feel like I was part of the scene, even though Ann's eyes were looking straight at me.

"Trudy, I hope you like chocolate," Ann said, strutting over to my desk. "I stumbled across the most fantastic candy store in Martinique and I couldn't resist." She paused and set the box on the corner of my desk and flipped the lid open. "You can afford the extra calories a lot more than I can," she said, displaying a smile so wide I could see almost every tooth in her mouth. Her head swiveled around, looking over my shoulder toward Wendy's cube then back to look in Pam's direction. "Pam, Wendy, knock yourselves out," Ann chirped, beckoning to Pam with a hand so animated it seemed disembodied. Wendy popped out of her cubicle like a jack-in-the-box. Pam skipped across the floor to my desk with an exaggerated grin, grabbing chocolate with both hands.

"Thank you," I mumbled. I didn't really care that much for choco-late, but I snatched two pieces at the same time, giving Ann a friendly but noncommittal look.

"Now if you all call in sick tomorrow, I'll know why," Ann said, rub-bing her palms together so hard I saw sparks. She spun around and left, floating across the floor like she was on wheels.

Wendy and Pam, with chocolate smeared across their lips, stared at me with anxious looks on their faces. "That was nice of Ann," I com-mented.

"Trudy, you ain't seen nothing yet," Wendy began. "The woman is like a fart in a windstorm. You'll never know which direction she's coming from or going to." Wendy's warning had such an ominous feel to it I couldn't even comment.

I appreciated Ann's gesture, but I couldn't help feeling apprehen-sive and suspicious of her motives. She had already made a lasting first impression on me. I couldn't wait to talk to Freddie.

"Girl, we need to talk. I am so glad you called. I'll meet you after work in your lobby. We can ride the bus home together," I said, whis-pering into the telephone on my desk an hour before quitting time. I had been too busy and nervous to chat with Freddie before now. She worked at Bank of America, three blocks and two streets over from my office. She was a bank teller so she spent most of her day at the counter. It wasn't that easy for me to call her at her work. When I knew she was on one of her breaks I called her on her cell. Otherwise, I had to wait for her to call me. "Where are you?" I asked, fanning my face. I knew that I was way too young to be having hot flashes, so I wasn't sure why my face suddenly felt like somebody was holding a flame in front of it. I was quite sure that it had something to do with Ann Oliver's odd behavior.

"I'm calling from that phone booth outside the Starbucks down the street from the bank. Is this about the robbery last Friday?" Freddie wanted to know. I had not even told her about what had hap-pened to me at the liquor store yet. But news traveled fast in our neighborhood.

With one hand cupped over my left ear, I pressed my telephone to the side of my face. It must have generated some heat of its own be-cause my face felt even hotter. I could feel sweat sliding down my cheeks and chin. "Uh, no. Worse. A personal issue." I lowered my voice even more. Both Wendy and Pam looked like they were trying to listen in on my conversation. "I might have made a mistake accepting this position," I whispered.

"Shit. You know I am dying to hear what's going on, but I can't meet you after work today," Freddie said with an apologetic tone. I didn't even ask her why she couldn't meet me. My girl had a huge plate and it was always full. I was just a small piece on it.

"I'll call you at home later on tonight. If I get a few things out of the way, and it's not too late, I'll drop by for a drink. You can tell me everything then. And it better be something juicy," Freddie teased.

Before I could even mention the subject, Ann appeared again. Without a word, she strolled over to my desk and stuck a yellow Post-It on the monitor of my computer. She didn't even look at me or say a word before she strutted back toward the elevator.

"I have to go," I sighed, lifting the Post-It. That hussy's handwriting looked like chicken scratch. It was a real struggle to read what she had written. "Freddie, would you believe that this heifer came all the way from the second floor to tell me to add toner to the fax machine?"

"What's wrong with that?"

I could hear Wendy and Pam snickering and clucking like old setting hens in a barnyard. I didn't bother to whisper anymore. "The damn fax machine is right outside her office. She had to walk right by it to get to me. She could have saved herself some time by adding that damn shit herself." I let out a snort that made my nose burn.

Freddie was snickering now. "Welcome to the real world, baby girl, baby girl," she chanted. "Now you know what I go through every damn day of my life. By the time they get through with you, girlfriend, you'll be running back to that counter in your daddy's liquor store."

"Now I don't know about all that," I protested. "I don't think this job here is *that* bad."

"Hmmm-huh." Freddie let out a huge snort. "Not yet. If I can, I'll call you tonight."

I stared at my monitor for about a minute more and would have done so longer if my phone hadn't rung. It was Ann.

"Trudy?"

"Ann?"

"Uh, yes . . ." Her hesitation confused me. For a full twenty seconds—I counted them on my watch—she remained silent. I knew she was still on the line because there was a faint hum with each breath she took. I didn't know where she was coming from or going to. She really was like a fart in a windstorm. "Trudy, did you see my note?" she huffed.

"Oh, yes. I was just about to go take care of that," I said meekly.

"Good. After you're done with that, swing by Starbucks and bring me a tall mild, a dash of half and half, no sugar . . . please. Thank you." She hung up before I could tell her that it was almost quitting time for me.

"She wants me to go to Starbucks to get her some coffee," I said to Pam, glancing at my watch. "I'm going to miss my bus." I sat there in slack-jawed amazement with my eyes blinking and itching.

"You're going to miss more than that by the time Ann's through with you," Pam predicted, shutting off her computer and struggling into her jacket at the same time. "When she gets her period, she gets so bloated she can't even button her clothes. That's when she turns into a real demon."

"How can you tell the difference?" I asked.

"Oh, you'll find out. Nothing you do will please her. She'll be as cold as ice. So during that time of the month, I advise you to dress warm."

Wendy trotted out of her cube, buttoning her sweater and shaking her head. "Look on the bright side, Trudy. Since your father owns a liquor store, you might want to bring in a few extra bottles yourself. I think you're going to need it."

The last thing I wanted to do was develop a steady relationship with alcohol like Wendy and Pam. From what they'd shared with me about their situations it hadn't really helped them that much. Both had told me more about their backgrounds than I wanted to know.

Wendy, the eldest of three children, didn't get along with her family. She was the daughter of a former coal miner and the town slut. She had been born and raised in the hills of Kentucky. She'd lived in California for ten years but still had a slight hillbilly accent. Her entire family, even her two teenage brothers, drank cheap whiskey like water and fought like cats and dogs.

Pam's history was even worse. Her epileptic husband had run off with another woman while Pam was in the hospital giving birth to their son. She hadn't heard from him since. Pam's mother had died in a mental ward and she'd never known her father. She had to have a drink just to get to sleep every night. Her six-year-old son was so incorrigible she had to change babysitters every three or four months.

My life was a bowl of cherries compared to theirs, and unlike them, I had a lot of pride and I was not about to let Ann Oliver ruin that.

Having to run down the street to Starbucks and add toner to the fax machine was going to make me miss my bus and I would have to wait half an hour for the next one.

Starbucks was two blocks away and I cussed all the way down there. I cussed even more when I got to the place because that was when I realized Ann hadn't given me any money, so I had to pay for her tall mild cup of coffee with money out of my pocket.

The fact that Ann was Black made it even worse. Sisterhood, and even brotherhood for that matter, took on a whole new meaning when I felt I'd been mistreated. Getting robbed and assaulted by that young brother at the liquor store a week ago was still fresh on my mind. I felt soiled. I knew I had to do something to make myself feel good again.

Every time that robber's face entered my mind, so did Ann's. I couldn't do a thing to get back at the robber. I'd have to take out my wrath on somebody else. When I look back on it now, I think that that was the moment when I got the notion in me that I could at least make Ann sorry for the way she treated me. I planned to do that by not allowing her to destroy what little dignity I had left. No matter how mean she was to me, and no matter how much it hurt, she'd never know it. But that depended on whether or not I remained on the job.

The way things were going, there was a strong possibility that I'd get fired first.

CHAPTER 10

It didn't take long for Bon Voyage to become an obsession with me. It filled a vacancy in my life that I had ignored too long. It didn't matter if I was on the premises or not, the place dominated my mind. Every time I saw a travel ad or a travel commercial on television, I thought about Bon Voyage. With just a little effort and imagination, in my confused mind it was my face on the bodies of the models stretched out under palm trees on the beaches in the ads. Or was it Ann's face? Sometimes I couldn't tell the difference. Even with a she-devil like Ann in the picture, to me, Bon Voyage was The Rapture compared to my old job at Daddy's liquor store. And, it was also a lot more interesting than every temp job I'd had.

Bon Voyage was more than a job to me. It was a distraction. The money was good, but not *that* good, so there was more to it than that. A lot of the appeal had to do with the fact that it was a travel agency. To me that represented *escape*. When I was in the office I didn't think about the robbery and assault as much as I did when I was at home. And when it did enter my mind at work it didn't seem to bother me as much as it usually did. One of the most important aspects of my relationship with Bon Voyage was that it helped me set aside my ongoing grief over losing my mother and my brother.

The office was closed on the weekends. It closed its doors to the public promptly at five P.M. every weekday evening, but we all had keys to get in after hours. As hard as it was for me to believe, some of the reps worked way past our regular hours. Often, they had the nerve to come in and work the weekends, too. Exactly what they did that kept them so busy was a mystery to me. Now, I knew that they traveled a lot and sat around negotiating all kinds of package deals with hotels, airlines, cruise lines, important clients and such. But they also spent a great deal of time socializing with each other during the day. Naturally, Ann was the leader of the pack. Her office was more like a clubhouse because that's where Mr. Rydell and the rest of the reps could usually be found, all at the same time.

When Ann wasn't on the telephone in her office yakking away to somebody in French (she could speak *two* foreign languages), or behaving like what Freddie called "the house nigger," she strutted around, showing off a different new outfit, fishing for compliments. I couldn't count the number of times I had overheard her ask somebody, "does this dress make my butt look big?" Ann did not have a weight problem and her round-sided, moderately extended butt, which was about the same size as mine, was typical for a Black woman. Wendy and Pam, and Joy Banning—the most likeable of the reps—all complained about being overweight. I could always count on seeing one of them poring over a diet book every day. The ones who should have been more concerned about their weight, plump Mr. Rydell and lumpy Lupe Gonzalez, nibbled and gnawed on something off and on all day long.

Dennis Klein, being the only male employee at Bon Voyage, except for Mr. Rydell, stood out like a lighthouse. He looked like a thirty-year-old version of Harry Potter and sometimes acted like one, too. Dennis behaved like a spoiled only male in a family of doting females. Even Ann catered to him. I often saw her brush lint off his clothes, straighten his tie and lapels, and smooth down his bowl-shaped hairdo with the palm of her hand.

This bunch was a real-life reality show. To them, vanity seemed like a job requirement. Next to Evian and coffee from Starbucks, Slim-Fast was the most popular drink at Bon Voyage. The whole crew swallowed cans of that stuff like it was holy water. Especially after gobbling up a croissant. But with Pam and Wendy, who both slurped at least one can of Slim-Fast a day, the bottle of vodka in Wendy's drawer was the top of the line.

A few days ago Ann requested coffee from Starbucks, again. It came as a complete surprise and inconvenience to me, again. As interesting as Bon Voyage was, I looked forward to quitting time each day. But it looked like my "quitting time" was going to vary from one day to the next.

When I got back to the office with Ann's coffee she was nowhere to be found. After I had checked her office, the ladies' room, the break room, and the other reps' offices, I assumed she was gone. But her coat and purse, as well as the personal belongings of all the other reps, were still where they were supposed to be. More puzzled than I was angry, I also searched the stairwell and the supply room. I did what I thought any other sane person in my position would do, I set the now-cold coffee on Ann's desk and I prepared to leave for home. Just the thought of leaving without knowing where Ann was made my head spin. Even though I had done what she had asked me to do, and something that was not really part of my job.

I sighed as I reentered the ground floor. Being in the reception area alone, not being bombarded with telephone calls, Pam and Wendy's catty chatter, and customers who couldn't make up their mind where they wanted to travel to, I felt totally different. Pictures of huge jetliners on some of the posters seemed to jump out at me. Even in the dim light, the reception area was mesmerizing. Pam had slapped some bold new posters onto the main wall that featured beaches from the Caribbean to Hawaii.

When I made it back to my desk I plucked the latest edition of the *Enquirer* out of my in box where Wendy had left it. Wendy and Pam, and now I, read every ratty tabloid and women's magazine on the market. Just as I was about to stuff the tabloid, which contained a cover that was lurid even by tabloid standards, into my purse, Ann stumbled in the front door dangling her keys. She stopped in front of me.

"Oh, it's you," I said, blinking stupidly.

"So?" Ann snapped, kicking the door shut with her foot. She opened her mouth to speak again, but stopped when she noticed my reading material.

She looked at me with an amused grin on her face. Then she made sure that I saw that the *Wall Street Journal* was the newspaper folded under her arm. She held it up and fanned her face with it.

"I left the coffee on your desk," I said, fiddling with the buttons on my jacket as I moved swiftly toward the door. "You asked me to . . . get you some coffee from Starbucks," I reminded her.

"I did?" she asked, her eyes rolling from side to side like marbles.

She had forgotten what she had ordered me to do that quickly!
"Hmmm," she said, scratching her head, flopping her newspaper in
front of her face, which now displayed a thin film of sweat. It was hard
for me to even imagine a prima donna like Ann experiencing a
bodily function as basic as sweating. "Are you sure?" She gave me a
look that would have made me feel stupid under normal circumstances. I had done more than my share of stupid things in my life.

This was not one of them.

CHAPTER 11

"Yes, I'm sure," I said firmly. "You were very specific," I insisted. Ann shrugged. "Well, today's my weekly evening appointment at the nail shop on the mezzanine across the street next to the boutique," she said, giving me a guarded look and waving her freshly polished hand. "Now, there are a few other things that you need to take care of before you leave today." She blew on her nails and waved her hand, beckoning me to follow her to her office. Walking behind her, I realized she didn't look as good from behind as she did from the front. Her butt was slightly lopsided and she had, of all things, flat feet. But what topped that were the hard-looking beads of nappy hair decorating the back of her neck like pebbles. I had to wonder if she would have thought so highly of herself if she could see what I saw. I had been taught to pity difficult people who couldn't see themselves the way others did. So despite her behavior, I pitied Ann.

She started to hum "Don't Worry, Be Happy," that old Bobby McFerrin song that had been sung to death. With her husky voice it sounded even more annoying. Then she gave me a two-inch stack of two-sided documents to photocopy and put into a binder, separating each section with tabs.

After the binder assignment, which took me an hour to complete, Ann handed me a bundle of new brochures to incorporate into the supply already on the rack by my desk.

To be on the safe side, I returned to Ann's office to see if she had any other chores for me before I left to go home.

"That's all for today, Trudy." She smiled. "I really do appreciate your help," she added as I handed her the binder. I was comfortable until she looked at my turtleneck sweater like it was a gunnysack. "Where do you live, Trudy, Oakland?"

San Jose was considered the distant, jealous cousin of San Francisco, two hours north. But Oakland, right across the bay from San Francisco, was often referred to as San Francisco's ugly stepsister. Mr. Clarke, the horny old man who helped Daddy run the liquor store, was from Oakland and was too embarrassed to admit it. Just from Ann's tone of voice, she made Oakland sound like a shantytown.

"South Bay City," I said flatly, bile rising in my throat. "I was born and raised there."

"Oh," she said, rubbing her nose. "Dennis got carjacked in South Bay. But I still don't think it's as rough as Oakland."

"No place is safe anymore," I said firmly.

She nodded and sniffed. "You know, I appreciate your staying late. If you can hang on for another hour or so, I'll give you a ride home."

Another hour or so. I was in such a state of disbelief that my head was about to explode and slide off my shoulders. And what was I supposed to do for the next hour or so? There was nothing on my desk that couldn't wait. I had a feeling that if I didn't make myself scarce soon, Ann would probably have me dusting the elevator.

Waiting for her to finish her work was one thing, but the thought of being stuck by myself in the same car with Ann Oliver made my stomach expand. "That's all right. I can wait for the next bus." I paused because I had to choose my words carefully. "I don't want you to go out of your way," I said. *I don't want you to see where I live,* was what I was thinking.

"Aw, shuck it, girl!" Ann shouted with a dismissive wave. "Take a cab. Get a receipt. I'll have Wendy reimburse you from the petty cash fund." She bowed her head and focused her attention on a sheet of paper on her desk.

"If you don't mind, I'd rather take the bus," I said with a broad smile. "Is there anything else you want me to do before I go?" I asked in a voice that was rapidly losing steam. Ann's sudden and unexpected kindness had thrown me off balance. "Your coffee's cold," I said, nodding toward the cup I'd set on her desk earlier. "Do you want another cup?"

"Don't mind if I do," she replied, not looking up. A few frighteningly quiet seconds passed by. When she realized I was still standing there, she looked up. "A tall mild, a little half and half, a dash of sugar," she told me, cocking her head to the side. A couple of dollars didn't mean much to her, but it did to me. At the rate I was going, I'd go broke supplying her with coffee with money out of my pocket. I made a note to avoid her around lunchtime. Knowing her, she'd have me picking up and paying for her lunch, too.

Starbucks had closed for the day. I scurried around for twenty more minutes before I found another coffee shop still open. I got back to the office just in time to see Ann and Joy leaving for the day. I attempted to hand Ann the coffee she'd requested. "I'm late," she snapped, giving me an exasperated look.

I shook my head as I watched Ann and Joy sprint across the street to the lot where they parked every day. I poured the coffee into one of Pam's potted plants and refilled the cup with some of Wendy's vodka. I drank until I'd swallowed every single drop.

I didn't just miss the bus I normally took home, I missed the next two that followed it, too, and had to wait another half hour for the next one. After plowing my way through a knot of rowdy teenagers, I plopped down on a backseat in a corner next to a large musty man in a trench coat. I felt totally overwhelmed, and in a deep state of disbelief. Several people on the bus turned to stare at me when I laughed out loud. I wondered if Ann was crazy, or if I was the one with the mental problem.

The musty man in the trench coat stared at me with a frown on his face but I kept laughing. He shook his head and moved to a seat closer to the door, still frowning at me. I didn't blame him. He didn't know what was wrong with me, and I didn't either.

I had no appetite when I got home, even though I had not eaten since noon. I was too tired to do much of anything. I didn't even protest when James called and said he was coming over.

I spent the evening in my nightgown, squeezed between Daddy and James in front of the television. You would have thought that I was invisible the way James and Daddy carried on a conversation that didn't include me. I prayed that Freddie would rescue me with a phone call or a visit. She did neither.

"Trudy, you ain't much company tonight. What's wrong with you?" Daddy asked during a commercial.

"I'm just tired, that's all," I replied, massaging my neck. "I had a long day." James slid his hand over mine and guided it to his thigh, giving me a knowing look. After the day I had had, sex was the last thing on my mind.

"You can't be that tired, baby. You are just a secretary. All you have to do is answer phones and sit at a computer all day," James decided with a patronizing grin on his face. Like so many men, James had made up his mind that any job a woman performed was not real work. "I should be so lucky." I was too tired to argue with him. The times that I did, he often didn't stop until he'd won. I just sighed and kissed him on the cheek. I was so preoccupied I didn't even know what was on television. But it didn't matter because James had something else on his agenda anyway.

As soon as Daddy left and closed the door to his bedroom, James was all over me, grabbing at my clothes, and moaning and groaning like a man who'd just been let out of prison.

About twenty minutes later we slid back into our clothes and resumed our sitting position on the couch in front of the television.

"Baby, that sure was good," he muttered, with a satisfied look on his face. Lucky for me, it didn't take much to please James when it came to sex. He slapped the side of my thigh and rubbed it so hard it throbbed. "There's nothing like a dose of pussy after a hard day's work. Believe it or not, Dr. Martin Luther King Jr. said something like that . . ." he whispered as he glanced toward the door to Daddy's room. When I didn't respond right away, he nudged my shoulder and gave me a sharp look. "What's wrong, Trudy? You having second thoughts about that job?"

"Huh? Oh, it's fine," I muttered. "I think I'm really going to like it." James didn't like gossip or any mean-spirited conversation. I couldn't discuss Ann with him but I did attempt to ease in a few negative comments anyway. "Some of the folks I work with could be a little nicer, though . . ." James gave me an anxious look.

I knew that I was lucky to have a man as dependable as James. I had had three boyfriends before him and each one had only stayed with me until they found someone they liked better. After ten years I knew James like I knew the back of my hand. I felt bad about it, but I couldn't change the fact that I didn't love him in the passionate way that I wanted to. He was too dull, familiar, and common for that. He didn't excite me. And to be honest, he never really did. With his tweed suits, his romance with beer, his relationship with the television, and his mama practically attached to him at the hip, he probably never would.

James's mother, Mavis, was a real piece of work. Like the brochure rack near my desk at work, that woman had been a huge pain in my butt from day one. We'd been playing tug-of-war with James for years and the only way I was going to win was to marry him.

More than one person had told me that I was crazy for letting James tie me down so early in my life. Even my girl, Freddie. She already had been married and divorced, and had lived with a slew of lovers. She was now in a committed relationship with her latest lover and had three kids with him.

Just in the last week, I'd decided that there was more to life for me, and I was determined to experience it.

CHAPTER 12

Socializing at work was a big deal with the folks at Bon Voyage. It seemed like every other day, they celebrated something. Just about anything was an excuse to have a potluck. The reps always had something going in their lives that called for a celebration. In the same week we'd gathered in the break room on the second floor to celebrate Joy Banning's five pound weight loss and Dennis Klein's dog's new puppies.

Pam loved to cook. Even when there was no potluck. Her desk was always cluttered with some of her baked goods right next to her daily can of Slim-Fast. The bookcase behind her desk had at least half a dozen cookbooks.

Pam had enough fashion sense to buy outfits that hid her potbelly, the only part of her body that she needed to be concerned about. Some days, especially when she wore T-shirts and jeans on casual Fridays, the bloated wheel of fat around her middle made it look like she was pushing a shopping cart.

The following Monday was Ann's thirtieth birthday. One bouquet of flowers after another was delivered for her. At lunchtime we all gathered in the break room where a table had been covered with casseroles and other party foods.

Mr. Rydell had a nearby bakery deliver a huge birthday cake. I could tell by the look on Ann's face that she didn't appreciate the face of the Black woman on the cake. And I didn't either. Not only was it three shades darker than Ann, but with the flaring nostrils and bulging eyes it looked more like that grinning mammy on the Aunt Jemima pancake box. Ann looked at me in a surprisingly conspiratorial manner and gave me a rapid blink. Then she puckered her lips in such an extreme way her mouth looked like it had taken the shape of a three-leaf clover. I nodded at the cake and shrugged, pleased to see her smile at me and shake her head. It pleased me to know that she knew what was on my mind.

"Ann, you don't look a day over twenty-five," chirped Lupe Gonzalez, gazing at Ann with a grin. Similar compliments from Mr. Rydell and the other reps followed and Ann lapped it all up. But she sliced into the cake like she was mad it, successfully removing as much of that annoying black face as fast as she could.

I glanced at Wendy, who was rolling her eyes. There was a glazed look on her face which told me she'd already whipped out the bottle from her desk drawer. Pam, holding the lowest of all our positions, snatched a huge piece of cake and skittered back to her desk to cover the reception area while the rest of us celebrated.

Ann had not spoken to me since the two coffee runs she'd sent me on. She stood less than two feet away when Lupe Gonzalez turned to me and gasped. "You know, you and Ann look enough alike to be sisters. Are you related?"

"Of course not," Ann snapped in such a hurry she almost choked on her own birthday cake. She couldn't resist giving me a guarded look.

After the little office party, it was business as usual. Without warning, Wendy slid her chair out of her cubicle and rolled over to me clutching a thick manila folder. She had a jaw full of mints but I could still smell the alcohol on her breath. Her red nose, shaky hands, and slurred words would have given her away anyhow.

She let out a loud hiccup and rubbed her nose. "Vodka's good for cramps, too" she explained. "Uh, listen up. This is important. From now on, you'll be in charge of paying all the bills, ordering supplies, rearranging schedules. All that fun shit," she told me, flipping open the folder on her lap. "We have four corporate credit cards. We'll share the grunt work"—she paused and leaned closer to me and whispered—"since the reps are too lazy to do it." She handed me two Visa cards. One was in Ann's name; the other was made out to Lupe

Gonzalez. "We order most of our office supplies from Office Depot, but every now and then we'll run out of something and it'll be easier for you to run out to that stationery store on Madison to pick up shit. You should carry these puppies with you at all times because you'll never know when you'll need to pick up a new briefcase for somebody or whatever else the hell they want." Wendy scribbled on a buck slip and handed it to me. "Memorize this number. It's the PIN number for the card made out to Ann."

I looked at the four-digit number on the slip of paper, then at Wendy. "What do I need a PIN number for?" I asked.

"Believe it or not, not every business accepts credit cards. How some of these pooh-butt places can stay in business in this day and age without accepting credit cards is a mystery to me." Wendy sniffed and let out an exasperated breath. "Anyway, say you need to pick up lunch from a specific place. Or flowers or whatever, and it just happens to be a place that doesn't accept credit. You'll need cash. You won't run into that much so I'll just give you the PIN to Ann's card. You can get up to a three-hundred-dollar cash advance a day from the ATMs," Wendy said, waving her hand. I could see that she was getting impatient but I didn't care because I felt it was important for me to know everything I needed to know if I was going to be responsible for company credit cards. I blinked and bit my bottom lip. It made me feel important to know that these people trusted me enough to authorize me to use the company credit cards so soon.

"Uh, will they issue a card in my name?" I asked.

"Yeah, right." Wendy giggled. "Not as long as you are just a secretary. Most of the places where we use the cards know us, so they won't ask for ID or anything. Whatever you do, please keep these cards in a safe place. The girl before you lost Ann's card one day after she had purchased lunch from the deli next door. Whoever found the card ran up six thousand dollars' worth of charges in just one day."

"Shit," I mouthed.

"But if that ever happens, you don't have to worry about them taking it out on you. Shit happens. These cards are all insured up the ass so Bon Voyage didn't lose a damn dime," Wendy told me.

Pam came and stood over my desk. She looked around first then cleared her throat. Wendy gave Pam a nod. "The good thing about it is, every time you have to make a run, you can always sneak a little something for yourself, too," Pam said in a low voice, barely moving her lips.

I looked from Wendy to Pam. "Are we allowed to do that?" I asked.

"Don't worry about it. For the cards you use, nobody'll see the statements but you," Wendy told me with a wink. "Don't look a gift horse in the mouth. Take advantage of this company. It's all part of the establishment that's been taking advantage of us little people since the beginning of time. Especially you minorities. The Black girl before you, she used to buy batteries for her vibrator with Ann's card."

After Wendy had explained the procedure of collecting the credit card statements and paying the bills, she snuck out to go meet her boyfriend for an extended break. Pam was still standing over my desk, as I slid the two credit cards into my wallet.

Wendy's suggestion that I take advantage of the company didn't mean much to me. My main concern was to do the job that I was being paid for.

And nothing more.

CHAPTER 13

Unlike the employees at some of the other companies where I'd done clerical work on a temp basis, the management employees at Bon Voyage were the most pampered group I had ever worked with. It seemed like all they had to do to persuade a large group to book an extensive tour was to hem their representative up in the reception area, wave a few brochures in a cute way, and grin. It wasn't even enough for the reps that they got to travel all over the world, they were too spoiled to even answer their own telephones.

In addition to my own line, the telephone on my desk contained business lines for each of the reps. The telephones in their offices each had one line, which the reps used to make and receive personal calls or to communicate with special clients.

When I didn't pick up a particular line after the fifth ring, the call went into voice mail. I spent a third of my day retrieving messages, typing them up on memo pads, and then delivering them to the reps' in-boxes on their desks.

It was no surprise to me that most of the messages I handled were for Ann. No matter how hard I tried to have as little contact with that woman as possible, I could not avoid her. It was just my luck to run into her in the ladies' room right after I'd dropped off a slew of messages. A few minutes earlier, she'd stormed into the reception area and shouted at Wendy for misplacing a file. It had amused me to see Wendy cower.

With a triumphant look on her face, Ann was now in front of the mirror primping when I came out of the stall. Standing next to her as I washed my hands, looking at our reflections in the mirror, I could see why Lupe had thought that Ann and I might be related. And, more than once we'd been mistaken for one another. Even by Mr. Rydell. She and I were the same shade and we did have similar features. I didn't consider myself a vain person, but it pleased me to see that I was better-looking than Ann. Her mouth was too wide for her face and she already had noticeable crow's feet around her eyes. She must have noticed that, too, because I detected envy on her face when she looked at my face in the mirror next to hers. "You have beautiful skin," she said.

"Thank you," I mumbled, surprised. When her eyes roamed up to my hair, I got suspicious. "I wish I could say the same for my hair."

She stared at my flat ponytail. "I see what you mean," she said, shaking her head. "A good conditioner would help those split ends but a wig would be even better . . ."

Like two confused warriors, we stood there sizing up one another. It was impossible to determine if what was on her mind was something that concerned me. And by the way she sighed and shook her head, while her eyes were still on my hair, I knew that it was not something flattering.

"I . . . know," I mumbled. A wig. I'd never worn fake hair before in my life. I didn't even bother with extensions when I wore braids. James's mother and some of her elderly friends were the only women I knew who wore wigs. "Where did you buy your wig?" I asked, letting the cat in me take over for a change.

Ann sucked in her breath and looked at me with her eyes stretched open as wide as they could stretch without popping out of her head. "This is my own hair," she declared in a worried voice. She patted her hair and let out a nervous laugh. "It really is," she insisted.

"Oh. I never would have guessed that," I said, feeling her hot gaze on my face. "It's beautiful," I added. Ann was like a lot of women I knew. All you had to do to distract her was to throw a compliment her way. Just like I'd done with Wendy.

"I spend enough on it," she said, beaming. She returned her attention to the mirror. "But I do own several hairpieces." She sniffed and smiled. "And where are you from?" she asked, surprising me with a gentle tone of voice.

"South Bay City." I was tempted to remind her that I'd already told her where I was from. "And you?"

"I grew up in 'Frisco," she announced, leaning over the sink to apply more plum-colored lipstick. Her next comment surprised the hell out of me.

"Girl, watch your back around these White folks." She glanced at the door. "Don't trust a single one of them."

"I won't," I said, more confused then anything else.

"They get their thrills by watching us fall on our faces. I learned that the hard way." Ann dropped her lipstick back into her purse, snapped it shut. She strutted out the door with her nose held so high in the air it looked like it was on top of her head.

I stood in my spot for a few moments, still trying to figure out where Ann was coming from. So far the only one at the company who had given me any reason to be watching my back was her.

I stopped off in the break room on my way back to my desk. Wendy was standing by the coffee machine stirring coffee into the mug with Ann's name on it. Her eyes were red, like she'd been crying.

"Are you all right?" I asked, knowing how angry Ann had made her. "Ann was pretty rough on you about misplacing her file."

"I'm used to it," she mumbled, barely moving her lips. "But payback is a bitch."

My mouth dropped open when Wendy reared her head back, cleared her throat, and hawked a huge dollop of spit into Ann's coffee.

CHAPTER 14

I believed that spitting in somebody's coffee was one of the meanest things a person could do. Even to a bitch like Ann Oliver. Especially when there were other ways to get back at her. One was to eavesdrop on her private telephone conversations like I decided to do shortly after I returned to my desk from the break room.

Business was slow that morning. The telephone on my desk had only rung a couple of times so far. Pam and Wendy were both occupied with their own personal telephone calls. Pam was on one of the office telephone lines whispering to one of her friends, glancing over at me every few minutes. Wendy was yakking away on her cell phone, revealing her business as usual, peeping out of her cubicle every few minutes. I had just buzzed Ann to see if she wanted to take a call from a man with a nice deep voice who refused to identify himself. "He has an accent," I whispered to Ann on line one, even though I had the caller on hold on another line.

"I know a lot of men with accents," she said, letting out a breath that made her sound just as impatient as the man I had on hold. "You know"—she paused and sucked on her teeth just long enough to get on my nerves—"you could take a few tips from Pam and Wendy when it comes to telephone skills. Not only do you ask the caller to identify himself, or herself, you need to ask the nature of the call. Do you understand, Trudy?" She pronounced her words like she was speaking to an idiot. I heard her slurp and swallow the coffee that Wendy had hawked so much spit into.

"I understand," I said firmly, bile so bitter rising in my throat I had to hold my breath to keep from throwing up.

"Now I want you to get rid of that rude caller and get back to work."

"Um, the man on hold did say that if you plan to dig a hole, dig it deep." I sighed.

"He said that to you?" Ann gasped.

"Not exactly to me. I think he was talking more to himself when he said it. He kind of mumbled it under his breath when I told him I had to check to see if you were available."

I heard a loud thud on Ann's end, like a stapler being hurled against the wall. Then she cussed so loud I thought she was coming through the telephone. "Put him through!" she yelled.

Twenty minutes later Pam, Wendy, and Ann were all still on the same calls. I had no interest in Pam's and Wendy's conversations, but I was itching with curiosity to know what Ann and the mean man with the accent were talking about. I gently lifted the line Ann was on, covering the mouthpiece with my hand. The telephone was hot against my skin as I listened.

". . . and how long have we been acquainted?" the man asked Ann. I was not good with accents. But when he mumbled something about a party in Montego Bay and then something about Kingston, I assumed he was Jamaican and that he was calling from the islands.

"Don't change the subject. You know you can trust me. I've never lied to you," Ann insisted.

"If you were here, I'd have you kiss me and kiss me hard," the man told her. "When I am being fucked, I liked to be kissed."

Both of my eyebrows shot up and I shuddered. I held the telephone away from my face and fanned myself with a travel brochure. It wasn't long before the conversation got even more personal.

"Ann, what color are the knickers you have on now?" the man asked, breathing loud and hard.

Ann took her time responding. "I'm not wearing any," she cooed.

My eyes got wide. I knew that in Britain they called panties knickers. Since Jamaica and England were so closely related, I figured it meant the same thing. I couldn't see myself leaving my house with no panties on! I felt naked enough when I wore my thong panties. Even the hookers I knew always had something covering their private parts, except when they were doing their business. "Ow! Aaaah . . . I could sop up your juices with my tongue! Just wait until I get my hands on you again! Aiyeeee, woman! Aaaaan!" The man was out of control.

"Is your dick in your hand?" Ann asked calmly. With all her prim and prissy behavior, she was just as straight-up nasty as me and Freddie, after all. Up until now, I could only picture Ann having sex by herself.

Not only was I excited, I was amused.

"Oh, yes! Oh, Ann . . . please be kind to me!" the man shrieked.

"Then you know what I want you to do, and I want you to do it right now. Do you understand? Pretend it's my mouth and not your hand on your dick." There was a long pause. For about a minute all I could hear was loud breathing and loud moans coming from the man. Then he yelled some gibberish so loud Pam heard him through the telephone, all the way across the room! She ended her call and trotted over to my desk.

"What the hell—who is that?" Pam asked, looking at the telephone with her eyes bugged out and her mouth hanging open. I was glad that my hand was still covering the receiver. All I needed was for Ann and her caller to hear Pam and me talking. "Is that your fiancé?" Pam wanted to know, a grin forming on her nosy face.

"Uh-huh," I said sharply, gently hanging up the telephone. I glanced over my shoulder to make sure that Wendy hadn't snuck up on me, too.

"You just hang up on him like that?" Pam waved her arm and nodded toward the telephone, her tongue sliding across her bottom lip. "He didn't sound like he was ready to get off the telephone," she said with a twinkle in her eye. "Shit, I was getting turned on," Pam admitted, blinking hard and rubbing the side of her hip.

I rolled my eyes. "You know how men are. He was feeling kind of horny. I'm on my period, so sometimes we get a little loose on the telephone."

"But I didn't hear you say a thing to him. At least not in the last five minutes." Pam gave me a suspicious look.

"He's the kind of man who likes to hear himself talk," I explained.

"Oh. Sounds like somebody I used to know." Pam sighed and cocked her head to the side, a bored look now on her face. "Men like that are usually selfish in bed," Pam suggested, returning to her desk. "It sure sounds like you're doing a good job on him. Phone sex is the next best thing if it's done right. I hope he keeps you satisfied," she added, shaking her head and staring at me with eager anticipation. It was obvious that she wanted to hear more about my sex life, but I didn't want her or Wendy to know any more about me than they already knew. With tongues as long as theirs, they'd have my business all over San Jose.

"Oh, he takes real good care of me," I said with a wink.

Pam wasn't the only one turned on. After hearing the man on the telephone reach such an intense climax, I had to stand up and compose myself. I was glad I did have on panties because I could feel myself getting moist between my legs. I practically ran to the ladies' room.

When I got there Ann was already leaning over a sink, wiping her face with a wet paper towel. I cleared my throat, unable to keep my eyes from staring at her butt. I didn't know what to think of her standing there in her expensive outfit with no panties on! I had to press my lips together to keep from laughing.

Ann turned around, looking me up and down like I was a tree. Then she left without even acknowledging my presence.

CHAPTER 15

Since the bank where Freddie worked was so close to Bon Voyage, we often had lunch together. We usually met at a halfway mark like Bobby's Bowl, a fast food joint tucked away in an alley next door to a shoe shop. The food was greasy, but it was cheap and tasty. And it was unlikely that we would run into any of the snobs we worked with in such a tacky place.

Our arrangement was that the one who made it to the restaurant first ordered for us both, which was easy because we always ordered the same thing every time. I had two cheeseburgers and two Cokes sitting in front of me on a small round table by the door when Freddie arrived.

Like me, Freddie shopped at discount stores. Even though she shared an apartment with her man, she had three kids so she had to watch how she spent her money, too. She wore a plaid jacket over a black jumpsuit which looked good on her because she was tall and slim enough to get away with a jumpsuit. Her shiny black braided hair, wrapped around her head like a basket, made her look younger than twenty-eight. Unfortunately, Freddie's look had not improved over the years. But her real mystique was her high level of confidence, which had increased over the years. This woman had enough self-love and charm for five women.

I didn't reveal all of the details when I told Freddie about Ann's telephone conversation with the man with the accent. Mainly because after the first few sentences, Freddie rolled her eyes and gave me a bored look. But she was appalled when I told her about Wendy spitting in Ann's coffee.

"You would have to tell me some shit like that while I'm eating," she complained, dropping her fork onto her plate. "That's nasty." Chewing so hard her big ears wiggled, Freddie kicked my foot under the table.

"Tell me about it. I don't care for Ann, but I would never do something as low down and funky to her as what Wendy did. Even though I know she doesn't like me." I paused and let out a deep breath, wondering if there was anything I could do to improve my relationship with Ann Oliver. "I got this feeling that Ann's trying to come up with a way to make them get rid of me. She's already pushed me to the point where I came close to slapping her," I mused. I was not a violent person. I would walk away in shame before I hit another person. Unless somebody forced me to defend myself.

"The utility company is hiring," Freddie quipped, her mouth full of burger meat. She'd never cared that much for bread. But that didn't stop her from ordering burgers with all the trimmings. She just stripped them and ate everything but the bread. How she could still be so slim after having three kids and eating like a mule was beyond me. I loved to eat but I had to watch what I ate to remain a size eight.

"And who would hire me when I tell them that I quit one job after only a month?" I stared at Freddie out of the corner of my eye, as she shrugged and snapped off another piece of her naked burger. "Besides, we both know that it's the same all over. Compared to some people, my job is a cakewalk." I sniffed and finished my drink. More than half of my cheeseburger was still on my plate.

"That's for sure," Freddie muttered, giving me a thoughtful look. "I know I work with some sick puppies, but the clowns you work with sound like they are a laugh a minute. I'd come apply for a job at that travel agency myself, if they got rid of Miss Thing."

Without asking, Freddie snatched the rest of my burger off my plate, wrapped it in a napkin, and stuffed it into her purse. She was the only person I knew who actually took a doggie bag home to a dog. Her man had a lazy, overweight, aging basset hound that would eat a rock if you put it in his bowl.

"You mean Ann?"

Freddie nodded and gave me a critical look. "I don't know how you can put up with all of the shit you put up with when it comes to that heifer. Back in school, you didn't even put up with that much mess from some of the kids from the projects."

"But I never physically fought anybody," I reminded her.

"You didn't have to. You ran before it got to that," Freddie said with an amused look on her face. "Or you tattled to the principal or somebody."

"Well, we are not in school anymore. And tattling is not an option. Our boss, Mr. Rydell, I think he's afraid of Ann. Wendy told me the other day that she walked past Mr. Rydell's office and heard Ann call him a motherfucker."

Freddie gasped. "Holy shit!"

"Freddie, she is one of a kind. I have never met a woman, Black or White, like Ann Oliver. Every compliment she gives, if you want to call it that, she follows it up with a slight insult." I laughed. "I hope I last long enough to see her fall off that high horse of hers."

"And you don't want to leave that job now?"

"No. I am going to stick around to see what happens next," I insisted. The whole situation with Ann Oliver gave me an odd thrill and some curious energy. I had come to look upon it as a project that I could not put aside until I'd completed it.

Before I'd left for lunch, Wendy informed me that during a ladies' room stakeout, she'd overheard an interesting conversation between Ann and Lupe. Ann had told Lupe that some big shot from the Japanese consulate had just invited her and Dennis Klein to spend a couple of days in Tokyo. And, the plump, wussy Mr. Rydell was leaving tonight to take his wife to Vegas for a few days. Joy was so quiet and meek; she was never a problem on a supervisory level. Lupe wasn't either, for that matter. She was always too busy trying to come up with ways to improve her looks. The fact that Pam, Wendy, and I often were the only ones in the office made the job that much more interesting.

It was payday. I had not cashed my check, but it didn't matter because Freddie was treating. I was in for a big surprise when it came time to pay the tab, which was just a little over ten dollars. Freddie's credit card got declined for a ten dollar charge!

"Girl, this is so embarrassing," she squealed. "Can you handle this?"

I pulled out my wallet, praying I had enough cash to cover the tab.

I didn't. Without thinking, I whipped out Ann's credit card and handed it to the red-faced waiter.

As soon as he disappeared, Freddie whispered. "What's up with that? I thought you filed bankruptcy and that cancelled all your credit cards."

"That's right," I said with a pout. "That's a corporate credit card," I added, sounding smug on purpose.

Freddie's mouth dropped open as she stared at me. "Hold on, now. What are *you* doing with a corporate credit card? You have only been at that job for a minute. And, you are just a secretary."

I let out a disgusted breath. If one more person reminded me that I was *just a secretary* I was going to scream. "The company has cards in the reps' names for us to use to buy office supplies and other shit." I rolled my eyes at Freddie and added, "Even though I am just a secretary, I am authorized to use the company credit cards." I let out a smug sigh and leaned back in my seat, enjoying Freddie's stunned reaction.

"To pay for your lunch, too?" she stammered with wide eyes and a rotating neck. "Girl, I am scared of you!"

"Uh-huh," I replied, nodding. I didn't like the hard, suspicious way Freddie was looking at me. Her eyes didn't move or blink. "Don't look at me like that!" I hissed. "You make me nervous."

"Couldn't you get in trouble using a company credit card for personal use? Whose name is on it?"

"Ann's."

"Shit. This is worse than I thought. What would she do if she knew you were charging your lunch, and mine, to her credit card, girl? That is fraud, you know."

"Only if they catch me," I said.

"And you're not worried about that?"

I shook my head and slid a stick of Carefree gum into my mouth, wishing that I had not requested extra onions on my burger. "Part of my job is to pay the credit card bills. Nobody except me will see the statements when they come in. All of the payments will be made online . . . by me."

"Don't the folks at your job keep files and shit? What if somebody needs to dispute a credit card charge six or seven months later? What will you say if they see something on a statement that shouldn't be there? Like this lunch."

"Didn't I just tell you that I'll be in charge of this credit card? I am the only one at the company who will be using it. It's just for office supplies and shit. If those reps never use it to buy anything, why would they ever dispute a charge?"

"What if they took a client out to lunch or something and wanted to charge it?"

"They have other credit cards for that. I could see Ann, with her stuck-up self, using the same card to pay for lunch with one of the CEOs at one of the big companies they work with that I use to pay for the Wite-Out and glue sticks." I had to pause and laugh because the thought was so far-fetched. "I swear to God, those people are from another planet. Flying from here to there, cruising all over every ocean in the world, they don't have time for anything petty. Shit."

Freddie nodded. "I know what you mean. Some of the folks I work for are pretty far off the radar, too."

I leaned across the table and whispered. "Then why are you still looking so nervous?" I asked, looking around to make sure that nobody from my office had wandered in. As predictable as those people were, they still surprised me from time to time. Just the other day at lunchtime I'd spotted Mr. Rydell himself ahead of me in a line at one of those "roach coach" taco trucks parked on the side of a street.

"Trudy, I just hope you know what you're doing. I would hate to have to visit you in jail," Freddie said with a worried look on her face. "You know how my father is. He still won't speak to my man unless he has to, just because he's got family members in jail. If you get arrested, our relationship would never be the same again."

I dismissed Freddie's concerns with a wave of my hand. "I got everything under control," I insisted, feeling so empowered I let out a deep sigh and stuck out my chest.

Just then the waiter returned with the credit card. "Thank you, Miss Oliver," he said, smiling as he stood there waiting for me to total the payment and sign the credit card receipt. He smiled even more because I added a twenty percent tip to the bill.

"Is there anything else you want before we leave?" I asked Freddie with a grin.

"No, thanks," she mumbled, blinking at me like she was seeing me for the first time. As soon as the waiter left, Freddie looked at me and sighed. "I'll have to remember to call you Ann Oliver when you use that thing."

"Who said I was going to use it again?" I asked with a sly grin, sliding the card and the receipt into my wallet.

Freddie shrugged. "Well, after what you just told me, I would. And I can't think of a better way for you to get back at Ann." Those few words out of Freddie's mouth made my mind light up like a burning bush.

"You know," I started, giving Freddie a thoughtful look, "I can't either."

CHAPTER 16

Ihad spent the rest of the afternoon after my lunch with Freddie thinking about what we had discussed. It had been so easy for me to use Ann's credit card to pay for our lunch! Because of the way Ann had decided to treat me I felt she owed me more sops than a greasy hamburger.

After the commute bus arrived at the bus stop where Freddie and I exited each day, Freddie and I had made a detour into Preston's Bar. It was a dark little hole in the wall where people went when they wanted to do nothing but chat and have a few drinks. We crawled into a booth near the ladies' room where we had three piña colada's each and some buffalo wings. Over the next three hours our discussion covered everything from our jobs to entertainment. The subject of the credit card didn't come up until the waiter had dropped our bill on the table. I whipped out my wallet and fished out the credit card again.

"You're really getting off on that shit, huh?" Freddie asked with an amused look. "I was just bullshitting you about it at lunch today."

I tilted my head and propped my arm up on the table, waving the card in Freddie's face. "I hope you have some cash on you in case . . . in case something happens," I said, beckoning the waiter with one hand, waving the credit card and bill in the other. "I'm fucked if he asks to see some ID," I mouthed.

Freddie tapped her fingers on the top of the table until the waiter returned. I held my breath until he handed the card back to me and waited for me sign the bill, and I did so with a flourish.

"Mmph! I'll say . . ." the waiter said with a sharp smirk. "You ladies have a nice evenin'!" he snapped. He rolled his eyes at me as he marched off muttering. Freddie and I looked at one another and shrugged, puzzled by the waiter's curious behavior.

"Shit! I was so nervous I forgot to add in a tip," I boomed, rising from the table, fumbling with my purse and jacket.

"I got it," Freddie said. She chased after the waiter and handed him a couple of bills. He grinned and invited us to come again.

"Before I had to surrender my credit cards, everywhere I went I had to show my ID. Isn't it ironic that nowadays I can go from one place to another, charge a payment with a credit card in another woman's name, and nobody even cares enough to check to see if I'm who I say I am," I said, giving Freddie an incredulous look as we walked down the street.

"America has become a crook's paradise," Freddie responded, sounding too serious for me.

I whirled around to face her. "I'm not a crook."

"I didn't say you were." Freddie grinned, gently tapping the side of my head with her fist. "You're not a crook until you get caught."

When I got home Daddy was in his nightclothes, stretched out on the living room sofa snoring like a buzz saw. He looked tired and much older than his sixty-four years. He often spent the night on the sofa, so I didn't disturb him.

I removed my shoes and tiptoed across the floor. I smiled when I noticed the jacket to Daddy's blue suit draped across the back of the sofa. The only times he wore suits was when he went to visit one of his lady friends.

After I checked out the kitchen and put away what was left of the dinner he'd prepared, I padded back through the living room and went to my bedroom.

I was tired, and more than a little drunk. After letting out a few loud burps, I dressed for bed and turned off my telephone so I wouldn't have to deal with James. I pulled out the credit card and looked at it long and hard, wondering just how far I could go with it and not get caught. A strange feeling that I had never experienced before came over me. It was a combination of guilt and anger. I had the nerve to feel guilty and be mad at the same time over the fact that it had been so easy for me to use Ann's credit card. Was it my fault that the temptation had been so great? It was no wonder criminals went on such rampages. It was so easy to do so! It was like leading a hungry hog to a trough full of food that you didn't want him to eat but you left him there alone anyway. How could he not take advantage of the situation?

If either of the two waiters I'd dealt with that day had even slightly questioned me about the credit card, it would have made all the difference in the world.

But they had not. Now my life would never be the same again because of those two waiters and Freddie. At least that's what I made myself believe.

I had already worked out a plan just in case one of my busybody coworkers discovered that I'd used the card for personal reasons. I'd claim I'd used it by mistake. I was pleased with the dialogue I'd come up with that played over and over in my head like a broken record. *Oh, my God! These credit cards all look alike! I didn't realize I'd used the wrong one! Don't worry. I'll pay off the charges as soon as possible. And it won't happen again. I'll be more careful from now on.*

I prayed that it never came to that. Especially since I'd already planned to use the card to finance a lot of necessities I felt I needed.

I had long vivid dreams that night. I saw myself shopping up a storm and feasting at the best restaurants in town. The strange thing about my dreams was the fact that nobody at Bon Voyage was in them. For once I was glad that I worked with such an oblivious, lazy bunch of folks. They didn't have time to be bothered with petty things like monitoring credit card charges. But Daddy was all over me in every one of the dreams I had that night, scolding me for spending so much money on frivolous things. "Trudy, you need to be savin' your money. You don't need all them frilly things you been buyin' lately. And eatin' out so much can't be healthy," he'd told me. It disappointed me to know that even in my dreams, Daddy was the same grumpy old man that he'd been in real life for years.

Daddy didn't like makeup and sexy clothes on women. At least that's what he'd always tried to make me believe. But I saw him smile and stare at women in makeup and provocative clothes every chance he got. Oh, he tried to be discreet. Especially when he checked out some of the hookers who breezed in and out of the liquor store between their dates. I knew that most men, no matter what they said, still liked to look at a flashy woman, as long as it wasn't their daughter or wife.

I was a long way from being flashy.

I didn't tell Daddy my plans before I went to the beauty shop at the mall that Saturday with a three-hundred-dollar cash advance from Ann's card. I decided to get myself a complete makeover.

After I got my face done I purchased a ton of makeup and a pile of provocative new clothes. I called to make sure Daddy was still at the liquor store before I rushed home and hid as many of my purchases as I could. But I couldn't hide my glamorous new face.

"Trudy, what in the world did you do to yourself?" Daddy asked as soon as he entered the house that night. "I know you didn't pay nobody to do that to you, girl."

"I had a coupon so I got a free makeover, Daddy."

"For what?"

"So I could look more like the women I work with. I couldn't keep going to work looking like a frump next to the other women. I deal with the public and they expect all of us to look nice and attractive."

"And lipstick, too?" Daddy asked, shaking his head. "I declare. I don't know if I like what that new job is doin' to you. Eye paint, face powder, rouge. You beginnin' to look just like some of them gals on the TV." In his own way, Daddy had sanctioned my new appearance. "You more like your mama than I thought, after all."

"Is that good or bad?" I asked, wondering where this conversation was going. "Mama was always trying to do things to herself and for herself that could make her happy," I said in a small, sad voice. A lump formed in my throat and I had to blink hard to hold back my tears.

"If it's somethin' that makes you happy, I guess it's a good thing." Daddy gave me a brief frown and then a broad smile.

The next day I had my trademark ponytail chopped off.

CHAPTER 17

A chic Halle Berry–type haircut did wonders for me. I couldn't stop looking in the mirror and I couldn't stop grinning. The beautician who'd tackled my hair commented on how good I looked. "Girl, the folks on them reality TV shows ain't got nothing on you. This is what I call an extreme makeover. You have been hiding your cute self for too long. I never would have guessed that there was such a fox hiding behind that ponytail and those granny glasses."

I was the first to admit that I looked a lot better, but my transformation was not that *extreme*. James didn't even notice the difference until our waitress paid me a compliment at the soul restaurant he took me to after picking me up from the beauty shop. And his only comment was that I'd already looked good enough for him.

That night when I got home, Daddy stared long and hard at my new hairdo with his hands on his hips and his jaw twitching. "Half of the Black gals on this planet is runnin' around wearin' weaves, wigs, and whatnot so they can cover up them bald, knotty heads they got. You was blessed with a head full of hair—*good* hair, at that—and then you go and cut it off!"

"It'll grow back, Daddy. Besides, I look better with short hair. Everybody tells me that," I said, smoothing the side of my head with my hand.

Daddy dismissed me with an abrupt wave of his hand, trying his best to make me think he was upset with me for cutting my hair. I picked up the extension in the kitchen at the same time that Daddy answered the call in the living room. I hung up when I realized it was one of his friends on the other end of the line, but I stopped on the way to my room when I realized from Daddy's responses that I was the topic of the conversation. "I know it'll grow back," he told his caller. But she do look like that Halle Berry and that's one pretty woman if you ask me. I'll tell James to his face, if he don't keep Trudy on a short leash, some other man'll grab ahold of her." There was a long pause before Daddy spoke again. "Yeah, she home. You want to come over here and look at her head? It is cute, but it looks like a onion." He laughed. I held my breath and ran into the bathroom, locked the door and turned on the shower. And that's where I stayed until I heard Daddy stumbling around in his room, getting ready for bed.

The next morning before I went to work he talked about everything but my head. I got more stares from men than usual on my way to work and I got a few compliments from Pam and Wendy. I couldn't wait to hear what Freddie had to say.

I met Freddie for lunch whenever I could. It was usually burgers and fries but this particular day we treated ourselves to lunch at an expensive Chinese restaurant near Freddie's bank.

She complimented my new look profusely and thought it was a hoot when I told her how often people at Bon Voyage got Ann and me mixed up.

"Well, you know how White folks think we all look alike. "Ann's lucky if she looks as good as you."

"Yeah, but don't let her hear you say that."

"I should be so lucky," Freddie said, a wishful look on her face.

"What do you mean?"

"Trudy, I know I could never win the crown in a beauty pageant. And don't tell me that crap about looks being only skin deep."

"I've never said anything about the way you look, good or bad. I don't care what you look like."

"Oh, girl, don't pay me no mind. I get this way every now and then. Especially when I'm around women like you."

I didn't know what else to say or think about Freddie's comments. If she was jealous of me, she had never shown it. If anybody had any reason to be jealous, it was me. Freddie still had both her parents, an exciting relationship with her man, and three beautiful kids. Not to mention the fact that her job was a lot more secure than mine. I would never intentionally do or say anything to make her feel bad about herself. I prayed that our friendship would remain as solid as it had always been. There was nothing I wouldn't do for my best friend. It pleased me to know that I could finally do some of the things for her that she had never been able to do for herself. Like treating her to expensive lunches.

"My mama would weep if she knew I was sitting up in here eating a plate of thirty dollar shrimp and sipping on eleven dollar glasses of wine." Freddie giggled

"Well, it's not costing you a dime," I reminded. "And you better lay off that wine. You are beginning to act and sound slaphappy." I shook my finger in Freddie's face. "If you get in trouble at work for fucking up at the teller's window by being drunk, I am not responsible," I scolded, fishing around in my purse for my wallet.

"Don't worry about it. I work better with a buzz."

As soon as I flipped open my wallet, Freddie wobbled in her chair, reached across the table and tapped the credit card with Ann's name on it. Our eyes met and I had to assume that we were thinking the same thing.

"I know a lot of people who would really do a job on that Ann if they were in your position." Freddie sounded seriously sober now. "Especially folks like us who have always lived from paycheck to paycheck."

"What do you mean?" I asked, giving Freddie a sharp look. I knew her well enough to know what she was thinking. The same thing was on my mind, too.

"Didn't you tell me you wanted Ann to pay for dissing you every chance she got?" Freddie's words had a sharp edge to them. Nobody would have guessed that she'd been drinking.

I nodded. "Oh, I do get back at her every chance I get. She ignores me, I ignore her."

"Is that what you call making some bitch pay for dissing you?"

"What else do you think I should do?" I asked.

"What's the credit limit on that card?" Freddie shifted in her seat and gave me a hot look before she took another sip of wine.

I cleared my throat and gave Freddie a pensive look before I answered. "Ten thousand dollars."

"How much credit is available on it?"

"Almost all of it. The cards get paid off in full every month. I just paid the bill for the first time myself."

"If that other heifer was brazen enough to buy batteries for her vibrator, you can do same thing."

"I don't have a vibrator!" I said quickly, almost losing my voice. "And I told you not to mention that other woman!" I hissed, looking around. We got quiet when the waiter approached and dropped the bill on the table.

Freddie waited until the waiter was out of range. "I know this loan officer at another bank. A real piece of work if you ask me. That woman would steal from God. She went on a Caribbean cruise last year and charged it to the bank."

My jaw dropped and I leaned to the side and narrowed my eyes to look at Freddie. There was an expression on her face that I had never seen before. In my opinion it did not represent greed or malice. It was a look that made Freddie appear to be a person who wanted to create some serious mischief.

I glanced away from Freddie's face for a moment. When I returned my attention to her she looked bored.

"And that loan officer got away with that?" I asked, looking around the restaurant to make sure nobody was listening to this incriminating conversation.

"That and a lot more. Her son's braces, repairs on her car."

"How did you find out?"

"One of the secretaries told me. She lives in my building and we do our laundry at the same time. She never misses a thing."

I let out a tired breath and sucked on my teeth. I gave Freddie a level look and shook my head. "And she blabs everything she sees. That's what happens when too many people know your business."

"Oh, Clare is not worried about getting in trouble or getting fired. She's been doing the boss for years and everybody knows about that."

"Freddie, nobody knows about me using Ann's credit card but you."

Freddie gave me a serious look and leaned over the table, talking in a low voice. "Trudy, if you are worried about somebody finding out, you better stop using that goddamn card now," she suggested. "I won't tell anybody. Not now, not ever. I know it sounds good and a lot of people are doing it, but what you're doing is some scary shit, if you ask me."

I gave Freddie's last words some thought, but not enough for it to make a difference in what I had already decided to do. "And I won't tell anybody about what I'm doing either," I said.

With a sigh, I whipped out Ann's credit card and dropped it on top of the ninety dollar bill for our lunch. I didn't know if it was the wine or my newly acquired confidence, but I was bold enough to leave a fifteen percent tip.

CHAPTER 18

Iknew that what I was doing was wrong. I knew it from the first
minute and it did bother me because I knew better. I rationalized
by reminding myself that we didn't live in a perfect world and it was
our nature to fuck up. As human beings we were *expected* to fuck up.
Every time I felt the slightest bit of guilt, I cheered myself up by treating myself to even more lavish lunches using Ann's credit card.
Dragging Freddie along whenever I could made it feel like a shared
responsibility. However, there were times when I regretted the fact
that I had revealed what I was doing to Freddie. One minute she was
as excited about it as I was. The next minute she was not. That confused me because she was the one who had put the idea in my head in
the first place! But I only took Freddie Malone's advice when I wanted
to and she knew that.

It wasn't long before the meals weren't enough. When I went shopping for more new clothes, I took Freddie with me and paid for her
purchases, too.

When she didn't have money to buy things for her kids, I paid for
that as well. The only thing that bothered me was the fact that each
time Freddie showed some resistance. "Girl, you don't have to do all
this for me. I was doing all right," she insisted, all the while grinning
and snatching.

"If you don't want these things, you don't have to take them," I told her each time. It did not surprise me that underneath it all, Freddie was like a lot of other people. She didn't want to pass up anything that was free.

I felt a little twinge of guilt every time I saw Ann, but I could always count on her to do or say something to piss me off. That made what I was doing seem justified. Besides, the payments weren't coming out of Ann's pocket.

According to Wendy, Bon Voyage had one hell of a budget. They had so much business that the reps were running themselves ragged. As hard as I worked and because of all the crap I had to take from Ann, I felt I deserved as many fringe benefits as I could get.

I wasn't the only employee who felt that way. Pam had friends in Hawaii and Florida. She made calls to her out-of-state friends and chatted for as long as she wanted to. She took so many office supplies home so often that I had a hard time keeping the supply room stocked. I got righteously annoyed when I found out what she was doing with them.

"Pam sells some of those supplies from a booth at the flea market every weekend," Wendy told me after Pam had helped herself to six reams of copy paper and a carton of staples.

"Now that's a damn shame," I said weakly. I knew that I was no better than Pam, but at least I wasn't reselling the things that I charged to Ann's card. I wasn't *that* greedy. My real fear was that Pam's greed would eventually be noticed by one of those busybodies on the second floor. Like Lupe. She was the only one who complained all the time about us running out of this or that. If Lupe or one of the other reps decided to scrutinize the situation with the supplies, what was to stop them from looking at other things? Like the credit card use. I made a mental note to keep my eye on this situation. Since I was in charge of the supplies, if something like that happened, I'd be the first to know.

"Don't look so sheepish, Trudy. Everybody screws their company one way or another," Pam decided, using me as a lookout while she stuffed her backpack with pencils and tablets and other supplies for her son to use at school. "Why pay for something that you can get for free?" Pam even stole toilet paper from the ladies' room and couldn't understand why I didn't do the same thing.

"But isn't this like shoplifting?" I couldn't believe the words coming out of my mouth. That same day I had charged a leather skirt to Ann's credit card. I never dreamed of telling Pam or Wendy about my own larcenous behavior.

"If that's the case, the whole world is guilty," Pam snapped.

I forced myself not to spend much time thinking about Pam's last comment. It was too ominous. Especially since I'd gone so far overboard. With the frequency of my purchases, I didn't even think that my ruse about using the wrong credit card by mistake was credible anymore. But because what I was doing was so easy, getting caught was the last thing on my mind.

Exposing myself to Pam was one thing—which was out of the question—but Wendy was the last person I would ever share the knowledge of my larcenous activities with. I knew she could not be trusted to keep her mouth shut. Especially after she'd had a few drinks. Besides, I didn't like a lot of the things she did and said. Her spitting in Ann's coffee was one. I drew the line with behavior like that. That's why I volunteered to do Ann's coffee runs myself. In my mind this little act of kindness made up for the credit card abuse.

Just like I had expected, Ann didn't appreciate my gesture. She took full advantage of it. She got to the point where the coffee we made in the break room just wasn't good enough for her anymore. Now *every* cup she drank had to come from Starbucks. And she didn't think twice about sending me out in the rain to get it.

"Freddie, let's have dinner after work at the Cowboy's Club," I said, whispering into the telephone. It was the same day that I had helped Pam haul a box full of toner for her home printer to her car. It was also the same day that Ann had sent me to Starbucks four times.

"Girl, that's way across town. A cab would cost us an arm and a leg," Freddie whispered back. "Even if I had that kind of money, I wouldn't spend it on a cab to take to a restaurant." She followed that up with a hollow laugh.

"Don't worry about it. You're going as my guest, woman," I hissed.

"In a cab?" she asked.

"Yep."

"That you're paying for?"

"Yep. They take credit cards," I told her.

CHAPTER 19

"Trudy, when do you plan to do the laundry?"

"Daddy, it'll have to wait until the weekend. You know how tired I am when I get home in the evening."

"I know you done let that job go to your head. You ain't got time for nothin' no more these days. You'll slow down when James start lookin' at other women. . . ."

I didn't have to worry about James, so Daddy's warning went in one ear and out the other. My man was always where he said he was going to be. Other than work, his mama's house, and my house to sit in front of the television with Daddy and me, James didn't go many places. He didn't even go to bars or any other place where he'd be tempted by strange women. I didn't worry about him fooling around behind my back. Especially as long as I showered him with nice gifts and kept him happy in bed. And I did that well.

When James complained about the cost of putting a set of new tires on his Sentra, I surprised him with a gift certificate from Grand Auto. It not only covered the cost of the tires, he was able to get some new seat covers, too. I didn't stop there. As a matter of fact, it was just the beginning of the many things I'd do for James to keep him attracted and distracted at the same time.

"Baby, I don't want you to be spending all your hard-earned money on me," he said two days after the Grand Auto gift certificate. He grinned as I handed him a new leather jacket from Macy's that he'd been admiring for weeks.

"Don't worry about it, honey. I like to do nice things for you." I had just surprised him by showing up at his apartment in a cab with the jacket under my arm, gift wrapped. I also had a huge bag of take-out food, with all the trimmings, from one of the most expensive Italian restaurants in town.

One thing I liked about James was that he appreciated a good meal as much as I did. But life was too short for anybody to settle for greens and cornbread most of the time like we had for so many years.

"And feeding me like a king." He grinned, wearing his new jacket to his kitchen where I had laid out our dinner on a table complete with candles. I could have screamed when I saw that the damn clerk at the mall had left the price tag on the jacket. James saw it before I could distract him long enough to snatch it off. "Six hundred dollars?" James was so taken aback he stumbled trying to sit down. "Baby, you can't afford shit like this," he hollered, waving the price tag at me.

Without missing a beat, I continued to spoon lasagna onto his plate. "It didn't cost me a dime," I chirped. "I won a raffle at Macy's."

"And the first prize was a leather jacket?" James gave me a confused and concerned look.

"Uh-uh. First prize was a gift certificate." I had never been a good liar. I had never had a reason to be. But since my new venture with Ann's credit card, lying seemed like second nature now.

James removed the jacket and draped it on the back of his chair, still looking confused and concerned. "Six hundred dollars is an odd amount for a gift certificate in a raffle."

I shook my head and sat down hard on the chair across from him, a fork poised between my nervous fingers. "Actually, it was just five hundred dollars. I paid the rest out of my pocket."

"A hundred dollars is a big chunk of change for you to be spending on leather jackets for me. I got a closet full of clothes."

"How long have you wanted this jacket?" I asked, chewing. I didn't give James a chance to answer my question. "You haven't bought anything for yourself in over a year." I didn't like the guarded look he gave me.

He finally started to eat. "And how much did you spend on this food?"

"Nothing," I said, my mouth full of lasagna and garlic bread. I was sorry that I had forgotten to include a huge bottle of wine with the meal. A nice buzz would have come in handy. Instead, I stumbled to James's noisy refrigerator and snatched out two cans of beer.

"Nothing? Don't tell me you won all this good food, too."

I drank half a can of beer before I responded. "Freddie gave me a coupon."

"Oh. Some greens would have been just as good," he said, plowing into the huge pile of food on his plate.

I reached under the table with my foot to massage James's crotch. "We'd better hurry up and finish dinner if we want to have some fun before I go home. I like doing nice things for you, baby," I said.

I liked doing nice things period. And it was a real treat to do it at somebody else's expense. Not a single penny of my money was being spent on the nice things I was doing for everybody. I wasn't even putting a dent in the Bon Voyage account.

"We need to be careful with our money, Trudy. I just don't want things to get out of control."

"I got everything under control," I insisted, starting to feel impatient. "Now eat your dinner and stop talking crazy," I scolded.

It didn't take long for things to get out of control. Before I knew it, I had run up Ann's credit card to its full limit. When I got the statement I almost fainted. I couldn't believe that I had spent almost ten thousand dollars in less than a month! I couldn't believe how easy it had been. However, I was too out of touch with reality to be too concerned. Not even when I had to use the other credit card that Wendy had given me to pay for our new copy machine.

When the bills came, I paid them on-line like I was supposed to, and I started charging all over the following day. Expensive lunches, cab rides all the way from San Jose to South Bay City, there was no limit.

There was a method to my madness and it went all the way back to my childhood. Mama's reckless spending had brought me out of the doldrums more times than I could count. Since I'd been treating myself and my loved ones so well, I had almost forgotten what it felt like to have the blues.

Things that happened at the office didn't bother me as much any more. And believe me, there was a lot going on at that place that got on my nerves. Like Mr. Rydell's rambling, long-winded speeches during our weekly staff meetings, and Ann's behavior. Since depression had become a thing of the past for me, I relied on other motivations to keep me going. Every time Ann pissed me off I went on a shopping spree, grinning when the store clerks called me by Ann's name. With my new wardrobe I finally experienced the kind of confidence that I'd wanted all my life. But it was more than that. It seemed like everybody looked at me in a different way. A way that made me feel as empowered and important as some of our biggest clients. Unlimited financial resources had such a strange effect on the human mind. Now I knew why rich people were so aloof and snooty.

It was amazing how good my new Prada outfit made me feel. But like with drug addicts, being high was only temporary, so I just kept spending. Each time, I had to do it a little more than the last time.

CHAPTER 20

Like Wendy had already told me when I'd first come to Bon Voyage, the reps I worked with were lazy as hell. Those people did things so dumb it would make an eel roll its eyes. There was a list as long as my legs of office bullshit that drove me up and down the wall.

The fax machine, the copy machine, and the break room were all on the second floor near the offices of Mr. Rydell and the reps. They would stumble into the elevator to come down one floor (they were too lazy to take the stairs the way Wendy, Pam, and I did) with a one-page document for one of us, usually me, to either copy, put in the outgoing mailbox, or to fax.

What was so ridiculous about the whole procedure was the same rep would escort me to the copy machine, mailbox, or fax machine and stand right next to me until the deed was done. Naturally, Ann was at the top of this shit list. One day, and only that one day, Wendy, Pam, and I all called in sick. When we returned the next day the break room looked like a train wreck. Coffee beans, half and half, water, crumbs, and just about everything else you'd expect to see in a kitchen were all over the counters and floor. One sloppy person had even peeled a boiled egg and left the shells in the sink. The cleaning woman had already done her chores for that day so all this had been left behind for Wendy, Pam, and me to clean up the next day.

Rolling up the sleeves of my new silk blouse, I headed for the refrigerator first. It was early and the office had not opened yet. Since we'd all called in sick the day before, by some strange coincidence, Wendy, Pam, and I had all come in a half hour earlier. That's why we were all able to be away from the reception area at the same time. One strict rule was, during office hours, at least one of us had to be in the entrance area at all times in case a client or a delivery person needed to get in.

Anyway, just as I reached for the milk container, Wendy cleared her throat. "I wouldn't drink out of that thing if I were you. Never," she said in a tone that had become quite familiar.

"Did you spit in this, too?" I asked. It concerned me to know about some of the spiteful things Wendy Barker did to her coworkers. Since I was a fine one to talk, I never addressed the situation with her.

"No, but Pam drinks straight out of the containers. There's no telling where her mouth has been. Haven't you noticed the scabs on her lips?"

"Thanks for telling me," I said, returning the milk carton to its place.

"I like you, Trudy, so you know I'll watch your back. And I expect you to do the same for me."

I had already made up my mind to keep my eye on Wendy Barker. She said and did too many unpleasant things for me not to. No matter how hard she tried to make it seem like we were on the same page, I didn't trust her. I'd worked with people like her before. I knew how treacherous women could be in an office setting. One jealous woman whom I'd worked with during my temp job at the phone company, a woman I'd considered a friend, used to sneak around to other peoples' computers and delete important files. She'd even done it to me once when I'd received a bonus. There were just some people who could not be trusted, no matter how friendly they acted to your face. Wendy was one of those people.

Wendy and Pam had instructed me to open and date stamp all of the mail that came in each day. Anything that was marked "personal and confidential" I was not to open. But Wendy and Pam did it anyway as they huddled behind the file cabinet next to Wendy's cubicle while I acted as the lookout. That's how we found out that Dennis Klein, the Harry Potter look-alike, was having an affair with the wife of one of his best friends. It was also how we found out that the two weeks Lupe Gonzalez said that she'd spent in Mexico visiting her sick grandmother was a bold-faced lie. She'd spent that time in a clinic in San Francisco getting bags removed from under her eyes by the same surgeon who'd removed some fat from Geraldo Rivera's butt and discussed it on Geraldo's talk show.

There were other situations going on at Bon Voyage that could best be described as "black humor." Last Tuesday I snagged the knee of my panty hose on the corner of my desk. I always carried an extra pair with me in my purse in case of an emergency, so it was no big deal. But since I'd already been on my morning break, I wanted to make my sudden departure from my desk look like it was business related. I fished the new panty hose out of my purse, still in the package, and slid them into an interoffice envelope. When I delivered the office mail to the reps, I always slid it into interoffice envelopes. That was the way the reps wanted it delivered.

On the corner of my desk was a half-a-foot-high stack of empty preaddressed envelopes, most of them for Ann Oliver, because being the diva she was, she received the most mail. A lot of it came from boyfriends all over the world, I might add.

Anyway, the envelope that I had just slid the new panty hose into was addressed to Ann. Before I left my desk I directed all of my calls to go straight to voice mail, like I always did when I had to step away. The last thing I needed was for Pam or Wendy to take a call from somebody about a purchase I'd charged. Last week some clerk at a fancy boutique had called to tell me that I'd left my credit card behind after I'd made a purchase! Luckily, I'd taken that dangerous call myself. Direct voice mail was the solution to that knotty problem. It was a pain in the butt to remember to direct all the calls to voice mail every time I left my desk, but I did it.

I took the stairs, entered the bathroom, and did what I had to do. With my fresh new designer panty hose hugging my legs and butt, I balled up the ripped old ones and slid them into the interoffice envelope. I returned to my desk and without giving it much thought, I dropped the envelope back onto my desk.

It got pretty busy and before I could deliver the mail Ann took it upon herself to check on it. She buzzed me on the line that I shared with Pam and Wendy. "Trudy." Ann often paused and sucked in a loud breath right after she said my name. As if she thought I was hard of hearing or dumb, or a combination of both, she repeated my name. "Trudy, do you know what time it is?"

"Uh"—I glanced at my watch and the big round clock on the wall above Pam's desk just to make sure—"it's three-thirty P.M.," I replied with a lilt in my voice.

"And what time are you supposed to deliver the afternoon mail?"

"Three P.M.," I replied.

"Thank you." Ann hung up without another word. I grabbed the envelopes, all of them bulging with all kinds of correspondence, and took the stairs two at a time. A minute after I returned to my desk the telephone rang. It was Ann again.

This time she didn't pause. "Trudy, will you tell me why you delivered me a pair of ripped panty hose?"

"Oh, my God! Oh, Ann, I am so so sorry. I snagged my panty hose and I had a spare pair so I could change them. I didn't want to carry my purse into the ladies' room, so I put my new panty hose into the envelope and then I—"

She cut me off with a sharp laugh. "I see," she said. "Well, is everything all right now?" Ann never ceased to amaze me. Sometimes she seemed genuinely concerned.

"Uh-huh. I'm just glad I had that extra pair with me," I added, thrown off even more by her interest in my wardrobe malfunction.

"Well, if and when it happens again and you don't have a fresh pair with you, I always keep a few extra pairs in the bottom left drawer of my desk. We're about the same size and color. Help yourself." She hung up before I could thank her.

I just didn't know what to do with this woman.

CHAPTER 21

I would go for weeks without having to deal with James's mother. I liked the woman and we got along fairly well, but the less I saw of Mavis, the better it was for me.

Mavis Young was a widow who had been looking for another husband since her first husband died at the age of thirty-five. She was somewhere in her sixties or seventies depending on who was telling the story. James said she was in her seventies; she claimed to be sixty-five.

In her long-range search for another man of her own, she decided she'd help James find a spouse as well. "God didn't mean for nobody to be alone," she told me during one of her visits to the liquor store, her roving eye looking from me to my daddy in his blue suit. "You and your daddy both deserve to be happy. You and my boy look good together, and while we on the subject, your daddy looks right dapper in his blue suit." Mavis spoke loud enough for Daddy to hear her comments. He promptly disappeared into a back room and stayed there until she had left. Having Mavis for a mother-in-law was one thing. Having her for a stepmother, too, was a hellish thought.

My mother had been the last woman whom I'd known to get and keep Daddy's attention. At least on any level to speak of. And certainly the last White woman. I'd overheard him once tell one of his friends that after the way Mama's family had treated him, he'd never get involved with another one. He had remained true to his word. It made him mad now when White women got too friendly with him. He'd kept company with a few persistent old sisters over the years, and he'd found something wrong with each one. It pleased me to know that Daddy had made it clear from the get-go that Mavis Young didn't have a chance in hell of landing him.

She had even set her sights on Mr. Clarke, the elderly man who worked part-time for Daddy at the store. A relationship between Mavis and Mr. Clarke was highly unlikely. Not as long as there was a massage parlor at his disposal. Every payday Mr. Clarke was up to his receding hairline in Asian hookers. And even though he'd made a few passes at me, Mr. Clarke often said, "When it come to women, I don't want nothin' black but a Cadillac." I repeated those words to him every time he came on to me. And, I reminded him of my plans to marry James.

Some people told me I was lucky that Mavis had sanctioned my relationship with James. Others told me the exact opposite. I was glad I had James to turn to after a hard day at the office.

The evening after the panty hose incident with Ann, I went to James's apartment before I went home. As dull as he was, every once in a while he provided the sexual healing I needed. However, that evening when I let myself into his place with my own key, Mavis was standing in the middle of the living room with her hands on her wide hips. She had on a floor-length flowered dress that made her look like a float.

"They tell me you done quit your job at your daddy's liquor store and hooked up with some outfit in San Jose," she said in a gruff voice, looking at me with small, slanted black eyes. The thick layer of makeup she wore didn't do much to hide the deep wrinkles and knots on her face this particular day. The fact that she was standing in some bad light made her appearance seem even more disturbing. And she was so heavy-handed when it came to perfume, I always had to breathe through my mouth when I was around her. It was no wonder she couldn't get another man.

"Yes, ma'am," I said sharply, quickly rerouting the conversation. "Uh, is James home?"

"Where else would he be this time of day? He got sense enough to come straight home from work like he supposed to every day." The false teeth in Mavis's mouth clicked like castanets. "You ought to know that by now." Mavis didn't make such remarks because she was a smart-ass. The things that slid out of her mouth, no matter how harsh, did so because that was just the way she was. Basically, she was a nice woman who would give you the wig off her head.

"Oh," I said, looking at my watch, then over Mavis's shoulder just as James exited his bathroom. "Hi, baby," I yelled. "Uh, I didn't know you had company. I thought maybe we'd go out for pizza or something."

"Sounds good to me. As long as it don't have no garlic on it," Mavis said quickly, raking her spotty fingers through her fuzzy gray and black wig. "Let's go now so we can get back in time to watch the *Golden Girls.*

When Mavis visited James she almost always stayed until the next morning, stretching out on his couch bed with enough pillows to prop up a horse. Even on the nights that he had to go to work the next morning. Tonight was no different.

After our visit to Round Table, and as soon as we got back to James's place and devoured the pizza, Mavis slipped into one of her many gauze nightgowns. She vacuumed James's carpet and dusted a few items with the tail of her gown, all within ten minutes. She spent the whole time mumbling about how she hoped I'd keep a clean house once I married her son and volunteered in advance to help me do just that.

Finally, wheezing to catch her breath, she turned to me. "Trudy, if you want to get jiggy with my son, don't let me stop you. I'll go in the bathroom and rinse out my hair. Tee-hee." For an old woman, Mavis could get quite bold at times. I didn't know if that was the way she really was, or if it was just the way some old women acted when they had been without a man for too long. She often crossed the line when it came to talking about sex. Like, I saw no reason for her to confess to me that she had not been fucked in twenty years. I had been praying for some man somewhere to crawl into her bed. I thought maybe it would make her behave more like a woman in her position should. Until then I would always be uncomfortable in her presence. Lately, when people made me uncomfortable, it compelled me to go do something expensive.

Last weekend Daddy got upset with me and complained of "severe chest pains" because I told him I was planning to spend that weekend in Vegas.

"Lost Vegas?" he hollered, looking at me like I'd just announced that I was going to Iraq.

"*Las* Vegas, Daddy," I said calmly. "Just for a couple of nights," I added casually.

"Oh. I won't live through the night," he whined, rubbing his chest and wheezing like a dying mule.

"You can stop talking foolish right now because it's not working!" I snapped.

Daddy gave me a defeated look, then blinked a few times before he spoke again. This time he used a voice that was so weak and low I could barely hear him. "Can you leave a telephone number where you can be reached?"

"Yes, I'll leave you the hotel phone number."

"Can you help me . . . get to the bed?" he asked, wobbling toward me. "And before you go to that Lost Vegas, make sure you leave Dr. Mason's telephone number where I can reach it."

I put my trip to Vegas on hold. I spent most of the weekend spoon-feeding Daddy chicken soup. As soon as he was able to get out of his bed, I fled to the mall and charged myself a new dress and shoes. "Thank you, Miss Oliver," the clerk had said. By now I was used to clerks and waiters calling me by Ann's name.

But during a telephone conversation with Mavis last Tuesday night, when Mavis had called the house looking for James, she referred to me as "Miss Ann." I had just told her in detail how exciting my new job was and how much fun I was having working with people who traveled all over the world and wore nothing but designer clothes. I almost choked on the pork chop I'd been gnawing on. "What did you just call me?" I asked, my hand trembling so hard I could barely hold the telephone still. It seemed inconceivable that Mavis would know Ann Oliver.

"I called you 'Miss Ann,' " she snapped, chuckling under her breath.

"Why did you call me that?" I asked, a thousand thoughts running through my head.

"Back home, that's what my mama, and all the old sisters, used to call them snooty White women they worked for behind their backs.

That's written up even in some of our books. They called us Sapphires behind our backs, and probably still do. Didn't your mama tell you . . . oh, I forgot."

There were times when Mavis made it seem like me being the daughter of a White woman was one of the worst things in the world.

I had let that comment go, as I did with most things when it involved Mavis. Like tonight.

CHAPTER 22

"Mama, please," James said, clearly embarrassed. "Please don't make a scene in front of Trudy again." I had to feel sorry for James for having a mother like Mavis. But my situation was not much better. James often told me how sorry he felt for me when Daddy said something stupid in front of him. With Daddy and Mavis both breathing down our necks, James and I had our work cut out for us. I figured that it was one of the things that kept us together.

One reason I was able to tolerate Mavis was because I didn't have a mother of my own anymore. The emptiness in my heart was sometimes so overwhelming that I would have traded places with James at the drop of a hat. In my mind, a mother like Mavis was better than no mother at all. That's why I was able to look at her with a smile on my face.

Mavis cackled. "Trudy know I don't mean nothin'. I'm just havin' fun with y'all."

It had been a long time since I'd experienced a night as uncomfortable as this one. The pizza that I'd eaten rose in my throat, almost choking me.

"I was just about to leave," I said weakly, coughing to keep from throwing up. "James can you drive me home?" I didn't have a problem getting jiggy with James in the backseat of his car. We'd done it before. Before James could answer, I read Mavis's mind. The anxious look on her face, and the way she glanced at her purse, told me that she planned to come along for the ride. "Mavis, I need to talk to James about something private, if you don't mind . . ."

James snatched his jacket off a wall hook and ushered me out the door before Mavis could react, putting it on in such a hurry he buttoned it wrong. As soon as we drove around the corner to a dark alley we had become quite familiar with, James took the jacket and the rest of his clothes off. We could have checked into a cheap motel or gone to my house to do our business on the couch, or even in my room, as we often did. Daddy was no doubt fast asleep—if he was home. Unfortunately, with Mavis waiting for James to return to his place we didn't have enough time for a real rendezvous.

Climbing into the backseat of a car and fumbling around in the dark like a couple of teenagers was one thing; getting naked was another. James and I rarely got completely naked when we made love. Even at his place. I figured it was because when we'd first starting having sex, when I was eighteen and he was twenty, I would only agree to remove my underwear. Even though he knew about the scar from where my appendix had been removed—slashed across my lower abdomen like a cruel smile—it made me self-conscious back then. Once it was decided that we would marry one day, my scar didn't matter so much.

But that was only part of the reason why I'd removed my clothes tonight. The fact of the matter was, wearing clothes on such an intimate occasion when the weather was hot was just too uncomfortable. Between the two of us we already generated enough sweat to wax a bus. Tonight was one of the hottest nights of the season and summer was still several weeks away.

"One thing I can say about that new job of yours, it's changed you in some ways," James noticed. He had turned on his car radio to a jazz station we both liked. There was just enough light from the dashboard and a dim streetlight for me to see the satisfied glow on his face as he bobbed his head to the beat of Grover Washington.

"What do you mean?" I asked, tweaking his nose and brushing pizza crumbs from his cheek.

He kissed my hand and sighed. "I don't know. You just seem . . . you know . . . different. Ever since you started that new job."

"Well, I am more relaxed than I was at the liquor store. I don't have to worry about getting robbed."

After we got back into our clothes, we tumbled back to the front seat, fanning our faces with the same napkins we'd used to sop up the juices still oozing from our crotches. Safe sex? I didn't have to worry about condoms. I didn't sleep around and I knew James didn't either. I was on the pill so getting pregnant was not one of my concerns.

I looked at the side of James's head as he started the motor. Sometimes my mind wandered. I could be in the middle of a serious conversation with somebody and be thinking about everything except what we were discussing. At that moment I was wondering if my children would inherit the shape of James's head. It was too long and narrow for my tastes. A boy could get away with having such a mean head, but a girl would suffer until the day she died. I had attended junior high with an unfortunate girl who had been teased and tormented so much about her elongated head, she committed suicide during the Christmas break. A sharp pain shot throughout my entire body.

"Did you hear what I just said?" James asked, still breathing as fast and loud as he had in the backseat.

"Yeah, I heard you," I replied, still buttoning my blouse and still wondering about the shape of my future children's heads. "What's that suppose to mean?" He was facing me now. His face was a much more pleasant sight.

"Well, the way you look, for one. And even the way you've been acting these days. If I didn't know any better, I'd swear you were . . . seeing another man or something." James shrugged. "Mama always says that a guilty conscience is one of the strongest motivators in the world."

"I don't have anything to be feeling guilty about," I mumbled, my hands up in the air defensively. That alone made me look guilty of something.

James laughed and tapped my head. "Girl, you know I am just fucking with you. I'm trying to make you laugh. I know you are still tense about that robbery."

"I'm fine, James. If I am acting different it's because things are different in my life now. I'm . . . we're getting older." James gave me a guarded look. I couldn't imagine what was going through his head. But my head was about to explode with all the thoughts piling up in it. And it seemed like they all involved Bon Voyage and Ann Oliver. I couldn't even begin to think what James would say or do if he knew about me using Ann's credit card for my own personal use. "I'm almost thirty, James. You don't want me to stay the same way I was when I met you, do you?" I asked, looking out the window. I pulled my jacket tighter when I noticed a light go on in the building in front of us.

"That depends," he mumbled.

I whirled my head around to face James. He was looking at me with such a strange look on his face, I got defensive.

"Depends on what?" I snapped.

"I fell in love with you back then because you seemed like the kind of woman I wanted to spend the rest of my life with. You were the sweetest, most humble woman I'd ever met."

"That part hasn't changed, James."

"You might not think so."

I looked away but I could see out of the corner of my eye that James was still staring at me.

"Trudy, if you ever fuck me over, I'll never forgive you," he said evenly.

"What in the world are you talking about, man?" I hollered, whirling around to face him again. "I have never cheated on you."

"I didn't say you had." He let out a deep sigh and rubbed my shoulder. "Just don't change too much more on me, Trudy." I was glad I couldn't read his mind. He looked at me a long time before he let out a laugh. "Girl, I know you wouldn't fuck me over. I guess Mama just got me riled up."

"That makes two of us." I grinned. "Now will you take me home? I have to lay out something nice to wear to work tomorrow. Some big shots from IBM are coming to discuss opening an account with us."

"Uh-huh. Well, don't wear nothing too sharp. You've hooked up some mighty sexy outfits lately. I know some dudes at IBM and they can really mess with a pretty woman's mind. I don't want you getting yourself involved in something you'll regret. That would be a crime."

I did not consider myself a criminal. At least, not a real one. I laughed when I realized that the only "real" thing I was, was a real fake. It helped knowing that the world was full of honest people who straddled that ultra thin line between right and wrong on a regular basis. My daddy was one of the most honest and dignified men I knew but that never stopped him from modifying the truth when he filed his taxes.

Then there was James and that mother of his. They had told a few lies—they called them fibs—to the Medicare folks about Mavis's "failing" health. Then they'd dug up a shady doctor who added a few lies of his own to Mavis's application so she could get better medical coverage.

I realized that the degree of the crimes other people committed varied from one crook to another, but a crime was a crime. I truly believed that I had nothing to be ashamed of so I kept telling myself that my real "crime" wasn't really that bad. At least it didn't involve me fooling around with other men. Nobody was getting hurt, physically or mentally, and the bills were being paid on time every month. I made sure of that. The best part was that it wasn't my money paying the bills that I racked up. But even with that, nobody was getting hurt. I'd seen the records so I knew that Bon Voyage was getting paid big time with all the tour groups and companies using their travel services. A few extra thousand dollars a month wouldn't even put a dent in a golden egg–laying goose like them.

I had everything under control so far. I ignored a little voice— along with a laundry list of other annoying things—that had settled in the back of my mind like a sore that wouldn't heal. The voice assured me that I was on a runaway train and it was just a matter of time before it crashed.

CHAPTER 23

Of all the people at Bon Voyage, Mr. Rydell was the one I liked the most. The fact that he owned the company and was filthy rich had a lot to do with his appeal. That surely got my attention. To me his wealth represented power, even though he cowered like a scared kitten when he was around Ann. But lately, having unlimited resources of my own to buy whatever I wanted made me appreciate power even more.

But it was more than that with Mr. Rydell. He was certainly no Adonis in the looks department. His round face, sad droopy eyes, and thick rubbery lips were all parts of a big knotty head sitting on a big body with no neck. He was barely five feet tall and looked to be as big around. But as hard as it was to believe, there was something about this troll that I found strangely appealing. He had a nice deep voice and I loved a man with a deep husky voice. It gave him presence. Even though he was in his fifties he still had a head full of hair. Unfortunately, all of it was as white as snow. When he spoke to me, with his eyelids lowered to half-mast, his hands clasped in front of his low belly, he made me feel important. Even when the subject was something mundane. "Trudy, did you get my memo regarding the Burrows account?" he had asked a few days ago. The way he had licked then pursed his lips made me recall a comment Wendy had made about his mouth: *I bet he gives damn good head.* I nodded at Mr. Rydell with a shy smile, recalling a convoluted memo suggesting that I organize a potluck to celebrate our landing a huge new account. Including Mr. Rydell and sex in the same thought embarrassed me. He was definitely not a man who I wanted to sleep with. Even though I found him strangely appealing, he also reminded me of a puppy that nobody wanted.

I didn't know why Ann was so fond of Mr. Rydell. But she glowed like a lamp when he came near her. And the feeling appeared to be mutual. They would strut out of the office to lunch or a nearby bar, arm in arm. Mr. Rydell was not that friendly with any of the other women he employed. "I bet Ann's sucking Mr. Rydell's dick," Wendy suggested at least every other day.

Mr. Rydell could afford to dress like a prince, but he always wore a black suit. I didn't know if it was the same suit or if he had a dozen of the same kind in his closet. As the owner of Bon Voyage, he had a lot to be thankful for, but all he did was whine about everything, from his two ungrateful sons and their children to his wife's spending habits. He kept a big white handkerchief in his hand to mop his face because he was always sweating.

Mrs. Rydell was an obese, loud, terrifying blond battle-ax with a face only a mother could love. She had tight suspicious green eyes and a nose like a fist. But she had enough style to dress like she was somebody's queen. She stormed the office at least twice a week to meet her miserable husband for lunch. She seemed nice enough to me and the other clerical employees, but she treated the reps like field hands. It was no wonder they all despised her. They would all run and hide in their offices with the doors locked during her entire visit. All except Ann. Mrs. Rydell spent as much time grinning in Ann's face as Mr. Rydell did. Just like Mr. Rydell had a strange appeal, so did Ann to some people. Wendy was right about Ann's butt getting kissed more than the Pope's ring. Mrs. Rydell acted like a groupie toward Ann.

The same woman who fawned over Ann Oliver was a totally different person with her husband. From what I'd heard and witnessed, she was positively fierce. Each time Mr. Rydell returned to the office after spending time with that big woman, he looked like he had been mauled. It was always just my luck to run into him in the break room soon after his difficult lunch with that big woman of his. Crumbs and red wine decorated his shirt and tie.

It had rained that day. Like a lot of men, Mr. Rydell was too vain to carry an umbrella. His hair, which was seriously askew, was still wet and plastered against the sides of his damp face. His nose looked like a glowing red ball. I didn't know what it was about White people and their noses. It seemed to be the first visible part on their body that showed signs of stress. "Trudy, as you grow older, always remember that the aroma of life is never as good as the actuality," Mr. Rydell told me in his smooth voice that afternoon. He swiped his shiny wet face and hair with his handkerchief and a paper towel. Even though he had just eaten lunch he snatched open the refrigerator and fished out a chunk of the sorry-looking coffee cake that Pam had brought in that morning. "Let that be your thought for today," he said, talking with his mouth full.

I had no idea what he was talking about. To me, Mr. Rydell's comments were usually nothing more than overstated gibberish. "My daddy tells me that all the time," I lied, hoping I could escape within a reasonable amount of time. The man held me hostage for twenty minutes, boring me with a convoluted conversation about his wife wanting a new car. Dennis Klein rescued me when he entered the break room and immediately started complaining about his wife. Compared to Mrs. Rydell, Mrs. Klein looked like she'd come from another planet. She was a soft-spoken, charming woman with long black hair, a figure to die for, and the face of a movie star. What she saw in Dennis was a mystery to me. And why he was having an affair with the wife of one of his friends was an even bigger mystery.

I had learned more about human nature in the few short weeks that I'd been at Bon Voyage than I had in the last ten years. Not just about my strange coworkers, but myself as well. It was like I was going through some kind of transformation. Like I'd told James, I was no longer the woman I used to be. I didn't know if the change in my personality was permanent or not, but I was curious enough to see where it would lead me.

One thing I did enjoy was the fact that I liked spending more time alone. I was amazed at how much I learned about myself during some of my more intense solitary moments. I looked forward to going shopping solo as opposed to dragging along James or a posse of two or three girlfriends. At home Daddy was always lurking around a corner, even roaming into my bedroom unannounced. If it wasn't him, it was James and his mama.

Everybody invaded my space at work. Even in the ladies' room. It was not unusual for Lupe or Joy to ambush me coming out of a stall and start up a lengthy conversation.

Freddie and I rode the bus together to and from work almost every day and we always had a lot of things and people to discuss. As much as I enjoyed Freddie's company and our colorful conversations, there were times when all I wanted to do was read the newspaper or sleep through the twenty-five-minute commute. So when Freddie wasn't available to have lunch with me, it didn't matter. I got used to eating lunch alone and I liked it. And the location of my solo lunches played a big role in whether or not I enjoyed myself.

To some people bringing a brown paper bag lunch to work—unless you worked in a factory—was the height of tackiness. That was the way the folks at Bon Voyage looked at it.

Pam, who brought in one of her baked concoctions almost every day, wouldn't be caught dead with a homemade lunch. Now, this was a woman so common she used Scotch tape to repair a loose hem in her skirt one day and staples to replace a button that had popped off the front of her too-tight blouse. Even Wendy, who was one generation away from poor White trash, looked down on folks who brought lunch from home.

The first time I brought lunch from home was a bad experience for me. Ann walked into the break room and immediately started to cough and fan her face. She didn't have to say one word, but she let out a gasp that could have spooked a ghost. And of all the days for me to have brought in a Tupperware bowl full of smelly turnip greens and hot-water cornbread!

The look that she gave me, and the greasy paper bag I'd left on the counter, said it all. But she had to say something, too. "What in the world is that I smell?" She stood next to me, rubbing her nose and still fanning her face. Then she reached around me and opened the refrigerator where Wendy had stacked a huge supply of Slim-Fast.

"Just some turnip greens and cornbread," I mumbled, my face burning with shame. I didn't know why I was so embarrassed about having a meal that most of the African Americans I knew enjoyed on a regular basis.

"You're going to eat all of that?" she wailed, fanning her horrified face.

"I have more than enough if you want to share," I mumbled.

Ann's mouth dropped open and she moved back a few steps. "What . . . you . . . you can't be serious," she stammered. Then she looked amused. "My grandparents used to cook that mess when I was growing up. Do people still eat that stuff?"

"Oh, I eat it all the time," I said proudly.

Pam walked in, fiddling with a loose thread on her sleeve. She looked around the room and sniffed. "Something sure smells good in here," she squealed, eyeing the bowl in my hands. "Can I have a taste?"

Ann let out an exasperated sigh and shook her head. Giggling like a child, she left with just a can of Slim-Fast.

I never ate my homemade lunches anywhere near the office again. All because of the way Ann had reacted.

Down the street from our office, about four blocks, was a small park. It was nothing fancy. It contained just a few benches, a lot of well-cared-for trees, a wishing well, and a Jacuzzi-size pond in the center with a few loud-ass ducks floating around in it. The only fly in the ointment was the half dozen homeless people always present. Each time when I arrived around noon hoping to enjoy my meal in peace, a few could still be found curled up on pallets made out of cardboard boxes and drab blankets.

Even as breezy as San Jose was throughout the year, you could still smell the cheap alcohol and body funk when you got too close to any one of the unfortunate folks who occupied the park on any given day or hour. But it was a nice place to sit on a quiet bench and read during lunch, which was what I usually did when I brought a bag lunch from home. As much as I enjoyed feasting on a T-bone steak or gobbling up lasagna at one of the many restaurants I went to, I still enjoyed an occasional bologna sandwich from home.

Anyway, there I was, sitting on a bench munching on my bologna sandwich that Monday afternoon. It was a few days after my romp with James in the backseat of his car. With my eyes on a page in the latest edition of *Today's Black Woman,* I sensed the presence of unwanted company. Before I even looked up, I was assaulted by an odor so foul it made my eyes water.

"Lady, I ain't had nothin' to eat since I don't know when," a gruff-voiced man whined, standing over me waving a plastic cup with a few coins in the bottom.

"You like bologna?" I asked, already handing him what was left of my lunch.

He looked at me like I'd offered him a mud pie. "Uh, it'll do, I guess," the man said, not even trying to hide his lack of interest. "I like them pizzas from across the street better, see." He sniffed and gave me a dry look.

"Well, I don't have any pizza today. It's bologna or nothing," I snapped, pulling my hand with the sandwich back. I had enough strange people in my life to deal with. The last thing I needed was attitude from a homeless man with high-maintenance expectations.

"I'll take bologna, then. Tell you the truth, I'd eat anything ain't movin' today, ma'am."

I gave up the sandwich and a stern look.

Within minutes, two other displaced individuals were in front of me, staring at me with pleading, teary, fish-like eyes. With more than thirty minutes left to go on my lunch hour, I ran to an ATM across the street and withdrew sixty dollars. I purchased sandwiches from a deli across from the park. I returned to the park with a bag of assorted sandwiches and distributed them. The way those poor people formed a tight circle of hope around me, wailing and praising me with their trembling hands reaching for food, I felt like I was Mother Teresa passing out rice on the streets of Calcutta.

I felt light-headed and proud of myself. I felt empowered. Nothing pleased me more than to know that I had brought somebody some joy. A sharp pain shot through my chest when I reminded myself of how I was able to be so charitable these days. I ignored the pain because it seemed like such a small price to pay.

So far, using Ann's credit card had done nothing but good.

CHAPTER 24

The homeless crowd didn't even notice when I slipped out of the park and walked to a bench near the ATM. I figured that I had enough time to finish reading my magazine. And I would have if I had not been interrupted again.

"Hey, wassup?"

I looked up into the face of one of the best-looking young Black men I'd seen in a long time. He had smooth caramel-colored skin and tight, shiny black eyes. Before I could respond, he plopped down on the bench so close to me our knees touched. "You work around here?" he asked.

I nodded. "Do you?"

"Uh, I'm between jobs right now," he said with a sheepish grin, which was just what I expected to hear. He sniffed, his eyes roving from my face to my breasts and back. "What about your man? He work around here?"

I shook my head. "Why do you ask?"

"Well, I thought maybe me and you could hook up sometime. I like what I see. Knowwhatumsayin'? Me havin' me a fine"—my admirer paused and looked me up and down, smiling when his eyes reached my legs—"me havin' a big-legged lady friend like you . . . that would be cool with me. Knowwhatumsayin'?"

One of the main things I noticed about the "new" Trudy was that I didn't feel I had to look at James as my only hope for a husband. It seemed like everywhere I went now, I had to practically beat the men off with a stick. Especially the type like the one sitting next to me now. I was streetwise enough to know a player when I saw one. But his loud red silk shirt, removable front gold tooth, earrings, ponytail that was obviously fake because it didn't match his real hair, and attitude were playing him more than he would ever know.

I let out a disgusted sigh and gave my admirer one of the sternest looks I could come up with. "You mean to tell me a fine brother like you don't already have a lady friend?"

He sucked his gold tooth and nodded, and gave his synthetic hair a quick pat. "I got me this old funky White girl, but . . . knowwhatumsayin'? Makin' love to her is like ridin' a mule. Knowwhatumsayin'? Them bitches ain't happenin' no more." He didn't wait for me to comment. "My White woman, she got her a good job and she real generous. But you look like you a smart lady, so I know you know how it is with them pale-faced skanks. They will do anything to hold onto a man." He clapped his hands and laughed. "Brothers and White girls, it ain't about nothin' but economics. Shee-yit!" He sniffed and wiped his nose, but not in time. I noticed the traces of white powder stuck to the ends of his nostrils. I had never done hard drugs, but I occasionally shared a joint with Freddie in the privacy of her apartment. Cocaine, other hard drugs, and the people who used them terrified me. I gripped my purse and moved it to the side, hoping that this coke fiend would get the message.

"Does your lady friend know what you really think about White women?" I asked, gearing up to make my getaway.

"Aw, heeeel no!" he shouted, waving his hands, which were both shaking so hard he could barely control them. "That bitch is so ignorant, she don't know if she comin' or goin'. She can't screw worth a damn, neither."

"Maybe you need a new lady, brother," I muttered. That put a smile on his face.

"Thank you. That's what I came over here to rap with you about. As soon as I seen you, I knew you was fly. When do you think me and you can hook up?"

"It won't be today," I snapped, shaking my head. I was not used to moving my head without having my brittle ponytail slap my neck.

Getting a smart new haircut was one of the best decisions I'd ever made.

"Well, when then?"

I sighed and looked at my new watch. My admirer looked at it, too. "You got somewhere to go?" he asked, wide-eyed and anxious. He started tapping his foot as he swiped his nose again.

"I do." I flinched when I noticed how bloodshot his eyes were.

One thing I knew about individuals such as this one was that it was not smart to provoke one. It could mean the difference between escaping unharmed or ending up in a ditch, naked and dead. "It was nice talking to you," I said with a smirk, rising.

His handsome face turned into an ugly mask of anger. "See there! Y'all Black bitches ain't never got no time for a brother. White girls always got time for us."

His outburst frightened me, but I refused to let him know that. Somehow I managed to keep a straight face. "I'm glad to hear that," I said in a humble voice.

"Be gone then, bitch! I was just tryin' to be nice. I didn't really want your black ass no how!" he bellowed, waving both hands in the air.

I got back to the office a few minutes before my lunch break was over. Wendy met me at the door with an anxious look on her pale face. Pam was on the telephone, but her attention was on me, too.

"Trudy! You missed all the excitement," Wendy roared, rotating her thin arms like a windmill.

"What happened?" I asked, brushing past her to get behind my desk. I could see the message-waiting light blinking on my telephone, which meant I'd spend the next hour retrieving messages for the reps.

"Where have you been! The cops were just here!" Wendy yelled.

My face and eyes froze. The rest of my body froze. Somehow I managed to move my mouth. "Oh, God. For what?" The words seemed to hang in the air as my eyes started to itch and burn. My heart was already racing so hard I was dizzy. Within two seconds I saw a vision of myself sitting on a hard, lumpy, naked mattress in a cell in a women's prison. "Were they looking for me?" I wailed, looking toward the door, wondering how fast I could run and where I could hide.

"Why would the cops be looking for you?" Pam hollered, rising from her seat.

"What were the cops here for? What's going on?" I asked, frantically looking from Pam to Wendy.

Wendy took a deep breath before she spoke again. "It's Ann!" she screamed.

"Ann?" I asked, breathing a sigh of relief. My legs were like Jell-O and my mind swirled with so much confusion I felt like I was in a whirlpool. "What did Ann do?" I whispered. Ann was a complete bitch. There was no doubt about that. But I couldn't imagine her doing something that would involve the police.

"Somebody attacked Ann with a baseball bat," Wendy said.

CHAPTER 25

As much as Ann Oliver irritated me, I immediately became concerned about her well-being. Even though I often fantasized
about slapping her face off myself. "Where is she?" As relieved as I was
that the cops had not come for me, I still had to hop and squeeze my
legs together to keep from wetting on myself like I'd done during the
incident with the robbers in the liquor store.

Pam joined Wendy in front of my desk. "They took her to the hospital," Pam replied, her nose as red as a strawberry. "I can't believe it,"
she sobbed, blowing her nose on a sheet of typing paper. Pam had
some odd habits. She filed her nails with a letter opener, chewed on
rubber bands, and watered the plants on her desk with leftover Slim-
Fast. Her using a sheet of paper to blow her nose didn't surprise me.
Her crying over Ann's misfortune did, though.

"What happened?" I asked, rubbing my chest. I felt bad for Ann,
but not bad enough to cry.

"She got jumped over on Leadly Street," Wendy revealed with a
squeal.

"What was she doing over there?" Leadly was on the other side of
town in one of the roughest, most drug-infested areas of San Jose. A
stylish woman like Ann would stick out like a lighthouse.

"She claims she was visiting an old school friend. But if you ask me,

I'd say she was over there to cop some blow. Just like everybody else that goes over there," Wendy decided, giving me a knowing look.

Lupe Gonzalez appeared out of nowhere with a wild-eyed look on her face. Even without the bags under her eyes, she still looked rather haggard and every minute of her forty years. She had on a long blue flannel skirt with a matching jacket. When it came to style, she was almost as chic as Ann. And why she'd recently dyed her jet-black hair blond was beyond me. When she stepped into some bad light, her hair looked green.

"Trudy, did the girls tell you about Ann?" Lupe asked in a voice that sounded like she was under water.

"Yes, Lupe. Is she going to be all right?" I asked.

"Our prayers are with her," Lupe choked. "She's a dear sweet woman and we all love her to death." Lupe paused long enough to catch her breath. "Ann will be taking a few days off. She asked that you bring these files to her condo this evening after work." Lupe handed me a stack of manila folders. "Wendy can give you her address." Lupe sniffed and burst into tears. "Excuse me, girls!" she cried as she spun around on a pair of pointed-toe boots and ran for the elevator.

I blinked at Wendy, who folded her arms and shook her head. Ann can't be that bad off if she wants to work from home," Wendy insisted. "I'd better go with you. She's real particular about who comes to her place."

"What do you mean by that?" I wanted to know. "She asked for me to bring her some work." I didn't need Wendy to remind me that I was not one of Ann's favorite people.

"With the mood she's probably in right about now, she might take her frustrations out on you. Don't you know by now that that woman hates your guts?" Wendy said to me with a look of pity.

"She was the same way with that other Black secretary we had," Pam chimed in. I didn't know if it was my imagination or not, but there were times when it seemed like Wendy and Pam enjoyed the way Ann treated me.

"I can handle Ann," I said firmly. "She can be nice to me sometimes."

"Uh-huh. And so can a cobra. Listen, my man is picking me up after work. We'll drive you home after we leave Ann's place," Wendy said.

The rest of the afternoon was pure torture. Mr. Rydell caught me in the break room and hemmed me into a corner so he could rave about what a wonderful person and employee Ann was. "So many of our clients will only deal with Ann," he informed me, stopping to blow his nose into his handkerchief. "I don't know where Bon Voyage would be without her."

The thing about people like Ann was she knew how to work the minds of the people who were important to her. I had to admit to myself that Bon Voyage would not be the same without her. Nor would I. I had come to depend on her credit card. Without it, I would be right back where I started: trying to live a champagne lifestyle on a beer budget.

I scolded myself for not informing Lupe that I had plans to meet Freddie after work for a drink. But, in a macabre way, I was curious to see Ann and the condo I'd heard her brag about so often.

Right at five on the dot that tense evening, Wendy grabbed her things and practically dragged me out the front door to the street where her man was waiting in her car.

For some reason, I expected Wendy to drive a raggedy pickup truck or an old van with mismatched doors and a taped-over window. I was surprised when she steered me to a shiny new Altima sitting by the curb outside our office with the motor running. I was even more surprised when I saw her man. He was not the greasy-haired, hatchet-faced, tobacco-chewing redneck I'd expected. He was much worse.

Wendy's man, the same one who she bragged about having to fuck every morning before leaving for work, was the same obnoxious young Black man who had tried to pick me up on my lunch hour in the park.

CHAPTER 26

Freddie had a theory about why bad things happened to good people. "They ain't living right," she once told me.

Despite the stupid things I had done, I still considered myself to be a good person. And I also felt that I was living right. It was so ironic that Wendy's man and the man who had accosted me in the park in such an unforgettable way were the same man. And here I was now, trapped in the same car with that man. I said nothing about our little session in the park when Wendy introduced him as "the sweetest chocolate chip since Famous Amos."

I simply smiled and nodded at Daryl Proctor, and pressed my lips together to keep from saying something I'd regret.

Traffic was always heavy in downtown San Jose. During the commute hours, it was a nightmare. Even though Bon Voyage was only about a mile from the freeway, it took twenty minutes for us to make it just that far. Having to listen to the unbelievably vulgar rap CD that Wendy had turned on made the journey seem even longer.

The ride to Ann's condo was uncomfortable to say the least. Not just for me, but for Daryl, Wendy's gold-tooth-flashing lover. I was in the backseat, hunched into a corner like a sack of potatoes.

Daryl drove, barreling through the city like he had the cops on his tail. Every time I looked up into the rearview mirror, his eyes were on me with that deer-caught-in-the-headlights look I'd seen on men's faces after they'd been busted. I stopped looking in his direction when he grinned and winked, all the while caressing Wendy's hair with his free hand.

For once I was glad that Wendy was the chatterbox she was. She dominated the conversation, which was mostly about Ann. She bitched about how bitchy Ann was to her and me. She was angry about Ann getting attacked, but not for the same reasons as everybody else at Bon Voyage. "I have a feeling that because of this thing, she's going to be an even bigger bitch," Wendy complained. She didn't like it when Daryl laughed about what had happened to Ann. "Daryl, what happened to Ann is not funny. She could have been raped or killed." I rarely heard Wendy speak in such a caring tone of voice.

"What the fuck do I care! That black-ass bitch looked at me like I stole something last year when y'all had that Christmas party," Daryl barked. "She had it comin'."

I had had time to give the situation a lot of thought. It had been selfish of me to be concerned about losing the ability to use Ann's credit card. But I could not overlook the few times she had been nice to me. "I just hope she's going to be all right," I said, genuinely concerned. "And I hope they catch the motherfucker that did this to her," I hissed. There was not a woman alive who deserved to be brutalized. Since I'd been there myself, I felt even more strongly about it.

Daryl parked the car on the street across from the large white building Ann lived in. Just as I'd expected, Ann's neighborhood was as glamorous as she was. Orange and lemon trees, and palm trees, and expensive cars lined the streets. Tall bright buildings scraped the sky. There were no rib or fried chicken shacks on the corners, just restaurants and boutiques with names I couldn't pronounce. I couldn't imagine living in such a place.

Within minutes after our arrival, a blond woman cruising by in a BMW rolled up her window as soon as she spotted Daryl's scowling face. "Bitch!" he spat, slapping the side of the steering wheel. "I ain't gonna be havin' no peckerwood cop comin' at me for bein' out here."

Wendy had already cracked open her door. "Honey, don't get excited. Nobody's going to bother you this time." Wendy paused and turned around, giving me a look of pity. "You, too, Trudy. Nobody's going to bother you . . . as long as you're with *me,*" Wendy said. That only angered Daryl more. The sad thing about White people like Wendy was she sincerely saw herself as being superior simply because she was White. It was no wonder she had a hard time accepting a Black woman on Ann's level.

"Kiss my black ass! I ain't stayin' around here so these cracker motherfuckers can do a Rodney King on me!" Daryl roared. He did nothing to hide the cocaine on his nose this time.

"Daryl, please. Honey, did you take your medication?"

Medication? Daryl's behavior was nothing new to me. My neighborhood was crawling with men just as rude and crude. But it never occurred to me that he needed to be medicated, too. His belligerence seemed natural. There was not much difference between his attitude and the man who'd robbed me. I thanked God every day for blessing me with Black men I could be proud of. Like James and Daddy.

Daryl slapped the side of the steering wheel again. This time so hard the dashboard shook. "Yeah, I took that shit." With an anxious look in my direction, he let out a deep sigh. Then, like a savage beast that had been shot with a tranquilizer, he softened right before my eyes. And for a split second, I actually felt sorry for him. I could imagine the sorry life he had. "Uh, if y'all don't mind, I'll come back in a hour. I got some business to take care of anyway," he purred, tickling the side of Wendy's neck. She closed her door and turned to him, draping her arm around his shoulder.

"We won't be but a few minutes. You can wait," she insisted.

"Naw, baby. I got places to go, folks to see," he insisted, glancing at his watch.

Wendy abruptly turned to me. "Trudy, do you mind if I don't go with you?"

I held up my hand. "Don't worry. Ann might not be up to much company anyway."

"You got my cell number. Call me when you're ready and we'll drive you home." Wendy rolled her eyes and nodded toward Daryl.

I nodded back and climbed out of the car so fast I didn't get Ann's unit number from Wendy. I was glad to see a smiling doorman in a uniform in front of the building. He directed me to the second floor.

The hallway reminded me of an expensive hotel. The maroon carpet was so thick I could not feel my feet on the floor. I couldn't wait to see Ann's place.

I wanted to see with my own eyes how a real Black American Princess lived. But I was nervous about seeing something else that Ann had that I didn't have. I knew that I would want that, too.

Just like that credit card with the ten thousand dollar limit.

CHAPTER 27

Ann was not the bloody mess that I'd expected to see when she cracked open her front door, but there was a purple gash on her forehead. She wore a pink housecoat over a pink gown.

"Hello, Trudy, come on in." Her voice was so hoarse, it sounded like she had a huge frog trapped in her throat. She waved me into a spacious living room that looked like something out of *Architectural Digest* magazine. She had plush blue couches with matching carpets, exotic African artwork on her walls, and posters from cities I'd never even heard of. I was surprised to hear Usher crooning from a CD player on a stand next to her couch. She seemed more like the type who'd be listening to Frank Sinatra or Englebert Humperdink. "Excuse the mess," she mumbled over her shoulder as I followed her to the couch. If she considered her place a mess, mine wasn't even on the scale.

"Wendy told me about what happened," I started, setting the files Ann had requested onto a coffee table with a smoked glass top and brass legs. I knew that the reps made good money, but Ann's place and her furnishings looked like she'd spent a king's ransom on it. On top of all that she had one hell of a high-maintenance wardrobe, too.

As she sipped from a flute of sparkling white wine and rubbed her head, I plopped down on the couch next to her wondering how in the world she could afford to live such a lavish lifestyle.

Ann sniffed and stared at the wall like she was in a trance. "Would you like some champagne?" she asked, turning to look at me with her neck moving like a robot.

"No, thanks. Uh, I just wanted to drop off the files and see how you were doing," I said, coughing to clear my throat. I was just as uncomfortable being alone with Ann as I'd been in the car with Wendy's boyfriend. Maybe even more so because I didn't have to work with Daryl or be around him anymore if I could help it.

"I'm all right I guess," she mumbled. Without any prompting from me she gave me an account of what had happened to her. "I'm walking down the street and the next thing I know, some Spic motherfucker with a baseball bat jumps out of the bushes and asks me for a light. I ignore him and the next thing I know, he has one greasy, smelly hand around my throat and the other on my purse. I gave that fucker everything I had and he still batted the shit out of me." A sob slipped out and Ann had to take a deep breath before continuing. "That punk! He didn't have to do what he did to me! I would have given him my purse anyway!" she exclaimed, shaking a fist in my face. I had never known a Black woman, or a woman of any other race for that matter, who could shift gears as fast as Ann. She could go from being a swan to a pit bull at the drop of a hat.

"It could have been worse," I said gently. I blinked and slid a few inches away.

If she had been anybody else, I would have hugged her.

"Oh, yeah? Well, I think he did a pretty good job of fucking me over."

"I know how you feel, Ann. I've been through this kind of thing myself and believe me, he could have done a lot more to you."

She sniffed again and gave me a distant look. "You? Oh, jeez, Trudy. What happened?" She asked in a gentle voice. Her concern seemed genuine, but I kept my guard up anyway.

I nodded. "A few days before I started working at Bon Voyage I got robbed, too."

"Oh?" Her eyebrow shot up. The same annoying way it did when she talked to me at work. Several dime size bruises dotted her neck in a shape resembling a cat's paw.

"My daddy owns a liquor store and I used to work in it. It's in a neighborhood that's kind of rough. It wasn't always that way, though." I mumbled. "It happened on my last day on the job." I paused and balled my hand into a fist and slammed it against my thigh. "The guy took the money, but that wasn't enough for him. That cheesy mother-fucker . . . made me suck his goddamn dick." I couldn't believe that I was sharing something with Ann that I had not even told Daddy or James. And as much information as I shared with Freddie, I still hadn't been able to bring myself to share all of the gruesome details of my ordeal with her.

"Oh, Trudy, I am sorry to hear that." If a bolt of lightning had struck me down, it would not have startled me as much as what Ann did next. She leaned over and hugged me. "Did they catch him?"

I was so taken aback by her show of affection that I had to blink to keep from crying. I was still in her embrace when she rubbed and pat-ted my back. "Not for what he did to me. But I'm sure that, sooner or later, he'll get caught for doing something to somebody else."

I had mixed feelings about what I'd just revealed. As unpredictable as Ann was, there was no telling how she would treat me now. I had seen enough movies involving rape to know how some people ended up treating the victims. Especially when it was a young woman. I *al-most* wished that Ann's attacker had sexually assaulted her, too. That way I wouldn't have to worry about her looking down on me even more than she did already. I was immediately sorry for having such a wicked thought, and I put it out of my mind as fast as I could.

"I'm truly sorry, Trudy. Did you get any help?"

"What do you mean?"

"Did you get some counseling? I have an appointment to see a ther-apist tomorrow."

"No, I didn't," I admitted, bowing my head in humble shame.

"Well, you should. Otherwise you will eventually act out your frus-tration in some other way.

If she only knew . . .

"Uh, I know. I do plan to talk to a professional . . . soon." I swal-lowed hard and bit my bottom lip.

Professional help would have done wonders for me. Not just for the robbery and assault, but also for the deep sense of grief that I still felt over losing my mother in such an unspeakable way. Right after the September 11 attacks I went into such a deep depression I couldn't eat or sleep for three days. The attacks were too similar to what had happened to my mother. As soon as I was able to crawl out of bed, I went on a four-day shopping binge. There had been no credit card in my possession to finance that frenzy. That time I'd used rubber checks. If I hadn't sold the jewelry that Mama had left me to cover the bad checks, I would have been sitting on a hard, lumpy, naked bed in a cell in a women's prison long before I got my hands on Ann's credit card. I had almost forgotten about that dreary chapter in my life. That was another thing that I had not shared with Freddie. Freddie was no angel, but she knew where to draw the line when it came to breaking the law. She would never pull some of the stunts I'd pulled.

"I know how degrading that must have felt. A cab driver raped my own mother six blocks from home. Lucky for her, they caught his ass. And Black men think they have it so hard."

"Does your mother live in San Jose?"

"She used to. But right after that traumatic incident, my father sold the house and they moved back to 'Frisco." Ann rose and started pacing, straightening pictures on the wall. "She was never the same after that. She sincerely believes that we Black women are destined to suffer. But then, most of our mothers end up thinking that way. Did you tell your mother about what happened to you?"

I shook my head. "My mama died when I was twelve. She was a flight attendant on that Pan Am plane that the terrorists blew up over Scotland."

"Oh. I didn't know that." Ann stopped, and stared at me. "Well, maybe she's better off anyway. Being a Black woman in this country can be a tragedy in itself. It's like we have the word victim written all over us."

"My mother was definitely a victim, but she wasn't Black." Both of Ann's eyebrows shot up as I continued. "Her folks were Dutch."

"I never would have guessed that. You don't look . . ."

I held up my hand and let out a sharp laugh. "I know I don't look half-White and I rarely bring it up. I was raised as a Black child and I never got to know my mother's family. After she married my daddy, they disowned her."

Ann shrugged and shook her head. "Well, I thank you for coming out of your way." She blinked and let out a loud sigh. "I plan to work from home the rest of the week. Direct all of my callers to Lupe, but if anything seems important, call me." She didn't have to say it, but I sensed that the conversation was over by the way she was walking toward the door.

"If you need anything else, let me know," I said, walking stiffly toward the exit.

A blank expression was now on her face. "Where did you park?"

"Uh, I don't have a car," I managed. "Wendy and her boyfriend, Daryl, drove me over here," I blurted.

Ann frowned, shuddered, and shook her head. As often as she shook her head, I was surprised that it hadn't fallen off. "Let me give you some advice, sister to sister. We are in the same book. Don't get too friendly with that White woman and that punk nigger boyfriend of hers. I don't like people like him knowing where I live."

"Oh, I got Wendy's number the day I met her, and a blind man could see what a hound dog Daryl is," I said, seeing no need to elaborate further.

Ann smiled in a way that I'd never seen before. There was something warm in her smile. Even with the bruises on her face she was absolutely beautiful. Her eyes contained some sadness, but they still sparkled like black diamonds. For the first time, I noticed a slight dimple on her left cheek. I was more than a little flattered to resemble her so strongly that some people thought we were related.

"Good-bye, Trudy." Ann gave me a pensive look. She quickly looked away, focusing her attention on the door.

I couldn't believe myself; I wanted to stay longer. I had just seen a side of Ann that I'd never seen before and probably would never again. I suddenly got misty-eyed, wondering what I could do to cultivate a real friendship with her. If only she would let me. I believed that it would enhance my life in tremendously positive ways if I had two sister-girl friends as diverse as Ann and Freddie.

Then, like Godzilla coming out of hibernation, she reared back on her legs and stared at me in a way that made me feel like I'd come close to crossing the thin line that separated women like her from women like me. It was a look of contempt if ever there was one. Even in my new Ann Taylor dress, that look made me feel like a pickaninny from the cotton field on a visit to the head nigger in the big house.

I was confused but I attempted to hug her anyway. She turned her head and moved away. I was horrified, but I didn't show it. I just smiled and walked away.

One thing was for sure: we were in the same book, like she'd just said, but on different pages. And she wanted to keep it that way. She would never accept me on her level and that thought brought me back down to earth.

That was why I didn't bother to wait for a bus to take me home. I took a cab all the way to South Bay City.

I charged the outrageous fare and twenty percent tip to Ann's credit card.

CHAPTER 28

Bon Voyage was a much more pleasant place when Ann was not around. At least it was for me. Her absence allowed me to be more relaxed around the clients and the rest of my coworkers. Dennis Klein was the only one who noticed a difference in my demeanor when Ann was not around. "Trudy, I've noticed that you seem a lot more animated and confident when Ann's not here. She can be intimidating, but you get used to it. I eventually did." Dennis's revelation in the break room a few days after Ann's attack enhanced my ability to tolerate Ann's foolishness, as well as other coworkers'. Especially Wendy Barker.

But the next day after my joyride with Wendy and Daryl to Ann's place, Wendy parked her tired body in front of my desk and started to brag about her man with so much vigor that she gave me a pounding headache. "Daryl's father owns a limo service. His mother is a nurse." Weeping with delight, dabbing away her tears of joy with a paper towel, Wendy went on to brag about how crazy Daryl's parents were about the two children she had by Daryl. She didn't stop bragging until she had described his dick in detail.

By the time Wendy had finished with me, my head felt like somebody had filled it with rocks. I swallowed some Tylenol and when that wore off, I took some more. The only reason I didn't deaden my pain with alcohol was because Wendy had already drained the bottle. Pam, smarter than I'd given her credit for, had slapped on a pair of head-phones as soon as Wendy lost control of her tongue.

Wendy sighed so hard she almost fell across my desk. "Oh, Trudy, Daryl's family is so good to me. Because of me, Daryl's the first one to give them some light-skinned grandkids."

If Mr. Rydell and Joy Banning hadn't entered the reception area with a client and immediately started to fiddle around with the brochures on that overloaded rack, Wendy's last comment would have pushed me over the edge. It reminded me that my mother's family had rejected my father, and they had shown no interest what-soever in me.

One of the many things that never ceased to amaze me was how easy it was for some Black folks to accept members of other races, White especially, into their families. The way Wendy made it sound, Daryl's family was at the top of the list.

As much despair as Black people already had to endure, it sad-dened me to know that some still placed so much importance on light skin when so many other things in their lives were so bleak. I had a very dark-skinned relative in Lubbock, Texas, who had told my daddy, right in front of me on the day that I graduated from high school, that nature had played a cruel joke on him by letting him have a daughter with a White woman who had come into the world looking so *black*. It was the only time I ever saw my daddy punch somebody in the nose.

One thing I had learned early in my life was that stupidity was an equal opportunity condition. But I had much more important things in my life to deal with. Like keeping in focus the things and people who meant something to me. Daddy, James, and Freddie were always going to be on my list of priorities. But after I'd addressed my own needs.

It had become a habit for me to treat myself to something nice whenever I got bored, anxious, angry, or restless. Sometimes I experi-enced all four at the same time. Like the following Tuesday when Ann returned to work.

"Trudy, my files are a disaster. I can't find a damn thing. I'd like for you to get me a new file cabinet and set up a color coding system," she told me, standing in front of my desk decked out in a pink silk dress with a bandage covering one of the spots on her head where she'd been hit. Despite her injuries, she still looked like a fashion plate. She had on more makeup than usual. Her hair, glossy and blacker than usual, which meant she'd had it dyed, was in braids. That was a surprise to me because I had assumed that she considered braids too ethnic. "Do you know where Office Depot is?" she asked, her face showing no emotion whatsoever.

"Yes. I've been there several times," I said with a mild smirk, rolling my eyes up at the ceiling. I had to wonder how she could have forgotten all the times she'd already sent me to Office Depot to pick up a this or a that because she had been too antsy to wait for us to order from our regular supplier. "That's where you sent me to get that new hands-free mouse last week," I reminded her. "Don't you remember? You requested a yellow one to match your yellow mouse pad. You sent me to Office Depot to get that the week before last." Ann's whole body seemed to stiffen right before my eyes. Even her face. I didn't think that I was being a smart-ass. But from Pam's muffled snicker and Ann's glare, that's what I must have sounded like.

Out of the corner of my eye I saw Pam give me a thumbs-up sign and a vigorous nod. Even though I couldn't see what Wendy was doing behind me, I could hear her squeaky chair moving around so I knew that she was peeping from her cubicle.

After Ann had almost stared a hole in my face she cleared her throat. "I'd like this taken care of by noon tomorrow," she said, giving me another look I'd come to hate. Her lips were swollen. I hadn't noticed until now. She pressed her lips into a thin line and narrowed her eyes as she started to tap her foot. It took me a few moments to realize she was waiting for a confirmation from me.

"Uh, yes. I'll take care of it as soon as I can."

Ann rubbed her eyes and gave me what passed for a weak nod before she whirled around and returned to the elevator.

As soon as it was safe Wendy jumped in front of my desk. "Too bad that mugger didn't bop her in the mouth," Wendy said with a smirk.

"From the looks of her lips I think he did," I suggested. I don't know why, but for some reason I suspected that the mugger had done more to Ann than she'd admitted. I found it hard to believe that a maniac wielding a baseball bat would do so little damage to his victim.

"You wouldn't be saying that if it had happened to you," Pam said, giving Wendy a mean look.

"Go get fucked, Pam," Wendy snarled. "It'd probably do you some good." It was rarely discussed, but Pam hadn't been with a man in over a year.

With all the gossip and catty remarks that they dished out on other people, I witnessed Pam and Wendy lock horns from time to time. Even though Wendy was a lot more malicious than Pam, Pam could be pretty vicious herself. She stood up and slapped her hands on her hips. "Ann's the one who recommended you for your promotion and you might remember that sometime. She could have been really hurt or killed." Something told me that it was Wendy's offhand remark about Pam's sex life that was really bothering Pam.

Wendy and Pam were still at one another's throat when I left to go to Office Depot, but by the time I returned they were acting like best friends and were even discussing a double date with Daryl and one of his friends. They didn't even notice the terror on my face.

The purchase that I had attempted to make at the office supplies store had been declined and it was my fault.

CHAPTER 29

One thing that kept me going was the fact that I knew most smart people were usually still fairly clueless. Especially when it came to things they considered mundane and beneath them. I had a feeling that I could really pull some major wool over Ann's eyes if I wanted to. With all her education and global savvy she didn't even bat her long curly eyelashes when I told her that the items she'd wanted me to purchase were out of stock. "The clerk told me that they just sold the last set ten minutes before I got there," I explained. Ann barely looked at me as she stood in front of a bookcase, dusting it with a cheesecloth that she held in a pinch between two fingers like it was contaminated.

Even if the reps didn't have nameplates on their office doors, and photographs of family members on their desks, it was easy to tell which office belonged to Ann. She had a huge bowl of potpourri on top of a file cabinet so her office always smelled like roses. Her shiny wooden desk was neatly organized and not cluttered with unnecessary knickknacks. The screensaver on her computer monitor contained flying doves clutching olive branches between their beaks. The other reps had offices that looked like train wrecks. Dennis Klein's trash can was always filled to the brim with soiled tissue and leaves from his dying plants. So was the floor immediately around it. Crumbs and half eaten pastries covered Lupe's desk throughout the day, every day. Joy Banning was somewhat neater, but she liked to walk around without her shoes, so her office always smelled like her feet. Mr. Rydell was as sloppy as he was oafish. One day when I delivered the mail to his office, I noticed a swarm of gnats buzzing around an apple core on his credenza. And every afternoon I could always tell if he'd had red wine with his lunch by the stains on his tie and shirt.

As pleasant as Ann's office looked, I never felt comfortable in it. There was something haunting about it. Even when she was gone. The knowledge that I'd have to set up and organize a new file system in her office made me shudder.

"But I ordered a new set of files and a cabinet for you anyway." I had done all of the talking so far since I'd entered Ann's office. I decided to pause long enough to allow her to join the conversation. All I got from her was a long bewildered stare. "Uh, right . . . well, the order should arrive in about two weeks," I stammered, praying she would not send me to another store. My stomach was in knots, my heart was thumping so hard and fast it felt like it was going to relocate.

Finally, Ann cleared her throat and spoke, sounding tired, bored, and indifferent. "That's fine. In the meantime, you can put in a service request for the guy to come out and take a look at my computer. It's been slower than usual, and today it shut off by itself. I lost some very important data. Charge it to the credit card. ASAP."

"I'll take care of that right away," I said with a smile, tempted to give her a salute. Her attitude was often so rigid it had a military feel to it. I turned to leave her office so abruptly I ran into the wall. To play off that display of clumsiness, I turned back to Ann, grinning like an idiot. "Is there anything else?" I asked dumbly.

"One more thing," she said, with her eyes glistening as she snorted and looked around the room with a slight frown. "Pick up some more cheesecloth and desk wax. When you have the time, hit a few spots in here." She slid a finger across the top of her desk. "Just look at this. I'm going to speak to Marty about getting rid of that lazy-ass cleaning woman. This place looks like a dust bowl. The first time *my* girl does such a lousy job cleaning my place I will tell her to start stepping . . . all the way to the unemployment line." I felt sorry for the woman who cleaned the offices for Bon Voyage. And any other cleaning woman who had to cross Ann Oliver's path. I didn't see a speck of dust on Ann's finger as she waved it at me like a wand.

I nodded obediently, hating the fact that I'd allowed myself to be pushed into such a deep hole of servitude. "Is there anything else?" I asked, unable to hide the smirk in my voice.

Ann gave me a blank stare. Without turning her head, she shifted her eyes toward the front window, which had a few light smudges. Then she cut her eyes back toward me. She must have read my mind, or the incredulous look on my face, because she didn't ask me to do what I thought she would: clean her office windows. "That's all for now," she said. She gave me an uneasy look before she dismissed me by nodding toward the door.

I added this encounter and its outcome to the list of indignities that I couldn't share with Freddie. I didn't want her, or anybody else for that matter, to know that I'd been reduced to a maid. But that was the least of my worries. I couldn't charge anything else, and that included the cost to have Ann's computer serviced, to her company credit card because it was up to the limit. For me, the walk from Ann's office back to the reception area had to be almost as difficult as the walk on the green mile on death row. I could barely lift my feet.

I returned to my workstation rubbing my forehead. I fell into my chair wheezing like a woman three times my age.

"What the hell is the matter with you?" Pam asked, an amused look on her face. "You're sweating like a pig."

"I'm fine," I managed. "I . . . I missed a step on the stairs and almost fell," I claimed. "Uh," I continued, turning to Wendy, behind me, with an inquisitive look on her face. "Ann wants me to call the guy to come look at her computer. She told me to charge it."

"You should use the card in Lupe's name to pay for that," Wendy said, startling me out of the black funk I had slid into. "It's easier to keep track of repair charges that way. Besides, there's a higher credit limit on Lupe's card."

"Oh. OK," I mumbled. Wendy had just saved my hide, so to speak. I knew I couldn't use Ann's credit card again until I paid the bill. And I was scared to death that I'd be put in another situation where I'd be asked to use it again before I could straighten out the mess I'd made.

I did decide that the smart thing to do was to not use Ann's company credit card again after I paid it off and to take my scheme one step farther. It was time to "diversify." I would apply for *another* card in Ann's name. It would be even more valuable to me than the first one, because it would not be connected to Bon Voyage.

CHAPTER 30

Staying a few steps ahead of the people who issued credit cards was so easy I could have done it in my sleep. It amazed me how they were able to stay in business. They had nobody to blame but themselves when they got scammed. Freddie agreed with me.

"Trudy, you wouldn't believe how easy it is for people to get credit and house loans and shit. Banks are getting 'robbed' left and right, and it's their own fault because they make it so easy for the *wrong* people to get credit." Freddie was right. Some stupid bank had sent a preapproved credit card, with a five-thousand-dollar credit line, to Freddie's two-year-old daughter! Freddie was too afraid to use it, but she held onto it in case she did get up enough nerve.

I gave Freddie one of my most serious looks. "So I shouldn't have any trouble getting another credit card in Ann's name?" I asked during our bus ride home a few days after I had done some light cleaning in Ann's office. It was a struggle to keep my lips from curling up into a smile

"Not if you're smart enough. Not if you use a different address," Freddie said.

"I rented one of those mail box things today," I confessed. "And," I continued with a flourish that impressed even me, "I also got a voice mail message number. I applied for two credit cards in Ann's name."

For a moment, Freddie just stared at me like she was having a hard time absorbing what I'd just shared with her. "What about her job information?"

"I said she's self-employed," I said with a shrug. Freddie raised both eyebrows and gave me a sideways glance. "They didn't even call to verify her employment." I gasped. "I mean, these banks are begging for it."

Freddie shook her head, a disgusted look on her face. "That's the shit I am talking about. With the way things are in this world today, you would have to be a complete idiot to not verify that everything a person puts on a credit application checks out. Even if Ann's credit is solid gold they should still at least verify her employment."

"Do you think a woman like Ann would have anything less than an A-one credit rating?" I scoffed. "That woman is on top of everything. Did I tell you she's got the nerve to have a maid come clean her condo?"

Freddie rolled her eyes and made another disgusted face. "That uppity heifer."

I had come up with my latest scheme even before discussing it with Freddie. Using the company credit card had gotten too risky. I knew I couldn't get a credit card in my own name because I'd fucked up my credit last year. Uncle Pete, daddy's brother, had talked me into taking out a ten thousand dollar loan for him to pay for some surgery.

Uncle Pete had always been a shiftless alcoholic who couldn't be trusted. He had not only stolen money from his own mother's bosom while she'd slept, he busted his sons' piggy banks when they were still toddlers to get money for more whiskey. For years Daddy had bailed my useless uncle out of one mess after another because nobody else would. When Uncle Pete went to Vegas to gamble with money that Daddy had loaned him to pay his rent, Daddy vowed that he would never give him another dime. And he'd kept his word.

Even though my ne'er do well uncle's son, Dwan, sent him money from his military pay in Iraq, Uncle Pete just couldn't seem to make ends meet. He could barely pay his rent, but he was determined to have his surgery, which, by the way, I never did find out exactly what type of surgery he needed. Just that it would cost ten thousand bucks. Anyway, I got the loan and paid off his bill before they released my uncle from the hospital.

My uncle died anyway and Daddy ended up having to take out a loan for him after all to pay for his funeral. As far as Daddy was concerned, this was the final insult. "If that no-good rascal wasn't already dead, I'd kill him myself," Daddy said right after my uncle's funeral. "He done cost me a few more thousand dollars, which he wasn't worth when he was alive."

"You could have had him cremated for a lot less money, Daddy," I said, missing my useless uncle already, and feeling so sad I couldn't think about him without tears sliding down my cheeks.

Daddy shot me a hard hot look, folding his arms. "Cremation? Girl, I wouldn't let nobody burn up my dog, let alone a blood relation. That Pete, he wasn't such a bad egg when he was a young boy . . ." Daddy admitted with a gentle tone, unable to hide his own tears.

I was sorry to lose my uncle but I was pissed off as hell that he'd stuck me with that huge bank loan. The first time I missed a payment, a few months after Uncle Pete's funeral, the bank collector started harassing me and threatening to bitch-slap me with a lawsuit. I was still grieving so I wasn't thinking straight during the time.

I ignored the bank's demands for their money. And the same day their collection agency served me with a summons, I filed for bankruptcy. That shot my credit to hell. I had attempted to obtain new credit at various stores and banks but it had been a waste of my time. As long as that bankruptcy charge-off was on my credit report—ten years—I wouldn't even be able to get a postage stamp on credit.

"You had all the information you needed about Ann?"

"Like what?" I gave Freddie a stern look and lowered my voice. "And don't talk so loud," I commanded.

"Well, like Ann's Social Security number," Freddie whispered.

"I even got her mother's maiden name. Everything I needed was right in her personnel file. Even her real age, which by the way is not thirty. That heifer is thirty-five." I laughed. "And guess what else I found out?" I didn't even wait for Freddie to respond. "Her full name is Annie Lou. Like calling herself a snooty white girl name like Ann makes up for it."

"Must I remind you that Ann is also my middle name?" Freddie snarled, jabbing me in the side with her elbow.

"Sorry, Freddie Ann. I forgot. Anyway, it was one of those instant credit deals that you get by E-mail. I should have the new card real soon because for a thirty-five-dollar fee, they will do a forty-eight-hour turnaround. You want to go to Reno with me to break it in?"

I didn't like the way Freddie hesitated or the worried look that appeared on her face before she answered. "You know I do, girl."

"I know you wouldn't do what I'm doing, but I don't want you to feel bad for me. I know what I'm doing," I said with confidence.

"I sure hope so, Trudy. I sure hope so. You just better hope that Miss Thing never requests a copy of her credit report."

My mouth dropped open. "What do you mean?" I gasped, blinking so hard my eyes burned.

A look of surprise, that turned into a look of exasperation a split second later, crossed Freddie's face. "Girl, every time you apply for a credit card or any other kind of credit, it gets reported to the credit bureaus." Freddie swallowed hard and tilted her head to the side. She seemed to enjoy telling me something I didn't know. I just wished that she had told me sooner.

"Now you tell me!" I hollered.

"Now you keep your voice down," Freddie scolded, looking around the bus. "You don't know who these people on this bus know."

"What about a credit bureau?" I hissed in a low but firm voice. I could barely get the words out without choking on them. I blinked fast and hard, looking at Freddie like she was the one responsible for my sudden fear. "What can the credit bureau do?"

"They put everything we do on a report when it involves credit. You didn't know that? Girl, I work in a bank. I know I told you that bank employees are stupid as hell, and most of them are, but they still got enough sense to report that shit. Even the little poo-butt department stores report credit activities to the credit bureaus."

Freddie sighed and pursed her lips. I could tell that she was getting frustrated and impatient. But this was valuable information to me. What I knew and didn't know could make a difference in whether or not I ended up in jail! "Why would a person want to see his or her credit report?" I asked in a feeble voice.

Freddie bit her lip and glanced around the bus. "There are a lot of reasons why a person would want to see his or her credit report. For one thing, they might want to see if there is any, uh, unusual activity on it."

I gave Freddie a thoughtful look before I forced myself to smile. "But if they didn't have any reason to think that, they wouldn't want to see their credit report," I said hopefully. "I got a thing in the mail one day offering me a free copy of my credit report. I just threw it away."

"I'm sure you did," Freddie said, an amused look on her face.

"That's because we both already know that your credit report looks like a shit list." Freddie shook her head and gave me an exasperated look. "OK. Say Ann was buying a new house, or a new car."

I shook my head. "Ann just got a new car last year, and she's already in a condo that she's buying."

"Then let's go back to what I said first. What if Ann wanted to check her credit report just to make sure it was accurate? From what you've told me, she sounds like the type who would want to keep everything in her name up to date and accurate."

"Shit," I said through clenched teeth. This new worry gave me something else to be concerned about. "What if I cancel that new credit card when I get it without using it?"

"It doesn't matter. You've already put in the application and you can't stop them from putting that on Ann's credit report. It's too late now."

"Dammit. Well, when I get the card, I'll just cancel it anyway. They will show that on the credit report, too, won't they?"

"Uh-huh. But as long as they can't prove you are the one applying for credit in Ann's name, you have nothing to worry about. Did you show your ID when you rented that mailbox?"

"They didn't ask for it. Well, the first place did. I told them I didn't have it with me. So I went to another place and they didn't ask."

"Then relax, girlfriend." It pleased me to see such a huge grin on Freddie's face. "You don't have a thing to worry about. When did you want to take me to Reno?"

CHAPTER 31

"What kind of trainin' program you need to go to when you already been workin' at that travel agency job all this time?" Daddy asked when I told him that I had to go out of town for the weekend. "If you ain't trained enough to do that job by now, you need to start lookin' for a job you *can* do."

The thing about walking on the wrong side of the law is it's hard to know when it's time to quit. Part of the reason for that is you never know when, or if, you will have to "pay the piper," so to speak. Each time I'd made a purchase with Ann's company credit card in a business establishment, or charged an elaborate meal in a restaurant and made it safely out of the door, it gave me a rush that felt as good as any high I'd ever experienced. That type of high seemed even more intense when it piggybacked on one of my highs after a visit to a restaurant with a bar.

On one hand, I had thoroughly convinced myself that I would never get caught. Every time I had entered a business with Ann's credit card in my hand, I felt like I was in total control of my life. I felt as invincible as I would have had that credit card been a gun. I could purchase almost anything I wanted.

At times I felt as good as I'd felt when Mama and I had patrolled the malls and bought ourselves some happiness. But the more I bought myself, the more I wanted. That scared me. In a way, I was glad that my mother wasn't around to see what she'd started.

I was so excited about going to Reno with Freddie that I could barely contain myself. I couldn't even eat the pork chops and collard greens that I had prepared for dinner that Thursday evening.

"It's not really a training program, Daddy. It's more of a . . . a . . . special project. Uh, a retreat."

"Say what?" Daddy's hand, clutching a large mug of hot tea, froze in midair. He looked at me like I'd just revealed an evil plot. "Gal, what in the world are you talkin' about?"

"Uh, the training program they signed me up for is a special project that they also call a retreat," I offered, setting the platter with the pork chops on the table in front of him. Daddy glanced at his dinner. He smiled and took long loud sniffs as he fanned steam that rose from the thick pieces of pork that I'd stacked like a small mountain. Despite the mesmerizing aroma I still could not work up an appetite.

"You still ain't told me nothin'," Daddy snapped. He speared a piece of meat with his fork and attacked it with his sharp teeth, chewing so hard his eyes watered. As the suspicious look on Daddy's face intensified, so did the web of deceit I'd started to spin.

"A lot of companies require new employees to get on-the-job training," I insisted, sitting down hard onto the chair across from Daddy.

Like with so many things I'd done lately, it felt like I was pulling things out of thin air with a sleight of hand that made me look like a magician. As I continued the walk of shame that was taking me to an unknown destination, my level of deceit became sharper and sharper. I didn't know if that was something to feel good about, or bad. I wondered at what point a person in a position similar to mine considered him or herself a "success"? Was it a success to get away with something? I truly felt like I was there. And, because it was quite an accomplishment, was it something that one was supposed to be proud of?

"Well, what else they want you to do? And they better be payin' you if they got you doin' somethin' extra," Daddy quipped, waving his half-eaten pork chop in my face. "Ain't nobody gwine to take advantage of my girl." With a sparkle in his eye, Daddy tilted his head to the side and stared at me in a way that made me feel warm all over. This was one man that I would not trade for the world. Daddy wasn't perfect, but compared to some of his peers, he was an honorable man. I knew that he would not approve of what I was doing. As a matter of fact, it was the kind of thing that would devastate him. I just had to make sure he never found out.

"When new hotels open up, the agency sends one of us to check them out. The hotels pay all the expenses and it's usually just for a weekend," I said proudly. All this was true except the part about the agency sending "one of us" to check the new hotels out. The only people that Mr. Rydell assigned to do this were the reps. And, like I was often reminded, I was just a secretary.

"Why they sendin' you? You ain't nothin' but a secretary."

"Well, all of the travel reps are too busy to go. And besides, they had told me when I interviewed for the job that there would be a little traveling. Didn't I tell you that?"

"No, you didn't. You told me they said you and your family members could travel on a discount. Which is a waste of time because you know I ain't fin to wanna go nowhere if it involve climbin' up on a airplane." Daddy had never been one to want to travel much. Even before the tragedy that had taken my mother. But after September 11, he wouldn't even get on a train, let alone a plane. "How you gonna get to Reno?"

"Freddie's renting a car," I lied, forcing myself to eat. I was the one renting the car—with the new MasterCard I had just received with the five thousand dollar credit line.

Daddy gasped so hard he sucked in so much air he started to choke. I had to lean over and pat him on the back. With a frown he motioned me back to my seat. "That Freddie," he muttered, shaking his head. "How did she get caught up in this?" He gave me an accusatory look, making me feel even more deceitful than I already felt. "Shouldn't James be the one gwine with you?"

"James volunteered to work this weekend," I said with a sigh of relief. "Freddie was going up that way anyhow to see her cousin. You remember her cousin Butchie Malone with the Indian wife?"

Daddy just rolled his eyes and dismissed me with a wave of his hand.

Later that night I told James the same lie I'd told Daddy. "It's about time you took advantage of some of the benefits of working for a travel agency," James told me with a proud sigh.

Even then I wondered what James and Daddy would have said if they had known just what kind of advantages I was taking.

CHAPTER 32

The new MasterCard had arrived just in time for Freddie and me to hightail it to Reno for the weekend. We won a little money, checked out a comedy show at Harrah's, and ate at some of the nicest restaurants in Reno.

When we returned from Reno I checked my new mailbox before I went home. Lo and behold, there was *another* credit card waiting for me with Ann Oliver's name on it. One that I hadn't even applied for! This one was a Visa with roses on it. It was lovely. It was definitely the style of card that Ann would have requested. I called Freddie from my cell phone as I was walking down the street to catch a bus home after I had returned the rental car to Hertz. "Why would this other bank send me a new Visa, too?" I yelled at Freddie, talking so loud other people on the street thought I was talking to them. As soon as I reached my bus stop I plopped down on the bench and started to speak in a much lower voice. "I didn't even apply for this card," I told Freddie. My heart was racing, I was sweating. I was glad to have yet another card but I was confused. And, I was paranoid. In the back of my mind I had formed a thought that the credit card people were on to me. By sending me a card in Ann's name that I had not asked for, they were setting me up so they could build a case. I dismissed that thought almost as soon as I'd come up with it. I had to keep reminding myself about how stupid bank employees were.

Freddie let out such a deep gasp she whistled. "That woman must have some dynamite good credit. When you apply for new credit and get it, the bank you got it from shares that information with other banks. The other banks send you their credit cards, hoping you will keep them so they can make them some money off you, too. It's like a courtesy or complimentary move on their part. They know that most people are stupid enough to accept the cards."

"But isn't sending credit cards at random a *stupid* thing for the banks to do? How do they know I am not some shylock just waiting to take advantage of their stupidity?"

"I just told you. Another bank sent you a new credit card just because some other bank already did."

"Freddie, are bank people that desperate for new customers?"

"They must be. It didn't used to be like that, though. Back in the day my daddy couldn't get one single credit card because he didn't have an A-one credit history. Now with computers running the world, banks are getting fucked left and right by crooks like—" Freddie stopped so abruptly she started to cough.

"Crooks like me?"

"You know what I mean." Freddie got quiet, waiting for me to speak again. I didn't know what to say. "You know, for a woman doing what you are doing, you are way too sensitive."

"I'm not a crook, Freddie. You know me better than that."

It took Freddie a long time to respond. "I know that. One good thing about it is, as long as you pay on those cards that proves that you are not trying to defraud the banks."

"What? You know, I don't like some of these words you are using. Crook. Defraud."

"Shut up and listen. You know I'm on your side. Now don't quote me on this, but I think they would charge you with something less serious as long as you do pay the bills."

"*If* they catch me," I said, feeling light-headed. I was beginning to wonder which one of us had the mental problem, me or Freddie.

"I could be wrong. The bad thing is, you are posing as another woman."

"But she doesn't know that and the banks don't know that," I wailed. "Besides, I haven't missed one single payment."

"Anyway, the banks are just as much to blame for the credit card nightmare this country has gotten itself into. Banks don't need your business; they are just greedy as hell. They like having a lot of people at their mercy to pay that high-ass interest to have those cards. That alone should tell you how gullible banks are. But for them to send my baby girl a credit card, they gots to be asking for trouble." Freddie laughed. I waited for a few moments and then I laughed, too.

"Apparently, they can afford taking chances like they do," I said.

"And that's why they got so much insurance. They aren't so dense that they don't cover themselves in case they hook up with . . . with," Freddie couldn't even finish her sentence so I finished it for her.

"People like me," I said. I was ready to hang up after that.

By the end of the month I had two more credit cards. I also had my eye on a new car, but that was more of a pipe dream than a reality. Without the proper ID I knew that I couldn't coordinate a scam of that magnitude. But I knew somebody who could.

Logan Botrelle, better known as LoBo, was the love of Freddie's life. She'd been with him for seven years and they had three adorable kids. Unlike Freddie's former husband, a straitlaced, churchgoing man whom she had married right out of high school and divorced the same year, LoBo was all about the streets.

LoBo had come from an even rougher neighborhood than mine, so he was pretty savvy when it came to the ways of the world. He always had a hustle going. He was a low-level thug who took care of his business without interference from the cops. Though he had several relatives who were in and out of jail on a regular basis, he had never even been arrested. He prided himself on being too slick.

Despite the fact that he was moderately corrupt, LoBo was good to his mama, Freddie, and the kids. Like Daddy and James, he was a family man. He had a job that he didn't like to reveal unless he had to, because it embarrassed him. As hard as it was for me to believe, some thugs had pride. LoBo was a garbage man, but he referred to his line of work as "waste management." After a few drinks he described himself as a "sanitation engineer." He made decent money, too. But because he liked to live high on the hog and everywhere in between, even with Freddie's salary, they lived paycheck to paycheck.

People contacted LoBo when they needed something they couldn't afford. Like a new television set, or a new DVD player. LoBo always seemed to be present when something "fell off a truck." Even large appliances like refrigerators and stoves. He had furnished the apartment that he shared with Freddie with items that had fallen off trucks

He only dealt with popular brand names so people knew that if they bought something from LoBo it was going to be worth every nickel that they paid for it.

After work the next day, I accompanied Freddie to her apartment on Blane Street. The section of town that Freddie lived in was one step, and I do mean *one* step, above my neighborhood. There were half as many liquor stores and the crime rate was lower, but it attracted a lot of hookers. And there was a massage parlor that attracted a lot of men. Old Mr. Clarke, Daddy's horny employee, was seen stumbling into that particular massage parlor several times a month when he should have been at the liquor store helping Daddy.

I sat next to LoBo on the brocade couch in Freddie's neat little living room. She had only two bedrooms, and her kitchen was barely large enough to accommodate a table and four chairs. She had bar stools, but no bar. Freddie sat across from me and LoBo, perched on one of her high-back brown leather bar stools, looking from LoBo to me. She wore a white turban that had slid high up on her head. The turban, her big ears and her narrow face made her look like an extraterrestrial.

Even with Freddie's plain looks she always managed to snag some of the best-looking men in town. LoBo was tall and well-built from working out at Gold's Gym five days a week. He liked to show off his body by wearing outfits like the sleeveless shirt and tight jeans he had on now. He had a nice neat goatee and a smooth bald head that he had Freddie shave and wax with lotion on a regular basis. It had been years since I'd seen a strand of hair on his head. His smooth dark brown skin and baby face looked like they belonged on a man ten years younger. LoBo was thirty-five. The three kids he had by Freddie, all under the age of six, were in the back bedroom quietly watching television. Freddie had three of the best-behaved kids I knew. I hoped to be as lucky some day.

"LoBo, can you get me a fake ID?" I asked in a determined voice.

CHAPTER 33

LoBo gave me a serious look, rubbing and thumping the top of his shiny head like he was inspecting a melon. Freddie had shaved and oiled his head just before I'd arrived. But small dots of shaving cream clung to his ears and the sides of his face. "Girl, I can get you anything you want. A fake ID won't be no problem at all." Lobo gave me an odd look. His eyes got big and his lips quivered like he was holding back a laugh. "Can you tell me why you need a fake ID?" he asked, scratching his chin and giving me looks that made me suspicious and nervous. I just sat there for a few uncomfortable moments, blinking and trying to decide what to say and what not to say. LoBo coughed and glanced at his watch. "I'm listenin'."

I slid so close to him our knees touched. "Uh, do you remember how I had to file for bankruptcy when my uncle died and left me with that outstanding loan I got for him?" I slowed down long enough to lick my lips and reorganize my thoughts. "Well, because of that I can't get credit in my name for a while," I said, choosing my words carefully. "Ten years! Ha, ha, ha. I'll be almost forty. I don't want to have to wait that long just to get more credit. That's . . . why I need a fake ID." I didn't want to reveal any more information to LoBo than I had to.

LoBo nodded. "From what I hear you seem to be doin' all right," he teased, giving me a suspicious look and a wink. I looked at Freddie.

"He knows. I told him," she confessed. Her eyes glanced at the floor, then back up at me with a mild smug that irritated me in a major way.

I gasped and shot Freddie a blistering look. That was enough to let her know that I was not too pleased with what I'd just heard. *"You already told him?"* I blinked at Freddie so hard my eyes watered. I knew that if I expected LoBo's assistance I had to tell him what I was up to. But when and how should have been my choice, not Freddie's. That's what was so upsetting.

"My woman tells me everything," LoBo hollered, waving his hand. "And I tell her everything." He shifted in his seat, crossed his legs, and gave me a sideways glance. LoBo looked like he had been working out more than usual. His shoulders and arms seemed bigger and more defined, making his head look smaller. He must not have noticed the change in his appearance because a vain man like him wouldn't do anything to minimize his good looks. With his overdeveloped body and small head, and Freddie's big ears, they made an interesting-looking couple. It didn't matter that some people compared Freddie's looks to a cyclops; LoBo still treated her like she was the most beautiful girl in the world. They were made for each other. It was no wonder she worshipped the ground he walked on. However, that didn't make me feel any better about Freddie blabbing my business to her man without checking with me first.

I felt slightly betrayed by the only woman in the world who I trusted with some of my deepest and darkest secrets. A painful lump formed in my throat. When I swallowed I lifted my chin, but the lump still hurt. It helped when I sucked in a deep breath and counted to ten in my mind, but even that didn't ease my anger. My eyes were on Freddie's face as I replied. I wanted to see her reaction. "Yeah, but this was supposed to be between me and Freddie. I tell my man everything, too, but I didn't tell him about this." I hissed the last sentence and enjoyed watching Freddie flinch, squirm, and cast her eyes toward the floor. She had made it clear that she didn't like what I was doing with Ann's name. I decided that she thought that by sharing the information with her man, she could feel less guilty about not turning down the gifts and lavish lunches that I bombarded her with.

It would do me no good to get upset with Freddie. I knew I was still her girl, but she had more of a vested interest in LoBo than she did me. After all, she lived with him and was the mother of his babies. I respected that. She was a woman in love. She and LoBo shared the kind of passion that was missing in my love life. Love, and money, made us do some pretty crazy shit. I was just sorry that finance was more of a weakness for me than romance. Had I been totally in love with James, or any other man, I probably would not have stolen Ann Oliver's identity. Sometimes I envied Freddie's position. I gave her a dirty look anyway.

"Freddie, who else did you tell?" I wailed, looking at her through narrowed eyes. Freddie was particularly close to her parents and siblings, her father especially. She had told her daddy stuff about me that I hadn't authorized her to. My jaw twitched while I waited for her to respond.

Freddie looked at LoBo before she answered. "LoBo is the only person I told." She paused and left her mouth hanging open as she gave me a pleading look. "I had to tell him," she insisted.

Freddie had already told me a long time ago that she and LoBo didn't have any secrets between them. He had confessed to several one-night stands, but Freddie was fiercely faithful to her man. She went out with her girlfriends and flirted with other men, but sleeping with them was something she would never consider. LoBo meant that much to her. It went without saying that no matter what I told her, she'd tell her man sooner or later, no matter how confidential it was.

I had no intention of ever letting James, or any other man, have that much power over me. I only had one daddy and keeping him off my back was a full-time job.

I wanted to slap Freddie for having such a big mouth, and for having such a committed relationship with her man. Her life was so much fuller than mine. In some respects, I would have given anything to trade places with her. Especially now that I'd stepped into a situation that I wasn't sure I could control.

"Don't let the air out of your titties, Trudy B," LoBo said casually, holding his hand in front of my angry face. "I know all about that bitch you work with. She thinks everybody wants a piece of that uptown pussy of hers. Me, I wouldn't touch her with another man's dick. If I was in your shoes, I'd be doin' the same thing to her, maybe even more. Shit." LoBo snapped his fingers and clucked his thick tongue. In a much more controlled and softer voice he told me, "You know me well enough to know I ain't gonna blow your cover. You done stumbled up on a chance of a lifetime. The Mother Lode. Girl, get all you can, while you can. You deserve it." LoBo cleared his throat and gave Freddie a thumbs-up. After she blew him a kiss, he turned back to me. "Now exactly what do you want?"

"Can you get me a driver's license in Ann Oliver's name?" I asked in a shaky voice. Freddie gave me an incredulous look, but she remained silent.

"Done," LoBo said, letting out a huge belch and massaging his chest with his fist.

"You may as well get the whole package?" Freddie said with a heavy sigh. It was bad enough that I had dragged her into the hole I had dug. Now here she was helping me dig that hole even deeper. However, she had a choice: fall in with me, or climb out while she still had a chance.

I looked at Freddie with a curious expression on my face. "What do you mean?" I asked sharply, surprised that she would encourage me to do anything more than I had already done.

"If you are going to do this thing, you should do it right. Get a copy of Ann's birth certificate. If that travel agency lets you take some trips out of the country, you'll need a passport," Freddie said, twisting on her stool, and crossing her legs at the ankles. She snatched off her turban and dropped it to the floor, revealing one of the meanest hairdos I'd ever seen. Her braids looked like horns, but that didn't stop LoBo from looking at her like she was something good to eat.

I cleared my throat to get the attention back on me. "I won't take trips through the company in Ann's name," I said quickly with an anxious grin. "That's hitting too close. I'm not that bold . . . or stupid." I gave Freddie a thoughtful look. Then I looked at LoBo. "Never mind! Get me the whole package," I said, speaking so fast my words almost ran together.

Each time I made a move in the wrong direction I immediately gave it more thought just to be sure that I was aware of what I was doing. After thinking about a passport for just a few moments, I realized that it was a much more serious document than a credit card.

"Uh, never mind about the passport," I said, rubbing my neck. "I don't know about that. Those passport people are pretty sharp. Ann travels a lot, so her name is probably in computers everywhere from here to Nome, Alaska. If something happens to me while I'm sipping margaritas on a beach in Mexico, while I'm traveling under her name, I could get in a serious mess. Then they would find out everything."

"You don't want nothin' then?" LoBo asked, frowning. He was clearly disappointed.

"Just the ID and the birth certificate for now." My eyes burned when I blinked.

CHAPTER 34

There were a lot of people in South Bay City who would not have been caught dead in my neighborhood. Mainly because "dead" is how they predicted they would end up if they based their beliefs on our history.

We had gone from a slow, peaceful, quiet little dot on the map occupied by a mostly minority, blue-collar crowd, to a hellhole overrun with baggy-clothes-wearing gangbangers. Hardcore rap music, in Ebonics and Spanish, could be heard blasting from everywhere all hours of the day. Our house, a no-frills stucco on West Cambridge Street, had even been burglarized a few times.

Even when we averaged a murder every other week during a three-month period a few years ago, Daddy refused to consider moving. I could still hear his words ringing in my head: *Them crooks could steal my bed with me in it but I ain't gwine noplace.* He tried to pretend that staying in the house was all about economics, but I knew better. There was a lot more to it than that. I knew Daddy better than he knew himself. Except when it came to me, Daddy was not one to show his true feelings too freely. And I knew that our house meant a lot to him. For one thing, it was a huge investment. Not just money, but feelings and history. It was the one thing left that connected us all together: himself, Mama, my late brother, Gary, and me.

Before Daddy had even paid off the mortgage, he'd remodeled the kitchen, added a bedroom, and had a new roof installed. The sentimental value meant even more to him whether he admitted it or not. It was the first and last place where we'd all been together at the same time. Mama and Gary were gone physically but their spirits could still be felt in every room. My brother's spirit had even been seen once, by me.

I had been alone in the house at the time. Daddy was outside in our driveway with all kinds of tools in his hands doing whatever men do under the hoods of their cars. It was a Saturday morning in July when I was fourteen. My brother, nineteen at the time, had not come home the night before from a party he'd attended in Sacramento with a bunch of his homeboys.

After losing Mama, Daddy got real possessive when it came to the important things in his life. Gary, being a boy and older than me, had more freedom than I had. He could pretty much come and go as he pleased, day or night. He could also stay away from home as long as he wanted to. All he had to do was call to let Daddy know he was okay.

Gary had never stayed out all night without calling home. When he had not called by the time Daddy and I got up that Saturday morning, Daddy grabbed his tool box and headed out to the driveway, instructing me to stay off the telephone so that the line would be free for my brother to get through.

Fifteen minutes after Daddy had shuffled out of the house with an extremely worried look on his face, I walked out of the kitchen into the living room and there was my brother. Gary was even darker than me, but he had blond hair and blue eyes like Mama. Females of all ages and races loved him to death. He stood in the middle of the floor dripping wet. It looked like he had been swimming in his clothes.

"Gary, boy are you going to get it!" I hollered, hopping from one foot to the other, pounding my fist against the palm of my other hand. "You didn't call home last night like you were supposed to, and now here you are getting water all over the floor!" I yelled, more relieved than angry.

That year, July was one of the hottest months in the South Bay area. Even with our windows open and a fan whirling in almost every room, our house usually felt like an oven during the summertime. That morning, with Gary standing there soaking wet, the living room felt as cold as Siberia.

"Trudy, I just wanted you and Daddy to know that what happened wasn't my fault," Gary said in a voice so hoarse and low I had to lean forward and cup my ear to hear him.

There were three entrances into our house. The back door through the kitchen, the side door connected to the garage, and the front door leading into the living room. The only time we used the back door was to take out the trash or to go into the backyard for some particular reason, like to barbeque on the grill that Gary and Daddy had built. There was no way my brother could have entered through either the side or the front door without running into Daddy in the driveway. I assumed that he had come in through the back door. However, that seemed unlikely because our backyard had a high fence around it and was always locked from the inside.

"Did you tell Daddy that?" I asked, rubbing the goose bumps that had popped up on my bare arms from the cold. Before Gary could respond the telephone rang. At the time the only telephones we had in the house were in the kitchen and in the hallway leading to the bedrooms. I smiled at my brother before I galloped across the floor toward the kitchen with my well-worn house shoes flapping like long tongues.

I grabbed the telephone on the third ring, expecting to hear Uncle Pete's voice. He'd called several times to check to see if we'd heard from Gary even though he had his own problems. His oldest son, Curtis, had caused the whole family a lot of concern. In the past few years, the boy had become far too familiar with drugs and the outside activities that went along with them. Cops in three different states were looking for him. Curtis had been on the lam for over a year, calling every now and then from locations he refused to reveal. But the important thing was, we all knew that my wayward cousin was all right.

The phone call was from Mr. Hardy, the daddy of one of the boys who had gone out with my brother the night before. Mr. Hardy reported that my brother had lost control of his car during the drive back from Sacramento while crossing the Sacramento River. The restored Mustang that my brother had always been so crazy about had ended belly up in the river. Almost choking on his words Mr. Hardy said, "All four of them boys drowned."

With a deep sigh of relief I pressed my hand against my budding breasts. "Uh-uh, Mr. Hardy. My brother's here . . . right now," I said, twisting my head around to face the doorway. I dropped the telephone and ran back into the living room. There was no sign of my brother. But there was a wet spot in the middle of the floor where water had dripped from his body.

We had his funeral three days later.

CHAPTER 35

My father believed me when I told him about my experience with my brother's spirit. But it upset and frightened him so much that he made me promise not to tell anybody else, or even mention it to him again. I couldn't even bring myself to tell Freddie. "News like that could be a real shock to a person's system. Most folks ain't strong enough to hold up under too much stress, like me and you," Daddy decided.

Daddy wasn't as strong as he thought he was. Three years ago on a Saturday night he had to go to the hospital with what he claimed was a heart attack. It had been brought on by a situation that a lot of people would have ignored. That morning, before we went to open up the store, a dusty moving van had pulled up and parked in front of the little beige stucco house next door to ours. Up until that point a quiet elderly couple had occupied the dwelling. They moved to Oregon, hoping to get away from the crime-filled streets of California.

Just as Daddy and I pulled out of our driveway about a dozen loud Harley-Davidson motorcycles roared down our street and stopped in front of the moving van. Long-haired, rough-looking white men jumped off of the motorcycles and started unloading bulging boxes and battered furniture from the van.

"Oh, no they ain't!" Daddy hollered, his eyes bugged out like they were about to pop out of his head. "I know ain't no bikers movin' up into this neighborhood to finish drivin' everybody crazy!"

But that was the case. Lawrence "Spider" Smythe, a bonafide Hell's Angel, became our new neighbor. Daddy was horrified. He raised such a fuss, he collapsed a few hours later. He stayed in the hospital overnight and came home with all kinds of pills. "If I got to live next door to them scalawags, I'm gwine to stay medicated until the day I die, or the day they move," Daddy vowed.

Within days bikers by the dozens invaded our neighborhood, parking their Harleys on the street, in the new neighbor's driveway, and even on his lawn. People hung out of their windows, some peering through binoculars. Everybody was too afraid to say or do anything that might be interpreted as an act of aggression. Nobody in their right mind would do anything to provoke the Hell's Angels.

Spider, with a long stiff ponytail hanging off the back of his head like a brown snake, surprised everybody when he promptly went around the neighborhood introducing himself to anybody who was brave enough to open their door. Bikers were as common on our block as a flock of priests. I gave Spider a sincere welcome and I think it helped warm the chilly reception that Daddy had offered with a frightened and suspicious look on his face.

Spider's race was not an issue; there were White folks already in the neighborhood. What concerned Daddy, and other people on our street, was the fact that Spider was a member of one of the most notorious groups of people in the country. Tattoos that included a snake with its mouth stretched open, a big-breasted woman, a dagger with blood on its tip, and a skull covered Spider's muscular, weather-beaten arms and hairy chest. "I hope we can become friends, dude," Spider said in a gentle but raspy voice as he shook Daddy's limp hand. I stood behind and off to the side of Spider, giving Daddy stern looks. I felt like a parent secretly encouraging a reluctant child to welcome and accept the new, but ugly, kid to the block.

Spider's friendly gesture caught Daddy completely off guard. "Well, as long as y'all don't start no mess, won't be no mess," Daddy responded. To my surprise, and to Daddy's relief, the bikers were a quiet bunch who kept to themselves. Instead of boasting about all the outlaw activities that the bikers were famous for, Spider bragged to Daddy about his job as a construction worker. But Daddy literally glowed when Spider talked about his grown daughter who was, of all things, a grade school teacher. The fact that a man like Spider thought so much of his daughter was all it took to win Daddy over.

Daddy started bragging so much about me to Spider in my presence it embarrassed me to the point where I had to leave the room. Daddy even allowed some of Spider's biker friends to park their Harleys in front of our house and in our driveway. There were days when our front yard looked like a scene out of a biker movie.

A few months after Spider moved to the neighborhood, and before Daddy had the bars put on our windows, another lowlife decided to pry open one of our back windows and help himself to our belongings. This one got more than he bargained for. As he was crawling out of the same window he'd crawled in, clutching a pillowcase full of various items, Spider and six of his ferocious friends were waiting for him. They called the police after they'd given that punk a mild whupping. The news spread throughout the 'hood like wildfire. The break-ins stopped shortly after that incident, and Spider became one of Daddy's closest friends. Cynthia, Spider's "old lady," had even asked me to cornrow her frizzy brown hair. It pleased me to know that once people of other races took the time to get to know one another, they realized how much easier it was to be friends than enemies.

I was glad to have the bikers next door. I knew that when I was not around they would look out for Daddy. James was somewhat skeptical and even paranoid about the bikers at first. "Those people will lie, steal, and attack Black folks for no reason," James declared. After a few weeks when none of James's predictions came true, he joined Daddy and Spider in our living room. And if James's meddlesome mother had not interfered, he would have purchased a motorcycle of his own, as he had threatened to do more than once.

When I got home from my visit with Freddie and LoBo, Daddy and Spider were sitting on the living room couch watching *Cops*. The coffee table was lined on both sides with beer bottles. Greens and neck bones were simmering on the stove in the kitchen. My cell phone started ringing just as I made it to my bedroom.

It was Freddie. She immediately started to whisper into the telephone. "Trudy, LoBo just got off the phone with his connection. He said for you to get some pictures of yourself to him as soon as you can. You know the kind, the color type that they put on a driver's license.

The stuff you requested will be ready by Tuesday. If you still want it."
Freddie's words made my ears buzz.

On my way home on the bus from Freddie's apartment I had given
a lot of thought to what I'd asked LoBo to do. At first, I was not comfortable with him even knowing about how I'd already scammed Ann
Oliver. A voice in the back of my mind had told me to cancel the deal.
"Tell him to hold off for a while. Let me give it some more thought,"
I replied. "I need to sit on this for a few days," I said, easing down on
my bed, my eye on the door to keep a lookout for Daddy.

Freddie was quiet for a long moment. "If you are having second
thoughts about this, you should say so now," she advised me, sucking
in her breath. "And if that's the case, don't do it, girl."

"What would you do if you were in my place?" I asked. I knew that
no matter what Freddie suggested, I was still going to do what I
wanted to do. That's what I'd been doing so far anyway.

"Trudy, you know what a fraidy-cat I am. I got three babies to raise,
so I am not about to do anything that might send me to jail."

"What's wrong with you, girl?" I yelled, with the muscles in the back
of my neck aching from all the tension I'd brought upon myself. I
rubbed the back of my neck, my head, and my face.

"What?" Freddie asked with a gasp. "What are you talking about?"

"Please stop mentioning jail! You said that if I was smart and careful, I wouldn't have to worry about getting caught."

"That's right," Freddie hollered. "And I still think that."

"But you wouldn't do it?"

"I just told you why. I got too much to lose. My daddy and mama
bent over backwards to raise us to do the right thing," Freddie announced.

"My daddy did, too. This has nothing to do with the way I was
raised. I want you to know that now. My daddy did his job as a parent
and he did it well." I lifted my chin and rubbed it. For some reason I
felt like I had to keep my hands busy. After I finished rubbing my
chin, I started scratching the side of my neck. "This . . . this is all
about me and my choices. I know my daddy would have a horse fit if
he knew about this."

"Girl, we are getting way off the subject. Now if you want my man to
help you with this scheme of yours, you do what I just told you to do.
You get him those pictures and he will take care of the rest. Do you

hear me?" Freddie hollered. I didn't know how to respond to Freddie's outburst. Crazy thoughts started to flash throughout my head. That kept me silent until I heard LoBo mumbling in the background. "Trudy, LoBo says to tell you he is a businessman. You know him well enough to already know that, but I'll mention it anyway. If you want to do business with him, you better say so now. He's got other people waiting."

"Okay. Just tell him to give me a little more time to think this through." I raked my fingers through my hair and glanced toward my bedroom door to make sure Daddy had not eased it open, which he often had a habit of doing at the most inconvenient times. He'd seen me naked more times than James and my doctor put together. It pleased me to know that, unlike some of the girls I knew, my naked body didn't provoke Daddy to have even a slight bit of sexual interest in me.

"Time is money to LoBo, girl," Freddie reminded. "You know how he is . . ."

"Well, tell him that whatever he charges me, I will throw in a bonus for making him wait."

CHAPTER 36

I spent the following weekend with James at his place. A lot of that time was spent in his bed, because that was one place where James and I seemed to get along, most of the time. When we were not in bed we spent our time in his living room watching TV.

Most of the time I didn't even know what show we were watching, and I didn't care that I didn't know. Even though this was something I'd been doing for ten years—and it bored the daylights out of me— it was a welcome distraction from my other activities. Of course, being as nosy as he was, James just had to comment on how preoccupied I was. "Trudy, your body is here, but your mind is somewhere else tonight," he told me. I heard him, but I didn't respond. My brain was working overtime trying to process some of the other things on my mind. I just blinked when James jabbed me in my side with his elbow.

With all of the dramatic changes in my life, being with James now was like taking a break. The mild guilt that I did feel was more for what I was doing to James than it was for Ann.

Identity theft seemed too mild a description for my situation. I was maintaining two roles with James and two with Ann; so in a way I was maintaining four different personalities. I couldn't tell myself enough, but at times I thought I'd lost my mind. The reasons that I should have stopped masquerading as Ann Oliver just didn't seem strong enough. At least not yet. Besides, I was having too much fun treating myself to things that I would not have had access to any other way.

By Saturday I couldn't even remember what James and I had eaten for dinner that Friday night. And I was the one who had done all of the cooking!

"Trudy, will you please tell me what is bothering you?" James pleaded.

"Nothing is bothering me, honey," I said in a mechanical voice. I stood in front of his living room window peering through the cracked curtains like a guard dog. James was so close behind me that I could feel his body heat. I didn't like the look that suddenly popped up on his face. His eyebrows shifted lower on his face, and closer together, almost forming a V above his eyes. This unattractive grimace did nothing for his face except remind me of an owl. His lips were dry and ashy, and on the verge of forming a scab. But I leaned to the side and kissed him on the mouth anyway.

James reared back, his head touching the window that I'd steamed up with my own breath. He slid his tongue across his lips. "I feel like I'm having a conversation with a shadow. Now I want you to tell me what the hell is going on, and I want you to tell me right now," he demanded. A deep sigh followed. His Adam's apple expanded, looking like a large rock lodged in his throat.

"Nothing. Why . . . why do you think that?" I blinked hard as I looked toward the television screen, trying hard to concentrate on yet another program I could not even identify.

"Well, for one thing, your lovemaking has changed. And not for the better, I might add." James blushed, and gave me a sheepish look, like he'd just told me that I had bad breath or a foul body odor. I had on one of his robes and a pair of his well-worn house shoes. His busybody mother had taken it upon herself to haul all of the lounging clothes that I kept at James's apartment to her house to "give them the washing" she felt they needed. She'd accidentally tossed my old house shoes into the trash because she couldn't believe that anybody would still be wearing house shoes that flapped so much. Especially a young woman with a good job.

"Can you be a little more specific?" I snapped. I was the first to admit that I didn't have that much experience in the lovemaking department. And since nobody had ever complained, until now, I had never had a reason to expand my sexual techniques. "You've never complained before and I am not doing anything now that I haven't been doing."

James sniffed and let out a mysteriously long breath, rolling his eyes up at the ceiling, then around the room before returning his attention to me. That owlish look was still on his face. "That's part of the problem. I had hoped that by now you'd do more than just roll around in the bed like a loose wheel."

I gasped. The sixteen-year-old boy who had charmed me out of my virginity with a bottle of pop and a moon pie when I was fifteen had told me that I was the best "piece of pussy" he ever had. His own virgin status had nothing to do with his opinion. "Boys are born already knowing a good pussy from a bad one. Girl, you the best . . ." he'd huffed right after his first orgasm had snuck up on him. With that validation, I had decided right then and there that there was nothing else I needed to do to satisfy my partner.

My second lover had made a similar statement. He advised me to increase my desirability by adding blow jobs to my list of "things to do" to keep a man happy.

By the time James entered my life, and body, I assumed that I knew, and did, everything it took to make a man happy in bed.

It was a rude awakening to hear that I'd been wrong all these years. "What more do you want me to do, James? I've already said I'd marry you. And, even now, I do all I can to make you happy." I cleared my throat. "Are you trying to tell me something else? Are you ready to move on?" As odd as my relationship with James was, I didn't want to give it up. Not yet.

Like Daddy, James had been like a life jacket for me for so many years, I didn't know how I'd survive without him. However, the way things had been going in my life lately, I had gained some much-needed strength and confidence.

"No, I am not ready to move on!" he exclaimed, an incredulous look spreading across his face. "I don't want to move on. Not now, not ever. You are the woman I want to spend the rest of my life with." He leaned over and gave me a few sharp, quick, loud little kisses on my cheek, pecking me with his lips like a woodpecker.

"Then what's the problem?" I asked. I was as confused as I was disappointed.

James held his breath for a moment. It seemed like he couldn't control his eyes. He looked at the ceiling, his feet, behind me, and around the room before his eyes settled on my face. He shrugged and scratched his chin. "Your mind is definitely not on me tonight. You have totally ignored several things I've said in the last few minutes. I just asked you if you wanted to go with me to look at those new houses on Market Street."

"Huh? What houses?"

"See what I mean." James lifted his chin and flashed me an angry look. "I've spent the last ten minutes telling you about my meeting with that realtor. Three months ago when this subject came up, you told me to my face not to even think about buying a piece of property without you being in on it. You forgot that, too?"

With a firm grip on my arm, James pulled me from the window back to the couch where we plopped down so hard and fast I was all but on his lap. I couldn't remember going to the window in the first place. My memory lapses gave me something else to be concerned about. I promised myself that I would be more alert, no matter what I did. Losing my memory at the wrong time was dangerous and it could alter things for me tremendously. I had a flash of myself forgetting to use the right name at the right time. I even felt the imaginary shame, embarrassment, and fear.

I spun around and rubbed James's shoulder. "I didn't forget," I said with an exaggerated grin, pulling him closer. I rubbed his chest, too, which was somewhat thicker and softer than I remembered. It was no wonder with all of the gourmet meals I'd been treating him to. Some I'd even served to him in bed. Unfortunately, our sex wasn't vigorous enough to burn many calories.

"Did you forget what I told you about Mama?"

"What about your mama?" I peeled his fingers from around my arm, irritated just by him mentioning his mother during one of our most tense conversations.

"She wants to sell her house." There was now a guarded look on James's face, and he still had trouble controlling his eyes. He stared at the wall as he continued. "She wants to be close to us when we get married." His voice had dropped to a whisper.

"What?" My words felt trapped in my throat. I coughed to keep from choking. "How . . . close?"

"Well, I told her not to get her hopes up until I discussed it with you. But the thing is, she thinks it would make a lot of sense for her to move in with us once we get married." James held his breath and scratched the side of his face, looking at me with wide-eyed anticipation.

"That close, huh?" I said with a sneer.

"Um-huh." He nodded. His eyes seemed like they didn't want to move. He kept his gaze on me, looking at me for a long time without a single blink.

I blinked so hard an eyelash fell off and into my eye. "Live with Mavis?" I asked, rubbing my eye. "Honey, I love your mama to death, but I don't know if I could live with her. You know how old people are."

James gently removed the lash from my eye with the tip of his shirt-tail. "I figured you'd feel that way and I told her just that. But will you at least think about it? Mama's old. She shouldn't be on her own too much longer."

"My daddy's old, too. Should we move him in with us, too?" I knew that that was a dumb question. Daddy would rather get a whupping than move out of his beloved house.

"I wouldn't have a problem with that."

"We need to give ourselves some time to think about what we are planning to do. Getting married, buying a house, raising kids. That's a lot of responsibilities, James."

"We've been giving all this some thought for ten years. How much more time you think you'll need?" he hollered, stomping his foot so hard on the floor the lamps rattled.

"I don't know, James. I just need a little more time to think things through again," I told him, waving my hands and shaking my throbbing head. A massive headache had eased its way into the mix, making me feel even more agitated.

"Trudy, don't make me wait too long. I've been more than patient with you. Against my better judgment, I agreed to let you get a job and work for a while. Mama told me that was my first mistake."

CHAPTER 37

"James, let's get one thing straight right now: the year is 2005, not 1905. I am not your property so you didn't *let* me do a damn thing." I stabbed James in the chest with the tip of my finger as I spoke, making him flinch. I looked him straight in the eye and didn't shift my eyes until I said everything I had to say. "You got that? My daddy's name is Otto and his job of raising me is over. I don't need permission from him to do what I want to do, and I damn sure don't need it from you." I said such a mouthful I almost lost my breath. I had to lean forward and rub my chest to keep from having an anxiety attack.

With his jaw hanging open, James bowed his head and raked his fingers through his hair. "I didn't mean for that to come out the way it did. I don't like to see you like this."

"Well, if you don't talk that kind of shit to me, you won't see me like this," I said evenly.

I had reached a crossroad in my life and I didn't know which way to turn. All I knew was, I wanted to enjoy my freedom a little longer.

My plans were too complicated at the moment for me to focus on James. But I had to give some serious thought to the fact that if he irritated me now, what would it be like to spend the next forty or fifty years with him if we got married?

There were things that I had to get out of my system first. I'd never been able to afford some of the things I had and did now. I had to take advantage of every opportunity I had. As soon as James took me home later that Saturday night, I called up Freddie.

"Tell LoBo I'll give him the pictures he asked for tomorrow," I said, blurting out the words while she was still talking.

"You better be sure now. Don't you have my man going through all the trouble of hooking you up with all this shit, and then you back out," Freddie warned.

"I won't back out," I promised. "I'll throw in another trip to Reno for you," I added. It did a lot for my ego for me to be in a position where I could do nice things for my friends.

"Well, I could sure use a trip to Reno," Freddie squealed with delight. "I've had one hell of a week."

After I hung up the telephone, I slept like a baby. I couldn't wait for Monday to arrive.

When it did, I got to work an hour earlier than my usual time. A red-flagged E-mail from Mr. Rydell to the entire staff, that had been sent even earlier, informed us that Ann was going to be out of the office for the next week. She had left the night before to accompany a country club group on a cruise to the Mediterranean, a trip that Mr. Rydell had been scheduled to take himself.

I found out the rest of the story from two of the reps later that morning. While I occupied a stall in the ladies' room, Lupe and Joy entered, already involved in a juicy conversation. "What a shame. Marty's wife should get herself a job for a change so she can stop telling Marty how to do his," Lupe said, sucking on her teeth as she spoke. "Does this dress make my butt look too big?"

Joy cackled first then spoke in a low, but very serious tone of voice. "Oh, Marty's just a big pussy and he's getting fucked inside out. Ann wanted that trip to Greece in the first place. I knew that when she invited Marty's wife to dinner at her condo the other day, she was going to cook up more than a meal. She got that trip to Greece, and Marty has to stay here to fight with that behemoth he married. Tsk tsk." I held my breath as the two women moved across the room with their high heels click-clacking across the tiled floor. "It's the mirror that makes your butt look too big. Look at my nose; now look at it in the mirror. Big difference, huh?" Joy said, expelling a loud burp and excusing herself. "I had a burrito for breakfast," she explained.

I waited until I heard Lupe and Joy leave the restroom before I flushed the toilet. I didn't realize I was humming until I made it back to my desk.

"You sure are cheerful. Especially for somebody who looks so bloated today," Pam said, straightening the brochure rack. Her last comment must have slipped out by mistake. With her own stomach looking like a melon, Pam rarely called attention to that part of a woman's body. "Uh, are you glad that Ann's going to be out of the office for a week?" she asked meekly, a pleading look on her face. One thing I tried my best not to do was to degrade another person to his or her face. There was a lot I could say about everybody I knew, especially my coworkers. But I chose not to. I felt better about myself knowing that there was at least one positive thing that set me apart from them.

"You could say that," I said with a grin. I stopped and helped Pam straighten brochures on the rack, something I'd never done before.

Two days later LoBo supplied me with a brand new California driver's license. Unlike the sour-faced picture on my real license, where I looked like I was posing for a mug shot, on my bogus license I had a grin on my face that reached from ear to ear.

CHAPTER 38

The following Friday, LoBo informed me at the last minute that he was going to accompany Freddie and me to Reno that weekend. I was not too pleased to hear this, but under the circumstances, there was little I could do to get out of it.

"Lord knows I could use me a little R and R, and Reno is just as good a place to do it as anyplace," he told me. "Besides, I need to keep a eye on my woman," he said gruffly, winking at me as he slurped his fourth rum and Coke. "I got a lot invested in this girl." He grinned and gently rubbed the side of Freddie's head. Her face lit up like a streetlight. I sat across from them at a wobbly table in a sleazy bar that I didn't want to be in in the first place, down the street from their apartment. Freddie and I had joined LoBo right after work. "Do I smell buffalo wings?" LoBo's left eyebrow shot up as he tilted his head to look at me out of the corner of his eye.

I shook my head. "I don't smell anything," I snapped. We had already racked up a long tab in my name. Well, actually, the tab was in Ann's name.

LoBo snapped his long ashy fingers. "Well, could I smell some buffalo wings?" LoBo grinned and squeezed Freddie's shoulder. "I promised my honey she wouldn't have to cook tonight."

"They do serve some screaming snacks up in here, girl." Freddie nodded as she reached across the table and patted my hand.

Before I could say another word, LoBo summoned our waiter and ordered another round of drinks. Freddie put in an order for almost every snack on the menu. With a whisper she said, "*We* may as well get in the mood for Reno." I knew then that LoBo and Freddie had cooked up their own scheme for him to get a free trip to Reno on me, too.

Freddie had a large poster tacked on a hallway wall in her apartment of her and me made up to look like Thelma and Louise. There was another poster facing it that depicted Freddie and LoBo as Bonnie and Clyde. Although the posters were a bit extreme, I couldn't think of anything that represented us three "outlaws" better.

I could not believe how potent greed was. It had me acting like a fool, and that was bad enough. But it seemed like no matter how much I gave LoBo, he always wanted more. Even though I had treated him and Freddie to snacks at the bar, LoBo decided he was still hungry. I treated him and Freddie to a late dinner at an Italian restaurant across town later that same night. He had stuffed so much food into his mouth that he was in pain. But he still had the nerve to order food to go, too! We didn't even discuss me gassing up his car. He just pulled up at a service station on the way home and turned to me with his palm open.

I had paid LoBo five hundred dollars for the fake ID and birth certificate. His trip to Reno was a bonus he felt he deserved. His behavior annoyed me. It ruined what might have been a wonderful mini-vacation for Freddie and me, had she and I gone to Reno alone like we'd originally planned.

What made it even worse was the fact that I couldn't discuss Bo's behavior with Freddie. I knew I couldn't cross certain lines with her. The last thing I wanted to do was put her in a position where she had to choose between her man and me. It took a lot of discipline, but I managed to keep LoBo happy. I didn't like giving in to him. I did it because I wanted to stay on his good side in case I needed his services again. Besides, he had the resources and connections to get me any- and everything I needed to keep my scheme going well.

So that everything would be consistent, I had chosen to go along with Ann's real birthday. Which meant that under my new identity I was thirty-five.

"I don't like being that old," I whined, admiring the new license as I slid it into the new sealskin wallet I'd purchased the same day we went to Reno. "Some people don't even believe I'm twenty-eight. My real age."

"That should be the least of your worries. And I'm tellin' you right now, if you get caught, you don't know me," LoBo warned with a threatening look and a finger in my face. "I done stayed out of the joint all these years, and I ain't fin to go now on account of this bull-shit you got me caught up in."

"Brother, you know I'd never rat you out," I said, meaning every word.

LoBo nodded, but there was a stone cold look on his face. "I'm just lettin' you know the real deal now so you don't get confused," he told me. "Do you hear me?" There was an ominous tone in his voice and that frightened me, but just a little. I'd known LoBo for years and had never known him to do anything violent. He was just a crook, but he had better morals than a lot of honest people I knew. He loved his woman, his kids, and the rest of his family. LoBo even treated his dog, an aging basset hound named Lucille, as well as he treated his kids. As a matter of fact, he claimed Lucille as a dependent on his taxes, and even had a MasterCard in that long-eared dog's name. I had to ad-mire a man with that kind of devotion.

It didn't take long for me to regret that I'd recruited LoBo into my scam. I knew that I would have to work hard to keep things in order. There were times when those credit cards actually felt hot in my hand. In Reno every time I pulled one out to pay for something, my hand flinched. Even though I was having a good time I couldn't wait to get back home where I could hide out in my bedroom and orga-nize my next move.

As soon as I made my way from my second floor suite to the casino on the first floor at Harrah's to join Freddie and LoBo, I had to with-draw three hundred dollars from an ATM to give to LoBo. It was an-other bonus that LoBo decided he deserved. "Girl, that Ann Oliver heifer is one cow that *we* need to milk till she can't be milked no more." He laughed, dancing a jig and balancing a drink in one hand, the fifteen twenties from me in the other. I didn't agree with his com-ment about Ann. Well, she was a heifer. I agreed with that part, but the money was *not* coming from Ann's pocketbook so she wasn't being milked. If anybody was, it was me and LoBo was the one squeez-ing my titties.

I had given LoBo the money anyway because I wanted to keep the peace, and he'd already lost all of his own money playing blackjack.

It was worth it to me because I couldn't stand to see a grown man pout. At least that's what I explained to Freddie when she told me I was spoiling her man.

CHAPTER 39

Reno was usually a nice place to visit. But it was always nice to return to California. Especially after losing a fortune in the slot machines the way Freddie and I did.

"In less than two days I lost more gambling than I make in a month on my job," Freddie complained, a worried look on her face. "Do me a big favor, girlfriend, don't make it so easy for me to 'borrow' money from you in the future. Those cards you got in your purse are getting dangerous."

"I am beginning to think that same thing myself," I replied. The fact that I'd gambled and lost and had nothing to show for it bothered me. "We'll have to be more careful next time."

"Next time? Girl, how long do you plan to do this thing? This shit is truly crazy. Now you do know that, don't you?"

I gave Freddie a thoughtful look, dismissing her with a wave of my hand. "But I don't plan on doing it too much longer, anyway. Let's just have a little fun while we can. This might be the only chance we get to live like queens."

Freddie occupied the seat next to me on the plane back to California from Reno. LoBo was in a window seat behind us, sipping on his third glass of wine in the last half hour. He was disgusted because he had lost so much money. But he was not half as disgusted as

I was. While he had thrown away money with both hands, playing the tables and ten dollar slot machines, Freddie and I had stuck to the nickel machines. First chance I got, I pretended to be asleep. I stayed like that all the rest of the way home.

When I walked into the house that Sunday night, Daddy was in the kitchen scrubbing a scorched skillet with a Brillo pad. "Wipe your feet and get on in here and call that James back. He been callin' here every hour on the hour," Daddy said, glancing at me over his shoulder. His face was covered in grease and sweat. A soiled dish towel was draped around his shoulders like a stole. He paused long enough to swipe his face with the dish towel. "Did you hear what I just said, gal?"

"Yes, Daddy. I'll call James before I go to bed," I moaned.

I fled to my room, still wrapped up in the new nylon jacket that I had purchased for my trip to Reno. My mood was dark and I had to be alone so that I could sort out my feelings. I had to think about what I'd let happen in the last couple of days. It was enough to make my head spin. Not only had I lost a great deal of money in Reno, I had paid for three round-trip plane tickets, our meals, the hotel rooms, room-service charges for the four adult movies LoBo and Freddie watched in their room, LoBo's airport parking, and the small fortune that I'd given to him and Freddie to gamble with. I plopped down on the side of my bed. It was only then that I noticed I had put my new pumps on the wrong feet before leaving Reno. I noticed something else that disturbed me: my hands were trembling. I balled my hands into fists, hoping to make them stop shaking. When that didn't work, I grabbed a pillow and hugged it against my chest. My diagnosis was that I was having an anxiety attack. Just as I was getting really worried, the telephone on my nightstand rang. The Caller ID identified Freddie's telephone number so I grabbed it immediately.

"Thank . . . thank God it's you," I said, my voice trembling as much as my hands.

"You sound delirious. Are you all right? You seemed worried on the way home. LoBo noticed it, too. He told me to call and check up on you," Freddie told me in a genuinely concerned voice.

"I'm fine. I was just a little tired from all the running around we did." I paused and let out a sharp, hollow laugh. "And I was ticked off because I lost so much money in those damn slot machines."

"Oh. Well, we had a good time and we wanted to thank you again.

Me and LoBo don't get to get out of town much since we had the kids. We appreciate everything you do for us."

"Thanks, Freddie." An uncomfortably long moment of silence passed before we spoke again. I didn't know what else was on Freddie's mind, but I had a feeling it was something I didn't want to hear. "Freddie, are you still there?" I asked dumbly.

I could hear background noises and Freddie's loud breathing. She followed that up with what sounded like a symphony of gibberish. Before I could ask her to speak more clearly, she cleared her throat and spoke not only more clearly, but in a voice so loud I had to hold the telephone away from my ear for a moment. "Now don't get mad," she began in a stilted voice. "But I've been meaning to ask you something."

"What is it?" I braced myself.

"How much does James know about . . . you know?"

I sucked on my teeth. "Why would I get mad about you asking me something as lame as that?"

"Well, with him being your man, I would think that you tell him certain things. Like I do with LoBo. How much have you told him?"

"Nothing. And he never will know about . . . you know, the credit card thing. He would have my head on a platter if he knew I was doing something so, um, you know."

"You can't even say it, can you?"

"What do you mean?" I asked in a voice so small I hardly recognized it as my own.

"It's called identity theft, Trudy."

"I know what it's called," I snapped.

"It's been in the news a lot lately. *Associated Press, Time* magazine. There are whole Web sites devoted to it. Millions, and I do mean millions of folks have been victims."

"Why are you telling me all this shit, Freddie? I read. I watch the six o'clock news. I already know what's going on."

"Then I guess you know about all the folks doing time for stealing other peoples' identities. One woman in D.C. stole her own daughter's identity. A man right here in California fucked up all of his young kids' credit by using their Social Security numbers and names. I just thought that you should know all that."

"I know all I need to know. Anyway, I don't plan to do this too much longer. I'll stop before it gets out of hand . . ."

"Like I said, I appreciate all you've done for us," Freddie said, sounding tired. "But if you do get caught, I want you to know I won't turn my back on you the way some friends would."

I was glad when Freddie hung up. She had given me a lot to think about. I was not in the mood to talk to James so I didn't bother calling him that night. I needed more time to think things through anyway.

CHAPTER 40

Most of the people I knew hated for Monday morning to roll around because they didn't want to go back to work. I was glad to return to work that Monday morning after the trip to Reno. The only thing I didn't look forward to at the office was Ann's return, which was supposed to be the following week. I was surprised when she didn't return as scheduled. Wendy and Pam didn't know any more about Ann's absence than I did. "I even asked Lupe and she hasn't heard from Ann either," Pam informed me.

No matter how big of a thorn Ann was in my side, I didn't want anything else bad to happen to her. But the mugging that she had survived would seem like a walk in the park compared to some of the things that could have happened to her during her trip to Greece. With all of the current terrorist activity, we all had some concerns when it involved travel. It was an especially sensitive subject with me. There was not a day in my life when I didn't think about how my mother had died. Being the victim of a terrorist attack was something that I would not have wished on my worst enemy.

Around nine-thirty that Monday morning, Mr. Rydell fired off another one of his red-flagged E-mails to the whole staff. He advised us all to meet him immediately in the reception area for an announcement he had to make.

One thing I had learned was, when you become part of the criminal element, and if you have a conscience, paranoia becomes part of your everyday routine. As soon as I heard about the impromptu meeting, I suspected the worst. I thought that somehow I'd been found out. My heart was beating a mile a minute as I stood by the side of my desk behind Lupe, wondering what was so important for Mr. Rydell to call us all together. Wendy stood next to me, breathing like a seal. Apparently, I was not the only paranoid member of the team. Wendy looked downright frightened and so did Pam, for that matter. The three of us remained silent as the reps mumbled among themselves. My mind was such a ball of confusion that I didn't try that hard to listen to the muffled conversations around me. I was just alert enough to determine that the reps' speculations had nothing to do with me. But that didn't mean anything. None of us really knew why the meeting had been called.

As urgent as he'd made it sound, Mr. Rydell was the last to arrive. Looking like a white-haired penguin in his black suit, he waddled into the reception area from the elevator, huffing and puffing like he had taken the stairs. The reps stopped mumbling and suddenly everyone stood ramrod straight.

Mr. Rydell looked around the room, his gaze settling on me. I held my breath as his rubbery lips began to quiver. I didn't know if other Black folks realized it, but whenever a situation involved one of *us*, attention was focused on the rest of *us*. Not only was Mr. Rydell paying a lot of attention to me, but Dennis was, too. In less than one minute he'd adjusted his Harry Potter glasses twice and stared in my direction, looking me up and down in a way that made me feel like I'd come to work naked.

Mr. Rydell finally cleared his throat to get Dennis's attention off me. All eyes were on Mr. Rydell as he began to talk in that low, steady voice that people used to deliver difficult news. "Ann . . . our dear sweet Ann, has suffered another blow." He stopped to blow his nose into a large white handkerchief, making a face that upgraded his plain features to fiercely ugly. Joy patted his back, blinking rapidly as if to hold back her own tears until we found out exactly what had happened to Ann this time.

With his eyes shut, Mr. Rydell rubbed his nose with the back of his thick hand but that didn't stop him from letting out a honk that sounded like the distress call of a goose. "Please excuse me," he said, forcing a smile. After licking his lips and composing himself, he continued. "Ann's . . . her sister was found dead last night," Mr. Rydell stated, mopping his face with the same large white handkerchief that he'd just blown his nose with. I gasped along with everybody else.

"What happened?" I heard somebody ask.

Mr. Rydell blew his nose again and rubbed the back of his head before responding. "I don't have all the details yet. But as some of us know, Ann's younger sister was leading a troubled life. Drugs were part of her problem so something like this was bound to happen sooner or later. Anyone interested in attending the funeral services along with me is welcome to do so. Time off with pay, of course," he added, looking from one face to another.

There were a few mumbled comments and a few choking sobs from the women. I looked at Wendy standing next to Pam with her arms folded and a bereaved look on her face. I didn't know if Wendy's sorrow was genuine or not, but mine was. I knew all too well what it was like to lose a loved one.

"So out of respect, we'll close the office for the remainder of the day. That will be all," Mr. Rydell croaked with a dismissive wave of his hand. He blew his nose one more time before he stumbled to the elevator.

Dennis Klein took off his glasses and rubbed his eyes. Joy muttered gibberish under her breath, shaking her head so violently her French twist came undone. And Lupe boo-hooed so hard and loud that people walking by outside on the street heard her. The three grieving reps walked behind Mr. Rydell in a single file with their heads bowed like convicts. It was a sight to behold. And it was all because of Ann.

As soon as we were alone, Wendy padded over to my desk. "If this doesn't knock Ann off her high horse nothing will," she said sharply, with a loose grin on her malicious face.

Wendy often said mean things about other people in my presence that rubbed me the wrong way. I always managed to hold my tongue. Until now.

"Show some respect for the dead, girl! You might be next," I snapped. Wendy was so taken aback by my outburst she ran back to her workstation in tears.

CHAPTER 41

There had been some tension between James and me since I'd returned from Reno. He didn't like the fact that my new job had already taken me away from him for two whole weekends. Chills ran up and down my spine when I tried to imagine what James would say if I told him the truth.

Especially the part about Freddie and LoBo going on a "retreat" to Reno with me. James had a problem with my choice of friends. That bothered me because I didn't associate with just anybody. I chose my friends carefully, so the few I had meant a lot to me. James tolerated Freddie, but he looked down on LoBo. Not because LoBo hauled trash for a living, but because LoBo was on the shady side and had family members in prison. James took a lot of pride in the fact that nobody in his family had ever been in jail or purchased any of the hot merchandise that LoBo could get his hands on at the drop of a hat.

I had tried to reach James at home that evening after we'd heard about Ann's sister, but his mother had answered his telephone. "I thought he was with you," she muttered, sucking on her teeth and pausing long enough to annoy me. "But then, you been mighty scarce lately. Scarce as hens' teeth. You the only person I know that got to go on retreats to keep a job . . ."

"I work for a travel agency, Mavis. We have to keep coming up with new ways to attract business to keep up with the competition," I snapped, making up things as I went along. "At our retreats we create scenarios and do exercises to evaluate our public relations skills. Travelers, especially large groups from big corporations, want to feel that they are in good hands when they travel."

"What is bein' a secretary got to do with all that?" Mavis barked. It amazed me how ignorant most people were when it came to what a secretary did or did not do. Some people believed that secretaries had it as easy as housewives, another essential but unappreciated group in our society. I had to admit that there was a time when I thought that all secretaries did was answer phones, file, type, and flirt with their bosses. But the truth of the matter was, secretaries and other clerical employees had a lot of hidden talent and power. A few years ago a temp agency offered me a position with a company that had almost closed after their three disgruntled secretaries walked off the job.

"I have to know what is going on at the company so I can do my job, Mavis. If my boss thinks that I should attend the retreats, I think so, too. And anyway, management people don't know the first thing about arranging meetings, setting up conference calls, maintaining office equipment and supplies, filing—"

Mavis clicked her teeth and cut me off in mid-sentence. "Organizing potlucks, making coffee . . ."

"I do all of that, too. But in the future they will train me to do what the travel reps do, too," I claimed.

One thing I knew I had to do soon was to organize my lies. At the rate I was going, it was just a matter of time before James or Daddy caught me in one of my own traps. If it could happen with them, there was no telling what kind of mess I could get myself into posing as Ann Oliver. I hung up before Mavis could annoy me further.

Before I could get comfortable and start dinner the telephone rang. It was Daddy calling from the liquor store. "James just got here. He'd already been by the house looking for you," Daddy told me.

"I spent a little time at the mall this afternoon and then Freddie and I went out for a drink after she got off work," I explained.

After Mr. Rydell had closed the office out of respect for Ann's latest tragedy, I had taken a bus to the mall to get my nails done. Then I did do a few hours of window-shopping. I saw a lot of things that I wanted to buy, but couldn't. Not because I didn't have the credit cards with me; I never left home without them. But because of something so off-the-wall it would have been funny had it not been so serious to me at the time: I was superstitious.

For some reason the news of Ann's sister's death had given me such a creepy feeling that I couldn't even bring myself to charge any of the lovely items I'd admired. But I hadn't felt that morbid feeling until I reached for the credit card when it came time to pay for the lobster lunch I'd gobbled up. I didn't know what Ann's sister looked like, but my mind had suddenly flashed on a younger version of Ann lying in a coffin. The vision actually made my hand throb when I touched the credit card. With the impatient waiter glaring at me, I fished out a fist-ful of five-dollar bills instead. It was painful for me to have to pay for such a lavish meal out of my own funds.

I had drifted in and out of several stores until it was time for Freddie to get off. I was standing in front of her building when she left work. She had had a hard day and needed a drink as much as I did. Surprisingly, I didn't have a problem paying for our drinks with the same credit card I had not been able to use at lunchtime. But my being slightly tipsy helped. I made a mental note that if there was ever another time when superstition interfered with my shopping plans, I'd take care of that worrisome condition with a few drinks.

"Gal, why you spendin' good money on alcohol at a bar when I got enough here to light up Mount Rushmore?" Daddy laughed, inter-rupting my thoughts.

"Uh, it's not the same thing, Daddy. I . . . I heard some bad . . . bad news today," I said, with a deliberate stutter.

"What?" Daddy asked, his own voice shaking.

"One of the ladies I work for, her sister was on drugs real bad. Well, they found her dead," I stated with a sob.

"Hmmm." Daddy let out a deep breath. "I'm glad I didn't never have to worry about you doin' nothin' that stupid. You ain't perfect but I'm real proud you my gal."

"Thank you, Daddy. Anyway, I was feeling kind of down about it, so Freddie took me out to talk about it over drinks."

"You all right? Did you know the dead girl?"

"Uh-uh."

"Why don't you come out to the store and relax till I close up, baby. I don't like you bein' by yourself when you got the blues. Besides, James is here and I'm sure he'd love to give you a hug."

"Oh. Well, I'll have to take a cab over there. But I'll get there as soon as I can."

Cab drivers didn't like to come into my neighborhood after a certain hour. This was one time that I was glad they didn't. I waited an hour before I called the liquor store.

To my everlasting horror, Mr. Clarke, the horny old man who worked for Daddy, answered the telephone. "Well, hello there, Miss America. I ain't seen you in a while. With your sweet self."

I had not been back to the store since the robbery, but I'd caught glimpses of Mr. Clarke every now and then. Usually from the living room window at Freddie's apartment as Mr. Clarke made his way to the massage parlor near her place that he couldn't seem to stay out of.

"Hello, Mr. Clarke. I know you are busy so I won't take up your time. Will you put my daddy on the telephone?" I said in a rush. The next voice I heard belonged to James.

"I thought you were on your way over here," he said gruffly.

"I thought I was, too. I called for a cab an hour ago. I called to check on it and they didn't even have a record of my call," I said, sounding annoyed. I had called a cab but then I called back five minutes later to cancel it.

"It's just as well, your daddy's about to close up anyway. You want some company?"

"Did Daddy tell you about my coworker's sister?"

"Uh-huh. And that's a damn shame."

"I'd like to just stay on home if you don't mind. We'll do something real nice in a day or so. Is that all right?"

"I guess it'll have to be, won't it? You've been doing what you wanted to lately anyway."

"James, don't you start that shit again," I said through clenched teeth, rubbing my eyes with my knuckles. "I am not in the mood to fuss with you tonight. All I can think about is that poor girl dying. It makes me think about Mama and Gary . . ." I was prepared to release a few sobs if I had to.

"I'm sorry, sugar. Look, you get some rest and I'll talk to you tomorrow." James hung up so abruptly I sat staring at the telephone until I could no longer feel it in my hand.

CHAPTER 42

Wendy and I were the only ones who didn't go to Ann's sister's funeral before coming to the office that Thursday morning. I had sent flowers to the funeral home that I'd paid for out of my own pocket.

When Mr. Rydell and the rest of the staff returned to the office that afternoon, everybody was understandably in a dark mood. Mr. Rydell had on his black suit as usual. But it was strange to see the rest of my coworkers dressed in black from head to toe all at the same time. They filed in, heads bowed, right before lunch.

Pam, holding a crock pot that contained what was left of some mysterious stew she'd taken to Ann's condo, burst into tears and ran for the elevator as soon as Wendy asked about the funeral. Pam sobbed off and on for the next two hours. Finally, Mr. Rydell gave her a hug and sent her home.

There had been a lot of tension between Wendy and me since I'd scolded her about making light of Ann's misfortune. She'd been unusually quiet for a change and I liked that. She only addressed me when she had to, and always about business matters.

Somehow we made it through that miserable day. The next morning when Wendy arrived, I was already at my desk finishing up my coffee. A recently divorced woman with a notion to take a cruise to an exotic land to celebrate, had come in and snatched a fistful of brochures from the rack. Wendy stumbled past my desk, almost colliding with the recently divorced woman on her way out.

"Wendy, are you all right?" Pam yelled, concluding a lengthy, loud telephone conversation with one of her out-of-state friends. She got her hair tangled in the telephone cord trying to get off the telephone so fast. I was surprised at how fast Pam had bounced back to normal after her crying fit the day before.

"I'm fine," Wendy said quickly, pausing by the side of my desk. Her hair was askew and her makeup was smeared, which was unusual for so early in the morning. Even for a crude woman like Wendy. "Trudy, I need to talk to you about something in private." She plucked a tissue from the box on my desk and blew her nose. It was then that I noticed that she had also been crying. Her nose was red and her eyes were red and swollen.

I shrugged. "Sure." I glanced at Pam who sat listening. I turned my attention back to Wendy. "You want to take our breaks together in a couple of hours?"

She gave me a hot look, staring way too long for my tastes. I stared back, with one eyebrow raised. That shook her up enough to soften her face and even offer me a smile. "I'll need more than a fifteen minute break. How about lunch? My treat. We can go to the deli next door." Wendy's smile didn't hide the fact that something was bothering her. She was distracted and nervous. She stumbled and dropped her purse twice.

I nodded. "That sounds fine. Do you . . . do you want to tell me what this is about?" I asked. I had already assumed that it had something to do with the way I had yelled at Wendy. She wanted to clear the air, make peace. I was all for that.

"I had a long conversation with Daryl last night," she said in a voice that was similar to a growl.

I looked from Wendy to Pam. Pam widened her eyes and shrugged. I turned back to Wendy. "And?" I said, more than a little curious now. I couldn't imagine what a conversation with a fool like Daryl had to do with me. Then it dawned on me. Like a lot of White women I'd worked with, Wendy wanted to use me as a sounding board—like a mammy. This was something that a lot of Black women experienced. Freddie worked with a lot of White women who would get hysterical over just about anything. They often took her, or one of her Black female coworkers, aside to weep on their shoulders. Just the thought brought a smile to my face. My own mother, as Black as she had tried to be, had been the type of White woman to cry on the nearest Black woman's shoulder.

"And this is rather sensitive and urgent so we have to talk abut it today. Lunchtime," Wendy told me. She whirled around and rushed back into her cubicle.

For a fleeting moment a hellish thought crossed my mind: Somehow Wendy had discovered my deception. That thought didn't stay with me long because Wendy had been the one to encourage me to use the company credit card for personal reasons in the first place. She couldn't expose me without cooking her own goose.

I convinced myself that whatever it was that Wendy needed to discuss with me, it had nothing to do with the credit card.

CHAPTER 43

It was a busy morning. With the telephones ringing off the hook and customers in groups of three and four dropping by, Wendy, Pam, and I were too busy to do much of anything else but what we were being paid to do, for a change. With the exception of Dennis Klein going out to meet his wife for a cup of coffee around ten, Mr. Rydell and the rest of the reps remained in their offices until just before noon. Then they strutted through the reception area like a bunch of hens.

Wendy waited by the side of my desk for Pam to run out and get her lunch. She was anxious to get me to that deli to have that mysterious discussion with me. During these few minutes, Wendy gave me quick hard glances, looking away each time I looked up from my desk and caught her looking at me. I didn't know what it was she needed to discuss, but the sooner we got it over with, the better.

"Wendy, can you give me a hint as to what this is all about?" I asked in a gentle voice, cupping my hands on my desk.

"Trudy, this is hard enough for me. As a matter of fact, I need some air so I can clear my head and get my thoughts together," Wendy replied, deepening the mystery. She spun around and ran to her cubicle, dashing back out with her purse. "I'll see you at the deli," she mumbled, running out the door.

As soon as Pam returned, a few minutes later, I joined Wendy at the

deli next door. She was already seated at one of the tiny red plastic tables in a corner, with a grilled-cheese sandwich on a plastic red plate
in front of her. Now that I had become accustomed to eating at the
more upscale restaurants, I felt out of place in a cheap deli. Getting
used to the "good life" had not been an easy thing for a person like
me to do. Somehow I had managed to do it, and I enjoyed every
minute of it. However, now when I had to backslide to the way things
used to be for me, I realized how much I had changed. I had to con-
stantly keep in mind that the lavish lifestyle that I had borrowed for
myself was still just that: borrowed.

Borrowed and stolen.

I never would have guessed that the private conversation Wendy
wanted to have with me was about her love life. I was understandably
surprised when she began. "Daryl broke up with me," she announced,
talking before I could even sit down in the weak-legged red chair
across from her with the sandwich and bottle of water I'd grabbed. It
had been a while since I'd sat on such a wobbly, cheap chair.

"I didn't know that," I said in a low voice, sincerely concerned. A
couple at a table close to ours had turned to look and listen as soon as
Wendy opened her mouth to speak. "Are you all right with that?"

I was hungry but not for what was on the plate in front of me. You
would have thought that I was staring at a grilled mouse instead of the
lopsided ham sandwich I'd selected. I made a mental note to treat myself to a lobster dinner with all the trimmings and a huge glass of
champagne soon.

Wendy shrugged and blew her nose into a napkin and blinked.
From the look of her face and the way she twisted and turned in her
seat, she was in great pain. "The relationship wasn't going to work
out. I've known that for a long time. Long enough to have two kids."
Wendy sniffed and shook her shoulders and head, as if she could
shake away her pain. "Besides, I always knew that a woman like me
could do a lot better." For the first time, I saw a side of Wendy that
made me feel sorry for her but that didn't last long. Nothing could
have prepared me for the bombshell she hit me with next. "Trudy, I
know how you went after Daryl."

"Excuse me?" I used my tongue to push the food in my mouth to
one side. I had to cough to keep from choking. As soon as I was able to
swallow, I left my jaw hanging open as I stared at Wendy with an incredulous look on my burning face. "Why . . . I . . . I can't believe my

ears," I stammered. I shifted in my seat and had to struggle to cross my legs. I held back a grin that was threatening to take over my face. "Please tell me you are kidding," I said seriously, glancing around the room.

Wendy gave me a hot look. She sucked in a deep breath and fixed her eyes on me, shifting her gaze to every twitch my face made. "That's what I wanted to talk to you about."

"Wait a minute. Let's back up here," I said, holding up my hand and trying not to laugh. "You wanted to talk to me about me going after Daryl?" I had to stop talking long enough to laugh. It wasn't just a chuckle it was a guffaw that brought tears to my eyes. "Where the hell did you get that idea?" I asked after I'd composed myself.

"Trudy, I can understand why a woman like you would go after a man like Daryl." I didn't know how to take the forlorn look Wendy gave me. She was the last person I needed to pity me. She snapped off a chunk of her cheese sandwich and washed it down with a huge swallow of Snapple. "It doesn't matter." She was serious.

"The hell it doesn't!" I exclaimed. "What did Daryl tell you?" I was still more amused than I was angry.

"Do you deny that day in the park with him? He told me all about how you came on to him. And how you wouldn't let up even after he told you all about me." Wendy sighed, and then an unbearably sad look crossed her face. "I tell him all the time that he's too pretty for his own good."

"Look, let me straighten out this mess right now. Daryl came after me with both guns blasting. He told me he had him a White woman, but he never mentioned her name." It was on the tip of my tongue to tell Wendy everything that Daryl had said about her but under the circumstances, I couldn't. Her life was miserable enough. "And for the record, Daryl is not my type. I wouldn't—I *didn't* give him the time of day." By now I was too angry to laugh again.

"Daryl has never lied to me," Wendy said weakly. "He says he doesn't even like . . . Black women. Especially ones that look like you."

I tilted my head and stared at Wendy's face for a long time. My ears were literally ringing. "Wendy, you can believe whatever you want. But if you think for one minute that I would go after a punk like Daryl, you are sadly mistaken. He has nothing I'd want and from what he told me, he has nothing to offer you either."

"He loved me," she said in a small voice. "He must have told me a thousand times."

"I bet he did. And you believed him?"

"Of course I believed my man."

"Then why are you wasting your time asking me what happened?" I sneered. My face felt like it was hot enough to fry an egg.

"I wanted to see if you'd be honest with me . . ." Wendy's voice sounded so weak and pathetic, and she looked so neglected. I *still* felt sorry for her.

"What difference does it make? If you believe Daryl over me, why do you even ask?" I pushed the plate in front of me away. "This lunch was not a good idea," I snapped. Surprisingly, I found myself wondering how Ann Oliver would have reacted if she had been the one who Wendy confronted. For one thing, I didn't think that Wendy was stupid enough to believe that a woman like Ann would even speak to a man like Daryl. It bothered me that she thought I was. I started to rise. "We have to work together so I suggest we forget this conversation ever took place. As you know, there is enough drama going on with my job in other areas." I didn't have to spell it out. She knew I was talking about Ann.

"Trudy, please don't go," Wendy wailed, touching my arm.

"I think I should," I hissed. "I need some air now."

"I didn't want to bring up this subject, but you seemed like the kind of person I could talk to woman to woman. Please don't go. Please try to forget about Daryl."

"Oh, I already have."

"You are one of the few Black women I can call a close friend."

I gave Wendy a look that could have melted steel. If I was what she called a close friend, she was worse off than I thought. "Wendy, like I said, let's forget this conversation about Daryl ever took place. There are more important things we can talk about other than Daryl. And if you want my opinion, dumping him was the smartest thing you've done since I met you."

"I didn't dump him, he dumped me," Wendy admitted with an extreme pout. I was surprised that she wasn't rolling on the floor crying like a baby.

"Well, either way, you are rid of him. You deserve somebody who appreciates you."

"That's the other thing I wanted to discuss with you," Wendy said, suddenly blinking and grinning. I couldn't believe how fast and far her moods could swing. It usually meant she'd had a few drinks. But there was a sparkle in her eyes that I had never seen before. "I've already met someone else anyway. Actually, I met him a few weeks ago. He made it clear that he wanted me to be his woman, even then. I'm a one-man woman, so I held him off until . . ." Wendy paused and actually looked embarrassed for a split second. "I couldn't get him off my mind. That's when I realized that things were not going to work out between Daryl and me. Lord knows I tried. I tried to the very end. You saw how sweet I was to him when we took you to Ann's place. Well, he told me to my face to leave him alone and that's just what I plan to do," Wendy sniffed and lifted her chin, like she had just won a battle. "My new friend will be here any minute," she squealed, clapping her hands together.

Before I could respond to Wendy's announcement, a tall Black man in a dark gray suit entered the deli. He looked at me first as he started walking toward us, smiling and strutting like he owned the whole block.

A lot of men like him had been coming on to me since my makeover. But none I really liked enough to risk losing James over. I prepared myself to deliver the usual brush-off, but it wasn't necessary.

This gorgeous, well-dressed Black man wrapped his arms around Wendy's shoulders from behind and kissed the side of her face.

CHAPTER 44

"Hello, sweetheart. How are you today?" He had a nice deep voice and there was a lot of sincerity and passion in the look he gave Wendy. I was positively amazed. My jaw got so tight that I was afraid I might not be able to open it again.

Wendy sucked in her breath and turned to face the handsome Black man. "Hi, baby," she cooed. Turning to me she said, "Trudy, this is Mark. He works at the bank next door. Mark, this is Trudy."

"How you doing, sister?" Mark smiled, returning his attention to Wendy before I could respond. "I can't stay, sweetie. I have several appointments I have to prepare for."

"What about tonight?" Wendy whined, looking like a frump with mustard lining her thin lips.

"I'll see you tonight just like I said I would. But I really do have to get back to the office." Mark glanced at me and gave me a casual wave. "It was nice meeting you, Trudy." Just like that, he was gone.

"What do you think?" Wendy wanted to know. There was a wide grin on her face, but her eyes seemed flat and empty. It was the same look I'd seen on the faces of too many other women, Black, White, and everything in between. It was the look of desperation. It bothered me to know that some women placed so much importance on having a man. But I had to admit to myself that I didn't know how I would behave if I hadn't already stashed James so firmly into my hip pocket.

"He's a step up from Daryl," I smirked, no longer interested in my ham sandwich. And, no longer upset over Wendy's outrageous accusation. "Is it serious?" A great sadness hovered over my head like a heavy black cloud. Culturally, I was as Black as I could get. Biologically, half of the blood that flowed through my veins was White. I had no idea what it was to be a White woman in America and probably never would. I was happy with what I was, as far as race was concerned. Despite the fact that my daddy had chosen to marry a White woman, he had taught me to have a lot of racial pride. Therefore, as a Black woman, I shared the same frustration that a lot of other Black women I knew experienced on the subject of Black men with White women. On the other hand, the only reason I had not dated White men was because the right one had not approached me.

"I hope so." Wendy placed her elbows on the table and gave me a thoughtful look. "My folks don't like me dating Black men," she announced, not waiting for me to comment. "I gave them hell for years. After the drugs, the drinking, and everything that goes along with it, I lost a lot of my self-esteem. When I thought I was ready to settle down, I didn't have the nerve to go after any decent White men. I decided that only a Black man deserved what was left of me."

"And they all seem to think the same thing," I remarked, wondering if my White mother had thought the same of herself. "Despite what you think of yourself, you don't seem to have any trouble attracting the kinds of men you like."

"Before Daryl I was with a dentist. For a Black man he was as fine as they come," Wendy stated with a wide smile on her face.

A dentist! A shiftless bum like Daryl was one thing. He was unemployed and crude. He was the kind of man who would go after a snake as long as it had a job and a pussy. But for a woman like Wendy to attract the cream of the crop of Black men it was a mystery and an insult to me and all other Black women. I couldn't wait to discuss this indignation with Freddie.

Freddie was already at the bus stop when I got off work that day. As soon as we'd settled into our usual seat in the back, squeezed so close together on the lumpy seat that I could feel her breath on my face, I told her about my lunch with Wendy. I repeated word for word everything Wendy had said—except the part where she accused me of making a play for Daryl. I couldn't bring myself to share something that ridiculous. I couldn't stop myself from laughing when I told Freddie what Wendy had said about herself and Black men, but Freddie didn't see the humor.

"That is not funny, girl. I can't believe you let that skanky White bitch sit there and talk that shit to your face," she scolded.

"Why should I care about her and that banker? I don't want him and I doubt if he wants me." I sniffed. "Or any other Black woman."

"You should have said something. Especially when she said that shit about only Black men deserving what was left of her blond beauty. I hope that banker's got a teeny-weeny dick."

"Wendy and I were the only ones from the office who didn't go to Ann's sister's funeral," I said, hoping that the change of subject, especially one so morbid, would calm Freddie down.

"That Ann," she said softly. "Now that's a sister with a basket full of curses. First she gets mugged, now this. She must not be living right." Freddie gave me a strange look.

"What's wrong?" I asked, wiggling my nose as Freddie breathed on my face.

"I hope you don't take on any of Ann's bad luck," Freddie replied, giving me a curious look.

"Why would you think that?"

"Fate is some tricky stuff, girl. You going around using Ann's name and pretending to be her could open up a big old can of worms in the luck department. You don't think about that?"

"No, I don't. I wish you wouldn't think about it either. Bad vibes attract bad vibes."

"Well, let's hope that's all it attracts."

I gave Freddie an exasperated look. "Since when did you get so philosophical?"

"I'm not. I'm just trying to help you keep this thing in perspective."

"Well, you can stop that. Everything's under control," I said.

I didn't know if it was what I said that made Freddie give me such a hopeless look or the uncertain voice that I'd said it with.

CHAPTER 45

Ann returned to work the following Tuesday looking good for someone in mourning. As a matter of fact, the woman looked downright dazzling. She waltzed through the reception area wearing a bright yellow silk dress with black polka dots that made her look like a cute bumblebee. She looked even better than she normally looked. Her eyes were nice and clear and her skin had a fresh dewy look about it. Not that I was looking for signs of decay, but I could have sworn that before she left, she'd had some faint lines and moderate crow's feet on her face. Now she looked like she had had a weeklong Swedish facial or something even more extreme. And I was not the only one who noticed it.

"I bet she's had a mini-facelift," Pam decided with a nod after Ann had passed us. "She looks five years younger."

Slithering from her cubicle like a serpent, Wendy joined in the conversation. "Ann is one of a kind. Black women are generally more concerned about politics, relationships, raising kids, church, and stuff; not vanity—except for the celebrities. It's nice to see a regular Black woman who really works hard at her appearance like Ann," Wendy said, looking straight at me as she spoke. Her eyes roamed over my entire body, making me squirm. "And, Trudy, if I had half the butt you have, I'd walk around naked every chance I got." That Wendy. I gave her the most dead-pan expression I could come up with before I dismissed her with a wave so aggressive it made my arm hurt. I could have been a lot more abrasive, but trying to check a woman as far gone as Wendy was a lost cause. After the things she had said to me during our lunch at the deli I should have put her on my shit list. But as hard as I tried to ignore and dislike Wendy, I couldn't.

For some strange reason certain things didn't bother me the way they would have before Bon Voyage became part of my life. Things like Daryl's bold lies and the confrontation about him with Wendy. As a matter of fact, I had to laugh every time I thought about Daryl. The only feelings that I had for him were feelings of pity. Most women like Wendy eventually came to their senses. Either that or they moved on to another man that they could take care of.

Ann had arrived an hour later than her usual time. She mumbled a greeting to Pam and ignored me completely. But I didn't hold that against her because I knew from experience how deep a tragic situation could sink a person.

She stood in front of one of the mirrors in the ladies' room with water running in the sink. She was applying lipstick with one hand and clutching her cellular phone in the other. I let the door slam on purpose so she would know she was not alone, but that didn't stop her from yelling at whoever was on the other end of the telephone. "Look, I know what I get paid to do! I've been doing this for you long enough to know all the rules." I approached the stall farthest away from Ann, gently opening the door as she continued to yell into her phone. "No! I don't want to come down to the islands! What? How dare you call me that! I'm not one of your shoeless island girls—" Ann finally realized she was not alone when she saw my reflection in the mirror. She whirled around and faced me, with her mouth hanging open and a frightened look on her face. She let out a loud sigh and clicked her telephone off, folding it and clutching it like it was trying to get away from her. "Trudy, how long have you been in here?" she asked with a forced smile, shutting off the water in the sink. I could see that she was nervous.

"I just walked in," I muttered, blinking at the telephone in her hand.

"Girl, I've been on this phone all day trying to get a good deal on a headstone for my sister's grave," she stammered, waving her cell phone like it was a rock that she wanted to throw at the wall.

"Did you get one?" I asked lamely.

"I'm working on it," Ann stammered. She left the ladies' room in such a hurry, I had to jump out of the way to keep from getting mowed down.

When I returned to my desk, I looked at the telephone and noticed that Ann was on her private line. If Wendy and Pam had been paying more attention to me, I would not have picked up that line again. I held my breath and pressed the receiver close to my face with my hand covering the mouthpiece. Just as I had suspected, Ann was talking to that same Jamaican man I'd eavesdropped on before. It didn't sound like he was masturbating this time.

"So you want to challenge me? Is that what you have on your agenda?" the man asked, talking loud. "I warned you when we first became close, I will not tolerate such behavior. Especially from a woman!"

"Well, I won't tolerate your threats. You need me more than I need you. And please don't forget one thing—I know all of your business!" Ann yelled. I sucked in my breath and held the telephone away from my face, staring at it like I was seeing it for the first time. I cut a glance in Pam's direction. She was too involved in her own telephone conversation to notice me. I placed my hand back over the phone and scooted down in my seat, turning my head so Pam wouldn't be able to see much of what I was doing.

The Jamaican snorted and mumbled some gibberish under his breath. He cleared his throat before he spoke again. "Yes, lady. You do know where the bodies are buried. But must I remind you, there's always space for you in the same place." If that was not a serious threat I didn't know what was. I had heard enough.

I hung up the telephone and made a promise to myself that I would not listen in on any more of Ann's conversations. I also promised myself that I would not share any of the information I had heard so far. Since I had only heard bits and pieces of the conversations I had no idea what it was I had stumbled into. It would be just like Freddie to blab to LoBo if I told her. And the way people talked, how was I to know that it wouldn't get back to Ann? Not to mention that scary Jamaican man. I had already placed myself into a shaky position by including Freddie and LoBo in my credit card scams.

I put Ann out of my mind for the time being and I called up Freddie at her job. "Girl, Ann looked right at me when she arrived this morning and ignored me completely. I let that slide. I figured because of her sister's tragedy she was too preoccupied to notice me—

even though she did speak to Pam. But when I went to the break room a little while ago, she was all over the place thanking Lupe and Dennis for sending flowers to her sister's funeral. She looked right at me and didn't thank me for sending flowers. And when she got mugged, I sent her flowers then, too," I said with a pout. "She didn't thank me that time either."

"Yeah, but you paid for them with her credit card," Freddie reminded.

"She doesn't know that," I hissed, glancing up to make sure Pam was not listening to my conversation. "But I did pay for the flowers for her sister's funeral with my own money." I tapped my fingers on the top of my desk. "Maybe I should have been the one to say something," I said, propping my elbow up next to my computer keyboard. "I still feel sorry for her."

"Trudy, how can you be feeling so sorry for that woman. I mean, yeah, even I feel sorry about her getting mugged and losing her sister. But she's *still* acting like a bitch and treating you like shit."

"The woman can't help herself, Freddie," I snarled.

"And you can't either, I guess. I know what you need to do. You need to use one of those credit cards to pay for some therapy." Freddie yelled, talking fast because she was on her cellular phone in a stairwell at her work.

"You sure are in a foul mood this morning. I'll talk to you later." I hung up before Freddie could get in another word. I was in a fairly good mood and I wanted to keep it that way.

I was glad that I was finally beyond being bothered too much by some of the hurtful things that Freddie or Wendy said to me. However, I could not say the same thing about Ann. No matter how nice she treated me from time to time, she continued to annoy and frustrate me even more.

Ann and I shared more than looks, ethnicity, and the same name on some credit cards. There were times when I had to stop myself from imitating her walk or the way she waved her hand back and forth when she spoke. There were times during my most extravagant shopping sprees when I had to remind myself that I was not the real Ann Oliver. I was not the Black American Princess that I posed as. Instead, I was the Cinderella version, who was living a lie that was so big it could no longer be measured. And the sad part about it all was

I was enjoying every minute of my masquerade. The only time I felt like myself was when Ann was around.

I was sorry that Ann had returned to work. And I was sorry for feeling that way. I decided to do whatever I had to do to keep things in the proper perspective no matter how painful it was. It took just as much energy to be positive as it took to be negative. At least it did in my case. I would treat her the way I wanted her to treat me: with dignity and respect. She had no use for me, but I still had a vested interest in her.

The colorful posters and large, healthy-looking green plants decorating the lobby and administrative area of Bon Voyage didn't do much to liven up the mood in the office. Everybody was dragging along in a sorry mood with a long face. Every now and then somebody muttered something about how important it was for us to cheer up "poor Ann."

As often as I could I waited until Ann was safely out of her office before I delivered her mail. But whether she was present or not I never felt comfortable in her space. Today was no different.

Just before my lunch hour I decided to deliver the mail and telephone messages to the reps. I stepped out of the elevator and almost fainted from a sweet aroma that was so potent it made my eyes burn. I didn't even have to guess where it was coming from. There were floral arrangements of every kind on Ann's desk, on her floor, even on top of her file cabinet. There were roses of every color, as well as types of flowers that I'd never seen before. A stack of sympathy cards half a foot high, and a small music box with its mouth cracked open playing "You Light Up My Life," sat on the desk on top of Ann's twenty-one-inch computer monitor.

After setting a stack of telephone messages on top of her neatly arranged desk and the *Wall Street Journal,* I padded to the file cabinet in the corner by the window. The same file cabinet I'd purchased for Ann from Office Depot a couple of weeks ago.

Unlike the offices of the other reps, Ann's didn't have a CD player or a cute little radio sitting on a credenza playing easy listening music. Except for the loud ticktock coming from an L-shaped clock on her desk, her space was unbearably quiet. The smell of flowers and the unnatural silence reminded me of a funeral parlor. If that wasn't disturbing enough, it suddenly felt like the room was closing in on me. I shuddered and started moving toward the door.

I hurried out of Ann's office as fast as my numb legs could carry me. I deliberately kept my eyes on the floor in case I ran into one of the other reps before I could escape back to my workstation. I didn't like to stand around talking to my coworkers unless I had to. Their conversations, which were usually centered on them, bored me. It was bad enough when one of them called me Ann, even though it had only happened a few times during my first couple of weeks. My being called Ann was ironic considering the circumstances. But I didn't like being called "Judy" instead of Trudy, either. And a few times I'd even been called the names of former African American employees.

I breathed a sigh of relief when I made it to the ladies' room without getting ambushed by Lupe, Dennis, Joy, or Mr. Rydell. The handicapped stall was occupied, and embarrassingly noisy.

As I stood over the sink washing my hands, the handicapped stall door swung open and Pam stumbled out. There was a severe frown on her face, which was as purple as a plum. Her eyes were bloodshot and puffy. "Hmph!" she muttered, with a tortured look spreading across her face. She let out a deep breath and patted her chest as she stopped in front of me and shook her head. "I never know how my body is going to react to Chinese food," was all she said as she pressed her bloated belly with both hands.

"Are you all right?" I asked.

"I am now," Pam mumbled, massaging her neck with a wet paper towel, then fanning her face with it. "You can have the rest of my fried rice if you want it," she offered.

"Thanks, Pam. But I had my mind on steak and French fries for lunch."

Pam shrugged. "If you change your mind, stop by my desk and get it before it gets too dried out." Still frowning and fanning, Pam left the ladies' room without washing her hands.

CHAPTER 46

As hungry as I was, there was no way I was going to eat Pam's left-over lunch. There was no telling what I'd pick up from her unwashed hands.

I'd also declined another free lunch from Wendy. She had attempted to woo me with the promise of a pizza if I'd escort her to her doctor's office, located in the tall building at the corner by my bus stop. To my horror and disbelief, Wendy was already trying to get pregnant by her new lover. She'd thrown up two mornings in a row and had dreamt about a fish. To her that was reason enough to start looking at baby clothes and see her doctor even though she'd only been with her new man a couple of weeks. I didn't want to mention it to her, but I realized that if she was already pregnant, there was a chance that Daryl was the father.

I was not in the mood to spend time feeding the homeless people in the nearby park. They had all but adopted me, and therefore expected me to dole out food and money every time they saw me. There was also the danger of my being accosted by another Daryl in the park, or even Daryl himself.

I ended up grabbing a meatball sandwich from a restaurant across the street and the latest issue of *Essence* magazine from the corner newsstand, and returned to the office within ten minutes.

"If you change your mind about the rice, let me know. Otherwise, I'll take it home to Boo Boo and Too Sweet. Cats are like men, they will eat anything." Pam gave me a wink and a knowing look so I assumed her last comment had something to do with sex. "I put a coffee cake on the table in the break room. I made it last night. If you want a piece, you better hurry on up there. You know how greedy the folks around here are," Pam told me, pausing in front of my desk to take a sip from a Starbucks cup. "Last week I caught two of those creeps from the insurance company on the second floor slicing up that pound cake I made—before any of us could even get a piece!"

"Thanks, Pam," I said. "I think I'll pass this time," I added with a smile. Pam looked like a clean woman. But Osama bin Laden looked like a nice man. Looking clean, or nice, didn't mean a thing. I'd seen Pam, with my own eyes, stroll out of a stall and leave the ladies' room without splashing a drop of soap and water on the very hands that had caressed and, I hoped, *wiped* her behind.

I'd never been to her apartment but I knew she got very affectionate with her two cats, Boo Boo and Too Sweet. She had shown me pictures of her kissing them on the lips. And cat hair often draped her clothes, not to mention an occasional flea.

After that session with Pam in the ladies' room, I knew that I would never again eat anything that she brought from home. Mainly because of a big news story in California a couple of years ago. A woman had died right after eating in a Mexican restaurant near San Francisco. An autopsy revealed feces in her system. The woman had literally eaten shit. After a bunch of other patrons who had also eaten in the same restaurant had to be rushed to the hospital, there was a big investigation. As hard as it was to believe, the investigators found traces of feces in other dishes at the same restaurant. One of the kitchen employees admitted that he had rarely washed his hands when he used the rest room. The scandal had almost caused the restaurant to close, but it remained open because people were still stupid enough to keep eating there. Recalling that detail made me wonder if it would do any good for me to tell anybody about Pam's nasty self.

The minute I walked into the break room and saw Ann standing over the counter with a knife slicing into Pam's coffee cake I reacted the way a responsible person should have.

"Ann, wait!" I yelled, holding up my hand. "Please don't eat any of that cake!"

Ann Oliver was one of the best-looking Black women I had ever seen in person. But for her to be such a pretty woman she sure knew how to make some ugly faces. She screwed up her face and looked at me like I was speaking Gaelic.

"What the hell are you talking about?" she asked, placing the hand with the knife on her hip.

"Remember that big newspaper story a while back about that Bay Area woman who died after eating in that Mexican restaurant?"

Ann gave my words some consideration. "I was in Rome when that happened, but I heard all about it when I got back," she said, an inquisitive look on her face. "So what?"

I glanced at the door before I inched toward her. I stopped with my face just inches away from hers. "Pam's not the cleanest person in the world," I said in a voice just above a whisper.

Ann gave me a bewildered look and a mild shrug. "And you know this for a fact?"

"I do," I said, with a vigorous nod, my eyes on the floor. "And take my word for it; you don't want to know the details. You don't want to eat anything Pam Bennett cooked."

A slight smile appeared on Ann's face and she tilted her head to the side, staring at me out of the corner of one eye. "Are you just saying this so there'd be more cake for you?"

Her unexpected smile made me feel more comfortable. "I don't want any," I replied.

"Oh, well, that's that." Ann dropped the knife back onto the counter. "I don't have much of an appetite these days anyway." She backed to the nearest of the bright blue plastic tables decorating the break room and slid into a matching chair.

As I was about to leave, I took a deep breath and faced Ann. "I am really sorry about your sister. If there is anything I can do, just let me know." Before I could make it out of the door Ann released a tortured moan. I turned sharply to face her again. Tears had already filled her eyes, but she managed to hold them back by blinking hard and fast.

"I am really going to miss my baby sister," she told me. I took this as an invitation to stay.

"Ann, your sister is out of her pain," I said gently, giving her hand a light squeeze. Her response almost gave me a heart attack.

"Trudy, I don't know of an easy way to say this, so I'll just say it." Ann paused and shifted in her seat, looking me straight in the eyes. "I know you're trying to be me," she announced.

The words hit me like a Mack truck. I froze and stopped breathing.

CHAPTER 47

"What . . . what do you mean?" I managed. I developed an acute case of tunnel vision. For a quick moment I couldn't see anything in the room except Ann's face. There seemed to be darkness all around me.

"That didn't come out the way I wanted it to." Ann cleared her throat and beckoned me with her hand. "Have a seat, Trudy."

Like a zombie, I moved to the table and tumbled into the seat across from her.

"You remind me of my sister and a lot of other women. Women who all want to be *like* me. Limitations have kept you from experiencing a lot of the things that life has to offer. I am where you want to be. I can tell that much by the way you look at me. My sister had that same look in her eyes every time I saw her. Some people call it envy, I call it ambition. With more education and experience, you could really go places, too." Ann gave me a triumphant smile and snapped her fingers. "I am the woman whom women like you and my dear baby sister—may she rest in peace until I get there—want to be. I am proud to say that because I've paid my dues and worked hard, I deserve every damn thing I have. Sure I can be a ball-breaking bitch, but it's the squeaky wheel that gets the oil."

I breathed a sigh of relief. "Uh-huh," I mumbled.

"My sister tried to dress like me. She tried to act, talk, and walk like me. But she had too many limitations! I used to tell her all the time to just be herself. Life is so much easier that way. Do you understand what I am saying?"

I nodded hard, and smiled even harder. "Oh, I understand. I understand completely."

Ann gave me a pensive look, then without warning she threw her head back and laughed. I laughed, too. Even though I didn't know what we were laughing about. Ann wet her lips before continuing. "Let me share a funny, but cute, little story with you. When my sister was a baby she got attached to one of my daddy's relatives. Cousin Bett was in her forties. She'd had polio for years so she dragged her left leg when she walked. My sister was just learning to walk at the time. For the first few weeks, she walked just like Cousin Bett, dragging her leg behind her."

"Your sister had polio, too?" I asked, surprised that I was enjoying this rare interlude.

Ann shook her head and waved her hand. "Not at all. The doctor called it, uh, oh, hell, I forget. But something about mimicry. Truly impressionable people, like my sister, like to mimic the people they adore. My sister was so fond of Cousin Bett that she wanted to be like her, disability and all. Once Cousin Bett moved away, my sister started to walk like a normal toddler." Ann paused and an unbearably sad expression slid across her face. In a voice that was one step from a whisper, she told me, "I tried to help my sister be herself. All her life." She sucked in a deep breath and looked at me with tears in her eyes. "I did all I could do for that girl. But . . ." she paused again and dabbed at her eye with the tip of her finger. "You can't help somebody who can't be helped."

"I know just what you mean," I said. It was only then that I realized we had on identical sweaters. The only difference was mine was blue and hers was black. If Ann did notice that coincidence, she did not react. I knew it was in my best interest not to bring it to her attention. We couldn't have looked more like one another if we had tried. I felt at ease for the moment. But I had learned to stay alert when it came to dealing with Ann Oliver no matter what the situation was.

"My folks worked their way up from the farms of North Carolina," she said proudly. I never would have guessed that her family had come from the South. That explained her full name being "Annie Lou." A faraway look appeared on her face as she continued. "They worked their way through law school, moved to California and raised my sister and me in one of the finest neighborhoods in San Francisco." She talked in a slow, level way that made it seem like she was talking to herself. Her eyes drifted around the room. The few times she directed her attention toward me, she blinked and stared for a few moments before looking away again. But each time she did that, she smiled. "My sister did everything she could to keep our house in an uproar. Drugs, convicts, you name it. No matter what we did to try to help the girl, it did no good. Delores was her name. She dropped out of school in the tenth grade and had two babies before she was eighteen. Mom, well both of my parents really, told her that if she couldn't live by their rules, she couldn't live in our house." Ann excused herself and got up to get a bottle of Evian from the refrigerator. Returning to her seat with her eyes on me and a mysterious grin on her face, she said, "The ungrateful wench cussed out everybody in the house and left that night. Three years went by and we didn't know if the girl was dead or alive. Daddy hired a PI and they found her living in a garbage-strewn *barrio,* on welfare with an ex-convict, in one of the worst parts of Oakland. She came home only for a minute. Just to get money and to cuss us all out again. My folks gave up on her after that."

"Sounds like my Uncle Pete," I said.

Instead of commenting on my comment about my wayward Uncle Pete, Ann just gave me a blank look and continued. "I was the only one she kept in touch with and that was only because I was the only one in the family who was still fool enough to give her money. A thousand dollars here, a thousand there. It was never enough. I helped her out for years and she was as bad off when she died as she ever was before. A few weeks ago, she got a job working the counter at a Starbucks. The discount stores, K-Mart, Starbucks. Places like that were the best she could do with her education and attitude. She called me and demanded money so she could move. I went to take her the money the same day. She moved into another dump of a neighborhood. Most of her neighbors were on welfare, Section Eight, food stamps, crack. Oh, but you would have thought that place was Shangri-la if you had seen the ever-present grins on some of those tortured faces. Delores was working the morning shift at this Starbucks. One of her neighbors had enough sense to open a day-care center in her apartment, so she kept my sister's kids. My sister had to catch one

bus at four in the morning and transfer to two more just to make it to
work by six." Ann paused again and screwed up her face like she was
in pain. She rolled her eyes and sucked in a deep breath before continuing. "I hate to keep bringing it up, but my sister lived in one of
the most obscene and dangerous neighborhoods in San Jose. A snake
pit has more class! Piss-stained old couches were on the ground in
front of the buildings! Old mattresses were piled up on the ground
between the buildings. One night when I was over there I saw a
hooker—one of my sister's friends—doing her business with a trick
on one of those mattresses!" Once again, Ann had to pause. This time
to catch her breath.

With tears in her eyes, she cupped her hands and rolled her eyes
up toward the sky, as if she was about to pray. Her eyes flashed angrily
when she looked back at me. I shifted in my seat. I was anxious to
leave, but my curiosity forced me to remain. "On any given day you'd
see *naked* kids in the middle of the streets bouncing around like mon-
keys! Those same kids, some as young as five, would run up behind
me and try to snatch my purse. They all looked alike so I couldn't
even identify them well enough to call the cops! I was visiting my sister in that jungle that day I got mugged."

Ann gave me a defiant look before taking a long drink of water. She
set her bottle down so hard the table shook. "I bought my sister a car
so she wouldn't have to stand out on that dangerous curb at four in
the morning. One morning when I was leaving her place, the girl who
babysat for Delores told me that that lowlife punk she had living with
her made her leave the car at home during the day so he could get
around to the bars and wherever the hell else he went while she was at
work! So she was STILL taking a bus to work at four in the morning.
That punk-ass nigger, who never got out of bed before noon every
day, was more important to her than her own damn safety. That was
the last straw. When I took the car back, she stopped speaking to me.
But not before telling me that I was just jealous because she had a
man and I didn't." Ann's last sentence was funny but she didn't laugh,
and neither did I. She narrowed her eyes and continued. "My sister
went from bad to worse. When that punk dumped her and moved in
with the woman in the apartment across the hall from her, she went
off the deep end. I don't know if she overdosed on purpose or not."
Ann got frighteningly quiet. As a matter of fact, the room was so quiet
all I could hear was the hum of the refrigerator.

"I am so sorry to hear that," I said, meaning every word. "What about her kids?"

"They're with my folks."

"Ann, if there is ever anything I can do for you, please let me know," I said, rising.

Ann blinked at me and nodded, with her lips pressed into a tight line. "Trudy, thanks for that tip about . . . Pam," she said stiffly. "I kind of need someone to look out for me for a change."

I smiled and leaned over to give her a much needed hug. At first, she whimpered and turned away, rejecting me the same way she had the day I visited her condo. But then she rose and wrapped her arms around me, giving me the longest, hardest hug I had ever received. "Thanks again, Trudy," she whispered, her voice cracking.

On my lunch hour I took the credit cards, the ID, and the birth certificate in Ann's name out of my purse while I occupied the handicapped stall in the ladies' room. I cut them all in two.

I could not bring myself to use these particular cards anymore, and I planned to pay them all off no matter how long it took. But I didn't feel like I had turned in all of my chips. I still had some leverage as far as I was concerned. After what I had learned about how convoluted, weak, and inconsistent the whole credit system was, I knew that I could always get more credit cards if I wanted to.

CHAPTER 48

Because of my chat with Ann in the break room I already felt like a totally different person. I no longer felt like the lowly servant girl she had made me feel like on too many occasions. Now I felt "sisterhood" toward this mysterious woman even though I did so with some apprehension. As strange as it was, it seemed like Ann and I had bonded.

The fact that I had destroyed all of the fraudulent credit cards and the rest of the documents that I had obtained in her name was proof that I'd undergone a major transformation.

So many thoughts crowded my mind, my head felt like it was going to explode. There were valid reasons for my behavior. I was still lucid enough to know that I'd been raised right. My daddy had been and still was a good role model. I had not been raised to be greedy and deceitful, or a crook. It was important for me to convince myself that I was not a bad person. But something beyond my control was responsible for what I'd done to Ann.

The trauma of losing my mother, my brother, and my Uncle Pete (even though I was still mad at him for leaving this planet owing me ten thousand dollars) were the things that made me so angry at the world that I lashed out the only way I could. I had convinced myself that my encounter with the robber in the liquor store had been the straw that broke the camel's back. It was a twisted thought but I felt that there should be something good in my life to make up for all the bad things that had happened to me. Ann Oliver's good just happened to be in the wrong place at the wrong time.

As far as I was concerned, the party was over. The biggest problem I had now was paying off all the debts I had run up. It was going to be a huge job, but not impossible.

Before I left work, I hid in the handicapped toilet stall again. This time I took out my pocket calculator and figured out how much I could pay each month with just my income, and how long it would take me to pay off the money I owed. The results were mind-boggling. According to my calculations, by making only the minimum payments on the credit cards in Ann's name, it would take me *twenty* years to pay them all off. I went over the figure three times and each time I came up with the same results. I got so light-headed, I almost fainted.

I was so upset I made myself sick. By the time I returned to my workstation I was almost delirious. "Pam, I don't feel well at all. Will you let Mr. Rydell know I went home sick?" I said, grabbing my jacket. Pam gasped and put a personal call on hold. I was out of the door before she could get out of her seat.

Because I'd left work early, I rode the bus home without Freddie. It was just as well. I was not in the mood to discuss my latest meeting with Ann with Freddie anyway.

I cried myself to sleep that night. I felt better by morning knowing that I'd made a constructive decision about something. The biggest beast on my back now was the staggering amount of money I had to pay out over a twenty year period to pay off the credit cards. To my surprise, the more I thought about that the less painful it felt.

I took an earlier bus to work than my usual one. That's how anxious I was to get to work. However, sharing my revelation with Freddie would have to wait until lunchtime or the ride home.

Later that morning when I arrived at Ann's office with my hands full of brochures, interoffice envelopes and other items addressed to her, she concluded a telephone conversation by slamming the telephone down. A split second later she greeted me with a stiff smile. Even though I had not listened in on this conversation, I was certain that it was the mean Jamaican she had just hung up on.

"Would you believe I am still trying to find a headstone for my sister's grave," Ann said in a nervous voice. I couldn't figure out why she felt she had to explain herself to me. She had made it quite clear that had no value in her book. But I went along with it anyway.

"I hope you find what you're looking for," I offered, going along with her lie.

I gently dropped all of Ann's correspondence into her in box and held my breath because a bold thought pushed its way into my mind: I was going to invite Ann to lunch and I was going to pay for it with my own money. And instead of comparing sob stories about the misfortunes we'd both endured, I would encourage, no insist, on hearing about some of the exotic cities she had been to. I would get more information from her about the complimentary trips that I would eventually be able to take, per the company's policy. Here I was working at a glamorous travel agency where I would eventually get to travel real cheap, or for a fraction of the cost, to the far corners of the world. I would meet some truly interesting people for a change. Poor Freddie. I was so sorry for her because she had to work at a boring bank at such a dead-end-ass job as a bank teller. But that was life.

I had to remind myself to get a passport. In *my* name, of course.

"That's a nice color on you, Ann. Not everybody can look good in that shade of yellow," I said, making a mental note to go shopping soon to get myself some more yellow items. I would go back to shopping at the discount stores from now on, though. Or at least until James and I got married and he added my name to his credit card accounts.

"Thank you, Trudy. Uh, I was just about to call you," Ann said, caressing her chin. There was a stony look on her face that made me have some concerns right away.

I stood as straight as an arrow in front of her desk. "Oh? Did you need something?"

"You might want to shut the door," she sighed, raking her fingers though her hair. She took a swallow from her tall Starbucks cup and cleared her throat and smiled some more. I smiled, too, wondering if this was about the raise they told me I might receive after completing three months. I was certainly going to need the extra money now that I didn't have those dangerous credit cards to fall back on!

Not taking my eyes off Ann's face, I backed to the door and shut it with my foot. "Is something the matter?" I figured that was the most appropriate thing to say. Bringing up my raise would probably make me sound too mercenary. Wendy and Pam had told me that during one of their bathroom stakeouts they had overheard Lupe tell Ann that one of the other women they'd interviewed for my position had ruined her chances by bringing up money and benefits too early in the interview.

"I think you should sit down for this." Ann waved me to the chair facing her desk. She sat ramrod straight, her chin held high as she placed her hands palm down on the desk like a sphinx.

I eased down onto the seat across from her, positioning my butt so close to the edge of the chair, I had to cross my legs to keep from sliding off.

With a straight face she told me, "Trudy, I'm going to recommend that you be terminated."

CHAPTER 49

I could not believe that I was in the presence of the same woman who had shared such a painful part of her life with me in the break room the day before. I could not believe what I had just heard. I still could not believe my ears when she repeated herself. "I am going to recommend that you be terminated."

I let out a gasp that almost choked me. I know that it is impossible for time to stand still. But for a few moments I was frozen in time. When things started to move forward again, like my legs, I asked, "What did you say?" It felt like a sledgehammer was pounding around inside against the walls of my head. I immediately developed a head-ache that was so severe, the throbbing could be felt at the base on both sides of my skull. I couldn't take my eyes off Ann's face. There was emptiness in her eyes that I had never seen before. It was like she didn't have a soul. "I'm going to be fired?" A sharp cackle tumbled out of my mouth. "What did I do?" I started to rise, my jaw still moving but no words coming out. Ann motioned me back to my seat. But I ignored her. If they were firing me I had nothing else to lose by being defiant.

"It's not what you did. It's what you didn't do," she said stiffly with one eyebrow raised so high it looked like a horseshoe. She waved me back to the chair again. This time I sat back down. Not to obey her but because I was so stunned I felt like I was going to fall flat on my face.

Clearing her throat she plucked a Palm Pilot out of a drawer and then a spreadsheet from a manila folder. The spreadsheet had already been filled with items on every single line from top to bottom. Pecking on the screen of her Palm Pilot with the tip of her claw-like nail, she licked her lips and began to chew me out. "On a regular basis you did not write down the telephone numbers of some extremely important prospective clients. You didn't arrange the limo service requested by members of the Second Baptist Church during their trip to Jamaica. They had to take a gypsy cab from the airport to their hotel." Ann held up a finger and shook it at me. Then she made a fist and slammed it down hard on the top of her desk. "A *gypsy* cab, girl! Driven by one of those patois-speaking, nappy-headed Rastas with a bad attitude. I don't even ride in cabs myself, period! Can you imagine how hellish and uncomfortable that must have been for them? Six little old sisters in their seventies! Grandmothers! That's reason enough for them to be treated special; which is why they came to Bon Voyage to book their travel plans in the first place. We are unique because we are more client-focused than our competitors. Our purpose is to please our clients!" Ann paused and returned to her sphinx-like position and gave me a steely look. "You made a flight reservation to New York for a regular client sending him to La Guardia when he specifically asked for Kennedy. He didn't realize the mistake until he was already at the airport. He missed a very important business meeting." Ann rolled her eyes up toward the ceiling and shook her head. "I don't know how we are going to make that up to Mr. Meacham." She stopped long enough to clear her throat and give me one of her penetrating stares. "Now"—she sighed and cracked what she tried to pass off as a smile—"would you like to get a cup of water before we continue? You look like you could use it." She looked over my shoulder and nodded toward the door.

"I'm fine," I said with as much coldness as I could come up with on such short notice. I folded my arms and looked her straight in the eyes.

"Next," she said, glancing at the spreadsheet in front of her. "You seem to have a problem with punctuality. You missed most of the last two staff meetings."

My mouth dropped open and stayed that way for a few seconds because it took a lot of effort for me to speak again. "The first time I was late was because my daddy had chest pains and I had to take him to the hospital. Last week I was late because an eighteen-wheeler jack-knifed on the freeway and my commuter bus couldn't move for two hours. I explained all of that to you." I gave Ann an incredulous look. She glared at me and blinked. "You even made a joke about how old the buses in this area are, how you see them broken down on the streets all the time," I reminded her.

"Well, this is no joke," Ann said evenly. "Several clients have complained about your telephone manners." She scanned her spreadsheet. "Here we go. Rude, impatient, abrupt. Ooh wee—we can't have that!" She clicked her teeth then looked up at me. "You've written telephone numbers down incorrectly and mispronounced names. I could go on and on. The bottom line is, Marty worked hard to get this company up and running. He put his own money on the line. I don't want to see Marty get hurt." Ann said the last part with what sounded like a sob. Maybe she was sucking Marty's dick, just like Wendy said. Either that or she was one hell of a house nigger. "We have a reputation to consider. And with the economy being what it is we can't afford to lose business." Wiggling in her seat and lowering her voice she added, "And speaking off the record, I think that Affirmative Action has done as much harm as good. I've told Marty that many times. My own sister pestered me to get her a job here. There was not a chance in hell of that happening. Can you imagine what it would have been like around here with that greasy slug she was in love with hanging around every payday?"

"Maybe she'd still be alive if she'd had a better job," I snarled.

Ann let out an exasperated sigh. "I doubt that very much," she said, looking at her watch. "I am sure you know how White folks think. No matter how friendly they are, they still have that fear in the back of their minds that we are going to make them look bad if they don't keep an eye on us. And, unfortunately, they are right too often." Looking straight in my eyes, she said in a stone-cold voice, "Some of us don't belong in certain work environments."

"I know just what you mean," I managed.

"Is there anything else you'd like to say?" she asked with a simmering smirk.

"I don't think there is anything else I can say. At least not something you'd want to hear," I sneered. My words didn't even seem to faze Ann. The smirk that I had come to hate was still on her face.

"Trudy, if you have something else you'd like to say, now is the time to say it. One thing I can say about you is, at least you do want to work. That's more than I can say for a lot of people, Black or White."

There were not enough words in the English language for me to say what I wanted to say. I still could not believe what I'd heard so far. Here was this woman telling me that I was being fired for some petty, off-the-wall mistakes that anybody could have made. The irony was, my real crime was ten times worse! It was downright funny. I couldn't keep from laughing. I threw my head back and cackled like a magpie.

The horrified look on Ann's face made me laugh even harder.

CHAPTER 50

"Do you think this is funny, Trudy?" Ann asked, her lips quivering. "Is that your response?" She looked at me with her eyes stretched open so wide she looked frightened.

I stopped laughing and gave her a serious look. "I'll be up out of here in ten minutes," I said levelly, rising. I looked at my watch, glad it was one of the more expensive items I'd charged to her name.

"Hold on now," she waved me back to my seat. "You don't have to leave."

"Why would I want to hang around here? What else do you have on your agenda? Do you want me to dust the elevator before I go or were you planning on doing that yourself? I know how hard you work to keep Massa Marty happy."

Ann screwed up her lips and looked at me with contempt. Then, like it took a lot of effort on her part, she folded her arms and reared back in her chair. "You don't have to be sarcastic."

"I don't have to listen to anything else you have to say, either."

"Trudy, I am not firing you. I am not authorized to do that."

I had to shake my head and box my ear to make sure I was hearing her right. Her words made my head feel like it had been hit up one side and down the other. "Then what in the hell is this all about?"

"You'd be wise to watch your language, sister. I am not authorized to fire you, but I can persuade Marty to do a lot of things," she said, shaking a finger at me.

"And I bet he can persuade you to do a lot of things, too," I hissed, looking at her with my head tilted to the side.

A confused look appeared on her face. "Do you want to tell me what you mean by that?" Ann didn't let me answer her question. "Never mind," she said, waving her hand.

Not taking her eyes off me, Ann sucked on her teeth as she picked up her telephone and pecked out an in-house extension. "Marty, you can join us now."

In less than a minute Mr. Rydell came stumbling in huffing and puffing. I had not given much thought to Ann's odd relationship with Mr. Rydell lately. I had gotten used to their curious behavior, like them fawning all over each other and taking three-hour lunches together. I had even gotten used to hearing Ann cuss at Mr. Rydell. A few days ago, Pam saw Ann throw a stapler at him and chase him out of her office. I saw Ann kiss him on his pudgy cheek later that same day.

"Hello, Trudy," Mr. Rydell said, his moon face looking like a huge strawberry. Beads of perspiration dotted his forehead. Still huffing and puffing and wringing his pawlike hands, he stood in front of my seat, leaning to the side like an old tree. This was the same man that I had once thought of as appealing in a dark way. He was anything but that now. Now all he was to me was a man with a lot of power who let Ann Oliver have her way because she was probably sucking his dick. "Did Ann explain everything to your satisfaction?" His voice was raspy and hollow, and he was close enough for me to smell his foul breath.

"Do I still have a job or not?" I wanted to know.

"Most certainly! As long as you understand that you must improve in every area outlined in Ann's performance evaluation," Mr. Rydell said with a reckless smile. "We believe in giving second chances if we feel an individual has potential." He cleared his throat and looked at Ann. She shrugged and nodded. "However, because of your shortcomings, we cannot offer to increase your salary at this time."

I managed to maintain my composure. "What happens now?" I asked. "This is the most interesting job I've ever had and I would like to stay here," I said in the most humble voice I could conjure up.

"Well then, you'll sign your evaluation indicating that you agree with everything that's been addressed. And"—Mr. Rydell grinned and clapped his hands together like a lobster—"you are free to return to your workstation. Have a nice day!"

I was still in too much of a state of shock to do anything else but sign the piece of paper Ann waved at me. She signed her name below mine then passed it to Mr. Rydell for him to sign. Then she rose and smiled at me. "I really want to see you succeed, Trudy," she said, extending her hand for me to shake. I refused to accommodate her so she waved me to the door.

I walked like a zombie to the stairwell. But by the time I reached the first floor I was clip-clopping across the floor like a Clydesdale. Wendy's head popped out of her cubicle. Pam rushed somebody off the telephone and rose. "What happened?" she demanded, rising from her seat. I ignored Pam as I walked by my desk and didn't stop until I was in Wendy's cube.

I gently pushed Wendy aside as I snatched open her drawer and snatched out that popular bottle and a Dixie cup.

Pam rushed over to Wendy's cube and stood next to her as they watched me.

"What the hell happened?" Pam whispered, looking over her shoulder toward the elevator.

"Ann just gave me my performance evaluation," I said, twisting the cap back onto Wendy's bottle as I let out a major belch. Pam massaged her belly and let out a whimper. "Ann wanted to fire me," I reported, my eyes stuck in one position. I blinked and looked from Wendy to Pam. One looked as horrified as the other.

"That bitch is a . . . a . . . bitch!" Wendy hissed.

"I guess that means you didn't get your three-month raise?" Pam asked, rubbing my arm.

"I don't need it. I don't need it at all," I said. Out of the corner of my eye I saw Wendy look at Pam and shrug. Pam stood with her arms folded and her mouth hanging open.

The sneer on my face turned into a wicked smile.

CHAPTER 51

I was not surprised when Ann buzzed Wendy instead of me around ten and asked her to go to Starbucks to get her the usual tall mild cup of coffee. As strange as it was to me—especially after my latest round with Ann—I still hoped that Wendy didn't drop any spit, or anything else into Ann's coffee.

Just before noon Lupe offered to buy lunch from the deli next door for Mr. Rydell and the other reps. She waddled into the reception area with her pad and pen poised. "Can I get something for you girls, too?" she chirped, paying more attention to me than usual. She batted her eyelashes and spread her lips into such an unnaturally large smile I could see most of her gums. We all knew about Lupe having bags removed from under her eyes, which was why she batted her lashes the way she did. She did that a lot these days, especially in the presence of our male customers. But the big smile was a new part of her ongoing makeover. Nobody had mentioned it, but it was obvious that she'd had her mouth upgraded, too. She had replaced a set of thick gray snaggletoothed choppers with a mouth full of small, pearly white false teeth that looked like they belonged on a doll.

Wendy and Pam leaped at the chance to get a free lunch. They both placed the same order: a grilled cheese sandwich on low-carb bread, Doritos, coleslaw, two brownies each, and Diet Cokes. I shook my head, offering Lupe a weak smile. "I'll order a few extra snacks anyway in case you change your mind later," Lupe told me, as she patted my shoulder. The look of pity on her face told me that either Ann or Mr. Rydell had discussed the meeting that they'd had with me. And the way the other reps liked to gobble up gossip, that information had probably been shared with them, too.

As soon as Lupe left, Pam shot from her seat and skipped across the floor to my desk. "Omigod! Lupe got her teeth done!" Pam said in a subdued yell, glancing toward the elevator.

"And it's about time," Wendy said with a shrug. "I'm surprised she didn't have the dentist add any of that gold metallic stuff that the rest of those people have put in their mouths, as if all that grease and beans wasn't enough. Last week at the flea market there was a tribe of Mexicans walking alongside me and Mark. There had to be at least ten or twenty of them. Every last one, including a little girl in a diaper, had two or three goldplated teeth," Wendy announced with a shudder, running a finger across her own front teeth and making a sucking noise.

"No wonder you see them grinning all over the place. They like to show off all that gold. Even on *Cops* when they're in handcuffs," Pam added with a sigh of pity. "Trudy, I see a lot of Black folks running around with those gold teeth, too. Do you know any people like that? I hope not."

"I've seen a lot of people with gold-capped teeth. The only one I know personally is my neighbor Spider's girlfriend. But she's White," I scoffed. Pam and Wendy looked at me with blank faces.

I excused myself to go to the ladies' room. This was one morning when I was not in the mood to listen to the usual catty chatter that Pam and Wendy subjected me to every day.

Dennis Klein had volunteered to pick up the lunch from the deli next door. He walked past my desk with his head bowed and the legs of his baggy suit pants flapping like flags. I didn't know if his long face was on my account or because his mistress had threatened to dump him. Wendy and Pam continued to share information about Dennis and his affair with me. Letters full of sexual comments and X rated cards from a tacky adult store from his mistress were still being mailed to him at the office. Pam and Wendy still opened them and used a glue stick to reseal them.

When Dennis returned he stopped in front of my desk. "Trudy, I really like having you around. I hope you will be with us for a long time to come," he said, with a blink and a sniff.

"I will," I said with a forced smile. One thing I had learned about some people was that when they seemed nicer to you than usual, they had other motives. Dennis was no different.

"Uhhhh . . . Trudy, I'm expecting some correspondence from a . . . uh . . . client named Nancy . . . Myers. Uh, it's coming by FedEx so when it arrives, would you deliver it to me immediately?"

I saw Pam's eyes widen as she focused her attention in my direction. "Of course," I told Dennis.

Knowing that I was still in a funky mood, Wendy and Pam didn't badger me much for the details of my meeting with Ann and Mr. Rydell. Instead, they spent their time trying to figure out why Dennis's mistress was sending him something by FedEx. The more time passed the calmer I felt.

Three hours had passed since my meeting with Ann and she had not shown her face on the ground floor yet. When I had to deliver the FedEx package that Dennis had been expecting, Ann was in his office. She occupied the wing chair facing his desk. She was so kicked back with her shoes off and her jacket draped across the back of the chair, you would have thought that she was in the comfort of her own home. She ignored me completely.

"Trudy, I appreciate your help. By the way, I didn't realize that National Secretaries Day was last month!" Dennis exclaimed with a guarded glance in Ann's direction. "My wife brought it to my attention. She used to be a secretary so she knows how important that day is to the clerical community. I'd like to treat you to a belated lunch soon," Dennis said, his eyes darting from my face to Ann's. "Let me know when you are available, please."

"I will. And thank you," I said sweetly. For a split second Ann's eyes met mine, but she quickly looked away as if it hurt her to look at me. I hoped it did because if things went the way I wanted them to go, I was going to become her worst nightmare. The only thing about that was she would never even know.

I'd spent my entire lunch hour in the park down the street sitting on the bench I'd become so familiar with. I cursed because I had left my cell phone at home so I couldn't talk to Freddie until on the bus home. I was in such a bleak mood that I ignored one of the homeless, nameless men who had come to expect a generous handout from me as he approached my spot with a long face and an empty can.

The rest of the afternoon dragged by so slowly that at one point I thought my watch and the big clock on the wall had both stopped at the same time.

My mind was a cesspool of confusion. I didn't know what to think about anything. One minute I was thinking about James, glad that I had him to fall back on. The next minute I was thinking about my job and how I was not going to give it up without a fight. I could not wait to get some advice from Freddie. Even though I knew that no matter what my girl advised me to do I was still going to deal with my situation the way I wanted to.

Freddie was not at the bus stop when I got off work and she didn't answer her cell phone when I tried to call her from a pay phone on the corner. I rode home alone in a daze. Instead of going home, I went straight to Freddie's apartment.

"Where's Freddie?" I asked LoBo when he cautiously cracked open the door, cradling his two-year-old son LoBo Jr.

"She had a hair appointment. Her and some of her girls from the beauty shop suppose to be at Harvey's gettin' drunk," he told me. "What you been up to, sister girl? How are things goin' at work with that bitch?"

"LoBo, I need your help again," I blurted, shifting my weight from one foot to the other. I felt so heavy I could barely stand without leaning. He led me into Freddie's cluttered little living room where he gently placed the baby on the couch. "You are not going to believe what that woman tried to do to me."

"Oh, yes, I would," he chuckled. "I deal with women like Ann Oliver on my route all the time. I haul garbage, but I ain't garbage. You would think I was, though, if you heard some of the shit I put up with. So, yes, I would believe whatever it is you got to tell me about that wench you work with." LoBo gave me a brief hug. "Make yourself at home, sister, and lemme get you a drink. You sure look like you could use one." LoBo disappeared into the kitchen and I dialed Freddie's cell phone again. She answered on the first ring. "I need to talk to you."

"What's up?" Freddie slurred. I could hear reggae music in the background.

"When are you coming home?" I asked. I clutched the telephone in my hand so hard I got a cramp.

"Not for a while. Today's Sarah's birthday. You know, the sister who does my hair. Why don't you come over here and join us so you can tell me all about it."

"I will. But I'm at your place with LoBo right now. I need to discuss a few things with him first." I glanced at LoBo. "I hope you don't mind." One thing I knew for sure was that Freddie trusted me. Even though LoBo had been unfaithful to her she knew that there was no way in hell I'd ever do anything inappropriate with her man. And I felt the same way about her and my man. But I knew how James felt about Freddie. She could get in the bed with him naked and he wouldn't touch her body with a torch.

"As long as he doesn't mind, I don't mind." Freddie sighed. "Take care of your business and come on over to Harvey's when you finish. We'll keep the bar warm," Freddie said.

It took me three beers and an hour to tell LoBo everything that Ann had said to me. I'd repeated the worst parts with so much emphasis, LoBo offered to have some of his homeboys burglarize Ann's residence. "That heifer workin' both sides of the street, ain't she?" LoBo said, scratching his head. "If I was you, I'd teach her a lesson she'd never forget."

"Well, she's too slick for me to come up with a plan that'll hit her where it hurts," I snarled. That was the problem. I had to keep reminding myself that there was no lesson I could teach Ann that I could let her know about. Sure, I wanted to scratch her eyes out, but losing my job and getting arrested for assault didn't appeal to me. Something told me that she was the type who would have me arrested rather than fight me back. I knew I wouldn't rest until I got back at her in a major way, whether she knew about it or not.

And there was only one way that I knew of.

Staying on at Bon Voyage was going to be a real challenge. The last thing I wanted to do was give in too soon. I was proud of the fact that I had hurled a little bit of anger in Ann's direction during my meeting with her. I'd surprised the hell out of her. I wondered which one of us would give in first. She would win the battle if she succeeded in getting me fired. And, for the life of me, I couldn't figure out what satisfaction she'd get out of that. But then, there was no rhyme or reason involved when people went off the deep end. I was proof of that.

My mind wandered off in so many directions, I had a hard time keeping up with reality. Somehow I managed to make some sense out

of my actions. If I managed to hold onto my job, it would do wonders
for my morale and self-esteem. Life had beaten me down enough so I
had to grab happiness where I could find it. Since I had managed to
remain intact after the assault I'd endured in the liquor store, there
was no way I was going to let a woman like Ann get my goat.

"After the mess she just went through with her sister, I felt so sorry
for her, I threw away all that shit you got for me. I even cut up the
credit cards I already had!"

LoBo gasped. "Why you do some stupid shit like that for? I went to
a lot of trouble to hook you up."

I nodded. "I know you did, brother, and I appreciate it. But I am
going to need you to hook me up again."

"That wouldn't be no problem. No problem at all. But it's goin' to
cost you more this time . . ."

"I don't care what it costs me. I can afford it. You got a passport?"

"Yeah. Why?"

"As a bonus for the new documents you get for me, I'm going to
treat you and Freddie to a weekend in Mexico. First class," I said.

CHAPTER 52

When I arrived at Harvey's an hour after my meeting with LoBo, Freddie, and Sarah and Lisa Wright were all loud and tipsy. They stumbled around on the small dance floor, dancing in a circle with their arms around one another. I stood by the exit until they wobbled to a booth next to the bar. The other few patrons paid no attention to Freddie and her crew, or me.

The way I staggered across the floor you would have thought that I was drunk, too. But the beers that I had consumed with LoBo had only sharpened my senses. I joined Freddie and the other two women as soon as they sat down.

"Trudy, Freddie told us all about that boot-licking-Uncle-Tom–house-nigger-bitch you work for," Sarah yelled, flashing her waist-length dreadlocks. "You want me to kick her ass?" Sarah was a size two but as rough and tough as they come. I had seen her lock horns with women and a few men twice her size and walk away unscathed. She'd de-balled a former boyfriend by biting into his genital area when he made her perform oral sex on him after he had already dumped her. He was too embarrassed to press charges, but everybody in the 'hood knew about it. The rumor was that he could no longer produce children, and he would have to use a big cumbersome pump-like thing to help him get an erection from now on. He was a lonely man these days. I had always wanted to be more like Sarah. Had I been, the day that that sucker made me suck his dick in Daddy's liquor store, there would be at least one more man walking around with a pair of useless balls.

Lisa was Sarah's mother but a lot of people didn't know that. There was only a thirteen year age difference. They co-owned the beauty shop where we all got our hair permed, braided, weaved, or whatever. I admired strong successful women like Lisa and Sarah, but they were more Freddie's friends than mine. However, they always made me feel welcome when I was around them. I also chatted on the telephone and went shopping with one or the other from time to time. I felt comfortable sharing information about my personal life with Lisa and Sarah because I knew that no matter what, these were the kinds of women who took a lot of pride in the fact that they supported other sisters that they considered their homegirls. But it was a different story when it was a sister who didn't know how to behave like one.

"That Ann Óliver sure don't sound like nobody I know, but fighting never solved anything," Lisa insisted, adjusting the San Francisco Giants baseball cap hiding her short Afro. "The Latina girl who rents the apartment below me, she got her face all cut up when she tangled with a knife-toting, just-arrived-from-Tijuana *chola* heifer in Berkeley last year." Lisa was like a lot of pretty women I knew. The last thing she wanted was for somebody to disfigure her heart-shaped baby face. She sniffed and fiddled with one of her false eyelashes. "I say you should quit that damn job."

"Uh-uh. Don't you let that bitch run you off, girl," Sarah blurted, glaring at her mother. "It sounds like you just being there gets on her nerves. Stay there and make her suffer. Sneak into her office and delete some of her files. Send her anonymous threatening letters. Piss in her trash can. Mix up some Drano and water and pour it in her plants. Find out who her man is and fuck the hell out of him." We all laughed.

"Naw, that's all too tame. I got a better idea," Lisa said with a snort. "I can get you some dangerous shit that you can slip in her purse before she leaves for her next overseas trip. Then drop a dime and make an anonymous call to customs before she gets back. Tell them she's muling drugs," Lisa suggested, slurring her words. I gave her an exasperated look. She rotated her neck and gave me an exasperated look back.

"I could never do something like that to Ann, or anybody else," I admitted. I was proud of the fact that I still had some feelings of morality left.

"Oh, girl, you know I am just bullshitting you. I wouldn't do anything that deep to another woman either. But I would still give her a mild whupping," Lisa said with a great burp. She closed her eyes and gave her head a vigorous shake. "Y'all, I am not drinking anything else this week!" she declared with a raised fist.

Sarah cleared her throat to get some attention. "Trudy, while that Ann's off somewhere basking her black ass in the sun, call up and cancel her credit cards," Sarah advised.

Freddie looked at me with an amused look on her face. I shook my head and gave her a threatening look. The last thing I wanted was for the discussion to include anything about credit cards. Freddie must have read my mind. "Leave that job, Trudy. You don't have to put up with that shit when there are a lot of other places where you can work. Why you want to work anywhere in the first place when you don't have to is beyond me anyway. By the way, how is James?"

I was glad Freddie had steered the conversation away from credit cards. I didn't want Lisa and Sarah to know too much of my business. "James is fine," I said, sounding and feeling a lot calmer now that I was in the presence of a powerful support group. "He wants to go look at some property."

"Well, if I had a man like James, that's what I'd really be concentrating on instead of that bitch you work with. Men like him are so hard to come by," Sarah said with a tired voice, looking at her watch. At twenty-nine, Sarah had already been married and divorced twice. "I gots to run, ladies. My babysitter will have a cow if I make her miss another date. Little Mama, you going to give me a ride home?"

"Sure, baby. I need to get up out of here, too," Lisa replied. She looked toward the door, leering at a gorgeous man in jeans leaning against the wall. He waved to Lisa and tapped his watch. "Looks like I got a date," she announced, grinning and snapping her fingers.

Lisa and Sarah rose at the same time.

"Let's all hook up this weekend," Freddie yelled as the two women rushed away from the booth. As soon as Lisa and Sarah made it out the door, with the handsome man in jeans holding Lisa by the arm, Freddie slid across the vinyl seat closer to me. "Girl, what is going on with you and that crazy bitch?"

I made her wait until I picked up a round of drinks from the bar.

Then I told her the same thing I'd told LoBo. She shook her head and gave me a pitiful look. She surprised me with some comments that didn't support my mood. "You have to feel sorry for the woman. She got mugged, she lost her sister. Once she's over all that maybe she'll treat you better. After all, she is a *sister.*"

"Sister my ass!" I shouted. "Ann Oliver couldn't care less about a sisterhood. All she cares about is herself. You just wait. As soon as LoBo gets me another ID, I'm going to get me a new car and a ton of new credit cards!"

"And what is that going to prove? You'll be the one paying for all that shit you charge up in Ann's name."

I responded in a lower voice because people around us had started to look at us and listen. "I don't care. I did it before, I can do it again. She won't know about it, but I will. And you didn't have a problem helping me enjoy all that stuff I did with her credit cards," I reminded. "Don't go getting moral on me."

"I appreciate everything you did treat me to. And I don't really give a shit about Ann. But I just don't want you to get yourself into something you can't get out of. That's all. You have been damn lucky so far. You are still paying on those other credit cards, right?"

I nodded. "Through the teeth."

"Quit while you're ahead."

"I still have that mailbox," I told Freddie, with a gleam burning in my eye.

"So?"

"I can get more cards and when I get tired of paying on them, I can cancel that mailbox and the cards. And I won't pay a dime on them. You told me yourself how your bank writes bad debts off when they can't find people."

"Trudy, you're using the Social Security number and name of a real person!" Freddie hollered, giving me a disturbing look. "Girl, it won't take the banks no time to track the real Ann down."

"How can they prove that I'm the one who stole her identity?"

"If you're smart and don't blab to the wrong person, they probably won't."

"Exactly."

"But it won't be that easy if you get a car in her name. It would leave too much of a paper trail. Insurance, registration, fees. I thought you knew all of this shit already. I do remember discussing cars with you and telling you how risky that was."

I gave this piece of information some thought. "Then I won't get a car."

Freddie was surprised but she didn't resist when I paid our tab with the one credit card I still had in Ann's name: the one from work that I used to purchase office supplies.

"This charge won't show up on the statement?" she asked, giving me a worried look.

"Didn't I tell you that nobody sees the statements but me?" I reminded. "Now, let's go to that expensive Thai restaurant on Bancroft before it closes. You want some lobster?"

Even though Freddie tried to encourage me, very mildly, not to masquerade as Ann Oliver, she never turned down anything I offered. I knew that she didn't really approve of what I was doing, but *she* was the one who had led me in this direction in the first place! I had to keep reminding myself that all I had planned to do that day in the hamburger joint with Ann Oliver's credit card was pay for our lunch, just that one time. In a way this mess was all Freddie's fault, but I didn't have the nerve to tell her that.

"I . . . I guess so," Freddie said. "Will you cover a cab to take me home from the restaurant?"

"Uh-huh. No problem at all," I said, glad to see a broad smile light up Freddie's face. "What the hell."

CHAPTER 53

I was more than a little drunk when I got home. Daddy and Spider, the biker from next door, were in the living room mumbling about something. They both turned around and stared at me when I bumped into the wall.

Daddy had about as much in common with the Hell's Angels as I did. Other than drinking and watching television I couldn't figure out what he and Spider had to talk about so much. But Spider was in our living room almost every evening. He never said much to me other than a muffled greeting.

"Yo, princess," Spider greeted from a chair facing Daddy on the couch. Despite all of the bad press that bikers received, the ones I'd met had treated me with nothing but respect. It pleased me to have Spider around to keep Daddy occupied. It took some of the pressure off me.

Daddy and James didn't smoke, but most of Daddy's friends did. Spider smoked cigarettes and cigars, and I suspected something illegal. None of that bothered me. But the mess that smokers made did. Even with an ashtray as wide as a pie pan on the coffee table, there were at least a dozen burns on the table's top. Daddy didn't like for me to buy things for the house unless we absolutely needed it, but I made a mental note to get us a new coffee table on my very next shopping expedition.

"Yo," I said back, waving to Spider. "Hi, Daddy."

"I cooked some lima beans and cornbread, and me and Spider done et up everything but the plates," Daddy said with a chuckle, looking me up and down. "That's what you get for takin' your time gettin' home. Spider, you lucky you ain't got to worry about stuff like this with your girl. You got a real good daughter . . ." I saw Daddy wink at Spider out of the corner of my eye. I ignored the comment anyway. Rising with a groan and a frown, Daddy followed me to the kitchen where I dropped my purse onto the floor, spilling most of its contents.

"I had a late staff meeting to attend, Daddy."

"Uh-huh. Y'all drinkin' on the job?" he said, eyeing me suspiciously.

"Why do you ask?" I asked, holding my breath.

"Girl, alcohol is my business. I can smell it a mile away."

"Yeah, we had dinner and some wine delivered to the office. My boss treated us all."

"And who is Ann Oliver?" Daddy asked, following me on my heels to my room. I made such a sharp fast turn I almost fell. "That your boss?"

I stared at Daddy for so long in slack-jawed amazement that he waved his hand in front of my eyes. "Hello?" he said with a sneer. "You still with me?"

It took another few seconds and a lot of effort on my part for me to tune-up my mouth and speak again. "I'm sorry, Daddy, uh, I just had a sharp pain," I muttered, rubbing an imaginary discomfort in my chest.

"Well, that must run in the family. Next time you make another appointment for me with Dr. Scruggs, you better make one for yourself, too," Daddy said with his hands on his hips.

"Daddy, how do you know about Ann Oliver?" I asked with a huge lump forming in my throat.

He handed me the credit card receipt from the Thai restaurant I'd taken Freddie to. "This fell out of your purse."

"Oh," I said, snatching the piece of paper. "She's my boss."

"I thought your boss was a man. A Mr. Rydell."

"Huh? He is. Mr. Rydell is the main boss. Ann Oliver is his assistant. She helps him supervise things."

Daddy rolled his eyes and scratched the side of his face. "What you doin' with a credit card receipt with her name on it?" he asked, scratching the gray stubble on his chin.

"Uh, she was the one who paid for the dinner," I offered with a heavy tongue. I couldn't believe all the physical discomforts I experienced when I got stressed.

Daddy narrowed his eyes and gave me a hard look. "I thought y'all had food brought to the office this evenin'."

"We did! But a few of us stopped off at a restaurant for dessert after we left the office. Ann Oliver was a little tipsy and forgot to pick up her receipt. I'll give it to her tomorrow," I said over my shoulder, walking toward my bedroom with Daddy on my heels mumbling under his breath all the way. I gave Daddy a broad smile before I picked up the telephone on my nightstand and started dialing James's number, hoping Daddy would take the hint and return to his company.

"You might want to tell her to be more careful. If an itty-bitty piece of paper like this get in the wrong hands with her credit card number on it, that Ann woman'll be gettin' a big surprise when she get her bill." The credit card receipt felt like a hand grenade in my hand. Daddy looked at it, then at my face. "Why is your hand shakin' so hard, girl?"

"Huh? I got a chill from the night air." I folded the receipt into the size of a stamp and balled my hand, praying that James would answer his telephone.

"See there. That's what you get for tryin' to be cute and not wear enough clothes!" Daddy scolded, waving his hand in the air like a conductor. "Sound like you just as careless with your own business as that Ann woman is with her credit card paperwork. Remember that time somebody got ahold of my American Express number and charged some car repairs to me?"

"Yes, I remember that, Daddy." I sighed. I clutched the receipt and the telephone in my hand so hard my fingers got numb.

James didn't answer his phone but I pretended he did. "Hi, baby, did you make that appointment with the realtor?" I said into his answering machine.

A pleased look appeared on Daddy's face. He smiled and gently shut my door on his way out of my room.

CHAPTER 54

I arrived an hour early for our next weekly Friday morning staff meeting. Why Mr. Rydell wanted the clerical employees to sit in on these boring dog and pony shows was a mystery to me.

When Ann was in town, the staff meeting was nothing more than an opportunity for her to grandstand. She loved to be the center of attention, so in a crowd she was a very animated person. She liked to tilt her head and wave her hands when she spoke. When she really wanted to bring the house down, she got so melodramatic she shed a tear or two. She enjoyed regaling her listeners with stories even I found interesting for the most part. Once during one of her visits to Rome, she'd had drinks with a blind prostitute. In Paris a dog had followed her down a street and peed on her foot. And no matter where in the world she went, she had to beat the men off with a stick. Everybody predicted that eventually one of her dapper admirers would permanently sweep her off her feet.

When Ann was not putting on her show, Wendy, Pam, and I had to sit for a whole hour listening to Mr. Rydell and the reps yip yap about new hotels, new ad campaigns to attract more business, and ways that Bon Voyage could get even more discounts on their tour packages.

To my everlasting horror, somebody always had to suggest a potluck. The one planned for the coming Tuesday was to celebrate Ann's landing a huge contract with Mechtel Construction and Engineering Company. They planned to send engineers to Iraq to help rebuild the mess that the war had caused. America's current state of affairs was another reason we had our staff meetings.

When the conversation turned to politics at our latest meeting, I tuned out. Apparently, I made a gesture that drew attention to myself.

"Trudy, did you have a comment?" Dennis Klein asked, adjusting his glasses. His eyes were wide with anticipation. He had smoothed things over with his mistress after a weekend in Vegas so now he walked around grinning all of the time. Even over nothing. The flowery notes that his lover sent to him at the office were coming three and four at the same time now. "You've been awful quiet lately." Poor Dennis. He was looking more and more like Harry Potter every day. When people told him that, which somebody did almost every day, he did all he could to enhance the illusion. He wore more dark clothes than before and he went so far as to tack a Harry Potter poster on the wall in his office facing his desk. He had given his nephew the whole series of Harry Potter books at his bar mitzvah, but Dennis kept the books on a shelf in his office. I saw myself in Dennis. We were both imitating people we could never be.

"Uh, no comment," I mumbled, blinking at Ann who was looking at me with a look I could not interpret. She had been cordial to me since our meeting in her office. She'd even sent me out for coffee a few times, like nothing had ever happened.

"As you all know, Ann and Lupe will be heading off to Jamaica this weekend. Let's keep them in our prayers," Mr. Rydell said before dismissing us all.

Hearing that Ann was going to be out of the office for a while was the only thing that had come out of our latest meeting that meant anything to me.

"I think she's got a lover down in Jamaica," Wendy whispered to Pam and me on our way back to the reception area.

"Who? Who has a lover down in Jamaica?" I asked, like I didn't already know the answer.

"You know that sexy dude who calls here for her sometimes?" Pam said, rubbing her nose with her finger then wiping it on the side of her skirt.

"I don't know anything about any sexy dude," I said, trying not to sound too interested. I couldn't imagine how Pam and Wendy would react if I told them what I did know about Ann's personal life. She received more calls than all of the other reps put together. I had recently taken a few messages from a man who identified himself as a Mr. Giles. He had a nice, pleasant tone of voice and a deep Jamaican accent. Although I was not sure of it, I suspected that Mr. Giles was the same Jamaican who had called for Ann the times I'd eavesdropped on her telephone calls. The same man who had upset her so much. I knew for a fact that she had had some kind of an intimate relationship with the Jamaican. Especially after that time I heard her having phone sex with him that day she had him masturbating so hard. "Ann doesn't discuss her love life with me," I said, holding back a sheepish grin.

"Oh, you'd be surprised at what you can hear while sitting in a bathroom stall when she and Lupe are standing around running off at the mouth." Pam grinned as I plopped down into my chair behind my desk. Then she and Wendy hovered over me like magpies.

As attractive, stylish, and sophisticated as Ann was, because of her aloof behavior around me, I rarely looked at her from a social point of view. Common sense told me that she probably had a good man (more than likely, she had *several* good men) stashed away somewhere. I had assumed that much from her bragging about how men all over the world tried to seduce her. Women like her always kept a supply of well-heeled, generous male fools in line waiting their turn to be used. It would explain her extravagant lifestyle.

"Ann's got a man in every city in the world. Some Frenchman followed her back to the States last year when she went to Paris," Wendy said, leaning over my desk. "You should have seen the funny way she walked when she came back to work." Wendy and Pam guffawed.

"I bet he's the one who paid for her new BMW," Wendy whispered. "You will never catch her tooling around town in a Altima like me."

"I figured Ann used a broom to get around on," I said, laughing. Like a bad headache, Ann came out of nowhere and pranced over to my desk. As if on cue, Wendy and Pam scrambled to their workstations.

"Trudy, may I ask you to do me a favor while I'm in Jamaica next week?" Ann asked sweetly. She displayed a smile so thin I could see through it.

"Of course," I replied with a shrug. I was beginning to feel like one of the robotlike women in the movie *The Stepford Wives*.

Ann beckoned for me to follow her back to her office.

"Uh, if you receive any calls from a Mr. Giles, don't tell him that I'm in Jamaica," she said, closing the door so fast she almost caught my foot in the doorjamb. She mumbled an apology. "Even if he doesn't leave his name, you'll know him. He has a very thick Jamaican accent and he's very charming."

"Okay," I mumbled, standing in front of her desk as she slid into her chair. "But isn't he already in Jamaica?" I asked, rubbing my injured ankle with the toe of my other foot.

"Yes, he is. But I don't want him to know I'm down there, too. It's very important. If he insists on knowing where I am, tell him I'm in Paris with my fiancé. Michel Moreau is my fiancé's name, in case Mr. Giles asks."

I had been working with this woman for months and I'd found out more about her love life in the last few minutes than I'd learned in all that time. I was puzzled because Ann was obviously nervous. So much that her hands started to shake.

"And do me a favor and not discuss this with anyone else," she said, rising.

"All right," I mumbled.

"Thanks, Trudy. I owe you one," she said, patting my shoulder and opening the door.

I was curious but I knew not to ask any more than she'd told me. It didn't matter anyway. I was just glad that I wouldn't have to see her for a week.

There was a message from LoBo on my voice mail when I returned to my desk. "I'll have the stuff you requested by next week," he said.

I smiled and started flipping through brochures advertising weekend package deals to Mexico.

CHAPTER 55

I had not been to church on a regular basis in years. Before Mama died, we used to go all the time. But not to one of the loud, foot-stomping, all-Black Baptist churches like the one Freddie and most of the other Black people I knew went to. That was the kind of church that Daddy had attended before he hooked up with my mother.

As a bonafide hippie back in the day, Mama had had some strange notions when it came to religion. That was what I'd been told by my Black relatives. Mama had encouraged Daddy to desert the church he had been attending for years. One day, he slid into a dashiki and some sandals and accompanied Mama to the New Hope Temple, a non-denominational place behind a warehouse in south San Jose. People of all races congregated there to listen to a short, chubby White woman preach the gospel. It was the kind of place where you could "come as you are," so to speak. Mama would even let me wear pants or shorts if I wanted to. She and Daddy both drew the line the time I wanted to go to church in my one-piece bathing suit when I was eight.

I was just a toddler when Jim Jones led his flock on a suicide mission in the jungles of Jonestown, and I had heard a lot about it growing up. Daddy used to socialize with some of the relatives of the victims in San Francisco. Some people were convinced that the New Hope Temple and their short, chubby female preacher was an off-shoot of Jim Jones and his mess.

When Mama died, Daddy began to lose faith in religion. He'd stomp around the house complaining about one thing after another that God had let happen.

Uncle Pete, who had been one of the biggest devils in town, had the nerve to be a church deacon and I used to eavesdrop on him praying to God to let him win the lottery or to keep the cops off his back.

"God helps them who help themselves," Uncle Pete told me once. That was right after he had stumbled across a duffel bag full of money that had fallen off a Brinks armored truck in Oakland. That was the only time I ever knew about something that really did fall off a truck. Unfortunately, my uncle blabbed to his friends and even trusted one of his shady women friends to hide the money in her bedroom closet. When she blabbed to the wrong person the investigators came knocking at her door and hauled her off to jail. Uncle Pete hid out in L.A. until things cooled off. As soon as he returned to South Bay City he started looking for new ways to get rich quick.

James and his mother went to church every Sunday and every now and then they dragged me along with them. I had been avoiding James and his mama lately. Not because I didn't want to go to church with them but because I honestly didn't want to see them as much while I had so many other things to sort out

We had a Bible in the house but all it was doing was collecting dust on a shelf in our kitchen closet. When my brother and Uncle Pete died, Daddy gave up on God and religion forever. Or so he said. On more than one occasion I'd overheard Daddy praying in his room. The same night of my ordeal with the robber in the liquor store, I'd passed by Daddy's bedroom after we'd both gone to bed. With a sob in his voice, he had thanked God for sparing me and he'd asked that no harm come to me in the future.

I sincerely believed that God was looking out for me. Especially since He'd already let me down by taking my mama and my brother. God owed me. That's why I went to the ladies' room at the airport and prayed to God that I wouldn't get caught trying to sneak into Mexico with a fake passport that Friday night after work. My disastrous meeting with Ann was so fresh and potent on my mind that I wanted to get as much mileage out of my anger as possible. I couldn't think of a better way to do that than to use one of the new credit cards

I'd just received in her name to treat myself to a first class tropical weekend with all the trimmings.

Since I had never been to Mexico I didn't know what to expect. The June weather in Puerto Vallarta was brutally hot and there was an unpleasant odor in the air. I almost fainted as soon as I stepped off the plane and stumbled across the airfield into the airport behind a crowd of rowdy vacationers. Some of them had taken full advantage of the complimentary drinks during the flight and were already pitifully drunk. One blond-haired passenger was hauled directly from the plane into a police car by the Mexican authorities after he'd threatened one of the flight attendants. I had been too nervous to have even one drink. Even though alcohol gave me a false sense of courage, I wanted to have a clear mind in case the customs people asked me something complicated.

"Hello, *señorita*. Welcome to Mexico," the cute customs clerk at the airport entrance counter said with a broad smile as he stamped my passport. He didn't even look that closely at the picture. He just blinked at it. My passport could have contained a picture of Godzilla and it would not have made a difference. Instead, the clerk's eyes roamed up and down the low cut blouse I had on. He winked at me and sniffed real hard, causing his thick black mustache to wiggle. "Aaah . . . very nice perfume, *señorita*," he said.

I blushed and clutched the handle of my suitcase, which was filled to capacity with expensive new sexy lingerie and cute beach wear. *"Muchos gracias, señor,"* I replied, rushing away from the counter and out to the curb where a line of dull yellow cabs sat as if they were all waiting for me.

CHAPTER 56

The foul smell in the air seemed to be everywhere but I liked Mexico already. I had never traveled so far away from home by myself, and something told me that I was not going to regret my decision to finally do so. It already seemed like an adventure.

Most of the airport security guards, some armed with long rifles, stood around chatting and flirting with every woman in sight. One guard, his weapon propped up against a wall, was piled up in a lumpy foam chair sleeping and snoring like a bear. Stout, bowlegged women with Indian features, some with skin as dark as mine, roamed around the airport hawking everything from T-shirts to beads. It pleased me to see a lot of the local women with their hair in cornrows. Since so many of the Black women I knew wore cornrows from time to time, it made me feel right at home. Something told me that this wouldn't be the last time I slid south of the border.

A sweaty man dressed in dingy white shorts and a dingy white shirt followed me out of the airport trying to sell me a time-share. When I told him I was not interested, he tried to make a date with me instead.

My middle-aged cab driver, who wore a T-shirt that said *Americans Go Home and Take Me With You*, sped through the narrow, tree-lined streets, on the way to the Sheraton hotel, grinning all the way. He had to dodge frisky chickens and humpbacked old people leading donkeys and dragging goats down the middle of the road. He talked nonstop about any- and everything. "Ju like to dance, go to the Club Bonita. Tonight is lady night," he told me. I was pleased to see that so many Mexicans spoke English.

"Is it far from the hotel where I'll be staying?" I asked in a loud voice so I could be heard over the cab's loud, rumbling motor.

"No, not far. Ju tell me what time, I come for to pick ju up tonight. Ju okay with that? Oh—I am Carlos." Carlos looked in the rearview mirror and leered at me with his toothy grin. When I grinned back, he whirled around. "If ju want me to, I go with ju, *morena*," he said with a suggestive gleam in his eye. "*Ay Carumba . . .*"

"Oh, no, thank you, Carlos. I can go alone," I replied quickly and firmly. "Pick me up at nine."

The same night that LoBo had given me the fake passport, I'd decided to make plans to travel to Mexico. I told Daddy and James that I had another work-related retreat coming up.

Daddy's off-and-on lady friend, Miss Sadie, had been having more trouble with her grandsons lately so he had a lot on his mind. He just grunted and waved me out of the room when I told him. He came to my room later that night to inform me that Miss Sadie's two older grandsons had been convicted again and promptly sent to Corcoran, the most hellish prison in the state of California. It made San Quentin look like the Holiday Inn. And the guards were even more brutal and corrupt than the inmates. They entertained themselves by beating and killing the prisoners and putting them in situations where they would beat and kill one another. I could understand why Daddy was so preoccupied. I just didn't like him being dumped on so much by that woman. It was one of the main reasons I chose not to associate with Miss Sadie. "Now, where you say you was gwine, baby girl?" Daddy asked. "Sadie and them young'ns 'bout to worry me half to death. I can't remember nothin' you told me tonight. You did say somethin' about gwine away for the weekend, didn't you?"

"I'm going down to Mexico on business for a couple of days, Daddy," I said, holding my breath as I awaited his response.

"Okay, baby. Have a nice trip," he muttered. I didn't like the fact that Daddy had allowed other peoples' problems to crowd his mind. But in a way I was glad that he had something else to fret about instead of me.

I didn't tell James to his face. I was not about to let an interrogation spoil my vacation. And I certainly was not going to have James insist on going with me. I left him a message on his answering machine. I didn't return his call when he called me back ten minutes later.

Freddie's parents backed out of the babysitting commitment when she told them that LoBo was going to Mexico with us. Therefore, she and LoBo had to pass up a free trip. It upset Freddie and I promised her that I'd cheer her up with a trip to Hawaii soon. "I love my folks but I don't know what I'd do without you, Trudy," Freddie told me. Freddie's family couldn't figure out what she saw in LoBo, a man who hauled trash for a living and had no ambition to do anything else. But the worst thing about LoBo as far as Freddie's family was concerned was the fact that he was as "crooked as a hillbilly's teeth." None of that went over too well with Freddie's father, who was an accountant. I wouldn't have wanted LoBo to be my man, but he had some qualities that I did admire. He truly looked out for the people he cared about. A month before his high school graduation, his grandfather passed away. LoBo canceled a date with his girl at the time and took his grief-stricken grandmother to the prom. Teachers were still talking about it when I got to high school a few years later. I felt blessed to have LoBo as a replacement for my deceased brother. He always looked out for me.

"Girl, you best be careful down there in Margaritaville. Them folks down there make a habit out of gettin' loose. Don't drink out of no glass you let get out of your sight. Dudes are puttin' all kinds of crazy shit in women's drinks these days. And that date-rape shit dudes be usin', they sell over the counter in half of the drugstores in Mexico! And, girl, whatever you do, don't let nobody talk you into bringin' no package, not even no book, back to the States with you. If you was to get caught with some dope that somebody tricked you into mulin', your goose is cooked to a crispy critter," LoBo warned. With LoBo encouraging me and helping me pull off my credit card scam, his concern for my well-being in Mexico seemed contradictory.

I had two fresh new MasterCards in my possession that had been issued the same day I'd applied online. The banks were so anxious for me to start using the cards they offered to send them to me by overnight express mail. After I'd picked up the cards from my private mailbox, I immediately called a rival travel agency from my cell phone in my bedroom to make my travel plans. "Ann Oliver! Is it really you? I haven't seen you in ages," squealed the agent on the other end. I hung up so fast I dropped the telephone.

It had never occurred to me that people in the travel business, other than the ones at Bon Voyage, would know Ann! Then it dawned on me: If I was going to travel in Ann's name I had to make arrangements in bits and pieces. For each trip I would have to book flights with an airline on my own and get hotel information from the Internet. I would also have to bypass the countries that she frequently visited. It saddened me to know that if and when I decided to visit the Caribbean, I'd probably have to use my own name—and pay for it out of my own pocket! There was not much of a chance for that to happen any time soon, so I had to settle for places like Mexico. Right after the aborted call with the travel agent who knew Ann, I called Mexicana Airlines and made a reservation to fly to Puerto Vallarta.

Since I had made my plans on such short notice, I had to pay a huge fare. But I didn't care. I could afford it. It pleased me to know that Ann's credit history was so strong that she qualified for new instant credit cards with generous credit lines. Even before my bankruptcy, the highest credit line I had ever had was a paltry thousand dollars. The cards in Ann's name were all between five and ten thousand dollars! And the one that I considered the Holy Grail was a Platinum Visa with a fifteen-thousand-dollar limit that I'd just received.

I'd left work before noon that Friday and gone home "sick." I took a cab directly to the airport. I had breezed into Mexico that Friday afternoon like it was something I did every day.

With only a weekend to work with I had to squeeze in as many activities as I could. After checking into my lavish hotel suite, I enjoyed a scrumptious seafood dinner in my room, which included a view of the Pacific Ocean. I felt like a queen!

After my dinner and a brief siesta, I leaped into a round bathtub filled with rose-scented bubble bath. It was as spontaneous as a lot of things I'd begun to enjoy.

CHAPTER 57

The Puerto Vallarta weather was much warmer than South Bay City so I had on a pair of short shorts and another one of my new low-cut blouses. Sarah, from the beauty shop, had given me a perm the night before so I didn't have to worry about my hair sweating out and balling up on my head. I was pleased with my appearance.

Just as he'd promised, my grinning cab driver, Carlos, pulled up in front of my hotel at nine that night. He still had on the same T-shirt. The same foul odor that I'd smelled earlier was still in the air, though not as potent as it had been in the airport area. It no longer bothered me. I was feeling too good to let it.

As soon as I stepped inside the Club Bonita a handsome young Mexican darted across the floor and started pulling on my arm, begging me to dance. He was clearly disappointed when I politely turned him down. I sat down at the nearest vacant table and ordered a Piña Colada. This was the first time I'd ever gone to a nightclub by myself and it was a strange experience. Local men in groups of three and four, most of them potbellied, plain, and middle-aged, hovered over my table, smiling and saluting me with their drinks. Looking around my immediate area I realized that my table was the only one occupied by a lone woman. Every other woman I saw was either with a man or with a party of two or more individuals. It seemed like all eyes were on me.

I was pleasantly surprised when an attractive young Black woman in a bright pink blouse and matching shorts appeared at the side of my table. "Ain't you from D.C.?" she asked, taking a long drink from a tall glass.

"I'm from California," I replied cordially.

"Oh. You look like somebody I know back in D.C. You wanna sit with me and my crew? You gonna get eaten alive, girl. These Mexican men love them some Black women. Me and my girls, we've been beatin' 'em off with a stick all week."

"That's all right," I replied with a dismissive wave. "I'm only in town for the weekend and I think I can take care of myself," I said with a smile. "Thanks anyway."

"All right, now. Just be careful down here," the woman said, easing back across the floor.

Before the waiter returned with my drink, two tall, very dark-skinned men with kinky black hair came out of nowhere and pulled out chairs at my table. The cuter one dropped a rose on the table in front of me.

"Excuse me," I said, annoyed and flattered at the same time. The club was crowded. The music, the latest hip-hop tune from the States, was so loud it made my ears ring. Like it was with other nightclubs I'd been to, this one was a ball of confusion. I smiled apologetically and started to rise.

"And where are ju going?" one of the men asked, speaking with a thick Spanish accent. He firmly wrapped his long brown fingers around my wrist.

"I'm going to another table," I replied.

"No, ju are not," the man said, giving me a stern look. His fingers tightened around my wrist.

"Uh, is this your table?" I stammered, looking around for another vacant table or the table with the sister and her friends from D.C.

"It is now," the other man said. "I am Adrian. His is my brother Marcos."

"Oh. Uh, I'm from the States. Where are you two from?" I asked, looking from one to the other, expecting them to tell me they were from Panama, Honduras, Guatemala, or some other Spanish-speaking country with Black folks. It was hard to tell their ages in the dim light.

"This is home. Born here, raised here," Marcos told me, laughing. "Ju are surprised?" he asked with a raised eyebrow.

"You don't look Mexican," I said, reaching for my drink from my waiter before he could even set it on the table. Even the waiter was bold. It wasn't enough for him to just wink at me. With two big strapping men sitting on either side of me, the frisky waiter still tapped, rubbed, and pinched the back of my hand. I loved the attention. But I had to wonder about how sincere these south of the border men were.

"Lots of black Mexicans. Most of us come from Vera Cruz. *Blexicans* is what we are called." Marcos laughed again. "They don't teach ju in America about black Mexicans?"

"No, they don't," I chuckled.

"All of our people didn't end up in America, the Caribbean, and other parts of the world, ju know. Lots of slaves ended up in Mexico," Adrian added.

"Oh." I smiled, feeling warm all over. "I knew that," I said, clearing my throat and glancing around the room. The same Black woman who had invited me to her table stood along the wall. She gave me a cautious look and mouthed the words: *Be careful.*

Within minutes Adrian and Marcos told me their stories. They worked for Mexicana Airlines. I must have looked skeptical because they whipped out their airline photo IDs right away and waved them in my face. Adrian was a pilot, a *capitan* he proudly emphasized. Captain Adrian Gallardo's position was a dozen steps above a store manager in a discount mall like James was . . .

Marcos was a flight attendant. They had flown in from Mexico City where they lived. Neither one asked about my background, not even if I was married. As sheltered as my life had been so far I did know from racy conversations with Wendy and Pam that vacations usually included no-strings-attached flings with the locals. Within an hour Adrian had talked me into letting him spend the night with me. After being only with James for the past ten years, I was curious to find out what I'd been missing.

Adrian dismissed his brother and led me to a cab and accompanied me back to the Sheraton. He started nibbling on my ear and purring to me in Spanish as soon as the cab pulled away from the club. He started tugging on my clothes during the elevator ride to my suite, right in front of another frisky couple. As soon as we got inside my room, he snatched off my clothes completely, with me squealing like a peacock.

James gave me compliments every now and then, mostly about my cooking. Adrian complimented almost everything I did. When I accidentally belched he said, "Aaah, a woman who expresses herself in such a basic way is a natural treasure." He liked my firm breasts, my dark skin, and my big round ass. He was good with his tongue, but when he sucked my toes, one by one, I shivered the whole time. Before he could finish I had already planned my next trip to Mexico.

Adrian didn't prepare me for lovemaking by ramming a spit covered finger into my pussy and telling me to "brace yourself, girl," the way James did.

The first time Adrian's tongue explored my crotch was a major first for me. I lost control and screamed so loud the guests in the room next door banged on the wall.

"Anita, ju are the woman I make love to in my dreams," he whispered, with his big hand covering my mouth to keep me from disturbing the people in the room next door again. Now, what woman wouldn't want to hear words like that? And I loved the way he said my name: "Anita." *Little Ann* in Spanish. It would not have sounded as sexy if he'd called me by my real name. A name that I hardly recognized anymore.

Reality reared its ugly head when Adrian told me he had to call up his wife in Mexico City to check up on her and their three kids. As soon as the words left his mouth, he slid off me and reached for the telephone on the nightstand. That one gesture made me feel like a ten-dollar whore.

I knew enough about Latin men, married or single, to know some of them hopped from one woman's bed to another. Even though Adrian spoke to his wife in Spanish I didn't want to hear anything he had to say to her, so I wobbled to the bathroom and stayed there until he came to get me to take me back to bed. If James had ever been this romantic I probably would have been with him tonight instead of in Mexico wallowing around in a king-size bed with a stranger.

When it was over with Adrian, it was over, period. There was no mention of a future liaison, or even a "wham-bam-thank-you-ma'am." Adrian disappeared from my life as suddenly as he had come. The knowledge of that settled over me like a wet sheet.

The rest of my vacation went by in a blur. I spent a lot of time stretched out on a towel, lounging under a beach umbrella on the beach. I smiled back at all the handsome men who smiled at me but I didn't encourage any more than a smile. After my romp with Adrian I didn't want, or need, to be with anybody else. He had done his job well, and I wanted to isolate and savor the memory.

I was exhausted and sore. It was amazing how much good sex and a whupping had in common. Daddy hadn't whupped me since I was a child, but I could still remember the pain. But the pain of good sex was worth it. It was the perfect excuse for me to remain in the same spot on the beach for hours, slurping on one exotic drink after another and rubbing my sore spots. When the blazing hot sun began to resemble a huge orange ball sinking into the ocean, I took my drink and started to walk along the beach. By the time I decided to make a U-turn and return to my hotel room, my skin looked and felt like leather. The party was over and it was time for me to go home.

I stayed in my room until time to check out.

CHAPTER 58

If it had been left up to me, I would have stayed in Mexico for the rest of my life. I would have drunk margaritas from sunrise to sunset. I would have loved a life of lounging on a beach and spending passion-filled nights with handsome men who put no pressure on me to commit to anything more than a night or two. Except for my daddy, I didn't have much to go home to. That thought saddened me.

I liked my job at Bon Voyage, but I could have lived without it. I figured that if Ann eventually got her way I'd soon be living without my job at Bon Voyage anyway. I would leave with dignity no matter what happened. Even if Ann found out about me stealing her identity, and charging thousands of dollars worth of merchandise and services to her name.

One day when I am too old and feeble to be held accountable, I plan to share stories about my Bon Voyage escapades with my great grandchildren.

In addition to Bon Voyage being a major prop in my life, there was James. I looked at James from a whole different perspective now. He had become a cross between a savior and a beast of burden on my back. I was so confused, I had a hard time thinking straight anymore. I don't even remember the cab ride from the airport once I returned to the States. I got off the plane and breezed through Customs and the next thing I knew, I was dragging my feet toward the house I had lived in for almost thirty years. Right back where I'd started.

I couldn't locate my keys in the bottom of my purse so I had to knock on the front door. My rough, ashy, sunburnt hands looked like ET's feet. Daddy greeted me with a massive scowl on his face. "Gal, why you lookin' so much darker now than you was when you left here the other night? You look like you been workin' in a coal mine," Daddy said as he stood in the doorway like a sentinel. It was around ten that Sunday night and he was in his bedclothes. Daddy padded across the floor with his long bare feet looking less than human. The smell of greens and neck bones filled the air, as usual. I smiled because the smell reminded me of the unidentified odor I'd smelled the whole time I was in Mexico. Beer bottles lined up on the coffee table looked like brown bowling pins. Daddy's house shoes sat neatly in a corner under the coffee table.

"There was a pool at our hotel, Daddy. We spent a lot of time swimming." I sighed, dropping my suitcase onto the floor.

Daddy scratched his chin and gave me a puzzled look. With his head turned to the side, he squeezed his eyes into narrow slits. "Your job sounds more like a shindig, don't it? Them retreats don't seem to be doin' nothin' but givin' y'all a excuse to have a good time." Daddy followed me to my room, wrapped in the new blue terry-cloth bathrobe I'd bought him for Father's Day. His thin gray hair was shooting up all over his head, making him look like Medusa.

"You're right, Daddy. But you know how White folks like to get loose. One of the White girls I work with dared me to get into one of those tanning booths." I laughed, plopping down hard onto my lumpy bed. There was a good reason why I had not rewarded myself with a new brass bed or something similar. It was because I didn't want to get too extravagant when it came to buying things that Daddy could see. As clueless as he was in some respects, he was still sharp enough to smell a rat if the smell was strong enough. I didn't know how long I would be able to keep him off my back with stories about my job sending me on retreats. But I planned to enjoy things while I still could.

Daddy frowned and scratched his chin again. "You need a tan like you need another leg." He laughed and waved his hand. "As soon as you get settled, give James a call. He done left six messages since dinnertime. He said the least you could have done was call him from that retreat in Mexico."

"I will, Daddy." I looked at the framed Polaroid of James and me on my nightstand. It had been taken during last year's Fourth of July picnic at Mavis's house. In the background, peeping out of her kitchen window, was Mavis. That same picture said it all. It represented my future. If something drastic didn't happen, I was going to spend the rest of my life with James . . . and Mavis. "Did anything happen while I was gone?"

Daddy grunted and threw up his hands in disgust. "Sadie just about done drove me crazy frettin' over them grandsons of hers," Daddy complained. "Every time she visits them two that's in prison, I have to peel her off the ceilin' the next day."

"What about that other one?"

"Kenny? Oh, he the only one ain't in jail. But he's a good boy, and he ain't gave Sadie no trouble . . . yet."

As soon as Daddy left my room, I turned the picture of James facedown and sat staring at the wall, rubbing the side of my arm. The memories of Mexico and my fling with the sexy airline pilot were so fresh on my mind I completely forgot about James until he called me.

He didn't even greet me the way he usually did. This time he mumbled some gibberish in a gruff voice. After a few tense moments, he cleared his throat and said very clearly, "Listen, Trudy, we are going to have to communicate better once we get married. How come you didn't tell me about this retreat sooner? I could have gone with you."

"Baby, this was work-related. Nobody brought their mates," I lied, listening to James, and still hearing the airline pilot's voice in my head calling me *Anita*.

"I could have stayed at a different hotel. Nobody but you would have known I was there. I want you to know that I don't like some of the things you've been doing lately, Trudy."

"Like what?" I asked in a crisp voice. I sat up straighter on my bed and crossed my legs, prepared to defend myself.

"I don't get to see much of you anymore. And when I do, you are too tired to do much of anything, and you look and act like you are bored most of the time. You are slow about returning my calls, you don't come by like you used to. What's happening to us?"

I let out a deep sigh and rolled my eyes, looking around the dreary bedroom that I couldn't wait to escape. Even if it was just to go back to work. "James, I'm tired. Can we talk tomorrow? I'll call you from work. No, I will call you as soon as I get home from work."

"See there! Now that's the kind of shit I'm talking about. Woman, I am your man. I'm going to marry you—at least that's what I thought."

"Let's talk about all this tomorrow, James." I let out a mighty yawn, hoping it was noticeable enough to encourage James to conclude the conversation.

"No, we are going to talk now. I'm coming over there!"

"James, I have to go to work tomorrow," I said. I had more of a whole life now. I had some real independence and financial leverage, if you could call using fraudulent credit cards that. I was now the one in control of myself; not Daddy, not James.

"I have to go to work tomorrow, too, dammit. I want to talk to you face to face. I'm coming over there."

"Don't you bring your black ass over here, mister. I will come by your place *tomorrow* when I get off work!" I yelled, shaking my finger in the air. I glared at the telephone as if I could see James's face through it.

There was nothing but silence for several seconds. Then I heard James suck in his breath. "Trudy, I love you. I have always loved you. I knew I wanted to marry you the first time I saw you and I thought you felt the same way. If you don't want to marry me, you need to let me know, and let me know now."

"I don't feel like talking about this now," I replied in a stiff voice.

"Woman, don't you hang up this telephone yet. There is something I need to know, and I need to know it now."

"What?" I asked with impatience and puckered lips.

"Is there another man?"

"What?" I hollered. "Who the hell do you think you are to be asking me something like that, man?"

"Scratch that. I'm sorry and I didn't mean that at all. I know you better than that."

"James, I'll come by your place tomorrow. We'll do something together real soon. Uh, I was thinking about inviting you to go to Reno or Vegas next weekend."

"We don't need to go running off to Reno or Vegas," James told me. "Besides, we need to be saving our money."

"Well, we can fly and it won't cost us but a few dollars to pay for the tax. And the hotel room will be free." I held my breath until I figured out the next thing to say. "I can use the employee discount now . . ."

"Oh?" James let out a sharp whistle. The kind people let out when something impressed them.

"Uh-huh," I said.

James was upset and it was because of something I'd done and said. I had to make up for that. It wasn't enough for me to just spend time with him anymore. I honestly felt that as long as the punishment fit the crime, it made everything all right again. With Ann Oliver's credit cards, I could afford to do just about anything I wanted to do for my man. James was my ace in the hole and I had to keep him happy.

"Let me think about it. I don't want to leave Mama by herself for a whole weekend right now. She just got over a mild case of shingles."

"If she feels up to it, she can come with us," I suggested, immediately regretting the corner I had backed myself into.

My life had become a raging contradiction. Even though I was in control of my life, my life was out of control.

I didn't know if I was coming or going. In my own twisted way I blamed it all on Ann Oliver.

CHAPTER 59

I was glad to be back at the office. It gave me the time and the space I felt I needed to reorganize my thoughts. It also gave me the opportunity to keep my eye on Ann.

I had stopped using her corporate credit card for my personal use, so there was no danger there anymore. And, I had used different telephone numbers and places of employment on the applications for the other credit cards. There was no chance that any of the new credit card people would call Bon Voyage. But for some reason, I still felt that for a while I needed to be in the office every day to screen Ann's mail just in case some suspicious busybody at the credit bureau sent something that I didn't want Ann to see.

I had to try extra hard not to make the same mistakes that Ann had already chastised me for. I paid more attention when I took telephone messages and I took an earlier bus to work every day now so I wouldn't be late. I even smiled all the time when I was in the office. Even when I didn't have anything to smile about. Like the following Tuesday when Ann returned from an extended weekend in Vancouver.

It seemed like the more I tried to avoid being alone with her, the more I ran into her. Like a ghost that could float through the wall, she appeared in the ladies' room or the break room every time I thought it was safe. That woman was everywhere. I got stuck in the elevator with her that morning on my way back to my workstation after distributing the mail. She started to look me up and down, with her eyebrows raised in a way that made me feel hostile and defensive. I was thankful that I knew how to restrain myself.

"How was Vancouver?" I asked. Initiating a conversation when I was alone with her made the ordeal less painful.

"Full of Canadians," Ann replied with a disgusted look. "No matter where I go it's always good to be back in the good old U.S.A." Her eyes were still roaming over my attire. "That's a nice blouse, Trudy."

"Thanks. Pam and I went shopping at Macy's after work yesterday."

"Well, you should shop at Macy's more often," she advised, straightening the lapels on her red blazer.

I could feel the heat rising to my face but I managed to keep my cool. "Did you have a good time in Jamaica last week?" My question seemed to startle her. She gasped and gave me a frightened look.

"Jamaica is not what it used to be," she said with a heavy sigh. When the elevator stopped she pressed the button to keep the doors shut. "Uh, remember what I asked you to do about any calls from Mr. Giles in Jamaica?"

"Yes. He called almost every day while you were down there."

"If he calls this week tell him I'm still out of the country."

"He didn't sound too happy the last time he called," I said, dying to know who this mysterious man was and what he meant to Ann.

I had studied Ann Oliver so much I could read her body language. She was nervous. She tapped her foot a few times. Then she folded her arms in such a clumsy way the fingers on both of her hands crossed. "He's an unhappy man and that's why I don't want to talk to him until I'm ready." The elevator door slid open and she marched off without another word.

"I don't know what is going on between Ann and that Mr. Giles in Jamaica. That woman is into something she shouldn't be in, and I don't know what it is," I told Pam and Wendy as soon as Ann waltzed out of the front door.

CHAPTER 60

Mr. Giles called again right after I returned from lunch, making my stomach churn the lunch I'd just consumed.

"Let me talk to Missee Ann Oliver straightaway!" he roared, not even revealing his identity.

By now there was no need for this man to announce his name. I had to ask anyway. "Who is calling, please?" I asked in my most pleasant and professional sounding voice.

"Giles!" he yelled, causing so much terror in me that I had to shift in my seat to keep from tumbling to the floor. In the background, I could hear the cling-clang of steel drums and a lot of other deep male voices with Jamaican accents talking and singing. It sounded like a beach party where everybody was having a good time except Mr. Giles. The threatening tone in his voice had me so scared by now that I couldn't imagine what Ann was going through.

"She's still out of the country," I told the angry Jamaican. There was a lot of static on the line, but his voice was so loud and angry I had no trouble hearing him. It was hard to believe that he was calling from an island country somewhere in the Caribbean Sea. It sounded like he was calling from next door.

"Ow!" he hollered, grunting under his breath like a hog. "And what is your name!"

My heart felt like it was marching across my chest. Even though this call had nothing to do with me, but because of my proximity to Ann Oliver, I experienced some level of fear myself. "I'm Trudy Bell," I said, making sure I sounded pleasant. One thing I didn't want was for somebody else to complain to Ann about my telephone manners. Especially somebody who sounded as beastly as this Mr. Giles.

"Tru-dee, you have de lady call me back de minute she returns! See to it!" Mr. Giles hung up abruptly, the way he had been doing the last few times he called. But there was something different about him this time. He sounded a lot meaner and more determined to talk to Ann. While I was still sitting there looking at the dead telephone in my hand it rang again. It was Mr. Giles. "Tru-dee, give Ann a message for me, please. Tell her I will not call again until I hear from her. If she refuses to call me back when she returns, she may suffer. That is all." Mr. Giles didn't slam the phone down like I expected. I could still hear him breathing and growling under his breath.

"Sir, are you still there?"

"I am," he said in a surprisingly gentle voice.

"I will give Ann your message."

"One more thing, Tru-dee. Tell her I know where she lives . . ."

This was one time when I couldn't wait for Ann to get back to the office. About twenty minutes later she sashayed through the front door, ignoring me completely. I jumped up and chased after her, catching up to her at the elevator. "Um, Ann, that Mr. Giles called twice while you were gone," I told her in a low voice. She whirled around and glared at me. "He gave me a . . . uh . . . message to give to you," I added with pleasure.

"What did he say?"

"He said to tell you he's not going to call again until you call him back." I paused long enough to catch my breath. "He seemed really upset, Ann," I added.

She shifted her eyes before she returned her attention to me. "Is that all?" she asked, her voice cracking.

I shook my head and swallowed hard. My throat felt like it had a lump the size of a golf ball in it. "I don't know what he meant, but he said if you didn't call him back, uh . . . you may suffer."

Ann's eyes got big and her lips trembled. For a few seconds she looked like a deer caught in headlights. She bit her bottom lip and looked around. Then without warning, she ushered me to a corner by the elevator. "Did he say anything else? It is really important that you tell me everything he said."

I nodded. "He said to tell you he knows where you live," I said, enjoying the look of terror on her face.

"Thanks, Trudy." Ann literally ran into the elevator.

Of all the good gossip for Wendy and Pam to catch from their hiding places in the ladies' room, I was disappointed that they hadn't heard Ann discussing Mr. Giles with Lupe or Joy.

Freddie had her own theory about Ann and the Giles man. "She probably fucked him and told his wife," Freddie said on the bus ride home that evening. "Or maybe she's got something on him and is blackmailing him."

I frowned. "Uh-uh. Blackmail victims don't try to get in touch with their blackmailers this hard." I was dying with so much curiosity I didn't have much time to think about my problems with James.

"Wanna go dancing this weekend?" Freddie asked.

"Huh? Oh, I can't. I'm treating James to Vegas this weekend."

"Well, ain't you sweet. I wish I could afford to be that sweet to my man."

I rolled my eyes at Freddie. "I'll go dancing with you next weekend."

I had a very ominous dream that night. In it, I saw a hulk-like, angry, shadowy man push Ann off a steep cliff with nothing but jagged, razor-sharp rocks below. It was the kind of endless cliff that nobody could survive a dive from. When the body hit the ground and landed on its back, it was me.

CHAPTER 61

From the minute I arrived in Vegas, knots started forming throughout my entire stomach. I had dismissed the dream I'd had and moved on to some real misery. I had James on one side of me and his mother on the other. Mavis had on one of her favorite wide-brimmed hats. She had placed it on her head at an angle to keep it from messing up the wig that I'd given to her for Mother's Day.

"You would think that that cheap travel agency you work for could have at least sprung for limo service," she complained. "Every time I visit Vegas I have a limo take me to and from the airport," she added with a look just harsh enough to annoy me.

"Mama, don't look a gift horse in the mouth," James scolded, helping Mavis into the backseat of a cab by the curb in front of the airport.

"And how come we stayin' way down at that old-time Stardust Hotel and not at the MGM Grand or the Mirage where all the action is?" Mavis continued, falling onto the seat with a groan. Of all the hundreds of people wandering about the airport, Mavis was the only one dressed like she was going to church. "If I had known y'all was gwine to drag me to a glorified flophouse like the Stardust, I would have got me a room somewhere else."

"Mama, the Stardust is one of the most popular hotel casinos in Vegas. People come from all over the world to stay there and see Wayne Newton's show," James said.

"And that's another thing!" Mavis roared, pouting like a two-year-old, giving the back of the cab's front seat a healthy kick with her round-toed pumps. "Just 'cause I'm old, don't mean y'all gotta carry me to see a old fossil like Wayne Newton. And how many Black folks come to Vegas to see Wayne Newton? Didn't I read somewhere that Prince or Gladys Knight was singin' somewhere at the other end of the Strip?"

"It was the only show I could get tickets for at such a late notice," I explained. At least that part was true. Here I was taking James and Mavis to Vegas at my expense, well, not really *my* expense, since the credit cards were in Ann's name. But I still felt the need to be apologetic. I don't know if it was a good thing or a bad thing, but I rarely spent my own money to finance my good times since I'd come into possession of the fraudulent credit cards. But I was the only one risking my neck. With that in mind, I could not believe the nerve of Mavis. She was getting a free trip to Vegas and still was not satisfied.

In addition to that, I'd gotten over a thousand dollars from several different ATMs which I'd slipped to Mavis behind James's back so she'd have money to gamble with. I had only two hundred dollars to gamble with myself. James didn't gamble, but since I'd told him I'd get reimbursed by Bon Voyage when I turned in an expense report, he decided we'd only eat at the most expensive restaurants on the Strip.

Summer in Las Vegas was always scorching hot. It was over a hundred degrees on this difficult day. The heat in Mexico had not been as intense. We were all dripping with sweat by the time we arrived at the hotel. Mavis was busy fanning her face with her floppy hat and complaining about other things all the way up to her room. To keep from saying something I'd regret, I left James alone with his mama while I went on to our room next door.

I enjoyed the few minutes I had to myself. It gave me a chance to inspect the room. It had cost almost as much as I earned in two days at Bon Voyage, so I wanted to make sure everything was in order. The bed, facing a large TV on a dresser, was large enough to accommodate a small family. The carpet was so thick I was tempted to lie down on it instead of the bed. The bathroom was so immaculate I felt like I was desecrating it when I squatted over the toilet to relieve my bladder. Even the toilet paper looked too good to use. The fact that Mavis had complained about staying at this particular hotel instead of one of the newer ones was outrageous It seemed all the more ridiculous because the shabby old Victorian house that Mavis owned and lived in was near a dump site.

By the time James joined me I had already popped open the huge bottle of complimentary champagne that I'd discovered in the room as soon as I opened the door. My head was already buzzing and my memory took me back to Puerto Vallarta, Mexico. I was so deep in thought, I didn't realize James had returned to the room until he was on top of me.

James was happy to find me stretched out on the bed on top of the covers with a wide smile on my face. "Girl, I need to get you off somewhere like this more often," he teased, his anxious hands rubbing me all over. He seemed pleased that I was already naked as a jaybird and wet between my legs. As much as I had going on in my life now, when I did find time to spend with James, I usually enjoyed it. The one thing about my masquerade was, I didn't know when it was going to end. But James was permanent. I had every reason to believe that he would be in that position for as long as I wanted him to. I had the best of both worlds. I planned to enjoy them as long as I could.

Before James could even get his dick hard, let alone get naked, Mavis called with more complaints. She couldn't find the TV remote control, she didn't have a nice view, and she had forgot to bring her blood pressure pills. It didn't do James much good to get her off the telephone by telling her he had to use the bathroom, because a minute later she was pounding on the door anyway.

That was the way it was the whole weekend.

CHAPTER 62

Right after James left our hotel room to escort Mavis back to her room, I started feeling guilty because Mavis was not having a good time. Without giving it much thought, I dialed her room. She answered immediately.

"Blood of Jesus." Mavis was not that religious, but whenever it suited her needs, she incorporated a higher power into her schemes.

"Mavis, it's Trudy."

"Uh-huh," she said in a bored voice.

"You seem a little tense," I said gently and with a smile even though she couldn't see it.

"You just now noticin' that?" she asked. As irritating as Mavis was, she was too pitiful to hate. Other than her son, she had no life. She didn't even have a lot of friends. In a sense, when it came to Mavis Young, I had the patience of a saint. But James didn't. I could hear him in the background scolding his mother like she was a naughty child. He had to do that a lot. It seemed like the older Mavis got, the more he had to treat her like a child.

"Well, I pretty much feel the same way myself. It's been a hard week for me. I was thinking that before we go back home maybe you and I could go get facials and a massage."

Mavis grunted under her breath before responding. "That sounds real nice and I could sure use some pampering. But I ain't got that kind of money."

"Oh, no. If you want to join me, it's on me," I offered quickly. An imaginary sound, one that resembled the ching-chang of a cash register, shot through my head like a random bullet.

"Oh. Well, when do you think we can get ourselves pampered?" Mavis chirped.

"When it's convenient for you," I decided.

As soon as I hung up, feeling a lot more relaxed now that I had soothed Mavis, the telephone rang again. This time it was Daddy, and he sounded totally distressed.

"What's wrong, Daddy?" I asked, my hand over my heart, expecting to hear the worst. "Did you take your pill?" I held my breath. "Is it Miss Sadie and her grandsons again? Don't tell me Kenny, the good one, is in jail now." I sighed.

"Kenny ain't in jail that I know of. But since you brought him up, there is somethin' about that boy I can't put my finger on. I would never bring this up to Sadie, but I don't trust that young'n. He ain't right. I can see it in his eyes."

"So why did you call, Daddy?" I asked. "Is something wrong?"

"Ain't nothin' wrong with me. I just called to tell you that old horny dinosaur Clarke is in jail," Daddy announced. His voice was smooth and steady but it didn't hide his exasperation and anger.

I had absolutely no interest in Mr. Clarke's activities. I rolled my eyes and sighed. "What for?"

Daddy groaned and clicked his teeth. "They raided one of them massage parlors he throws his money away in. The po'lice hauled everybody in there off to jail—where they belong! I done told him and told him to stay away from them hooker women."

"Who's minding the store?"

"Who do you think is mindin' the store? Me, that's who! Spider said he'd help out till Clarke gets his dried-up tail bailed out Monday mornin'. I'm tellin' you the honest truth, niggers ain't shit. I'm tryin' to help Clarke out with a little spendin' money, which he must not need that bad if he can spend it on them massage parlor trollops."

"Why don't you just let the man go. There are a lot of people in the neighborhood who would appreciate that job more. They would be glad to work for you."

I knew where Daddy was going with this even before he let it out. "That's what I called you for, baby," he admitted.

My heart started to thump. "Daddy, I am not coming back to work in the store. I already have a job, and I don't want to leave it until I am good and ready."

Daddy let out a dry laugh and cleared his throat. "Don't flatter yourself, gal. That ain't what I'm thinkin' about. You ain't the only person I know who can work a cash register."

I was puzzled. "Then what did you call me for?"

Daddy took his time responding. "How would you feel about me hirin' Spider on permanent? He can come work for me in the evenin' when he get off his construction job. My blood pressure done shot up. My heart been actin' up again. I'm tired."

"Then sell that place and retire."

"I ain't retirin' nothin'! I ain't *that* old!" Daddy howled.

"Then get somebody to run it for you full-time!"

"Hold on. Let me sit down before I . . . fall down."

"Are you taking your heart medicine?"

"I can't find it." Daddy's voice dropped to a weak whisper. "I hope I can hold out till you get back," he managed.

As much as I loved my daddy there were times when his comments about his mortality bothered me so much I wanted to finish him off myself. I didn't like feeling that way even though it was never a serious thought, and I would regret it immediately. "Find your medicine, Daddy. Now, I have to hang up."

It didn't matter if I was at home or away, Daddy, James, and Mavis were driving me crazy. My life was rapidly spinning out of control, so I treasured the few things that I did still have some control over. My love life was one. I couldn't stop thinking about my weekend fling in Mexico and what I'd done. I was twice as wet between my thighs by the time James returned from his mother's room an hour later.

He almost jumped off the bed when I tried to guide his head down between my legs. "You know I don't do *that*!"

I sat bolt upright in bed with my arms folded. "You seem to enjoy it when I do it to you," I reminded him. Oral sex had not been the same since I'd been forced to do it with a gun to my head. However, knowing how much it turned James on, I continued to accommodate him anyway.

"But you've never wanted me to do that to you before."

"I want you to do it now."

James shook his head and headed for the champagne bottle. "Nuh-uh, baby. Not tonight. Maybe some other time but not tonight. I am not ready to do that, Trudy." His words made me furious. Here was a man who liked to have his dick sucked in his sleep, but he had a whole different attitude when I was the one who wanted oral sex. He sat back down on the bed, sitting close to the edge. He looked nervous and wild-eyed. Like he thought I might straddle him and sit on his face anyway. He grabbed the remote control and spent the next two hours watching television.

Even though he hated champagne, he drank one glass after another until it was all gone.

It was my idea for us to skip the Wayne Newton show, even though we already had the tickets. I was not happy with the fact that I'd allowed Mavis to take control of the situation. As it turned out, we actually had fun drifting from casino to casino. We had even spotted a few A-List celebrities.

Every chance I got I encouraged Mavis to have a drink. Unlike some people, she was a lot more pleasant to be around when she was drunk. James didn't make love to me until the following night after we'd done some sightseeing, and more gambling, and dining. That was because by then I had plied Mavis with enough alcohol to get her out of our hair. By nine that Saturday night, she was splayed belly-up on her hotel bed, drooling and snoring like a pig.

Despite James's sexual limitations, he was a fairly good lover. He satisfied me most of the time. He surprised me when he threw back the covers and dropped his head between my thighs. But as soon as it was over he jumped off the bed and ran to the bathroom and rinsed out his mouth with Scope. And not just once. He didn't stop gargling and gagging until he had used half of a family-size bottle. That bothered me. For one thing, it was the same thing I'd done after the robber had assaulted me in the liquor store a few months ago. The other reason it bothered me was the fact that it made me feel unclean. As many times as I'd put my mouth on James's private parts over the years, I had never gargled afterwards.

I pretended to be asleep when he returned to bed, clearing his throat and coughing. He plopped down on the side of the bed and remained there for at least ten minutes. It wouldn't have bothered me as much if he had not continued to cough and clear his throat and swipe his lips with a hand towel the whole time. The more he did it, the nastier it made me feel.

Sex was one of man's greatest mysteries. I often wondered how something so good could be so bad. But that was only when it was used the wrong way.

It was one of the longest weekends of my life. I couldn't wait to get back home where the worst I had to deal with was Daddy and his heart problems and other ailments.

I looked forward to going back to work.

CHAPTER 63

There was another accident on the freeway that made me and Freddie late for work that Monday morning. She didn't have to worry about it because her bosses didn't arrive until an hour after she did anyway. But I ran all the way from the bus stop to the office, praying that Ann wouldn't notice me coming in late again.

Before I could even get inside and close the door, Wendy and Pam galloped toward my desk. One of Wendy's sharp heels caught in the carpet and she stumbled, but that didn't slow her down. She reached my desk before Pam did.

"Trudy, you are not going to believe what's happened!" Pam hollered. Her eyes looked like they were going to pop out of her head. I looked from Pam to Wendy as I struggled to remove my sweater. Even though it was the middle of summer, it was still chilly enough during certain parts of the day for sweaters or light jackets. For once in my life I was glad I lived in a part of California that had such odd weather. I had a lot of new sweaters and jackets that I wanted to show off. I couldn't wait for the weather to drop low enough so I would have an excuse to buy some new leather items.

"What's going on?" I asked, my head still swiveling around to look from one to the other.

"Ann's gone!" Wendy shrieked.

I froze. "Gone?" I gasped. I blinked so hard my eyes burned. "Gone where?" Within a split second my imagination ran amok. One of the first thoughts that came to my mind was that Ann had been kidnapped. With the mugging she'd survived, the messy situation involving her late sister, kidnapping seemed reasonable. I let out a long loud breath. "What are you talking about?" I mouthed. A taste slid throughout my mouth that was so sour it made me gag. I covered my mouth and cleared my throat, anxiously awaiting a response from either Pam or Wendy. "What are you two talking about?" I demanded. I got impatient and angry at the same time. These two women knew me well enough by now to know that I did not like being held in suspense.

"She quit! She called Mr. Rydell at home last night and told him she was not coming back to work! Ever!" Wendy yelled. "I just can't believe it! I didn't think dynamite could make that woman leave this place. She had this place and Mr. Rydell by the balls!"

"What?" I gasped. "Did something happen to her?"

"She's getting married," Pam mouthed in a quiet voice, a small smile on her face.

"Is that all?" I managed. "She quit just because she's getting married? She doesn't strike me as the stay-at-home type. How do you know she's never coming back? Are you sure?" I asked hopefully.

"Can you imagine a man desperate enough to marry a she-devil like Ann Oliver?" Wendy let out a long, low whistle before she laughed.

"Slow down. Who is she getting married to?" I asked with my head pounding so hard I had to grit my teeth. It was too good to be true. "How do you know she's not coming back?" I grinned. I don't know what came over me. I couldn't help myself. My lips curled up into a smile so extreme my eyes almost disappeared into my face.

"Remember that guy she met in Paris?" Pam said, nodding. "He's the only man I know of who is as mean as that Mr. Giles who calls for Ann from Jamaica. I wonder what it is about bitches and scoundrels that attracts them to one another." Pam paused as she wiggled, then rubbed her nose. "Well, he showed up on her doorstep last Friday and told her either she goes back to France with him so they can be married or it was over. At least that's what she told Mr. Rydell."

"And she said she wasn't coming back? Are you sure?" I couldn't believe what I had heard so far. That's why I had such an incredulous look on my face.

Both Pam and Wendy nodded with smiles like I'd never seen on their faces before. "Other than this job, what does Ann have to come back here for? She rarely spends time with her parents, and other than Lupe and Joy, she has no other women friends," Pam said, her mood making a U-turn. There was now a look of despair on her face that made it seem like she was talking about herself.

A gust of warm air caressed my face as I thought about Pam's words. Then, just as suddenly, a deep sadness came over me. I couldn't imagine life without my friends. True, Freddie was the only really close female friend I had, but there were other women I chatted with from time to time. I had to remind myself about all the misery Ann had caused me. I knew that to have a friend, you had to be a friend. I wondered if Ann had ever been a real friend to anybody. No matter how nice she had treated me from time to time, she had never been my friend. One time she had made me so angry that I had even fantasized about her getting drunk and falling off a cruise ship during one of her overseas escapades. The truth was, I didn't want any harm to come to her. I just wanted her out of my way. From the looks of things, one of my dreams had finally come true.

"Looks like Christmas is coming early this year." I grinned.

"If this doesn't call for a drink I don't know what does." Wendy laughed, already removing the bottle from her drawer.

"I thought you were pregnant," Pam said quickly. "Oops!" she added, covering her mouth with her hand as she shot Wendy an apologetic look.

"It's okay to tell Trudy. She knows I've been trying," Wendy said, patting her stomach. It did look pretty well-rounded.

I knew it was not my place to bring it up and I wouldn't unless she did, but if Wendy was truly pregnant already, Daryl was more than likely the father. It was something that had been in the back of my mind since the day Wendy had tried to get me to accompany her to her doctor's office. Unless, of course, she had been fooling around with Mark from the bank sooner than she'd led me to believe. I shook my head to rid myself of thoughts about Wendy. I had more than enough evidence to convince myself that I was living in a crazy world. Sadly, the insanity had rubbed off on me.

Wendy was too anxious and impatient to twist the top off her bottle. She bit it off. "One little sip won't hurt," she said, looking at Pam. She took a long drink and let out a loud burp before she waved the bottle at Pam.

I was too overjoyed to move. Pam almost knocked me down trying to get to Wendy to grab the bottle. As soon as she took a long swallow, she pushed the bottle toward me.

Pam and Wendy were both surprised when I held up my hand and shook my head. I no longer drank straight out of the bottle after Wendy, and especially Pam. Not after that incident in the ladies' room when she failed to wash her hands after an extensive episode behind the handicapped stall. I had an ample supply of Dixie cups in my drawer, but I wasn't going to need them any longer.

"I don't think I'll need that bottle to help me do my job anymore," I announced proudly.

CHAPTER 64

"There really is a God," I whispered to Freddie as soon as she answered her cellular phone. I had called her from my cellular phone while I was in the ladies' room at Bon Voyage sitting on a commode. One thing I always did before I called Freddie from the ladies' room was to squat on the floor and peep under the stalls to make sure I was alone. A few minutes earlier I had spied Joy's long bare feet in the stall next to me. As soon as I heard her leave I called up Freddie to tell her the latest news about Ann Oliver. Ann had become like a one-woman soap opera to Freddie. She waited like a spider on a vine from one episode to the next.

"You want to tell me what this is all about?" Freddie said eagerly, not even trying to hide the fact that she was anxious to hear what I had to say. "What's up?"

"Ann quit her job." I stated, giving myself a thumbs-up with each word.

"No, she didn't!" Freddie squealed.

"The woman ran off with some Frenchman and she's not ever coming back," I said, almost choking on my own breath.

"Now that's one man who must be some kind of a magician, witch doctor or something. From what you told me, that woman's from another planet." Freddie clicked her teeth. "Mmph! Girl, that's the biggest news since the parting of the Red Sea. To hell with waiting for the weekend to go dancing! We are going out to par-tay tonight if I have to carry you on my back."

"I guess if this isn't a reason to celebrate, nothing is. Uh, I don't want you to pick me up at the house, though. Daddy's been mighty agitated lately. His lady friend is worrying him to death over those crazy grandsons of hers. Our excitement—over something he'd call foolishness— might set off his chest pains. I'll be standing on the corner by that shoe shop at nine."

Ann Oliver's sudden and curious departure had taken everything in my life to a new level. The huge worry that I'd been carrying around on my back like a papoose about her finding out I'd been masquerading as her was gone. I would no longer have to put up with the cat and mouse relationship I had with her. Never knowing which direction she was coming from had taken its toll on me.

As if I wasn't already taking advantage of Ann, I made plans for the use of her name that I never would have come up with if she had stayed around.

The very next day after Ann's departure I spent my lunch hour poring over the classifieds, looking for a cozy little studio apartment to rent. I felt it would do me a world of good to have a place to go to when I needed to put some space between myself and Daddy, not to mention James. Besides, there were other things I wanted to get out of my system before I married James. Other men were one of those things I had to address. As flawed as James was, he still was a better catch than some of the husbands of women I knew. I thought that he was probably the best man for me. But just *thinking* that wasn't good enough. There was no way I could be sure if I didn't get a firsthand confirmation.

I didn't know what I would do if I stumbled across another man half as exciting as the sexy Mexican I'd met in Puerto Vallarta. Especially if it was a man who wanted to establish a real relationship with me. If that did happen I knew I'd probably be tempted to delete James from my life completely. Until I'd met the Mexican I'd been completely faithful to James for more than ten years. That was an accomplishment that a lot of married women couldn't claim.

Since my sexual experiences had been so limited before James, and even with James, I thought I owed it to myself to see what I had been missing. Not to mention what I would miss once James and I got married. One thing I'd promised myself was that I'd never cheat on my husband. It was one promise I planned to keep. That was why it was so important for me to get everything out of my system while I was still single.

I planned to pay the rent on my secret apartment with cash advances from the credit cards. I hoped to find a furnished place. That way I wouldn't have to use up any of my available credit on new furniture that I would not need after my masquerade had played itself out.

It amazed me how easy it was to rent an apartment. The first two places I looked at were nice. I selected the third one I looked at because it came with the cutest furniture. Also, because it was located in San Jose where I planned to do my socializing and entertaining. Not too many folks in San Jose knew me, so I would not have to worry about bumping into some blabbermouth who knew James or Daddy.

The apartment I'd selected was within a reasonable price range, not that the price was anything that I was too concerned about. I planned to keep the residence only for a few months, so the price range didn't really matter to me one way or the other.

If I told myself once, I told myself a thousand times that even though my masquerade was *wrong* I wasn't *hurting* anybody. Not Ann, not the banks, not myself. If anything, I had the same attitude that Robin Hood had: rob from the rich, give to the poor. The insurance companies, who had been "robbing" folks from day one, weren't even losing anything. All the money they collected—from hardworking Americans like myself— more than covered a few scams, in my book. As far as I was concerned, I wasn't "scamming" anybody. So far everything I had done had brought joy not only to me but to all the people who benefited from my generosity. Each time I withdrew a fistful of crisp twenty dollar bills from the ATM by the park and doled out some of it to the homeless people who patrolled the area, I felt like an outlaw and a hero at the same time.

CHAPTER 65

I couldn't figure out how real criminals maintained their sanity. The ones who weren't already crazy. Not that I considered myself a criminal on any level, but what I was doing was more like a job that I had to work in all three shifts. Even when I wasn't off on a shopping siege, I had to keep myself in check when I was alone in the house with Daddy or lying around with James. I got so used to signing Ann's name that when I prepared one of my checks to pay my utility bill I signed Ann's name! Thank God I caught my mistake in time. Then there was the time that Daddy had to call me several times before I answered because it took me a while to realize that I was Trudy and not Ann. "You talking to me?" I had asked dumbly, shaking my head to get out of my daze. It felt like I had rocks rolling around in my brain.

As long as I live, I will never forget the way Daddy looked at me, because it was a way he had never looked at me before. First, he rubbed his eyes and blinked hard. Then his face morphed into a frown so sour it made me flinch.

"Do you see anybody else settin' at this kitchen table but me and your crazy self, girl?" Daddy paused just long enough to suck his teeth and massage the side of his head. I felt and acted like a mute. I breathed just enough to remain conscious, but I couldn't even blink my eyes. "I don't know what's got into you these last few months. Seem like to me all y'all young people done gone stone crazy." Daddy gave me a grave look, giving me more to worry about. "Sadie found some funny white powder in her grandson's sock drawer last night." He lowered his head and rolled his eyes up to look at me, like I had something significant to add to his comment.

"Now that's a damn shame," I commented.

"Uh, *you* ain't crazy enough to be snootin' none of that powder mess up your nose, I hope," Daddy said with a stern look, his head turned just enough to the side where I could see the bloody veins on the outer sides of his fishy eyes.

"You know I'd never do cocaine, Daddy. That's not what's wrong with me. I just got a lot of things on my mind, that's all," I muttered, sniffing hard to hold back the mucus threatening to ooze out of my nose. When I rubbed my nose, Daddy's eyebrows shot up. "I have never done that stuff, and I never will." I needed to sniff again, but decided not to since Daddy was already suspicious about what I did with my nose.

"If you ever do, you better make damn sure I never hear about it. You won't live to tell about it," Daddy threatened. "I know I didn't raise no fool."

One thing I was certain of was that my daddy would never hurt me no matter what I did. But his empty threats had had a huge impact on me. I knew where to draw the line where my daddy was concerned so I'd never done drugs because I was no fool. Unfortunately, I was way beyond that. It took more than being a fool to do what I had done. I didn't want to think about the things I might have done had Daddy not been in my life.

By the time Ann had been gone a month I had so many irons in the fire I could barely keep track of my activities. I couldn't remember which credit cards I'd made payments on, and which ones I had not. My record keeping was a mess. I couldn't pay "Ann's" bills with my personal checks, and thank God I wasn't bold enough to get a checking account in Ann's name, too. Freddie had told me that even as dumb as some bank employees were, every now and then they did something smart. Like keeping microfiche copies of checks they'd cashed, comparing signatures, and other busybody antics.

Trying to lead the lives of two very different women kept me in a state of confusion. The only thing that kept me going was the fact that I had promised myself that I would end it all soon. I *had* to. The excitement had run its course. I had already taken too many risks. For instance: more than once I'd almost signed my real name to credit card paperwork when it came time to pay for something. I often misplaced receipts from the money orders that I paid bills with. It was just a matter of time before some meddlesome busybody stumbled across one of those misplaced money order receipts in Ann's name, dated after Ann's departure, and trace it back to me. There were times when the only way I could tell who I'd paid or who I hadn't paid was when a stern message for Ann from a bill collector turned up on the answering machine at the studio apartment I secretly rented.

I dodged James and his mama more than ever. To keep Daddy occupied, I encouraged him to visit Miss Sadie more often. "That grandson of hers could use a strong father figure like you in his life. Maybe it'll help keep him from joining his brothers in jail," I told Daddy.

"You might have somethin' there," he agreed. "But like I said, there is somethin' about that boy, Kenny, that makes me nervous. I like the boy, and I'll coach him when I go out there. I don't want to put a notion in his head for him to want to start hangin' around here. I don't want him to be gettin' under your foot," Daddy added, giving me a playful slap. "You done got to be right busy, gal."

I even encouraged Daddy to spend even more time with Spider so that I could have more time to do the things that had become so important to me. Even if it meant that a mob of Spider's brother Hell's Angels accompanied him to our house. The empty beer bottles, long stringy hairs shed here and there, and the musty masculine odor that bikers left wherever they went greeted me every time I left the house and came back. I didn't like it but since I was at least partially responsible, I didn't feel I had the right to say anything about it. Besides, getting all that attention from Spider and his friends kept Daddy off my back.

Bon Voyage seemed like a totally different place without Ann Oliver strutting around like an ostrich. Mr. Rydell replaced her with a quiet, moon-faced Japanese woman who tiptoed around the office like a geisha. Akira Tanaka was so tiny and perfectly groomed she reminded me of a doll.

I was concerned about attempting to enter certain foreign countries using my new passport. As much as I wanted to see the Caribbean and Europe, for free, for the time being I had to settle for an occasional jaunt to Mexico where I hoped to run into the sexy airline pilot again or at least another one as good as he was.

After just one weekend in Mexico with LoBo and Freddie in tow, I decided to restrict my excursions with them to Vegas and Reno. The whole three days that the three of us had spent in Cabo San Lucas, which was the Labor Day weekend, Freddie and LoBo spent most of their time running back and forth to the toilet, throwing up from both ends.

"Girl, you must have a cast-iron stomach if you can drink all this fucked-up water down here and not feel it," LoBo moaned after he'd run to my hotel suite to use my bathroom because Freddie was using the one in their room.

If the diarrhea wasn't bad enough, a few hours later an iguana entered Freddie and LoBo's room and crawled up LoBo's leg while he was in the bathroom prostrate with shame, throwing up so violently he'd turned blue. "Girl, I know it's time to get back to the States when lizards start crawlin' all over me," he complained, running into my room with a wet towel wrapped around his head. And that was another thing. Something had caused a nasty, itchy, disgusting rash on his bald head.

The only way I could calm Freddie and LoBo down was to get them out of Mexico as soon as possible. That meant we had to leave on an earlier flight, which I had to charge on one of the cards twice as much as our original nonrefundable, nontransferable tickets had cost.

I threw parties at the secret apartment, sometimes twice in the same week. I didn't like bringing the strange men that I'd met in bars to the apartment too often. It was too risky. A person didn't have to be a professor to know that millions, maybe even billions, of the people on the planet couldn't be trusted no matter how nice they acted or how innocent they looked. Just last month an eighty-two-year-old great-grandmother was arrested trying to cross the border from Mexico into Arizona with a hot water bottle full of cocaine strapped to the bottom of her wheelchair. I knew I didn't look or act like the kind of person who would do what I'd been doing.

In the long run, even knowing all the possible dangers involved, men seemed like a new toy that I wanted to play with as often and as long as I could. Sometimes it was just drinks and conversation. I'd strolled along Stinson Beach in the moonlight with a young dentist. If I really liked a particular man and was feeling frisky, then drinks, conversation, and a walk on the beach didn't satisfy me. I had to have more. But it had to be somebody I really liked for me to share my bed with them. The few that I'd shared my bed with, so far, had not done anything worth my inviting them back a second time.

I became a regular at some of the bars Freddie went to. A few times I went by myself, but it was more fun when I went with Freddie. I didn't realize how much I'd been missing by tying myself down to James for ten years. Ten long, dull years. Men had taken on a whole new meaning for me. I liked the attention I received when I wore provocative outfits in public. As unpredictable and frivolous as I'd become, I still had enough sense not to act or look too extreme when I was around Daddy or James. I chose to keep my most provocative outfits at the second apartment. There was no way I could explain what I was doing with a see-through blouse or a bustier to a man like Daddy.

CHAPTER 66

Six months after my transformation had begun, Freddie accompanied me to the apartment so we could get ready to go out to a club in San Jose that neither of us had ever been to. Normally, LoBo would tag along behind us making it hard for Freddie to really let her hair down. But with Christmas only three months away LoBo had a lot of orders to fill. It seemed like everybody who knew him needed a new computer or a new DVD player. Or something nice and expensive that they wanted to obtain the fast and easy way—not to mention, the cheap way.

In all the years I'd known Freddie Malone, I had never seen her naked until tonight. I gasped when I looked up at her standing in the doorway that led from the kitchen into the living/bedroom area of the tiny studio apartment I rented.

"That's some nice bubble bath you got in your bathroom," she said, sliding her hand across a belly that resembled a fish net.

"What the hell happened to your stomach?" I asked, my face screwed up like a can opener.

Freddie sighed and looked at the mess on the front of her body like it was the most normal thing in the world. "I hope you don't expect to look the way you do now after you have kids," she said tiredly. "You ought to see my ass. Worm city." She giggled and turned around and shook her naked, stretch-marked butt at me. I didn't bother to comment on the blue veins zigzagging up and down her thin, slightly bowed legs. I had another concern. Something I could not identify was distracting me. "What's the matter, Trudy? You look worried."

I shrugged. "I don't know. I have this real funny feeling."

"About what?"

"That's just it. I don't know. I just feel like something is not right."

Freddie excused herself and went to check her makeup. Not a minute later the telephone rang. The only people who had the number to the apartment were Freddie, LoBo, and the credit card companies that I'd received new cards from. Since it was a Friday night, and Freddie was already with me, naturally I assumed it was LoBo calling.

"Blood of Jesus," I said, mimicking James's mother Mavis and the way she sometimes answered her telephone.

"Is this 555-1028?" a cool, crisp female voice asked.

"Yes . . . it is," I said.

"And is this the residence of Ms. Ann Oliver?"

Right after I heard Ann's name, I held my breath and squeezed my legs together. My heart started banging against the wall of my chest so hard I had to breathe through my mouth. "Uh . . . huh," I muttered. "This . . . this is Ann Oliver."

"This is Angelina Loggia with the fraud division at Sunshine State Bank."

"Oh?" I said meekly, looking toward the bathroom door. Even though Freddie knew most of my business I didn't want her to see me in such a state of panic. "What's the problem?" I bleated.

"Hopefully, there isn't one. We noticed a lot of activity on your Visa card and we just wanted to verify some information."

"Uh . . . yeah. I just recently got the card." I didn't know where the investigator was going, so I knew it was in my best interest not to volunteer any information I didn't have to.

"Can you tell me the last time you used the card and the amount of your purchase?"

"Uh, I don't exactly remember the last time I used it. I've used it a lot lately. I . . . uh . . . took some friends to Mexico and I used it a lot there. I still have all of the receipts. You want me to fax them to you?"

The investigator laughed. "That won't be necessary. I just need to verify one other piece of information."

I felt like I was going to crack open and self-destruct. One thing I

had learned from shady people like LoBo was that if you ever felt like
you'd been backed into a corner, pull out the big gun: get defensive,
get ugly, get ghetto. Say whatever you have to say to get out of that corner. "Look, lady, if there is a problem with me having this card, I'll
cancel it right now! I have several other cards, and no fraud investigators from those banks ever call me up on a Friday night when I am trying to get ready to go to my grandparents' fiftieth wedding-anniversary
party."

"Miss Oliver, we don't want to lose you as a customer. But we want
to make sure that we protect your interests, as well as ours."

"Well, you are making me feel like a crook," I said, biting my bottom lip. "And I don't appreciate that. I don't want your credit card
that bad!"

"Miss Oliver, I apologize for upsetting you. For our records, I just
need to verify one critical piece of information."

"What else do you need to know?" I snapped. "I am Ann Oliver and
I did use the card a lot. In Mexico."

"Could you please tell me the state your Social Security card was issued in?"

"Huh? What do you mean? I live in California."

"Yes, but where were you living when your Social Security card was
issued to you?"

"Why do you need to know that?"

"I just need to make sure you are who you say you are."

The silence that followed was unbelievable. So was the flip-flop my
heart did with each second that passed.

"What state ma'am?"

"California?" I practically whispered.

"What other states have you lived in, ma'am?"

I recalled a conversation I'd had with Freddie several years ago.
Apparently, Social Security numbers were coded by state. A Social
Security number that started with the number five, like Freddie's and
mine (my real one), more than likely meant that the person had ap-
plied for and received a Social Security card in the state of California.
Ann's family was from North Carolina, but I didn't know if she had
been born in that state, or applied for her Social Security card there!
I had to assume she did. "North Carolina," I said stiffly.

"Thank you, ma'am. You have a nice evening."

I was still standing in the same spot holding the telephone when Freddie came back from the bathroom. "Trudy, I—what's the matter? You look like you saw Tupac's ghost."

"Nothing. I just can't shake this weird feeling," I admitted that much, but I couldn't bring myself to tell Freddie about the telephone call I had just received.

"Who was that on the telephone?" Freddie nodded toward the phone still in my hand.

"Wrong number," I said quickly, dropping the telephone before I returned it to its cradle.

"You are really making *me* nervous now, girl. Do you want to forget about going to the club? We can go to the movies instead."

I shook my head. "No, I think I really would like to go out. I might meet somebody who'll perk me up." Ann's departure was one thing, but I took the telephone call from the fraud investigator as a sign: I had to straighten out the mess I'd made, and I had to do it quickly. Like tonight.

CHAPTER 67

Sarah and Lisa from the beauty shop had wanted to accompany Freddie and me to the club, but Freddie had decided that it should just be the two of us. The Smart Set was a club that none of us had been to before. "Four women walking into a club together will scare off the men quicker than anything. From what I've heard about this place, it's not the type of place where you'd see men traveling in groups of three and four," Freddie told me, still walking around my apartment naked.

"You're right," I agreed, secretly wishing that Sarah and Lisa were coming with us. The disturbing telephone call I had just received had seriously frightened me. Having Sarah and Lisa along would have made me feel more secure. I was still nervous even though I seemed to have appeased the fraud investigator. But like I said earlier, leading a double life was a hard and full time job.

By the time we got to the club, after being lost for over an hour, weaving back and forth on Interstate 880, first south, then north, I was already tired. Not only that, James had left six urgent messages on my cell phone voice mail. I called home to make sure nothing had happened to Daddy and almost got cussed out for bothering him while he was getting dressed to go visit Miss Sadie. "I thought you was at a dinner party for your boss!" he snarled.

"I am. I just wanted to check to make sure you were all right. It'll be

late when I get home. If I get home at all. I might spend the night
with one of the girls from the office." Daddy was silent but he let out
an exasperated sigh. "Daddy, I'll see you when I get home. If James
calls, tell him what I just told you."

I knew we'd made a mistake going to the Smart Set club as soon as
we walked in the door. A puny, ashy-lipped man in a cheap-looking
blue suit came out of nowhere. He followed us to a booth near the
back of the club's main room. "I sure likes what I see up in here
tonight," he said, sucking his teeth and rubbing his hairy paws together. I sat down, ignoring the intruder.

Freddie, one hand on her hip and her neck rotating, faced him
with a scowl. "Brother, you ought to be ashamed of yourself, coming
at us like that! Is that the best pickup line you can come up with?
Because if it is, you ain't getting no pussy tonight!"

The man gasped, rotated his neck and placed both hands on his
narrow hips, looking at Freddie like she was the Bride of Franken-
stein. "What— Girl, I wasn't even talkin' to you with your mugly—and
I do mean *mugly* self. If they was to blow one of them whistles only
dogs can hear up in here, you'd be barkin' from now on. Get your
high-yella ass oughta my face!" He dismissed Freddie with a swift wave
of his hand and a look that made me cringe.

Freddie was so taken aback she could not speak. Out of the corner
of my eye I noticed a mean-looking, thick-necked man in a security
outfit just a few feet away. When he blinked and kept right on talking
to the man in front of him instead of coming to our aid, I leaped up
from my seat and grabbed Freddie's arm. "This is not the place for
us," I insisted, almost knocking down the man who had just insulted
Freddie. As soon as we got back outside, we galloped down the street.
We didn't stop running until we reached Freddie's car, three blocks
away, parked between two Dumpsters in a gas station parking lot.

"It's a good thing you got me out of that fucking place when you
did. I was just about to knock some of that fake gold out of that bas-
tard's mouth," Freddie said, trying to catch her breath. She massaged
her chest with her fist.

I took my time crawling into the front passenger seat of Freddie's
car. A deep sadness came over me. The fact that Freddie's car was on
its last wheels and here we were sitting in it between two huge garbage
cans, in a gas station parking lot, said it all. After all the money I had

spent, this was as far as I'd made it. And if all this wasn't traumatic enough, that telephone call from the fraud investigator had me thinking that there was a chance I might end up in jail!

"Let's get a bottle and go back to my place," I said, looking at my watch as Freddie sped down the street.

"Uh-uh. I have a better idea. Remember that club you told me Ann used to brag about?"

I looked at the side of Freddie's face. Freddie's plain looks and big ears were things that I had not given much thought since our school days. To me, she was such a beautiful person, her looks were incidental. She had had so many boyfriends who had been attracted to her for other reasons. If that crude man who had insulted her at the club had hurt her feelings she didn't show it. An insult like that would have reduced me to tears.

Freddie was brave to consider going to another club where she would probably get a similar reaction from another man. I'd been present when other men who didn't know Freddie had made insensitive remarks about her looks. Even though she never brought it up, I assumed that she was used to being dogged by men by now.

As Freddie's best friend I felt it was my responsibility to accommodate her whenever I could. However, going to a club that Ann used to go to didn't quite appeal to me. My biggest fear was that we would run into somebody who knew her. "You mean the Baby Grand club? You know I don't want to go anywhere where I might run into some of Ann's friends."

"They don't know you, or what you've been up to, so what difference would it make?"

"Well, none really. I just wouldn't feel comfortable going where I know she's been."

"Okay. Then let's go get a pizza, some beer, and go back to that apartment and get bloated and drunk." I could tell that Freddie was upset with me. She cleared her throat and gave me a quick glance, almost running up on the curb. "Uh, I am really curious to see this place. That guy who rates clubs in the *San Jose Mercury News* gave it four out of five stars . . ."

I blinked and let out a sigh. I knew when to give in. "All right. We could go and just stay long enough to have one drink. We don't even have to talk to anybody," I said, still feeling uneasy. "I can't imagine the kind of men we like going to a place that a snooty witch like Ann would go to." I sniffed and fished my compact out of my purse to touch up my makeup. Just in case.

Just in case the man who could change my life showed up at the same club. I would remember that thought for the rest of my life. Because it was the night that I met the man who changed my life. The only thing was, I almost didn't live long enough to tell about it.

CHAPTER 68

Unlike Freddie and some of the other women I knew, I had not spent a lot of time in nightclubs. Not even when I was younger when every other young person I knew was using a fake ID to run from one club to the next. Despite my limited experience and knowledge of the club scene, I knew a classy establishment when I saw one. The Baby Grand was at the top of the list.

The parking lot on the side of the club was full of expensive cars, including a few shiny black stretch limos. Beautiful women, dressed to kill in long dresses, their jewelry sparkling like fireflies in the night, strutted into the club on the arms of dapper men grinning from ear to ear.

"Are you sure you want to go into this place?" I asked Freddie. "So far it looks like it's out of our league." I cupped my hand to examine my breath then I checked to make sure my hands were not ashy or smudged with makeup.

We sat across the street from the club in Freddie's shabby old Escort, the loud motor idling and coughing like a sick old man. A smudged child's handprint on the dashboard, empty fast food containers on the floor, a baby's seat in the back, and a parking ticket still stuck on the windshield caught my attention and made me shudder. These things were grim reminders of what Freddie and I really were.

We had a lot of nerve coming to a club on the scale of the Baby Grand. I imagined every woman inside was a clone of Ann Oliver.

Glancing at the sorry state of her car and her chipped nails, then at me, Freddie said with a heavy sigh, "We don't have to stay long. I just want to glimpse how the folks with money party. Just this one time." There was a sad look on her face that was so profound it almost brought tears to my eyes.

"One time might be one time too many," I said, trying to add a spark to our lackluster moods. I squinted at a woman strolling past us in a full-length mink coat.

"And, I doubt if any of these men will insult us." Freddie's voice cracked, but she tried to cover it with a laugh. I laughed along with her. Not because I was amused, but to keep the sad look on her face from showing up on mine.

"Even the bouncers on the door are in suits and ties," I said, adjusting the strap on my dress. I sniffed under my arms to make sure I was still fresh enough in case a man did get close to me. Even though my new silk blue dress and matching shawl had come from Neiman Marcus, I felt cheap. "Let's park down the block and walk. The last thing we want is for somebody interesting to see us in this shit box of a car."

Freddie let out a grunt and slapped the side of the steering wheel like it was a ring of fire. "For somebody who rides the *bus* to and from work, you sure can be highfalutin at times!" Freddie snapped. Then she gently mauled the side of my face with her fist. "Don't you forget what you really are."

Freddie's car jerked and farted all the way down the street. I ducked down in my seat when I noticed a few people staring at us. I yelled when I hit my forehead on the dashboard but that didn't stop Freddie from mauling the side of my head again. "Girl, we are renting a limo the next time we go to a club like this," Freddie informed me with an anxious look.

"There won't be a next time. After tonight we will stick to the sleazy clubs we've been going to, in your car," I declared, meaning every word. Once I got myself out of the hole I'd dug, pretending to be something I was not, I would return to my old ways. As dull as it was, it was a whole lot less stressful. My nerves had already begun to fray before tonight, but the unexpected telephone call from that fraud investigator had helped me make up my mind once and for all.

I had resigned myself to the fact that once the masquerade was over, there would be no more men for me like the sexy pilot in Mexico. There would be no more extravagant shopping expeditions or exotic vacations—unless the cost was coming out of my pocket. It had been fun for a while, but now the whole situation seemed more like a chore than a thrill. My masquerade had pretty much run its course, and I had gone as far as I could go with it. Tonight seemed like a good time for me to bring things to a close.

We parked two blocks away from the club in a Safeway grocery store parking lot. With us both in heels, it was a long slow, painful walk to the club. Our feet were still in pain from us running back to Freddie's car after leaving the first club.

As soon as we approached the door to the front of the club, several attractive men with women already on their arms looked us up and down, smiling and nodding their approval. I was pleased that just as many men were looking at Freddie as there were looking at me.

"I guess men like these only come out at night," Freddie whispered.

"Why do you say that?"

"I don't see these kinds of men during the day and I work in a bank."

"You don't see them during the day because they don't see you. These same men act a totally different way at night in a place like this," I said, making things up as I went along, something I had become good at.

"Whatever you say." Freddie chuckled. I could tell from the grin on her face that she was as anxious to get inside as I was.

There was no cover charge but as soon as we got inside the front entrance a scowling doorman with a wide short body held up a thick hairy brown hand and shook his head.

"Oh, shit," Freddie whispered, stepping on the side of my foot.

"What's wrong?" I asked the doorman, clutching my shawl and shifting my weight from one foot to the other. We were dressed as nicely as some of the other women, so I knew there was no problem with our attire. My heart started beating hard and fast. "Is this club for members only?" I asked, in the sweetest most sophisticated voice I could manage. Like I said, lately I had become good at making things up as I went along. Even though this question just popped into my head, it sounded reasonable.

But the doorman's response sent a shiver down my spine. "May I see some ID, please."

CHAPTER 69

"ID?" I asked dumbly. I moved a few steps back from the door, ready to run if I had to. Even in my heels with my feet already feeling like they were on fire.

The doorman looked straight at me with a wide smile on his round shiny face. With his stump-shaped body covered in a black suit and white shirt, he looked like a penguin with a man's face. He was a black, younger version of Mr. Rydell. "You must be twenty-one or over to enter this club," he told us.

Any woman my age and older would be flattered to get carded. I was no different. It happened almost every time I bought liquor. I liked the way merchants complimented me on my youthful appearance when I had to show my ID. It was a different story when the ID I had in my possession was for another woman. Before I could steer Freddie away, she whipped out her wallet and flipped to her driver's license. The doorman took his time inspecting it before he turned to me. "You too," he snapped.

"Oh. Of course," I stammered. I slowly removed my wallet and flipped it open.

"Thank you, Ann," the doorman said in a flirtatious manner. It could have been my imagination, but right after the doorman waved us on, I saw him nod at a man lurking behind a large green plant in a nearby corner.

"Did you see that?" I asked Freddie.

"See what?" she whispered as we eased through the crowd toward one of the few vacant tables.

"That doorman gave a guy back in a corner a signal."

"Girl, you are so paranoid it's not even funny anymore. You know I don't tell you this often, but you are a good-looking woman, Trudy. You should be used to men doing all kinds of shit when you come around." With a chuckle Freddie added, "I should be so lucky."

For the first half hour it was just Freddie and me, and our drinks at our table. Not a single one of the men who had flirted with us asked us to dance. I laughed when Freddie lifted her arms and yawned. "This place is fancy and all and the drinks are good, but I don't think this is my kind of place. I've never waited this long to get asked to dance." Freddie let out a bored sigh and fanned her face with a napkin. She looked around, hoping to get somebody's attention. "At least we don't have to worry about falling asleep in any of the clubs we've been going to." Freddie groaned and looked at her watch. "If we leave now we might make it home in time to catch Jay Leno or David Letterman or whoever the hell is on late-night TV these days."

"As soon as I finish my drink," I said, my voice losing steam. My lips were still on the lip of my glass when he approached. He had dark, deep-set eyes that didn't blink as he stared at my face. He moved toward our table in such a smooth manner it was like he was on roller skates. I heard Freddie gasp before she kicked my foot under the table.

"He's coming this way!" Freddie said in a low voice. There was a look on her face that I had never seen before. Her lips were curled up at the ends in an exaggerated smile and her eyes looked twice their normal size.

He was the most breathtaking, dapper man I'd ever seen. He was tall with a lean body that sported a pair of broad shoulders like icing on a cake. He stopped in front of our table and actually bowed. "Excuse me, sisters," he began, looking from Freddie to me. "There is something I must know immediately." I didn't recognize his accent, but he definitely was not from San Jose or anywhere else in the United States. He paused, shook his head, and then wiped his forehead with a large white handkerchief. Freddie whimpered when he lifted her hand and kissed it, not taking his eyes off hers. Then he

looked at me and blinked before he lifted my hand, which was shaking like a sumac leaf, and kissed it. Freddie's mouth dropped open
and she gulped down the rest of her drink in record time. She was
unable to hold back a mild burp—even with her hand across her
mouth. He was the same man that the doorman had nodded to
when I entered the club. He was not a fraud investigator so I wasn't
worried about that. Whoever he was, he was too intriguing to ignore.

"What do you need to know?" I asked in a squeaky voice. My hand
was warm from his kiss. I was suddenly warm all over. My butt felt so
hot it seemed like I was sitting on a heating pad. There was a glow on
Freddie's face that made her skin look even lighter. She couldn't take
her eyes off the man in front of us. And neither could I.

"Is there some way I can contact your parents?" he asked me with a
pleading look in his shiny black eyes. "It is a matter of great urgency."

I looked at Freddie. She had a frozen grin on her face. She looked
at me and shrugged.

"Why do you need to talk to my parents?" I asked, trying to maintain a reasonable level of common sense. Especially considering how
deep I'd slid into so many black holes lately. The last thing I wanted
was to look and act like I wasn't used to gorgeous men coming on to
me. "Do I know you?"

He made a weird clicking noise with his teeth and tongue that
caused Freddie to let out a slight yelp. We both shrugged, then
quickly turned our attention back to the stranger as he hovered over
our table with his arms splayed like a large winged bat. "I grovel in
gratitude in advance," he said with a strained look on his face. He
clapped his hands together then rubbed them, causing so much fric-
tion I was convinced that the sparks I saw were real. I tried to imagine
what else he could do with those hands of his. Especially in a more romantic setting.

"Oh," I nervously scratched the back of my neck. "O . . . kay."

It had taken this man less than one minute to have me itching and
sweating so hard around my crotch that I had to crisscross my legs
and squeeze my thighs together to keep from doing something nasty.
I'd been with James for more than five years before I'd felt half as
frisky as I felt now.

Before the darkly handsome stranger said another word he covered my hand with his and squeezed. His flesh was so hot against mine I trembled. He shook his head and let out a sigh that would have blown me down if I hadn't already been sitting. "I would like to thank and bless your parents for honoring the universe with a goddess such as yourself, m'lady."

CHAPTER 70

I didn't like to go out with anybody and not have a good time. I felt the same way about the people I went out with having a good time as well. That included James, even though he was currently somewhere in the back of my mind. I hoped that wherever he was, he was having a good time. I made a mental note to call him up tomorrow. Since I had decided tonight that I would soon return to my old life, I'd have more time for James. But tonight was mine.

The thought that my life would once again be boring and predictable didn't appeal to me at all. For one thing, I knew in my heart that I had to make some adjustments in my love life no matter what I did. Whether or not it included James, I didn't know yet. The alcohol had me thinking strange thoughts. With such a man now sitting next to me, looking like something that should have been served up on a platter, James should not have been on my mind at all. Without warning, a weird feeling wrapped itself around me like a thick blanket: I didn't really want to spend the rest of my life with James! However, ten years was a lot of time to have invested in a relationship. Besides, I was not exactly a teenager anymore. And despite my frequent trips to the makeup counter and beauty parlor, I was no Miss America. If potential husbands hadn't been beating down my door before, I couldn't imagine they were all sitting around waiting for me now. I decided to deal with the present situation. I came out of my trance when Freddie kicked my foot under the table.

Even though the sexy foreigner had gotten all over me in record time with me loving every single minute of it, I was still concerned about Freddie enjoying herself as well. I didn't have to worry about that for long. In less than a minute after my admirer excused himself to go return a page, another man, not as handsome as mine, popped around the corner. He must not have considered me a blessed creature like my other admirer, because he just glanced at me with indifference. Then he leaned toward Freddie and whispered in her ear. She snapped her head around so fast a hairpin flew out of her hair. She displayed a grin so wide it almost divided her face in two. "You talking to me?"

"Would you care to dance?" he asked. This club obviously attracted a lot of foreigners. The man gazing at Freddie like she'd just dropped out of heaven had a British accent. The people in the booth next to ours were speaking what I assumed was Spanish.

"Uh-huh!" Freddie said, already half out of her seat, the man holding her hand. "Order me another drink," she yelled to me over her shoulder, as she strutted to the dance floor like she was on a catwalk.

Walking back toward me clutching two fresh drinks, the tall mysterious man smiled at me in a way that was as close to foreplay as I could get and still have my clothes on. His name was Anoseki. I didn't know if that was his first name or his last. When I'd asked him, all he did was laugh and tell me again, "Anoseki is my name."

Anoseki laughed a lot instead of answering questions. Even when I asked him why he'd picked me with so many better-looking, unescorted women in the club to choose from, he laughed about that, too.

When an extremely beautiful woman waltzed by and grinned in Anoseki's direction, he ignored her, too. I felt special, something that I rarely experienced.

"You chose me over *her*?" I teased, my knee touching his. His arm went around my shoulder and gripped me so hard I could feel his heart thumping against my chest. I sat as stiff as a mannequin, trying to maintain my composure.

Anoseki shared some intriguing biographical information with me. Somehow my weakened mind absorbed every word that came out of his juicy mouth. His full moist lips barely moved as he spoke. When he smiled, the shape of his eyes seemed to change, making them appear more slanted. His smile also made his high cheekbones appear even higher. I was glad that he was leaving for London in a few hours. If a man like this one stayed around me too long, I knew I wouldn't be responsible for my actions. In the condition I was already in, I would have given up my citizenship if he asked me to.

He was originally from Nigeria but had lived in London for several years. He'd moved to Jamaica six years ago, he said. He had stopped in San Jose to visit some relatives, on his way to London to visit some more relatives. His father was some kind of a diplomat. His mother was what he described as a *honcho* ("head nigger in charge" according to Freddie's crude, tipsy opinion) at some university in London.

He was obviously well-educated and -heeled. The diamonds on his long, manicured fingers and his designer suit must have cost a fortune. He had no siblings or wife. And the closest he came to being a parent was to a fleet of luxury cars stored in a garage in Montego Bay, Jamaica, that he referred to as his "babies." All I got from him was another smile when I asked his age. He looked to be about thirty-five.

"What made you decide to come to my table?" I asked, hoping he would do more than laugh.

"Because I only accept the best of everything. I would say that you are worth at least five of these other cheeky tarts combined and, as my father would say, a flock of sheep."

I was so overwhelmed and dazzled, my eyes burned. I blinked and sniffed before offering my best smile.

CHAPTER 71

Now I would like to say that I didn't consider myself a gullible or foolish woman. But smarter women than me had been mesmerized by men who looked more like frogs. Anoseki—even his name made me shudder—put so much emphasis on his words and he sounded so *sincere,* I soaked up everything he said like I was a big sponge. He acted like he couldn't take his eyes off my face. That made me even more receptive.

Anoseki took me by surprise when he hauled off and kissed me. It was a quick peck on my cheek but I could tell that it was the kind of gesture that could lead to something bigger and better.

I could not believe how well the night had turned out after all. It was like a fantasy come true. The kind that every woman deserved to experience at least once in her lifetime—especially a woman with a life as dull as the one I had to go back to. Since I believed that tonight would be my one and only chance to be so bold and loose with such a hunk of a man, I decided to leave no stone unturned. I knew I would never see or hear from him again. I decided to "play" my part in this unplanned drama and I intended to play it well.

"I work for a fantastic travel agency," I began, revealing the only part of my story that was true. I took a quick sip from my wineglass and reared back in my seat, all tuned up to spin a tale of mystery and excitement. Just like the real Ann Oliver used to. I wondered if Ann really was in Paris with her Frenchman. Despite everything she'd said and done to me, I still wished her the best.

Ann Oliver was a prize-winning heifer. But knowing her had enriched my life in a way that I could not have accomplished on my own. Having so much confidence in myself now, even though it had been formed out of a mountain of fraud and deceit, made me realize how much more I wanted out of life. I decided that after all I'd been through, I deserved more than I had.

Anoseki refused to take his eyes off my face, but that didn't bother me. As a matter of fact, him being so attentive gave me even more confidence. "My job as a travel representative takes me all over the world." I sniffed and pressed my lips together as hard as I could to keep myself from drooling.

As far as I was concerned there was not a man in the club who could compete with Anoseki. There was no way I was going to bore a man like him with the truth. Even *I* didn't want to hear myself talk about my daddy's liquor store, the gritty neighborhood I lived in, my likes and dislikes, my dingbat friends. I didn't even want to admit that I was just a secretary at Bon Voyage who delivered interoffice mail, added toner to the fax machine, and organized potlucks.

"Then you must have visited my country, yes?" he asked with the wide-eyed eagerness of a child.

"Nigeria? Uh, not yet. But I think that's where I'll be going in a few weeks. We have to go check out new hotels, new clubs, things like that."

Anoseki gave me a stern look and shook his head. "I didn't mean Nigeria. I have not lived there for years."

"Oh, you mean Jamaica. Uh-huh. I've been there many times!"

The look on his face changed dramatically. Instead of a cheeky smile, he now had a hard penetrating look in his eyes. "I see." He swallowed hard, and kept his eyes glued to my face. "And where did you go in Jamaica?" I was beginning to feel like I was being interviewed, but it didn't matter. I'd been interviewed before.

"Uh, Kingston, Negril. By the way, where in Jamaica do you live?"

"I have a house in Montego Bay. You've been there, too?" There was a look of anticipation on his face.

I nodded. "Some interesting people live in Montego Bay." I cleared my throat and repeated a variation of a tale that Ann had shared during one of our insufferable staff meetings. "I had drinks with a toothless hooker and a ninety-year-old pimp tried to recruit me in Montego Bay." I laughed and was surprised that Anoseki didn't see the humor. His face now looked like it had turned to stone.

"Where is your family?" he asked, looking and acting too serious now. I was afraid that he was losing interest in me already. I had not seen his smile in a while. There was now a noticeable grimace on his face, like he'd bitten into a lemon.

"My parents are both retired lawyers. My younger sister died a few weeks ago. Leukemia," I managed, blinking back a tear.

"I am sorry to hear that." He slid a finger across his lip and turned to look across the room. "Will you excuse me for a moment, please?" Anoseki didn't wait for me to respond. He eased up and strode across the floor and disappeared. Freddie stumbled back to the table about a minute later, fanning her face with a napkin.

"I thought he'd never leave," she said, groaning as she fell back onto her seat. "I'm ready to go when you are, Trudy."

"Don't call me by that name!" I hissed. "Not tonight. Call me Ann," I pleaded, squeezing Freddie's hand.

She gave me a guarded look. "Is that the name you gave to your third-world Romeo?"

"Yes. That's the only name I will answer to tonight. I don't want a man like this one to find out what a . . . a . . ."

"You don't have to say it. I know what you are. What I don't know is, why you care what this man thinks? After tonight you won't ever see him again anyway."

"I know that," I said with a wicked smile creeping up on my face. "But if he finds out I'm lying, he might lose interest before the night is over and move on to another woman," I insisted.

Freddie rolled her eyes.

I gave her a surprised look. "I thought you were having a good time," I said in a whiny voice, giving her a desperate look.

"Yeah, but—"

"Then why do you want to leave?" I wailed, looking at my watch. "It's still early. I am just getting to know Anoseki." Bobbing my head along to the latest from Toni Braxton, I was feeling better than I'd felt all night.

Freddie gave me a look that was a combination of surprise and amusement. "Why, you skanky ho, you. I'm surprised you didn't follow him to wherever he went. He is coming back, then?"

"I hope so," I purred. "Why?" Alarmed, I looked around the club. "Did you see him leave or something?"

"No. But I passed him in the lobby on my way back from the ladies' room, and he was on the telephone fussing and cussing at somebody."

"Oh. What . . . what was he saying? Did it sound like he was talking to a woman?"

"All I heard was him using some cuss words and saying "I will take care of everything" to whoever he was talking to. Then he—why do you have that goofy look on your face all of a sudden?"

"Are you going home tonight?" I asked, suddenly feeling flustered and horny in a way that I'd never felt before. Not even when I was with that sexy pilot in Mexico.

"Of course I'm going home tonight. Where else would I go?"

"What about that guy you've been dancing with? You two looked awful cozy out there on that dance floor," I teased.

"Now you know me better than that. I got my man at home waiting on me—and he's the only man I want to share myself with. . . . I do not cheat on him, and he does not cheat on me . . . anymore. As a matter of fact, I know where he is at all times."

I sucked in my breath and bit my lip. "Freddie, the only women who know where their men are at all times are widows," I scoffed.

Freddie let out an exasperated sigh before she shot me a hot look. "Look, if you want to spend the night with Kunte Kinte, go on and do it. I can get home by myself," she snarled.

"He's on his way to London," I said with a heavy sigh.

"So?"

"Like you just said, I'll probably never see him again after tonight."

Freddie shrugged and waved her hand. "Girl, you don't have to explain a damn thing to me. What you do is your business. If you want to fuck that man, go spend the night with him and fuck his brains out so you can get it out of your system."

"He hasn't asked me to spend the night with him yet. If he does, I'll probably say yes. I just—hush! Change the subject. Here he comes!"

As if on cue, another man invited Freddie to join him on the dance floor just as Anoseki made it back to the table. For a woman who claimed she was ready to go home, she sure leaped out of her seat fast enough.

"Here we are again, my dear," Anoseki said with an unnecessary wink. I was glad to see that he was smiling again. There was a mysterious look in his eyes as he whispered, "I missed you . . ."

I told myself that if I did decide to go through with my plans to marry a dullard like James, a night of passion with Anoseki would be the best way to end my masquerade. All he had to do was ask.

"Ann, as you know, I am on my way to London. I must leave tomorrow noon. My dear, will you bless me by sharing the rest of this special night with me?" Anoseki asked. His strong hand gripped, massaged, and parted my trembling knees.

He didn't even allow me to answer. The next thing I knew, he slid his hand up under my dress and tapped my crotch a few times before he nodded toward the exit.

And I nodded back.

CHAPTER 72

"On his way to London, huh?" Freddie couldn't even wait for us to make it to the ladies' room after I beckoned her off the dance floor. She pulled me into a corner near the exit. "What does he do for a living?"

"I don't know," I admitted. I'd asked but he just laughed and kissed me on the neck.

One thing I never could figure out about the club scene was how some men, with women already on their arms, could still leer at other women. The same man who had been dancing up a storm with Freddie strolled past us, looking in our direction with a look on his face that you'd expect to see in a strip joint. The beauty queen that he was leading toward the exit made Freddie and me look like hound dogs. Freddie looked at me with a stunned look on her face. "I'm glad my man doesn't go to clubs often." She let out a sigh of defeat and shook her shoulders. "Anyway, you say your new friend is on his way to London?"

"That's right. He has to be on a plane tomorrow by noon. I'm sure I won't hear from him again, even if he ever does come back this way."

"Well, like I said, what you do is your business. I just . . . I don't feel right about this one."

"What's wrong with him?"

Freddie gave me a sorrowful look. "I didn't say anything was wrong with him. Other than him being a stranger, he seems fine." A dreamy look appeared on her face and she gave me a knowing smile. "And he looks good enough to eat . . . if you know what I mean." She winked and licked her lips. "If I were you, I guess I would go for it, too. A one-night stand is a one-night stand."

"Then why did you act like I was about to run off with the big bad wolf at first ? You are making me nervous."

Freddie made no attempt to hide her impatience. She snorted and stomped her foot. "Trudy, will you make up your mind and do what you have to do. Leave me out of this mess. It's getting late and I want to get home to my family," she whined, looking at her watch and then the exit

"I'm *Ann,* girl," I reminded her through clenched teeth. "Can't you remember to call me that just for the rest of tonight?"

Freddie threw up her hands and released a tired sigh. "Whatever. You go on and have a good time. Call me in the morning and tell me all about it, Miss Ann." Freddie paused and a wicked smile slid across her face. "I hope that big bulge in his crotch is a balled-up sock that he stuffed down his pants. That's how LoBo got my attention."

I pinched Freddie's arm. "You go on home, you nasty heifer," I scolded. It was almost two in the morning, and the club was about to close. I gave Freddie a dismissive hug. "You all right to drive? I can charge you a room somewhere until you sober up."

Freddie shook her head and gave me a hug, squeezing so hard she almost cut off my breath. She leaned back and looked at my face so long and hard it made me apprehensive.

Somehow, I managed a smile anyway. "Calm down, girl. Don't behave like I'm about to go to the moon. I'm just going off for a few hours with a gorgeous Nigerian." I let out a hesitant chuckle. "He might be so bad—and quick— in the bedroom, I might make it home before you do."

"Let's just hope that a bad lover is the worst thing he is," Freddie said in a distant voice, making me feel eerie all over again. I had almost forgotten about the fraud investigator who had called me up earlier.

"Go on home, girl. Don't say another word," I ordered. "The more you say, the more nervous I get. If you don't leave now, I'll lose my nerve," I muttered, hoping Freddie would take my advice.

She gave me another hug, then she turned to leave, dragging her feet like she was disabled. Before she could reach the exit, an anxious man grabbed her by the arm. She shook her head vigorously and pulled away, waving to me as she trotted out the door.

Before I could move from my spot and return to the table, Anoseki appeared, holding my shawl. "Shall we go now, m' lady?" he asked. The corners of his mouth curled up into a broad smile as he draped my shawl around my shoulders. The light in the lobby area was brighter. Anoseki was not as flawless as he'd appeared to be in the dim light inside the club. His skin was not as smooth as I thought it was. His eyes seemed unusually dark. Not just a normal shade of black like mine and a lot of other people of African decent, but a shade of black so deep that there was no sparkle. And, I noticed, he didn't blink as often as most people. It was almost like he had the eyes of a dead man. If that didn't concern me enough, some disturbing scars on his forehead did. I had read an article somewhere about how some males in Africa had to go through a scarification ritual after they reached a certain age. I decided it was a tribal procedure that had to do with some rite of passage; therefore, it was nothing for me to worry about.

I dismissed the thoughts going through my mind, focusing my attention on something more positive. Like that nice bulge in Anoseki's pants. I didn't like to lie to Freddie, but whether Anoseki was good in bed or not, I had already decided to tell her that he was the best. That was the only way I knew how to keep Freddie from riding my back with an "I told you so" comment.

"What hotel are you staying in?" I asked, wrapping my arm around Anoseki's narrow waist as we exited the club. He wasted no time showing me that he was the kind of man who liked to be in charge. He removed my arm from around him, then looped his around my shoulder and guided me, plowing his way through the crowd blocking the exit.

"Ow! I hate hotels! They are too impersonal!" he hollered. He rubbed his chin and snorted. "You do have a place to yourself, yes?"

I nodded. "Uh-huh. But it's nothing fancy, see. Just a little studio apartment with the bare necessities. It's not far from here. I'm staying there because the . . . uh . . . condo I just purchased is currently being refurbished."

He pulled me closer and whispered. "Your studio has a bed, hmmm?"

I giggled. "Yes." I giggled some more. "And two bottles of wine in the refrigerator."

"Good! I give thanks. That's all we need!" he yelled, squeezing my waist. I didn't want to say it out loud, but I also kept a big supply of condoms at the studio.

I was led like a sheep to a black SUV with a sticker from a rental agency on the front window. After Anoseki asked directions to my apartment, he ignored me all the way there, even though I had my hand on his thigh the whole time. I could not believe that he was the same man who had swept me off my feet at the club. I blamed his fickle behavior on some cultural thing. What did I know about Nigerians? Nothing. But that didn't matter tonight.

I had seen a lot of romantic movies, and read a few romance novels. Whoever wrote that fluff had to believe in fairy tales, too. Things between a man and a woman rarely went as smoothly as some folks tried to make it sound. As soon as we entered my secret apartment and right after I flipped on the light, the man was all over me like a cheap wig. I wondered why he had bothered to ask if I had a bed. With the couch-bed already let out, he still shoved me toward the La-Z-Boy facing the couch-bed and bent me over the back of it. He slid my dress up to my waist, snatched my thong panties down to my knees and plunged in and out of me so fast I almost fell after he released me. I was stunned beyond belief. I was relieved to see a condom dangling off his thick, but short dick.

"Where is the loo?" Anoseki asked in a gruff voice.

"The what?"

"Rest . . . room is what you call it here," he said impatiently.

I nodded toward the area near the kitchenette. He gave me a quick nod and rushed out of the room. The walls in the apartment were thin. Not only did I hear him flush the toilet, I heard him talking on his cell phone. His conversation was not in English, so it didn't matter what I heard. I rolled my eyes, recalling how the sexy Mexican I'd spent the night with in Puerto Vallarta had called up his wife right after he'd made love to me.

By the time Anoseki returned, I had filled two glasses with wine, removed my clothes and stretched out on the bed on top of the covers.

"Is everything all right?" I asked, sitting up with a breast in each hand and a seductive look in my face.

Instead of answering, Anoseki marched over to me with one hand inside his jacket.

"If you do as you are told you will not be hurt," he grumbled.

"What . . . what do you mean?" In a split second fear consumed me. I swung my legs to the side of the bed. Before I could rise to my feet, he was in front of me pointing a gun in my face.

CHAPTER 73

I rarely talked about what had happened to me that day in Daddy's liquor store, but that incident was often on my mind. Just two nights ago I had a nightmare where my assailant had attacked me again. This time it was in my own bedroom and the shape of the birthmark on his face had changed from a half-moon to a dagger. Though my current situation was different I still felt like I had worked myself into the same position: my life was at stake again.

"My purse is over there," I croaked, pointing to the counter next to my sink. "I . . . I don't have much money."

"Listen, the games are over. I was sent to retrieve what you took and I will not leave without it," Anoseki said in a voice so smooth I thought he was joking.

"What do you mean? I just met you tonight. What do you mean you were sent? Sent by who? Sent from where and for what?"

"Look, lady. I have a job to do and I intend to complete it. You give me what you took and I leave immediately. Where is it?" He shook his fist and waved the gun so close to my nose I had to breathe through my mouth. "One million dollars is what you stole. I want it and I want it now! Or you will suffer in a million ways."

My eyes burned and a huge lump formed in my throat that almost choked the life out of me. It looked like I was going to die one way or the other. "I don't know what you are talking about. I don't have a million dollars. *I'm just a secretary.*"

Anoseki, the man I'd envisioned as my own personal knight in shining armor, slapped me so hard my face felt like it was on fire. "Bah! Where is it? Where is the money, woman?" he roared, looking around the room. His eyes alone were enough to scare the daylights out of me. Long, jagged red lines outlined his dilated pupils. His eyebrows merged and wiggled like one long, angry worm. "Where did you hide it?" Snake eyes. That was what his eyes looked like now.

"I don't know what you are talking about," I whimpered, holding the side of my head. The gun was still dangerously close to my face. My eyes felt like they were on fire as I blinked to look at him. "What makes you think I have that kind of money?"

"You stupid woman! I was told that you were a smart lady, but you are just like all the rest. A fool. You parade yourself around until some weak man mounts you so you can take advantage of him. Well, you've been mounted enough. Giles was a fool to involve himself with an American woman!"

"Oh, my God!" I shrieked so hard my tongue felt like it had frozen. "You think—you think I'm Ann Oliver! I spoke to that Mr. Giles several times."

"You did more than that for Giles, you cocksucking tart. It was because of your intimate talents, and his foolishness, that he thought he could trust you with his money! Now we know."

It took me a moment to realize that the cackling laugh I heard was coming from me. "I'm not Ann. I was just pretending to be her. See— I used her information to get credit cards and this apartment in her name! I was going to stop it all—"

"Don't play games with me, too!" Anoseki sprinted across the floor, leaping over an overturned end table with the grace of an antelope. He grabbed my purse, fishing out my wallet. He flipped to the fake driver's license bearing Ann Oliver's name and my picture. "Do you think I'm stupid?" Then he let out a weird laugh. He whipped out his own wallet and flipped to a picture of Ann wearing the same hairdo I had my hair in now. The resemblance was remarkable.

"Uh, she's older than I am. Can't you see that? Her nose is larger than mine," I cried, pointing to the picture. And look at the teeth— her teeth are smaller!" I lifted my head, clenched my teeth, and spread my lips open as wide as I could with my fingers.

"If you die tonight, it makes no difference to me. I will still get paid," he told me in a dead calm voice.

"Would you really kill me? Do you think you can get away with it?"

"Look, lady, this is nothing new to me. Don't flatter yourself by thinking that you are the first . . ."

I was spellbound. It felt like my spirit had separated from my body and was floating along the wall witnessing the latest nightmare I'd stumbled into.

Freddie's face flashed through my mind. "I know!" I shouted, waving both hands. "The woman who was with me tonight—she'll tell you my real name. She's known me most of my life," I hollered. I scrambled from the bed and ran to the telephone with Anoseki right behind me. I was so terrified I couldn't even remember Freddie's number. When I finally got it right Freddie's answering machine came on. "Freddie, if you hear me, please pick up the telephone. Please pick up, Freddie!"

The last thing I wanted to do was piss on myself again. But that's exactly what I did when Freddie answered because I was just that happy to hear her voice. "What's up?" she asked, sounding half asleep.

"Freddie, listen carefully. I want you to tell someone who I really am." I handed the telephone to Anoseki as I hopped from one foot to the other with urine still streaming down my legs.

He listened for a few moments with a cold expression on his face. After a few grunts, he said, "She *is* Ann Oliver, you say?" he said, nodding with a pronounced frown on his face. "I know she is. I thank you very much."

I grabbed the telephone. "Freddie, tell him the truth! Ann fucked up in Jamaica with that Mr. Giles I told you about and he sent Anoseki up here to take care of the problem. She stole a million dollars from these people!"

"Girl, what in the world is going on over there!" Freddie yelled.

"You have to tell this man that my name is Trudy. Tell him how I was using Ann's name! He's got a gun!"

"Shit! Put him back on the telephone!" Freddie screamed. I handed the telephone back to Anoseki. It didn't matter what Freddie told him. He grunted and hung the telephone up and grabbed me around my throat anyway.

"She is your friend and she lies for you now," he said, glaring at me. "She's a fool, too." He slapped me again. This time so hard I stumbled back to the bed where he beat me so savagely about my face I passed out.

I don't know how long I was unconscious but when I came to he was standing over me with that gun in his hand. "You want to tell me where the money is now?" He glanced at his watch. "Your time is running out, m'lady."

"I swear to God. I don't know anything about any money. I've never been to Jamaica. Why don't you call that Mr. Giles and let me speak to him. He'll remember me," I bleated.

"Giles is a busy man. He has no more time to waste with you."

"Freddie's probably calling the cops right now. Please go and leave me alone," I whimpered, forcing myself to remain focused on staying alive. It was hard for me to speak with a busted lip and a few loose teeth.

Anoseki nodded and caressed his chin. "I go, you go with me," he said, pulling me off the bed. He tossed my clothes at me but I just stood there holding them and shaking like a leaf. "Hurry, or I will shoot you down like a mad dog right now and leave you to fester! Go!"

I got into my clothes somehow, putting my dress on backwards and my shoes on the wrong feet. In less than five minutes he was pushing me out the door.

Just as we got to the parking lot, a familiar car drove up and stopped right in front of us. It was Daddy's car. As much as I resented "Old Bessie," I was never so glad to see that piece of junk before in my life. All four doors swung open, each one with a piercing squeak. Out tumbled Freddie, LoBo, Daddy, Spider, and James.

CHAPTER 74

"Trudy, what in the hell is gwine on here!" Daddy hollered. At the mention of my real name, Anoseki let go of my arm. The alcohol that I had consumed at the club was threatening to erupt out of my mouth. There was a lot of confusion going on, but a howling dog somewhere in the distance distracted me. It was an ominous wail and it made the current situation seem even more sinister. That distraction gave me enough time to pull my senses together long enough to keep from throwing up.

"Daddy, he's got a gun!" I shouted. Everything in front of my eyes suddenly seemed distorted. Daddy's face seemed unusually long and painfully sad. I felt so light-headed I thought I was going to faint and would have if I had not been so concerned about my daddy. With my legs wobbling and the foul taste of bile in my mouth, I looked Anoseki in the eyes and cried, "Please don't hurt my daddy. He had nothing to do with this."

Anoseki stomped his foot on the ground and muttered something under his breath in a language I did not recognize. Then he threw his head back and laughed. I doubt if it had anything to do with the fact that he was amused. He abruptly stopped laughing and looked at me with enough contempt in his eyes for five people.

"You miserable trollop!" he barked, grabbing my arm again, gripping it much harder now.

"Where the fuck is the damn cops I called?" Freddie screamed, looking frantically around the darkened parking lot. "Get your black hands off my friend!" she continued, pummeling Anoseki's back. As soon as he dropped the gun, James and Spider wrestled him to the ground. For a man who had already started to let himself go, James was reasonably strong. Spider was fairly strong for a man his age. Daddy, rubbing his chest and gasping for breath, was stumbling around more than I was. Anoseki bucked and reared like a wild stallion until James went flying one way and Spider went the other.

Anoseki retrieved his gun and aimed it at me. "There is no place you can go where I won't find you again," he vowed. With a maniacal grin, he waved his gun at me again. Then he ran to his vehicle and shot out of the parking lot like a missile.

James scrambled up from the ground and ran to me, brushing off his clothes. For a minute that seemed like an hour, he just stared at me. The pain in his eyes was tremendous. I had never felt more contrite in my life.

James's lips moved silently for a few seconds. It seemed like the harder he tried to speak, the harder it was for him to get his words out. All he could produce was gibberish. After several attempts he finally managed to speak coherently. "Trudy, what in the hell did you get yourself into? Why?" In all the years that I'd known James, I'd never seen him so horrified, confused, and hurt. He didn't even sound like himself. His voice was weak and hoarse, and so low I could barely hear him.

"I don't know," I sobbed, tears gushing out of my swollen eyes. "That Nigerian, he thought I was this other woman. He beat me. He thought I stole some money."

"It sounds like you stole more than money!" Daddy yelled, shaking a fist in my face.

"I didn't steal any money from him! It was the other woman!" I sniffed. "I . . . I was just trying to have some fun."

"Fun? Is this what you call fun, gal?" Daddy's words flew out of his mouth like rocks. "From what Freddie told us, you cooked up a lot more than that!" Daddy shouted. "I oughta whup your behind myself! Girl, don't you know you can go to jail for what you done?"

I looked at Freddie with my mouth hanging open. The look she gave me told me more than I wanted to know. She had exposed my crime to the last people in the world I wanted to know.

"Let's go inside and sort this mess out," Freddie suggested. LoBo, still silent, stood off to the side looking like he wanted to crawl into a very deep hole.

As soon as we all made it into my apartment, James, Daddy, and Spider started looking around the room. LoBo, who had been to the apartment before, went straight to the refrigerator and snatched out a beer.

"Trudy, I had to tell them everything," Freddie said, standing in the middle of the floor with her arms folded. She had a trench coat on over a long white nightgown. "I'm sorry. They know it all. They know every detail. The gifts you bought me, the trips to Reno, Mexico. Everything. It was the only thing I could do."

My face felt like it had been left out on the beach and burned by the sun. Every time I blinked, a sharp pain shot through my eyes, making me see colored auras around all the people in front of me.

"If I had known you'd get yourself into a mess like this, I never would have helped you get that shit in that other woman's name," LoBo said, wiping beer from his lips. "Brother Bell, James, Trudy didn't stir up all this mess by herself. I helped her get them credit cards," LoBo confessed, looking from Daddy to James.

"Logan Botrelle, I hope you proud of your part in this mess," Daddy scolded before he turned on Freddie. "And, Freddie Ann, I know you had more to do with this than you ownin' up to, gal!"

Freddie dropped her head and sniffed, then looked at me. "I *did* try to talk some sense into Trudy. I tried to talk her out of all this a long time ago." I couldn't get mad with Freddie because she was telling the truth.

"James, I'm sorry," I whimpered. James looked at me like he was seeing me for the first time. I couldn't imagine what was going through his head. Spider, the last person in the world I expected to rescue me, looked amused. "Spider, thanks for coming to help . . ." "Oh, this kind of shit ain't nothin' new to me. But if you want some advice, I suggest you choose your future men friends a little more carefully, darlin'." Spider waved his hand and laughed. It was the most he had ever said to me at one time.

"That ain't all she ought to do!" Daddy snapped, rubbing his chest some more, still looking around the apartment. "What possessed you to do such a foolish thing as this?" He waved his hand around the room. "What did you hope to gain by posin' as this other woman? What was you tryin' to prove, gal?"

I ignored Daddy and looked at James. He shook his head and turned away. "James, we can talk about this when we get alone. I'll explain everything." I was shaking so hard one of the teeth that Anoseki's fist had loosened popped out of my mouth and rolled across the floor like a loose coin.

"I thought I knew you, Trudy. I guess I was wrong," James said, his eyes following my runaway tooth, his voice cracking. "You had me fooled, too."

"We better get out of here before that motherfucker come back," LoBo said, looking nervously toward the door.

"That's the best thing I done heard all night," Daddy said, coughing and moving toward the door.

James drove with Daddy in the front passenger seat fussing all the way, repeating the same things he had already said.

I occupied the backseat, squeezed between Spider and LoBo, who held Freddie on his lap. She patted my knee and gave me an awkward embrace. "I'm glad this is all over. I knew it was going to end like this . . . or worse."

My right eye was swollen shut. I closed the other one, too. And kept it that way all the way home.

CHAPTER 75

James stopped the car in front of his apartment building. He mumbled something to Daddy then he climbed out without a word or even a glance in my direction.

"James, I'll call you tomorrow. We can talk," I yelled after him. But he didn't respond. He sprinted across the ground to his front door without even looking back. That was the last time I saw him.

Daddy got in the driver's seat and we drove Freddie and LoBo to their apartment in silence.

"Be cool, Trudy," LoBo said, giving me a thumbs-up as he exited the car pulling Freddie by the arm.

"Call me tomorrow," Freddie told me, blinking hard before the car pulled off. The streetlights behind her provided enough light for me to see the pain in her eyes. I knew she felt bad about having to "betray" me by dragging Daddy and James into this situation. But had it not been for her, Anoseki probably would have killed me. I knew that after tonight, my friendship with Freddie would never be the same again.

Daddy was still rubbing his chest off and on. Spider had to drive the rest of the way home.

"Dude, you might want to get some medical attention," Spider said, climbing out of the car.

"I don't need no doctor!" Daddy snapped, snatching me out of the car by my arm. Once we got in the house he just looked at me and shook his head. "Gal, I'm fin to get in the bed and try to get some sleep. You can make a po'lice report in the mornin'."

"I'm not involving the cops in this, Daddy," I said in a feeble voice.

Daddy stopped in the middle of the living room floor and gasped so hard he had to cough. "That foreigner beat you half to death."

"I'm fine," I sobbed, rubbing my sore face. "I just want to put this behind me."

"Well you got a whole lot of mess to put behind you. What you plannin' on sayin' to that other woman? This Ann." Daddy placed his hands on his hips and glared at me.

"She's gone, Daddy. She left the country and I have a feeling she won't be coming back anytime soon."

"That don't excuse what you done. How much money we talkin' about here?"

"I don't know for sure. A few thousand dollars."

Daddy moaned and rubbed his head. "What about that apartment? What you gwine to do about that furniture and whatnot?"

"The furniture goes with the apartment. I'll have Freddie go with me to get my few clothes from it. Then I'll mail the keys back to the landlord. The rent's paid for the month, and that's all he'll ever need to know."

Daddy groaned and muttered under his breath. "If I was James, I wouldn't have nothin' else to do with you and your connivin' self. Folks always said you was just like your dead uncle Pete. He was as crooked as a dog's hind leg, too."

"Daddy, please let me clean myself up and get to bed. We can talk about this in the morning."

"I ain't got nothin' else to say about this mess, because I don't know what else to say. You just better figure out what you gwine to say when them credit card folks come knockin'. You don't pay them debts you done run up, they will put you up under the jailhouse."

"Good night, Daddy." I ran to the bathroom and threw up all over the floor. While I was still puking, Daddy eased open the door.

"Put this on your eye to help the swellin'," he said, handing me an ice pack. "Uh, I'll go to the bank first thing Monday mornin' and draw out that insurance money."

"What?"

Daddy looked so old, hurt, and tired. That made me feel even worse. He was the last person I wanted to disappoint. "The money that I was gwine to give you and James toward the down payment on a house that y'all been savin' up for. It'll help pay off some of them charges."

"You don't have to do that, Daddy. I'll pay off those debts somehow."

Daddy gave me a warm smile and a look that made me feel completely redeemed. "It's your money anyway. I'd rather see you stay out of jail instead of in a new house. Besides, this house'll be yours once I'm gone." I was amazed when Daddy chuckled because I knew he was still angry and he had every right to be. "I don't know about James, but you still my girl . . ."

CHAPTER 76

As late as it was, I knew that I would not be going to sleep anytime soon. Curled up in my bed, still in the clothes that could have been my shroud, aching from head to toe, I had a lot to think about. The fact that I could now hear another dog howling out on the street that sounded just like the one I'd heard in the parking lot during the tussle with Anoseki, kept me from getting too comfortable.

Paying off the massive bills that I had racked up was the least of my concerns. Staying alive was more important. I had no way of knowing if Anoseki was out of the picture. If he had the resources to find me once, there was the possibility that he could do it again. Calling the police was out of the question. There was no way I could tell the cops what had happened without digging a deep hole for myself, too. By posing as Ann and forging her name I'd committed a crime. How the banks would handle it, I didn't know. I knew that I could buy myself some time and hopefully stay out of jail if I quietly paid them off. It just broke my heart to know that the money Daddy had held onto for so many years for my first house would now be used to pay for my greed and foolishness. I didn't know how I was going to repair my relationship with Daddy.

Even with the ice pack, my eye throbbed so hard I couldn't cry anymore without writhing in pain. I ignored the pain and cried until I couldn't cry anymore.

One thing I did know was that I could not return to work at Bon Voyage. As serious as the situation was I almost laughed when I thought about all the stories Wendy and Pam would come up with when I called to resign on Monday. And to keep from having to look at their nosy, gloating faces, I didn't even plan to go back to pick up any of my personal effects. What pay I had coming I'd have Wendy mail to me.

I couldn't believe how things had turned out! In a strange way Ann got the last laugh on me again anyway. Trying to be her had almost cost me my life. Annie Lou Oliver. She was even more of a mystery now. My curiosity was burning a hole in my brain. I wondered about that sister; where she was and what she was doing. And, I wondered if Mr. Giles and Anoseki would ever find her.

It was hard for me to believe what Ann had been accused of. Then it all made sense. Somewhere along the line, during one of her frequent trips to Jamaica, she'd been sucked into something she could only get out of by running away. My guess was that Mr. Giles was a big time criminal in the islands. He was probably dealing drugs, weapons, and whatever else men like him did to get rich.

A million dollars was a lot of money. How did Ann get her hands on it? Was she supposed to hide it or deliver it to launderers or something? It was no wonder Mr. Giles had tried to reach her so many times. I really wanted to know exactly what this woman had done that almost got me killed. I had taken so many messages from Mr. Giles that I had memorized his telephone number. But calling him, even to clear myself, was out of the question. I knew that unless Ann told me herself, I would probably never know all the facts. And as long as I was out of danger, I could live with that.

I glanced at the picture of my mother on my nightstand, wondering how my life would have turned out had she not been on that doomed plane. "Mama, Daddy did the best he could raising me, but I still made a fool of myself. I chased away a good man, too . . ." I whispered. "I am so sorry."

I didn't wait until morning to call James. I dialed his number as soon as I composed myself, now gazing at the picture of him next to Mama's. He didn't sound surprised to hear my voice.

"Trudy, I could never forgive you or trust you again. How many other men were you involved with? Huh? Were you laughing at me behind my back?"

"James, I'm sorry. I will never hurt you like this again."

"You got that right. I won't give you another chance to."

"Are you telling me it's over?"

James cursed under his breath. "Do I need to tell you it's over? There is not a man in his right mind who would overlook what you did. And I have a feeling there's more to this drama than what I found out tonight. Those retreats you claim your job sent you to, the lame excuses about where you went with Freddie, what you did, all of it was a lie. Wasn't it?"

"No matter where I went, what I did, and with who, I loved you and I still do."

"Mmmm-huh. I bet you do. You loved me enough to risk passing on some disease to me?"

"Now wait a minute! I never exposed myself to any disease! I would never do that to you. I'm not stupid."

"Trudy, listen to yourself. You don't even know what you are. But you know what? I do. You are nothing but a lying, whoring, hoochie mama. Just like my mama said you were. I wasted almost eleven years of my life fooling around with you. I could do a lot better and I plan to."

"So that's it. I don't get a second chance? We can't be lovers anymore?" I said, my voice cracking so hard it felt like I had a Jawbreaker rolling around in my mouth. "After ten years?" It was amazing how hard I was trying to hold onto James now.

"What! And it was ten years too long! Lovers? What— We can't even be friends now!" James boomed. His words hit me like a ton of bricks and I deserved every bit of the pain. "Now if you don't mind, I'd like to get some sleep. It's been a busy night."

"James, I am sorry. I really wish that you would let me make this up to you."

"Good night, Trudy. And good-bye!" James slammed the telephone down so hard I heard an echo.

I let out a sigh that was so strong it blew the hair off my face.

CHAPTER 77

I don't know what time I finally dozed off but when I woke up the next morning I could smell breakfast cooking. The aroma of bacon was so strong it made my eyes water. As I lay in the middle of my bed, wrapped and curled up among my covers like a caterpillar, I could hear Daddy banging pots and pans in the kitchen.

"Spider's gwine to help out at the store by hisself today. I'll stay close to the house in case that African tracks you down here," Daddy told me as soon as I entered the kitchen in a bathrobe that barely covered my see-through nightgown. "Them Africans is naturally sharp like foxes. They can track better than a bloodhound because of them bushes they grew up in. I got something for that jungle bunny if he shows up around here," Daddy said, lifting a butcher knife off the table.

"How are you feelin' today, princess?" Spider asked, waving to me from the kitchen table where a plate of grits with all the trimmings sat in front of him. Spider had never said anything inappropriate to me. But this morning his eyes roamed all over my body, forcing me to secure the belt around my housecoat and then button it up to my chin.

"My eye feels like a mule kicked it, but other than that, I'm fine," I muttered, pouring myself a much needed cup of coffee. "What happened to Mr. Clarke? He doesn't help out at the store at all anymore?"

"Yeah, Clarke closes for me now. Spider just got laid off from his job, so he need the money. Besides, he a lot more dependable than Clarke," Daddy explained.

"I . . . I can help out again," I said humbly.

Daddy looked at Spider, then at me. "What about your job at that travel place?"

I shook my head. "I won't be going back," I said. Daddy looked from Spider to me again. "That Nigerian and the man who sent him might visit Bon Voyage looking for Ann. It would be a disaster if I was there," I said meekly. "Everybody would know what I've done."

"Well, if any of them dudes come out here to mess with you again, they got me and my boys to deal with," Spider said, waving his fist in the air. I couldn't believe how much he had to say to me now. "My daughter had a nasty little problem a few years ago when I lived in Oakland. I took care of him, too. Permanently."

I smiled and returned to my room with my coffee. Freddie was the next person I needed to call up and talk to. "I didn't mean to drag you and LoBo into my mess. But thanks for being there last night," I said, clutching the telephone.

"That's what friends are for. How's James this morning?" Freddie asked, breathing hard into the telephone. LoBo was in bed next to her so she didn't have to tell me why she was breathing so hard.

"It's over," I croaked. "Everything is over. I am not going back to Bon Voyage."

"I'm glad to hear that." Freddie snorted and cleared her throat. "Now, don't you take this the wrong way, but that job was your downfall. None of this shit would have happened if it wasn't for that Bon Voyage."

"Uh-uh. It wasn't the job that made me do what I did. It was me."

"You need some help, girl. You need some professional help," Freddie suggested.

"I know that, too," I snapped.

"Listen, these kids of mine are tearing the house down. I'll call you later."

"I'll be here," I replied, rubbing my throbbing eye. Even though my vision was blurred, I refused to go have a doctor look at my eye. I didn't want anybody else to know that I'd been hit by a man I hardly knew.

I stayed in my room the rest of the weekend with an ice pack on my eye, nibbling on a piece of whatever Daddy brought into my room. As soon as Monday morning rolled around I called Wendy at the office.

"I've decided not to return to Bon Voyage," I said sharply, speaking so fast it sounded like one long word.

"Why?" Wendy gasped and cursed under her breath. "Shit, girl. Don't tell me you running off to get married, too."

"I'd rather not say why I'm quitting," I said firmly. "Just let Mr. Rydell know. Tell him I appreciate him letting me work there. I enjoyed it and I learned a lot. And tell everybody else I enjoyed working with them, too."

"Well, can't you tell me why you are quitting?"

"Something came up, Wendy," I snapped. "It's a personal matter and I'd rather not talk about it."

"Shoot. Well, I hope you will come back for my potluck baby shower that Pam's throwing in a few months. It's supposed to be a surprise but I overheard her talking to Lupe about it this morning in the ladies' room."

"Congratulations," I mumbled, forcing the word out. "I just might do that, Wendy." I knew I wouldn't. I didn't have anything against Wendy or Pam or anybody else at Bon Voyage. However, I knew that it would be better for me if I removed everything from my life that was connected to what had happened to me. "I have to go now, Wendy."

"You will come to pick up your last check, won't you? What about that picture of your fiancé on your desk?"

"You can mail me my last paycheck. You can toss that picture of James into the trash can."

Wendy gasped again, this time much louder. I could imagine the look on her face. "I knew it. He dumped you, didn't he? And you're depressed. I was the same way when I broke up with Daryl. But don't you worry. You'll find somebody much better. I did. You remember Mark from the bank next door, don't you? He proposed last night."

"That's nice, Wendy. Be good to him."

"Uh, he even knows that this is not his baby. It's Daryl's. But Mark said it didn't matter. He said to me, 'your kids are my kids,' and he meant it."

"Be good to Mark, Wendy. You got yourself a good man. I'm sure he's going to treat you like a queen." I sighed, trying to keep the sarcasm out of my voice.

I knew that my comment went right over Wendy's head. The truth was, I was happy for her and I wished her all the best. In her own way Wendy had been good to me and that was one thing that I would not take for granted. Then, all of a sudden, Wendy's feelings didn't matter to me anymore. I had to say what I felt. "No wonder you White girls are so spoiled."

Sadly, that comment went right over Wendy's head, too. She didn't even respond to it. Instead, she rambled on for another fifteen minutes about how great her life was and how I could change mine if I "applied myself." What she meant by that, I didn't know and didn't care enough to ask.

I didn't feel guilty about interrupting Wendy. "Wendy, I hate to cut you off, but I have to go now." I hung up before she could say another word.

day driving a cab four nights a week. I still owed a huge amount of money to the credit card companies, even after I'd applied the entire ten thousand dollars from the insurance money that Daddy gave me. But if I lived long enough, everything would eventually be paid in full.

A month later Freddie married LoBo and they moved to L.A. Just like I'd predicted, our friendship took a dramatic turn because of what I'd done. I hardly heard from my girl anymore. She'd been gone for two weeks before she called.

"I'm seeing a therapist," I told her.

"It's about time." She laughed. "I was praying for you to get some professional help."

"Well, you can keep praying. I'm *dating* a therapist," I explained. "I met him in the cafeteria at South Bay General when I went to get my eye checked out last week. Roy Middleton."

"Never heard of him."

"He moved here from Fresno. And, before you even ask, he knows everything about me."

"Everything?"

"Everything. He dragged a skeleton out of his closet, too. He told me that if he hadn't cheated on exams all through college, he wouldn't be where he is now. He didn't even try to pass judgment on me."

"My daddy always said we'll all reside in a glass house at least once in our lifetime. He's been straight ever since he got caught collecting unemployment and working at the same time. There are and always will be somebody doing something a lot worse than what you did. And don't think I don't feel guilty for accepting all the stuff you gave me. I just wish I'd have been more of a real friend and slapped some sense into that head of yours. I knew that what you were doing was going to end up a big mess."

"Well, it's all behind us now. I wish I hadn't hurt Daddy and James so much, though."

"Speaking of James; remember Sarah from the beauty shop? She wrote me last week and told me she ran into James and his new squeeze at the mall. They were holding hands and acting like a couple of kids."

"That's nice. Girlfriend, I'd love to sit and chat with you for a while, but I have to go. Roy's on his way to pick me up for dinner."

Roy was a therapist, and *did* give me professional advice on almost

CHAPTER 78

It had been two months since my night of terror in the apartment I'd rented in Ann Oliver's name.

Freddie did some snooping around and shared some interesting information with me. She had a friend in the credit card department at the bank where she worked who got her a copy of Ann's credit report. It listed all of the credit cards that I'd obtained as well as a few that Ann had had for years.

Ann had not made any payments on her legitimate cards, her condo, or her BMW since her abrupt departure from Bon Voyage! If I had chosen not to pay off what I'd racked up, I probably could have gotten away with what I'd done. But I'd made too many bad choices already. It was time for me to do the right thing.

I resumed my position behind the counter at Daddy's liquor store ringing up lottery tickets, spirits, gum, and cigarettes. With Spider working full time for Daddy now, and being behind the counter the same time as me, I felt safe. It helped for him to maintain a fierce scowl on his face and keep his Harley parked out front. The thugs and would-be thugs avoided us. I was glad that Daddy finally had a security camera installed. I was confident that we wouldn't be getting robbed anytime soon.

Daddy couldn't afford to pay me the kind of salary that I'd earned at Bon Voyage and I didn't want him to. I made a few more dollars a every one of our dates. Tonight was no different. "The trauma of losing your mom, your brother, and your uncle all so close together had a lot to do with what you did. It impaired your ability to know right from wrong. You were crying out for help and attention," he told me. We occupied a booth at Kincaids, a seafood restaurant in Oakland. "You risked losing a lot more by your actions. Identity theft is a serious offense. You did the right thing by paying off some of those banks." Roy had a receding hairline and blunt features. However, he was a man with a beautiful soul and that was what I needed in my life for a change.

"It seems like I'll be paying the rest of them from now on," I said seriously.

"The important thing is, you've learned your lesson." Roy dropped his gold American Express card on the table when the waiter brought the bill. A strange look came over his face. He glanced at me, then his card. He plucked the card off the table and slid it back into his wallet and replaced it with a hundred dollar bill. He gave me a thoughtful look before he laughed.

I laughed too. I knew what he was thinking. "You don't have to worry about me stealing anything from you or anybody else," I assured him.

"I hope not," he told me.

CHAPTER 79

Ididn't know that I was going to miss James as much as I did. He had
been in my life for a long time. Not enough time had passed yet for
me to put him out of my mind completely. I had strong feelings for
Roy and I was pleased that Daddy approved of him. I didn't know if
Roy was going to be the man that I spent the rest of my life with, but
he suited me for the time being. He was always there for me when I
needed him. Like when Daddy dropped the next bombshell on me.

"Sadie's grandson's dead," he announced. I had not heard him
open the door to my room. "And he was the only one in the bunch
she thought would amount to somethin'." Daddy pushed my bedroom door all the way open and shuffled into my room. I had just
come in from my date with Roy and still had my clothes on.

"What happened?" I asked, swinging my legs to the side of the bed.
I had been in my room for about half an hour, just going over my
thoughts.

"Kenny's dead."

I went from being groggy to being wide awake within a matter of
seconds. "Kenny? Isn't he the 'good' one?"

"*Was.* Listen, I'm fin to go out to Sadie's house," Daddy said. He
looked away and blew his nose into a large white handkerchief. "Poor
Sadie. Now she done lost all three of them young'ns. Them other two
that's in jail, they good as dead."

"Do you want me to go with you?"

Daddy held up his hands. "Naw, baby. You stay home for now. But I would appreciate it if you'd honor Sadie by going to the boy's funeral. It's just a cryin' shame that the first time you see Kenny is at his funeral."

"Of course I'll be there, Daddy. That poor woman. What happened to Kenny? Was he in an accident?" I yawned and rubbed my eyes.

"I wish it was somethin' like that. Like I told you more than once, there was somethin' about the boy that I didn't trust. He was sneaky and evil. I could see it in his eyes. I never told Sadie, but somethin' told me the boy was gwine to come to a bad end one of these days." Daddy looked at the floor and shook his head, rubbing his neck and moaning. "He fell in with a bad crowd, and they went and tried to rob somebody."

"Oh." I sighed.

"Like I told Sadie, you live by the sword, you die by the sword."

"You said he *tried* to rob somebody. Do you mean to tell me that the person he robbed is the one who killed him?"

Daddy nodded. "And who would have thought it'd be one of them little old Vietnamese gals runnin' a nail shop. That gal had been robbed one time too many so this time she was *packin'*. She was ready." Daddy whistled and started to walk away. "That gal grabbed a sawed-off shotgun and blowed half that boy's head off. Hallelujah! Don't wait up for me. I got a feelin' Sadie'll want me to stay the night and go with her to the morgue in the mornin' to identify that boy." I knew that Daddy was thinking about the day that he had to go to the morgue to identify my brother's body. He had made the horrific trip alone and had come home looking like a dead man himself. "That ain't nothin' nobody need to go through alone."

The boy's name was Kenneth Leroy Freeman. He was eighteen years old. Because of the damage the shotgun had done to his face, it was a closed-casket funeral. His high school graduation picture, in a silver frame, sat on top of his casket in the church, which was filled wall to wall with more than three hundred mourners.

It was a nice photograph of Sadie's grandson, even with the smirk on his face. That picture was worth more than a thousand words. I could see the confusion, defiance, and sorrow in Kenny's eyes. I could see the faint, half-moon-shaped birthmark below his right eye, too. Just as I'd seen it the day he had come in and robbed Daddy's liquor

store, and pressed a gun against my face and forced me to suck his
dick.

"Sister, you all right?"

"I'm . . . I'm fine," I said to the man in line behind me, his hands
on the small of my back, urging me to keep the line moving. I couldn't
feel my feet, but somehow I made it to the ladies' room in the base-
ment.

The light switch in the closet-size ladies' room didn't work, but it
didn't matter. I didn't need the light. I could see what I needed to see
even in the dark. *"Kenny, you son of a . . ."* I couldn't even finish the
sentence. But another sentence was running through my head like a
broken record. *"Kenny, how long did you think you could get away with robbing folks, boy? You should have stopped with me. Look at you now."*

I heard a woman laugh. It took a minute for me to realize that the
woman was me.

I rose from the commode and rearranged the simple black dress
I'd purchased from Wal-Mart for the funeral. As I opened the door, I
recalled the sneer on Kenny Freeman's face the day he robbed and
sexually assaulted me. I recalled a lot of other things that had occurred to me. The robbery/assault and my experiences with Bon
Voyage had come full circle. But something more important had occurred to me. My mother, my brother, and my wayward Uncle Pete
were gone and I had to let go of the lingering grief that had been partially responsible for the fool I made of myself. As far as I was concerned, the black cloud of pain and confusion that had plagued me
for so many years had moved on, and so had I.

Bon Voyage.

IN SHEEP'S CLOTHING

MARY MONROE

ABOUT THIS GUIDE

The suggested questions are intended to
enhance your group's reading of
IN SHEEP'S CLOTHING
by Mary Monroe.

DISCUSSION QUESTIONS

1. One of the reasons that Trudy's elderly father took advantage of her was because she was so convenient. Having her around made his life so much easier. Do you think that some parents expect too much from their adult children?

2. Do you think that Trudy took advantage of her longtime fiancé, James, and saw him more as a convenience, too?

3. Trudy had never met any of her father's lady friend's thuggish grandsons. Did you suspect that one of them was also the same boy who had robbed and sexually assaulted Trudy in her father's liquor store?

4. Do you think that if Ann had been nicer to Trudy, Trudy would not have stolen Ann's identity?

5. It is fairly easy to steal another person's identity. Have you ever been victimized?

6. Banks and department stores often send unsolicited credit cards to deceased people, minors, the family pets, and people with bad credit. Do you feel that these institutions are also responsible for so many cases of identity theft?

7. A lot of people are often tempted to do something illegal if they think they can get away with it. Trudy knew that what she was doing was wrong, but she felt that as long as she was paying the bills on the credit cards nobody was getting hurt. Have you ever been tempted? If so, how did you handle it?

8. Trudy's coworkers Wendy Barker and Pam Bennett annoyed Trudy with their gossip and bad behavior. It was Wendy who first encouraged Trudy to drink on the job and misuse Ann's company credit card. As corrupt as Wendy and Pam were, do you think that they would have been appalled if they had found out just how out-of-control Trudy really was with Ann's identity?

9. When Trudy started showering her father, her fiancé and her two best friends, Freddie and LoBo, with lavish gifts and exotic

trips, did you feel that she had crossed a line that might lead her to jail? Did you think she would end up in jail sooner or later?

10. Trudy eavesdropped on private telephone conversations between Ann and one of her foreign lovers. Could you tell from some of the things that Trudy overheard that Ann was involved in a messy situation herself?

11. Using another person's passport to travel these days can have some extremely serious consequences. Trudy's jaunt to Mexico and her fling with the handsome Black Mexican airline pilot was one of the best times she'd ever had in her life. But was she foolish to take such a big chance on losing her freedom and possibly ending up in a hellish Mexican prison?

12. Do you feel that if Freddie had been a true friend to Trudy, she would have talked her out of stealing Ann's identity? Was Freddie just as guilty as Trudy by accepting all those gifts and going on those trips with Trudy?

13. When the handsome Nigerian hit man first approached Trudy in the nightclub convinced that she was Ann Oliver, did you know then that the jig was up?

The following is a sample chapter from
Mary Monroe's upcoming novel

GOD DON'T PLAY

This book will be available in
September 2006 wherever books are sold.

ENJOY!

My worst nightmare began with a blacksnake and a cute envelope. I had no way of knowing that my life was about to fall apart on the most beautiful day that we'd had all year.

The bold morning sun was shining down on my freshly painted house like a lighthouse. I had just had some of the best sex that I had had in years, and there had been no one else in same room with me.

"You give good phone sex. You should call me up more often," I teased my husband, Pee Wee, as I'd struggled to catch my breath before hanging up the telephone on the wall next to the refrigerator in the kitchen. I couldn't remember the last time I'd enjoyed sex standing up, and nibbling on a Pop-Tart at the same time.

"Well, it is the next best thing to me bein' there," Pee Wee told me, whispering so that his cousins in the next room at his cousin's house couldn't hear him. "Did you get naked like I told you?"

"Uh-huh. Naked as a jaybird," I lied, smoothing down the sides of my muumuu. There was no way I was going to shed my clothes in the middle of my kitchen floor. It was hard enough for me to get naked in my own bedroom. But I did remove my shoes.

"Did you stick your fingers where I told you to stick 'em?" Pee Wee asked with a moan.

"Uh-huh," I mumbled, lying again. The only thing that I'd stuck my fingers in was in that Pop-Tarts box. However, I had massaged a few other spots on my body like Pee Wee had instructed, and that had been enough for me.

I had enjoyed my passionate telephone tryst with my husband, but I was glad when it was over. Not only did I feel downright ridiculous doing some of the things to myself that he'd ordered me to do, but I had started getting cramps in my legs. And I wanted to clean myself up and put on some fresh underwear.

With a satisfied smile on my face, I stepped out on my front porch to retrieve the mail. A large butterfly that had wings every color in the rainbow landed on my hand.

The sun felt good on my face as I clutched my mail and shook the butterfly off my hand. I waved to the friendly, good-looking White couple from down the street as they walked by, pushing their homely toddler in a creaky stroller. Everybody on our block, except for the husband, knew that the homely toddler's daddy was the homely insurance man who made house calls.

A large, light-skinned man that I didn't recognize, with his black hair in large pink foam rollers, waved to me from a shiny black Lincoln that was cruising down the street. I yelled at a stray dog who had decided to lift his crooked leg and water the prizewinning rosebush in my front yard.

My biggest concern that day was trying to decide what to do first: get my nails done, go shopping, do the laundry, or treat myself to lunch at one of my favorite restaurants. I was in a frivolous mood so I didn't want to do anything that was too serious, like go pay bills or visit my fussy parents. But the bizarre uproar that I was about to face would cancel everything else that I had planned to do on that beautiful Saturday. From that point on, my life would never be the same again. What happened to me on this day would haunt me for the rest of my life, because it was the beginning of the end for me in some ways. And it all had to do with a blacksnake and a cute envelope.

There was nothing that unusual about the cute envelope that had arrived in the mail that morning in late August. I had almost missed it among the usual stack of bills and other unwanted junk—like the Frederick's of Hollywood catalogue with the picture of a beautiful young blonde woman in a white negligee on the cover.

I laughed when I saw the catalogue, wondering what the world was coming to for *my* name to end up on the Frederick's of Hollywood mailing list. I had to give them credit for advertising muumuus, waist clinchers, capes, bras with cups large enough to hold forty ounces of beer, long flowing nightgowns that looked more like parachutes, and other inducements every now and then to appease us full-figured gals. But almost everything else that the mysterious Mr. Frederick— who probably looked like Buddha or worse himself—sold was for women half my size and even smaller. On the first page inside the catalogue were some "one size fits all" pantyhose. Yeah, right. The see-through gowns and low-cut blouses were outrageous enough, and I had absolutely no use for crotchless panties. I'd probably be wearing diapers again before I break down and put on a pair of crotchless panties.

I was not surprised when I flipped the catalogue over and saw that it was addressed to Jade O'Toole, my best friend's sneaky teenage daughter. Some of the clothes that the girl wore every day showed just as much skin as the frocks she ordered from Frederick's that she hid from her parents, so I didn't know what the big deal was. But I didn't have a teenager yet, so I couldn't really judge the behavior of the "in your face" music-video generation. They had their own culture and Jade kept it in my face. I had allowed her to take too many liberties with me so it was too late for me to revise my position in her life. I was no more of an authority figure to her than a cat was. She had started using my address without my knowledge or permission. I shuddered when I thought about what that girl might do next.